Delicate Armor

What others are saying about Connie Claire Szarke's *Delicate Armor*:

"... Szarke writes with compassion and artistry about a young girl coming of age. A keen-eyed observer of the challenges that confront her family, Callie takes us on a journey from joy to sorrow and back again. *Delicate Armor* is a compelling and deeply-absorbing read."
~ Brent Spencer, author of *Rattlesnake Daddy: A Son's Search for his Father*

"Huckleberry, Scout ... Callie ... She's a daddy's girl, intense with enthusiasm for her father's outdoor pursuits, and that father is worthy of her love for him. As an adult, despite experience that might have shattered her, Callie's good health continues, often expressed by the love and understanding she brings to the men in her family, especially the father who had so much to do with her ongoing wholeness. Szarke is above the cheap shots that other writers may have taken at these men, and Callie remains true to the child she once was, a not-so-common feat in the literature of our time ..."
~ Joe Paddock, poet, oral historian, environmental writer

"My affection for Callie, the feisty but tender-hearted narrator, grew with each chapter, as did my admiration for the author's ability to tell a good story and her wonderful ear for language ..."
~ Stephen Wilbers, author, syndicated newspaper columnist

"... Inducted into the outdoors world by her father, Callie Lindstrom witnesses firsthand the jealousies, losses, and tenderness that have permeated her family's history. Under Szarke's clear eye and deft touch, the reader follows Callie's growth from a cheeky tomboy to a self-possessed woman, cheering for her on every page."
~ Pamela Carter Joern, author of The Floor of the Sky

"The story in *Delicate Armor* could have been mine. As a son, I was raised to think that some day when I became a father, I, too, would have a son to pass on my love of outdoor pursuits ... Instead, my journey through fatherhood included two daughters who became my fishing partners, hunting companions, and morel mushroom stalkers ...What really matters is the ... journey through life so elegantly described by Connie Claire Szarke ... daughters can do outdoors whatever boys can do ..."
~ Ron Schara, host Minnesota Bound television show

"Move over, Mattie Ross of *True Grit*. Take a break, Huck Finn. Here comes Callie Lindstrom, as winsome a little mischief-maker as you'll ever want to meet. She's the star of Connie Claire Szarke's first novel *Delicate Armor* and once you've met her you're not likely to forget her."
~ Robert Lacy, author of *The Natural Father*

Delicate Armor

Connie Claire Szarke

Keep on rowing.
Connie Claire

Tranquil waters flowing

N S

NORTH STAR PRESS OF ST. CLOUD, INC.
St. Cloud, Minnesota

F
Sza

Previously published portions:
"A Flimsy Thread," *The Talking Stick*, Vol. 18, © 2009 Jackpine Writer's Bloc
"The Tackle Box," *Dust & Fire*, Vol XXII March 2008, © 2008 Bemidji State University
"School of Fish," *Lake Country Journal Magazine* July/August 2007 Vol. 11, Issue 4
"The Storm," *Lake Country Journal Magazine* July/August 2006 Vol.10, Issue 4

ISBN: 0-87839-440-0
ISBN-13: 978-0-87839-440-1

First Edition, September 2011

Printed in the United States of America

Published by
North Star Press of St. Cloud, Inc.
P.O. Box 451
St. Cloud, Minnesota 56302

www.northstarpress.com

To the memory of my parents.
And to my sister, Dixie Lee.

Table of Contents

❖ Part One ❖

 ❖ *Part Two* ❖

"I just ask for your recognition of me and you and the enemy—time—in us all."

~Madeleine Sherwood

Part One

One

N THE DIM BACK ROOM of the basement, where Mom did the laundry and Dad made repairs on whatever needed fixing, I stepped up on the Remington Express crate and reached for the string with the tiny silver tulip dangling from it. The workbench, covered with polished tools, lit up under the bare bulb.

I hopped down, moved to where the steel vise was bolted, and twirled its handle until the thick jaws opened wide. I inserted Grandad's shotgun shell, its puckered end aimed at where the wall met the floor, and tightened the vise, making sure the red paper didn't get squished or the brass head flattened. Then I raised a ball-peen hammer over my head and came down *bang* on the primer.

Actually, I never really heard the bang. But I saw stars. Zillions of 'em.

My ears rang and the smell of gunpowder hung in the air. Sprawled on the cold cement floor, I felt as though I'd somersaulted too many times underwater. The lump on my forehead was greasy with blood.

Within seconds, Mom, Dad, and Liz were kneeling around me, faces frantic, mouths going a mile a minute. Mom grabbed my left arm and began swinging it up over my head, then back down to my side, over and over again.

"I'm all right, Mom," I muttered, barely able to hear my own voice, trying not to cry.

"There's too much blood, Will!" she shouted. "I'm afraid to probe around her eyes!"

Dad carried me, lurching up the steps and out to the car. That's when it struck me that what I had done was serious, because we usually walked everywhere. I felt embarrassed and couldn't catch my breath.

"Lie down, Callie," he ordered, settling me on the back seat with my head on Mom's lap. She pressed a wet towel over my face so I had to fight for air. My eardrums hurt like the devil, like when Bobby Keeler sneaked up behind me at school and blew a high-pitched whistle in my ear.

For once, my big sister wasn't giving me any dirty looks. Kneeling backwards in the passenger seat, Liz reached down to grip my wrist. The way she kept repeating my name—*Callie, Callie*—reminded me of how she'd called out, *Penny, Penny,* when our dog got hit by a car and lay dying on the garage floor.

It took about two minutes to get to the small tan brick hospital at the edge of town. Dad drove like hell and when he let out the clutch and set the emergency brake, Mom jolted forward. I rolled onto the floor. Mom yelled, "For heaven's sake, Will, you'll have us all killed!" Then we scrambled out of the car and, after Dad made sure I could walk, paraded into the hospital in our pajamas. Mom and Liz wore raincoats over their nighties. Dad had grabbed his hunting jacket.

Old Doctor Dohms boosted me up onto a metal table in the operating room to inspect my body for shot. I began to shiver and breathe inward in short little bursts, which made my head keep jerking to one side. I grabbed at the doctor's white sleeve and tried to sit up.

"Callie," said Mom, gently pushing me back, "you've got to get hold of yourself."

"You mustn't cry," said the doctor, "or I won't be able to take care of you."

I remembered the dentist telling me almost the same thing. "I'll have to send you home with your teeth unfilled if you don't settle down." I let out a long, shaky sigh and focused on Doc Dohms's watery blue eyes and the bushy black-and-white eyebrows that matched his mustache. His breath smelled of peppermint.

"That's better, child. Now try to relax."

He rubbed a dressing on the powder burns and stopped the bleeding in my forehead. "How old are you, Callie?" he asked, tweezing a pellet from my cheek and one from my chin.

I reached up to touch the goose egg. "I'm gonna be eight."

"Well, you're a very lucky little girl," he said, pasting gauze pads on my face and wrapping my head as if I were a mummy. "You might have lost an eye. As it is, you'll have a slight scar, but if you wear *bangs*," he paused to chuckle, "it won't be noticeable."

I caught his little pun, but I didn't feel like laughing.

He turned to Mom. "I think it's best to keep her here for the rest of the night, quiet and awake, until we're sure there are no complications."

"I'll stay," Mom told Dad and Liz. "You two go back home for some clothes."

Dr. Dohms put an arm around Dad's shoulders.

"Will," he said, steering my dad away from the rest of us, "I'm sure sorry about your father."

"Thank you, Doc. It's been a rough day."

After that, I couldn't hear much of what they were saying, except, "shotgun shell" and "down the basement."

A short time later, Dad and Liz rushed into the room where the nurses had taken Mom and me. Liz started her goofy laughing when she saw my bandages.

"I can't wait to tell Brian about Callie's one-gun salute," she repeated until Mom made her pipe down. Brian was her boyfriend.

Mom sat rigid in the chair next to my bed, clutching my hand and dabbing at her eyes with a crumpled handkerchief while Dad told her what they'd discovered down the basement.

"The shell's load fanned out and fired into the ceiling and walls. Some of the shot hit the workbench and your washing machine, Emily, and then ricocheted back at Callie. The worst part was the brass head. It blew backwards out of the vise. That's what hit her just above the eye." Dad shook his head. "If she'd been two inches taller . . ."

"We found that part of the shell on the floor," Liz explained, "next to the cistern wall."

Mom stared at my bandages.

"I tried to get her to talk," she said.

And then, without warning, she jumped up and faced off with Dad, as if she were going to slap him.

"Will! Honest to God! Maybe it's time you teach this kid how to shoot a damn gun instead of blowing things up. This is what happens," she said, throwing her hands into the air, "when you keep shotgun shells in the house. We've just buried Vic. And now this!"

Liz's eyes grew wide.

"Mom!" I cried, tugging the crisp, white sheet up over my nose.

It had been a long time since I'd heard my mother shout at us. And she never swore. In fact, she'd washed my mouth out just yesterday for saying

"Damn it!" I couldn't even say "Shut up!" without getting my teeth filled with Ivory soap.

"That's enough, Emily." Dad's voice was stern. "Don't be so quick to blame until we hear the truth."

"I couldn't get her to tell me what happened!"

"In due time. For now, we'll let her be quiet and rest. No more upset."

"When I think of how this might have turned out." Mom's lips quivered. "I couldn't bear to lose another child."

"I know," Dad whispered. "I know."

He held her for a moment, and then reached out to Liz. Together, they huddled next to my bed. Liz started to snicker, I suppose at my wide, green eyes looking up from between bandage and sheet.

Mom sat down again, not bothering to put on the dress Liz brought from home. Dad stood with his hand on the bed railing.

"Thank God, it wasn't all black powder." He looked down at me with an expression I'd never seen before. "Good thing you had it clamped as well as you did, Callie." His chin trembled the way Mom's did when she was about to cry.

Doc Dohms came in to shine an extra-bright light at my eyes and said I could go home in the morning. Just before sun up, Mom and Liz decided to leave.

"I'll stay home from class," said Liz, poking my arm and flashing her dimples. "So I can help take care of the brat."

"I'm sure we'll manage while you're in school." Mom kissed the bandage above my eye. "C'mon, Liz. And Will, make sure she doesn't fall asleep."

Glad for a day away from my teachers, I stayed awake, listening to Dad snore as he sat slumped in the chair. Stuff from Grandad's funeral crept across my mind like a slow-motion parade: people lined up to stare at him lying in that casket, his suit rumpled and one eye a little open as if he were peeking at us. If he couldn't come back to life, why was he doing that? And there was Gram in those thick glasses that made *her* eyes look huge and empty; my cousin Jen, thin and sad, looking helplessly at the stain on her blouse; the whites of Aunt Eloise's eyes and her wide pinched lips like a red slash across her face; the way her shrill voice echoed through the church: "Shut up! Just shut up!" And all those nasty things she said about our town.

Just as first light crept into the sky, Dad awoke and jumped up to check on me.

"Hey, Snickelfritz." He leaned over the metal railing and stroked the top of my head. "How are you doing?"

"All right, I guess."

He was quiet for a moment before asking me what must have been on his mind the whole time.

"Callie, sweetheart, where did you get that live shell?"

"From out at the lake. It was Grandad's."

Y ESTERDAY, THE MIDDLE OF MAY, which my dad usually called the most beautiful month in Minnesota, I had stood near Grandad's coffin, imagining what he'd say if he woke up: "Yes, sir," he'd mutter in his deep, slow voice, "this is God's country."

Mom coaxed me forward, her hand against my back. "Go on, Callie. You can touch him."

Inching ahead, arms tight against my sides, I studied Grandad Vic. The way his hands were folded, one over the other, looked stupid. He'd never held his hands like that in his life. His gray suit coat and white shirt and blue-gray tie curved strangely over a barrel-shaped chest that he'd never had before. How did that happen? And where were his legs? After all, they were what took him through the fields and woods of "God's country," down to the dock and into his boat. He always wore khaki pants, baggy at the seat. Why didn't the undertaker show all of him? Didn't he bother with the suit trousers? What the hell had he done to my grandad? I hated Mr. Kimmel.

The soft silvery hair that fell onto Grandad's forehead when he was busy filing lead sinkers and polishing his guns had been combed straight back and looked like gray straw. His skin was like wax. Mr. Kimmel had done him up as if he were sending him off to Sunday school. I was noticing the wiry hairs in Grandad's large ears and the little white scars on his lips from smoking cigarettes down to nubbins, when the combined odors of carnations and roses and something strange and cold from inside the casket hit my smeller. I edged away.

Then I got really scared. Dad was leaning over Grandad, circling his arms around that barrel chest and scooping him up from the satin liner. Auntie Edna grabbed me and whipped me around, pressing my head so tight against her huge, jelly stomach I thought I'd suffocate. But her arms weren't strong enough. I twisted and turned until I could see it all. Like a big wooden puppet, Grandad was sitting up in his coffin, moving to the rhythm of my dad's shaking shoulders. It was as if the dead knew how to dance. Dad held him like that for a long time, until everyone around us began to fidget and exchange glances. Mom covered her mouth with one hand and stared at the floor. Liz backed away. Gram, tiny in her black dress and pillbox hat with the stiff netting over her forehead, rocked slightly on her old-lady shoes. Uncle Ray wore a bitter, sarcastic smile.

In that moment, I realized that terrible things were happening to my family, especially to the men in my family—those burly, happy men in hunting jackets and squeaky hip boots—those pipe-smoking men who cussed and talked about interesting stuff like the fights televised from Madison Square Garden and the monster northern pike that Uncle Ray had caught and strung up on the clothesline and how General Eisenhower, if he became president, would pull us together.

After a while, Dad eased Grandad back into his coffin. Mr. Kimmel, hovering on the sidelines, slithered over to smooth the hair, fuss with the tie and suit, and adjust the silky pillow. Grandad would have preferred a burlap bag to that frilly old thing. Just before Mr. Kimmel reached into his suit pocket for a tube of something, I saw Grandad peeking at me through a tiny slit in one eye.

I broke away from Auntie Edna, bawling until I thought my head would burst, and ran back to Dad. His face was so red and distorted, he looked as though he'd go down with a stroke right there, next to the casket.

"Come here, Callie," he said in a choky voice. Kneeling down on the floor, he wrapped his arms around me and kept repeating, "It's okay. It's okay."

He didn't sound very convincing.

Mom and Liz gathered around, teary-eyed. Uncle Ray, with a stony look, stood off to one side, next to Aunt Eloise and Jenny. Gram, standing alone, looked confused. We were like three islands in the middle of a lake.

I peeked at Grandad one more time. His eye was closed again, but his hair was still mussed and his tie crooked. At least his hands, no longer perfectly folded, looked the way I remembered them when they were alive: rough from summers in the fields and swollen from winters spent ice fishing. How could his fingers stand skimming ice out of augured holes and scooping minnows from buckets of freezing water? Gram had made him a dipper by crocheting around a piece of bent wire, but he hardly ever used it.

Now, at age seventy-five, he was dead—dead from a wrong-type blood transfusion after prostrate surgery. I looked the word up in the dictionary and wondered how anyone could die from lying face down until Mom told me to subtract an "r."

Dad tried to hide his heartbreak. For the longest time all he could say was, "It should *never* have happened. It *never* should have happened."

In 1952, small town folks didn't fuss over such mistakes—like the Swensons, for instance, who lost their little girl because of Doctor Nelson. Anyhow, Grandad, a second-generation Swede, had always lived close to the land, and so, since nothing could bring him back, my dad did what the men before him had done when troubles came to call: he took to the woods and the lakes and let it go.

I was a month short of eight years old the day Grandad died. If anybody ever asked me about him, here's what I would say: He's a crack shot at clay pigeons. He blows his nose outside in winter without a handkerchief. He ice-fishes until his fingers turn purple and white. He spends evenings next to a fire, checkering gunstocks and carving fishing lures. And he hardly ever speaks.

Mom said that he'd likely grown to be a man of few words on account of the shock when he was young, when his own dad (my great-grandfather) abandoned the family—that and the necessary quiet of hunters and fishermen.

Grandad mostly lived within himself and only paid us kids attention during holiday dinners or after a hunt. Sitting next to me at the table, he'd point to a tall stack of bread, then raise his bushy eyebrows and stare at me with eyes so blue they seemed almost white. When I nodded, he'd grab a slice, hold it high above my plate, and slap it down as if he were closing the trunk of a car. The first time he did this, I frowned, especially at the soft chuckle that went along with the slammed bread. Mom and Liz would grin. Gram, as usual, rearranged the food on her plate between bites. Dad always winked at me and helped himself to more pheasant or duck or goose. Eventually, I grew to expect our silly routine, reminding Grandad with a tap on the shoulder in case he forgot.

Fall days, he returned from Slaughter Slough and lined up his kill on the grass behind our cottage: mallards, teal, bluebills. He gave me pretty feathers and spent shotgun shells, eventually enough to fill a medium-sized burlap bag. The shell cases of burnished and cherry reds, forest green, midnight and cobalt blues, and their brass heads, shiny like gold, made me feel rich. By the strong smell of gunpowder residue and bits of wadding that clung to the openings, I could tell which ones had recently fired or fired some time ago. Each dent in a primer was slightly off-center. I made it a game to check every one to see if any of the dents might be exactly in the middle. They never were.

When I was five or six, I played with the shells on rainy afternoons, arranging them by color or mixing them up, designing trails and fences, trees and big animals. When I turned seven, I thought of filling them with something, because they seemed too hollow and light after hefting fresh shells whenever I came across a box of them. I loaded my empties with grains of rice or fine sand and pushed down hard on their puckered ends. The rice was all wrong and the sand eventually seeped out.

One afternoon, I found a box of loaded shells in Grandad's garage. They were smaller than most of my collection. Heavy with shot, their ends tightly crimped, they felt weighty and good in my hands. What would happen, I wondered, if a primer got whacked by a hammer? Before closing the box, I took one of the shells and dropped it into my bag along with the empties.

The day Grandad died, it never crossed my mind that I wouldn't see him again or that our family car would ever have to leave its garage and inch along behind a hearse on the way to the cemetery. After all, my friends and I counted on tried-and-true rituals to ward off old Devil Death. We celebrated when it passed us by with only a warning. Sometimes, the warnings turned scary, like the time Bobby Keeler was riding his bicycle down Maple Street.

"Here he comes, the big show-off," I said to my friend Valerie, as we pumped in unison on the playground swings.

"He thinks he's so smart," she said. "Let's pretend we don't see him."

From the corners of our eyes, we watched Bobby pedal hard, then hop into a crouch on the crossbar, as if he were riding a circus pony. He grinned at us under huge glasses that covered half his face. But he didn't smile for long. Glancing over his shoulder, he got spooked by the *Black Hell Hound* (the local hearse) bearing down on him and crashed into the bumper of Mr. Paulson's parked Buick. Valerie and I laughed like loons to see his bike bounce off the fender like a bucking bronco. Bobby crawled around on the tarred street, searching for his broken glasses, then turned his back on us and dragged his bicycle home. He looked as though he wanted to cry, but it was bad luck not to laugh, especially when death came sniffing around.

Whenever the *Black Hell Hound* interrupted our play, cruising the streets, creeping along, trolling for customers, we stood up straight with our fists in the air and chanted after the dark monster 'til it rounded the corner and rolled out of sight:

When a big black hearse goes by, do you think you'll be the next to die? They'll put you in a great big box and cover you up with dirt and rocks. The worms crawl in, your eyes fall out, the ants play pinochle on your snout.

"Away! Away!" we howled, shrugging off the interruption, certain that our chant had done the trick and everyone in town could go on living. Then we pumped higher than ever on the playground swings.

When I told Dad about Bobby crashing into Mr. Paulson's Buick and how Valerie and I couldn't stop laughing, he said, "It isn't for others to comment in the aftermath of a man's wounded pride."

I thought for a moment. "Or a woman's?" I asked.

"That's right, Callie. Or a woman's."

ALTHOUGH MOM EXPLAINED that Grandad was gone forever, that I was lucky to be eight and old enough to have "solid memories of him," the idea didn't take until we walked into the church and saw him in that fancy metal box. Before Grandad died, "forever" meant the impossibly long time between birthdays or Christmases and the forever wait until summer vacation when my friends and I could trade the dead air of a schoolhouse for the leafy, warm smells of fields and lakes and woods.

Seeing Grandad lying in his casket, I realized the end of him in a flash. He belonged with the wild game he and Dad brought home from a hunt—

ducks, geese, and cock pheasants lying on the ground in motionless formation.

Grandad would never be coming back to us. And the rest of our family, especially my dad and his brother, would never be the same.

The day of the funeral, we were to meet Uncle Ray, Aunt Eloise, Jen, and Gram in the church narthex. That's what my uncle called it—the narthex.

"What's a narthex, Mom?" I asked, watching her rouge her cheeks.

"Same as an entry, dear."

"Do we say that in Lutheran?"

"Not usually. I guess we call it a vestibule."

She smoothed powder over the rouge and reached for her tube of Tangee lipstick.

"Why would Uncle Ray call it a narthex? He didn't turn Catholic like Aunt Hazel, did he?"

"No. I don't know, Callie," she mumbled, applying the color to her stretched lips. "Maybe he's just being pretentious. Or funny."

"I don't know. Narthex. Narthex. Sounds like a sickness to me."

"Well, it'll become one if you say it often enough." She rubbed her lips together, then blotted them with a square of toilet paper. "Now hush up and get yourself ready or I'll give you a dose of something for your narthex disease."

I smelled my mother's fresh makeup as she laughed and kissed me on the forehead.

Excited to see Jen, I didn't mind wearing a dress and my new patent leathers. Shiny and black, with higher heels than usual, the shoes turned me into a tap dancer. But after I'd made several loud clacks around the kitchen, Liz scowled and said, "Callie, this is no day to be dancing." I guess the only good thing about the shoes that day was the extra height for seeing deeper into Grandad's coffin.

Before we left home, Mom squeezed a dollop of *Suave* onto her fingers and worked it through my hair. "Anything," she said, "to keep it out of your eyes."

In the church parking lot, she spit on her starched white handkerchief, the one with the yellow rose embroidered on one corner, and rubbed it over my nose and cheeks as if to erase my freckles.

Inside the church was when all that other stuff happened. Eventually, everyone sat down in a pew. Everyone, that is, except Mr. Kimmel. He kept fussing with Grandad. And I was trying to stop my short, jerky breaths left over from crying so hard.

"You sit still now during the service," Mom warned in an unusually stern voice. I think she was trying to bring me back from the upset of seeing Dad lift Grandad out of his coffin.

I felt better when my cousin Jen sat next to me in the front pew. We were soon swinging our legs and sticking them straight out to compare length and to show off our shoes. We tickled the insides of each other's arms and giggled at how old lady Swenson and some other woman seemed to be in a voice duel to see who could sing each hymn the loudest, especially the high notes.

"The storm may roar without me," they warbled, "bright skies will soon be o'er me ..."

I trilled a few notes of my own, which made my cousin laugh out loud.

"Shut up," hissed Aunt Eloise, slapping Jen's thigh extra-hard.

When she did that, it hushed me, too. My family never said "shut up" to one another, nor did my parents ever hit us. Jen lowered her head as if she were praying. I leaned forward to peek at my aunt. Her face had taken on a nasty, pinched look, and her dark eyes were darting from side to side as she twirled a hank of black hair around her finger. Pastor Gullsvig spoke from his pulpit, all the while keeping an eye on Aunt Eloise, who had started making strange noises, like hiccoughs mixed with goofy laughter. Finally, Uncle Ray stood up and led her outside. He must have had plenty of experience taking her away from places, calm as he was. But there was also a bitter and wary look about him, like on the faces of those churchwomen whose bad-tempered husbands were mean to them.

"Why is she crying?" I whispered. "What's wrong with her?"

Jen shrugged, "I don't know. She always does that when something upsets her."

Just then Mom held a finger to her lips and shook her head. I was glad when she reached over to pat Jen's knee.

"Why is she carrying on like that, Mom?"

With pursed lips, a slight frown, and a shake of the head, Mom let me know that this wasn't the time to discuss Aunt Eloise.

While the congregation sang "A Mighty Fortress Is Our God," I thought about the possible reasons for my aunt's behavior. I was sure it didn't have anything to do with Grandad's dying because I'd overheard Mom say to Dad, "Our family means nothing to that woman. Why bother to come for the funeral when she refused to see him while he was alive? She couldn't even show up for your folks' Fiftieth."

"Maybe Ray's trying to take charge," Dad had said, "include her, get her in line."

"Well, good luck," Mom shot back.

I finally decided that Aunt Eloise was just plain crazy, because after the cemetery service, things got worse. At a long table in the church basement, we sat across from Ray's family on wooden folding chairs, the rickety kind that creaked whenever someone shifted. Gram sat at the end, hunched over and forking her food around the plate, as usual. Dad and Uncle Ray had just started commenting on how, of all the brothers and sisters, Amer (their favorite uncle) had been the first and Grandad the last to die, when Jen spilled a big glob of cherry Jell-O on her new white blouse.

"Look what you've done!" Eloise shrieked, bringing quiet to about two hundred people. "You stupid girl!" she screamed, grabbing Jen's thin arm and jerking her hand away from her blouse. "Don't rub it. You'll only make it worse." She pushed Jen away from the table, hurling words after her like skipping stones: "Lavatory! Cold water! Hurry up! Git!"

I tried to follow my cousin, but Aunt Eloise told me to stay put. "She doesn't need your help!"

"Now look here," said my mother in a quiet voice. "That's no way to talk to the girls. Whatever has possessed you?"

"Mind your own business, Emily!" My aunt's eyes had taken on a wild look with so much white showing that they reminded me of the Halloween eyeball jawbreakers at Buckle's Five and Dime.

"You're out of line here," said Dad, jumping up from his chair so fast that it folded and crashed to the floor. "We just buried my dad and now this. What the hell's the matter with you?"

"Oh, Mr. Importance! Mr. Will Lindstrom! Top turd in this shit hole of a hick town!" Eloise threw her fork down so hard it bounced off the table and onto the green linoleum.

Uncle Ray, now looking worried, quietly gathered up their things and led Eloise from the dining hall, jerking her along toward the washroom where Jen had been standing the whole time. My cousin's face was as white as her blouse, and she looked sad. She gave me a little wave, and I waved back, wondering if I'd ever see her again. The last thing we heard echoing through the church was Aunt Eloise yelling, "Oh, shut up! Just shut up!"

Confused, I didn't know what to do. Liz scooted her chair closer to mine and put her arm around me. Mom and Dad looked flushed, as if they had a fever, and seemed ready to melt onto their wobbly chairs.

With some effort, Gram stood up. She'd taken off her pillbox hat, which left sections of gray hair scrunched against her head. Her eyes looked weird ever since she started wearing those creepy glasses after cataract surgery.

"I'm going out to say goodbye to Ray," she said. "You should too, Will."

"Nope." Dad shook his head slowly. "I warned him about that woman a long time ago."

Gram shuffled between the tables and went out by herself.

Eventually, the people found their voices again. Our neighbor, Mr. Ryan, approached Dad, nodded, and squeezed his shoulder in a friendly way. Others gathered round, including the ladies from Mom's 500 Club. Then everyone, except my family, lined up for more food.

How could anyone eat after that? And how could they eat after my grandad had just died and was left all alone in the cemetery? The crowd carried on as if they were at a party, laughing and chatting about the last time they'd seen each other, about the weather and getting the crops in. They scooped up tuna hotdish, stacks of string beans, escalloped potatoes, and buttered biscuits as if they'd been working all day in the fields. The strong coffee smelled bad, and the food looked yucky, especially that little dish of red Jell-O left in the middle of our table.

Sitting in the noisy basement, I thought about poor Jen and her awful mother. And what about Uncle Ray? And what if Grandad, locked inside that box, deep in the ground, might come alive again. And would my dad be all right?

The men in my family were disappearing. That's what was happening! There were plenty of women—my mother and sister, grandmothers, aunts, and cousins. But with both grandfathers gone (the first when I was three), there were only two men left that mattered to me—maybe one, considering Uncle Ray's troubles.

While listening in on my parents' private talks about him and Aunt Eloise (Mom referred to Ray as "a Steppenwolf, always coming and going, leaving us guessing"), I began to feel sorry for him, determined to figure him out.

But for now I needed to keep a closer eye on Dad.

At the end of his busy days auditing books at the courthouse, walking long distances, helping Gram, shooting and catching food for our table, spading and planting a big garden, he'd fall asleep on the davenport, looking as if he'd never wake up. I always checked his breathing as he dozed after supper, the evening paper draped over his chest. I'd call out to him. If he didn't budge, I'd poke at the paper.

"Well, hello, Snicklefritz," he'd say in a groggy voice, "is it morning already?"

"No. Still nighttime."

The night of the funeral, before I went down the basement with my shotgun shell, Dad was sitting alone on the couch with a far away look in his eyes. It was late and Mom and Liz had gone to bed hours ago.

"What are you doing up?" he asked.

"Can't sleep. It's so windy out, and I'm still thinking about Grandad."

"Me, too," he said, patting the cushion next to him. Snuggled into the crook of his arm, I was comforted by the scent of his skin and the sweet smell from the pouch of Velvet pipe tobacco in his shirt pocket. "It's hard to imagine him gone. We'll miss him like the dickens."

"What if he isn't really dead and tries to get out of his coffin?"

"No, Callie. That won't happen."

"How can you be sure?"

"Mr. Kimmel took care of him."

I wasn't in the mood to hear another word about that twisty-faced undertaker. I picked up the newspaper and handed it to Dad.

"Will you read me the funnies?"

Usually, he'd ask, "Don't you know how to read yet?" And I'd say, "Hell, yes, but I want you to do it." And he'd say, "You shouldn't swear, Callie." And I'd say, "I'll think about it." And he'd laugh and say, "I'll read a couple, then it's off to bed with you."

But this night, he held me in the tight nest between his arm and his ribs, and pointing to each word, slowly read, "Little Orphan Annie's come to our house to stay, An' wash the cups an' saucers up, an' brush the crumbs away."

I could not sleep that night, for I was bursting with sadness and scary thoughts of Mr. Kimmel hovering over Grandad, doing strange things to him. Even out at the cemetery, he kept checking the coffin lid. When would the gravediggers shovel dirt into the hole after the coffin got sealed in its vault and lowered into the ground? What if it hadn't been filled in yet? Who would do it? Worse still, what if Grandad hadn't been lowered and there he was all by himself in the dark, rocking in the wind. I wasn't allowed to see for myself. Mom had taken me back to the church before the lowering, saying it was just too much for me to watch. Now all I could picture was that long box perched high above a gaping hole in the ground.

Careful not to wake Liz, I crept out of bed, pulled my burlap bag of shotgun shells down from the closet shelf, knelt on the floor, and spread them out—all that was left of Grandad's hunts and the birds he'd brought home from Slaughter Slough: canvas backs, fat mallards with dangling emerald heads glinting in the sunshine, teal with patches of blue-green wing feathers that grew when you fanned them out. Gram used to laugh when she saw a skinny little teal in the bunch. "By the time I roast that," she'd say, "there'll be barely enough for Callie to gnaw on."

Sorting through my dozens of empty shells, I found the live one I'd stolen—a bright red case with a nice heft and the only primer in the whole batch without a dent.

If Doc Dohms or anyone else had asked me why I did this, I might have said, "I don't know," or "Because I was curious."

But they never asked.

Maybe I did it because I always wanted to go hunting with the men. And for Grandad—for his low, slow laughter and the pretty feathers and empty shells he gave me, and for all those slices of bread he slammed onto my plate.

Two

Call Me Cal

N THE NAME OF THE FEATHER, the sunny, and the whole goose," chanted the preacher man, pouring water three times over the tiny head bobbing around in front of the congregation. Listening to that screaming baby from our pew in the middle of the church made me wonder how cold the water was in the baptismal font. Wouldn't you think those pretty words would calm the baby? Of course, I knew a long time ago that "feather, sunny, and goose" weren't *exactly* what Pastor Gullsvig said. But I liked to think those were the words chanted over all baptized babies. He must have spoken them while pouring a river of water over *my* head. After all, that's the kind of language that made sense to me.

Desperate and angry cries from the baby bounced off the high ceiling.

"Mom, did I carry on like that when I was baptized?"

"No, Callie." Mom smiled and leaned close to my ear. "You flapped your wings and kicked your legs and laughed out loud. I guess you were in your element from the very beginning."

I sat up straight and repeated my own blessing after Pastor Gullsvig: "In the name of the feather, the sunny, and the whole goose."

Mom bumped shoulders and held her finger up to her lips.

Our church hymns invited different words, too, especially when Hulda Swenson warbled "Onward Christian Soldiers" in competition with the rest of the congregation, the way she sang at Grandad's funeral service. No one but my friends could hear me in the choir loft during the second service as I belted out, "Hellfire and Dam-naaa-tion marching as to war, with their guns and ar-rows killing as before . . ."

Parts of opera songs I'd learned from my grandmother worked, too: "*O mio babbino caro, mi piace è bello bello.*" Who knew what those words meant? After so many repetitions, they flowed from my mouth as easily as the Lord's Prayer: ". . . For thine is the kingdom, and the power, and the glory, forever and ever. Amen." These words sounded just as foreign to me as "*mi piace è bello bello.*" What and where was the kingdom? What did *piace* mean? How did the Lord use power and glory? Did *bello* mean what I thought it did? The glory and power of what? No matter if they were church chants or opera words, every bit of it sounded like beautiful nonsense that flowed and carried me away from the ordinary. Mostly, I liked my own versions the best.

Baptized Callandra Mae Lindstrom, third child of William and Emily Lindstrom of Maywood County, I came into this world on D-Day, "fat, squawking, and unexpected." So I was told by a couple of old busybodies. Although it took awhile, I eventually learned to ignore these women, paying attention, instead, to stories about the relatives who came before me.

In the 1800s, a slew of Swedish immigrants settled in southern Minnesota, including our town of Masterton, where Dad's grandfather, August, landed. I had him pictured as a gruff man with a long bushy beard until Dad showed me the tintype of a young man with a hank of black hair curling over his forehead from under a dress hat tilted back. His suit coat was snug over a white vest and white shirt buttoned tightly at the throat. Only a few inches of his necktie showed. The rest was tucked sideways into his vest. He looked jaunty and surprisingly handsome, with confident eyes. His wife, Ernestina, was a short, severe-looking woman with lifeless eyes and pinched lips, as if incapable of the slightest smile.

After several years, August Lindstrom moved the family, including my grandad Vic and Dad's uncle Amer, to a parcel of farmland west of Rockford, Illinois, where other Swedes had settled. Great-grandfather was a man of repute for three reasons: he'd shaken hands with President Lincoln, he'd fathered eight children (two died), and he abandoned his family.

"Where'd he go?" I wondered.

"According to relatives, he returned to the Old Country," said Dad. "At least that's what they thought at the time."

"What old country?"

"Sweden. But ..."

"But what?"

Dad shook his head. "I'll tell you more another time."

"When I'm older, right?"

"Something like that."

Grandad once told me that Lindstrom meant linden tree and stream. Because forests and water were important to our family, I thought it was a good name.

Although my mother was not Swedish, she could hold her own with the Lindstroms. I admired her for not backing down whenever Dad teased her. For instance, one evening, while we were wandering through neighborhood alleys in search of ideas for building a grapevine trellis in our back yard, Dad pointed at a rusty wheelbarrow propped against a lopsided wooden shed. "See that, Callie?" he said in his joking voice. "Be sure to ask your mother about it."

"About what?" I asked, figuring he was going to tell another of his silly stories. "An old wheelbarrow? What for?"

"That's how the Norwegians teach their children to walk."

I laughed at the image of my mother as a baby dressed in a red, blue, white, and yellow costume, toddling behind a wheelbarrow like a tiny drunken farmer.

Mom laughed, too, when I told her what Dad had said.

"There he goes again, making up stories. All right. Everybody sit down, because it's *my* turn to put an oar in the water."

She grinned at Dad.

"Now, I'm going to tell you about those boats coming over from Sweden. They were so loaded with plowshares, dinghies, oars, fishing poles, landing nets, hip boots, and shotguns that it was a wonder there was any room for the women. Why, if your great-grandfather had been captain of the *Titanic*, it would have been men and boys first. Men, boys, and their fishing poles!"

Dad smiled a kind of sad smile. Then they both grew quiet and their eyes met. They might have been remembering my shotgun shell, but I think they were also thinking of Billy.

Between my sister and me there was a baby boy who lived only a few weeks.

Liz had told me, "Mom and Dad were sad and quiet for a long time after Billy died. Eventually, they decided it was just fine that I would be their only child. But then you came along." Sometimes, if we were arguing, Liz would say this in a snotty way.

My sister was almost eight when I was born in 1944. When I was old enough to fight with her and she found ways to tell me that I wasn't expected, I thought of how exciting it was whenever unexpected company came to call, especially if they had little kids for me to play with. Sometimes, though, when Liz got really mad at me, she called me "a mistake" or "an accident." What the hell did she mean by "accident?" To my knowledge, I'd never been in one. And how could I be a mistake? I was here, wasn't I? And above normal, according to my teachers.

Whenever I told on Liz, complaining about the mean things she said, Mom would give me a little hug. "There, there, now," she'd say. "The stork simply got lost for a while, but eventually found his way to our house."

Imagine a bird flying around over swamps and cornfields for such a long time with a nine-pound baby tied up in a blanket, dangling from its bill. Dad said that the stork most likely put down in the marsh near Bear Lake woods for a good rest while I fattened up on fish.

I let them have their stories.

The truth was that Mom had to spend two weeks in the Old Home Hospital—a three-story, white frame building—recovering from the horrible and dire complications of my birth. That's how Aunt Hazel liked to describe it, while shuddering in an exaggerated way: "horrible and dire complications." Mom survived, of course, saying, "Compared to the conditions of soldiers returning home from Europe, my ordeal was nothing. Why, I saw our local boys carried into the hospital on stretchers, some without an arm or a leg."

Until I looked up Aunt Hazel's word, "dire," it never occurred to me that my mother might have died as a result of my birth.

Dad said to just ignore the woman because she had a screw loose. He had no patience with her. Once, when Auntie tossed her head back, as if to look into heaven, and told Dad that she felt born again, he asked her if she could handle it this time. He told Mom that he'd never seen anyone get religion as fast as Aunt Hazel when she converted so that Cecil McDonough would marry her. "She takes her instructions too seriously," he said, "going to Mass (Dad called it 'mass hysteria') twice a day." She preached purgatory and damnation to anyone who'd sit for it and called just about everything a sin.

Although I eventually figured out what it meant to come into this world as a surprise, I never felt unwanted, except by Aunt Hazel and one other woman: Hulda Swenson.

Lucky for me, Aunt Hazel didn't come around very often. When she did, I was usually outside, playing with my friends. But I couldn't avoid old lady Swenson's cold eyes, flaring nostrils, and vicious tongue. Whenever the 500 Club met at our house, Dad either went for a long walk or entertained his friends in the basement. I wanted to be with them but Mom wouldn't let me.

Instead, she made me take a bath, put on the shoes and navy blue taffeta dress I'd worn for Grandad's funeral, and pass out tallies to the women so they'd know where to sit. Each time I walked the circle of women, they wore tight little smiles and whinnied as they drew a numbered card from my fist.

For at least an hour before the assembly of fur coats or pastel swing jackets (depending on the season) and beautiful dresses and a dozen different perfumes trailed in through our front door, I protested, hoping to wear my mother down.

"I *hate* having to be polite and parade around the room in front of everybody."

"It's good for you, dear. Gives you some poise. It'll make a lady out of you."

"Don't *want* to be a lady if it means going through such stupid rigmaroles just to sit down at a damn table."

"Oh, for heaven's sake, Callie. Just pass out the tallies and keep still. And, honest to God, your swearing *must* stop!"

Because Mom was already dressed and made up, having taken special pains with her thick, dark-brown hair, I knew she wouldn't be chasing me through the house and grabbing the Lava—a gritty soap reserved for extreme occasions.

"Damn, damn, damn!" I shouted, dancing from foot to foot.

"That's it! You've got one foot in hot water already, Callie. Just keep it up and you'll be sorry."

She turned her back on me and went to check on her serving supplies: the good china dessert plates with the little African violets, gleaming forks from the brown box of wedding silver, cloth napkins, also with African violets. She plugged in the coffee pot and made sure the angel food cake was intact.

"I'm keeping a tally on your language!" she called out from the kitchen, "so you'd better watch it, missy!"

Meeting up with Hulda Swenson in church was bad enough. Standing in front of her was a nightmare. She nailed me with those hard hazel eyes and flared her nostrils enough to reveal little black hairs. Then she reached with long, bony fingers to pluck at my fan of tallies, all the while glaring at me as if I were a criminal. She'd cluck her tongue and whisper comments that varied each time: "You were a dickens, you know. Your poor mother. You put her through an awful ordeal. Still do, I understand." Then she'd screw up her nose as if she had to sneeze. As I turned away, she'd hiss, "And your fingernails need a good cleaning."

If anyone else heard her, they never let on. And when I'd tell my mother about it, she'd accuse me of making it sound worse than it was.

Mom, who felt sorry for anyone who suffered trouble (which was just about the whole world), said not to let any of it bother me, that some years ago "the poor soul" had lost her only child who was eight, like me. Afterward, Mrs. Swenson was afflicted by so many miscarriages that she couldn't ever get another baby.

"When that happens to a woman," said Mom, who, at the time of our conversation, was ironing the cotton sheets and pillow cases I'd brought in from the clothesline, "she'll veer one way or another or pull up neutral."

"What does that mean?" I asked, inhaling the delicious, warm smell of the iron on sun-dried cloth.

"She'll either be extra good to children or treat them badly. Or she might go through life showing no feelings at all and simply ignore the little ones."

"Well, I know how *she* turned out, and I don't like her."

"Just be civil, Callie."

"I *am* civil, Mom. It's old lady Swenson who's *not*!"

"Good for you, dear. Now, if you please, put these away for me."

I gathered up the folded sheets and pillowcases and buried my nose in them on my way to the linen closet. What was a miscarriage and why had that little girl died? I could look up the word "miscarriage" but I wouldn't know, at least for now, how Doctor Nelson's mistake caused the girl to die. All I knew for sure was that Hulda Swenson was mean and sour, especially around me.

As soon as I could read, I spread my large pink baby book out on the living room floor next to Liz's and saw that our mother had given them equal attention. She'd pasted the same number of scribble drawings next to our annual birthday pictures and poked common pins through the pages, fastening the same number of locks of our darkening brown hair tied with tiny pink ribbons. I fitted one finger into a yellow wool mitten that had slipped from between the pages, still crusty and shrunken from baby spit. Finally, after poring over detailed records of our first teeth, first steps, first words, I came to the conclusion that I was every bit as smart as Liz.

What about the messages, though, in Mom's cards? She'd tucked those into a separate album that I found squirreled away on the top shelf of the linen closet. There were a couple of nice notes—even one from Aunt Eloise and Uncle Ray, whose baby Jen was a year old when I was born. But the album held as many "Get well" cards as "Congratulations on your new baby" cards: *You poor dear, Emily,* read one. *First of all, what a surprise! Also, being confined to bed for a month must have been very difficult. Good that Will was so helpful through it all. And little Liz, too. Harry and I wish you a speedy recovery.* And another: *I know that you've been through an awful ordeal. Get well soon so that you can enjoy the girls. I hope Liz will be happy with her new baby sister.*

Liz *was* happy with me, most of the time, glad to have someone to boss around. With so many years between us, she often acted like another mother.

Now that I was nearly nine, Liz and her boyfriend didn't mind taking me to a show once in a while. Sometimes, they let me sit on the front steps with them just before dark on a Saturday night while they waited for their friends to drive by. Liz's girlfriends were nice to me, but I especially liked the boys who wore their hair in flat top crew cuts and drove two-toned Chevies and low-riding black Mercuries with the chrome stripped off. They always had interesting stuff in their trunks and backseats: kittenballs, baseballs and mitts, slingshots, wooden guns with clothespins that shot rubber bands, cap guns that looked like real pistols, rifles and shotguns and boxes of shells and hunting caps ("Keep my sister away from those shotgun shells," Liz teased), and jackknives for carving and for playing mumblety-peg. I especially liked to play mumblety-peg after Brian taught me how to let the jackknife flip into the ground from different parts of the body, beginning with the toes and knees and working all the way up to the top of the head.

"Careful," Liz warned each time the knife's pointy leather punch steadied on a finger above my eyebrow.

After my sister and her friends piled into cars and drove off to cruise Main Street, I stretched out on the lawn and tugged at blades of grass, slowly, the way Liz taught me, so as not to break them. I nibbled on their tender white shoots and watched firefly lights drift above the grass or among shrubs, guessing where they might glow next. Sometimes, if the stars were out, I fell asleep on the lawn, trying to understand the idea of a sky without any end.

One night in August, Liz came home with a huge blue bear she'd won at the county fair. I was supposed to be asleep. She asked Mom if she should give me the stuffed toy.

"No, Liz," Mom answered, "that's yours. You won it."

That's when I knew that Liz wasn't just another mother.

In the fall of 1953, I had to go through a really shitty evening (I can almost feel the suds in my mouth) with the 500 Club. First of all, the mix of perfumes drifting around our living room made me want to puke. While the ladies studied their tallies long enough to figure out which tables to sit at (which took forever), Mrs. Swenson dragged out her whispered comments to me in an especially sarcastic tone, ending with, "A pretty dress does nothing for scabby knees," which Mom overheard. Finally!

"Callie," she said for all to hear, "you look lovely tonight and we thank you for passing out the tallies." Then with a hug, she excused me and whispered, "I am *so* sorry. You'll not have to endure Hulda Swenson any longer."

Without bothering to change out of my stiff taffeta and good shoes, I hurried through the kitchen, eyes burning, gouged a chunk from the angel food cake sitting on the counter, stuffed it into my mouth and clomped down the basement steps, cursing "that nasty, rotten old Mrs. Swenson." Mom would probably be mad about the cake, but I didn't give a damn. I hoped Mrs. Swenson would get that slice.

Dad and Carl Ryan, custodian at the Worthmore Dairy and Meat Locker, and Ted Claussen, who lived across the street from us, were cleaning up after gutting and singeing the mallards they'd shot before sunset. The familiar smells of fresh duck and blood and the contents of their intestines mixed with the sweet tobacco smoke from Dad's freshly lit pipe. Mr. Claussen, never seen without a toothpick sticking out of the corner of his mouth, stopped wadding up soiled newspapers. He and Mr. Ryan looked at me as if I didn't belong there, as if they'd stopped short in the middle of a dirty joke. They glanced at Dad who smiled and said, "Hey, Snicklefritz. How's my girl?"

The others said, "Hello, Callandra," in a polite way.

"Are the ladies winning big upstairs?" Dad asked.

"That damned old Mrs. Swenson," I snarled.

"Callie," Dad said sharply, "that's no way to talk."

"She's a mean old hag."

"What did I just say?"

"Well, she's not very nice."

"Just ignore her then."

"That's impossible when Mom makes me pass out those stupid tallies every time. Old lady Swenson is nothing but a witch and I hate her!"

"Oh, Callie."

I felt a little better when Mr. Claussen couldn't hide a smile. Even shy Mr. Ryan was grinning, which stopped the nervous tic in his left eye for a minute.

Turning my back on the shotgun shell pock marks in the tub of Mom's ringer washing machine, I reached down to pick a webbed foot out of the pail of remains and tugged at the tendon to make its toes move. Sometimes, while Dad dressed out birds, we'd look inside the crop of a duck to find out what it had been eating. Usually there was corn, tiny stones, and seeds.

I tossed the foot back into the pail. "May I see the ducks you shot?"

Mr. Ryan, acting surprised, unwrapped the waxed papers that hadn't been taped yet. Six large drakes were lined up on a long board atop the old pop cooler that we used as a minnow tank.

I looked closely at the ducks and poked at the small wet tufts of gray down feathers carried into the skin by lead pellets, mainly along the sides and legs, and a few in the necks. With the pinfeathers gone and after a quick singeing, the skin felt soft to my fingers.

"At least the breasts aren't all shot to hell."

"Callie!" Dad gave me a stern look.

The others laughed.

"She talks just like you, Will," said Mr. Claussen. "A chip off the old gunstock."

And they laughed some more. This time Dad joined in.

"Do you shoot, little lady?" asked Mr. Ryan.

"Yes, I know how to shoot a .22. I hit a bull's-eye that Dad nailed to a tree. Hit it from fifteen yards."

"Is that a fact?"

"Yes, sir, that's a fact."

Dad assured him that I was telling the truth.

"These birds are as big as any I ever shot years ago," he said, rewrapping and taping the waxed paper, "when I used to hunt with my brother Ray."

The way Dad said, 'when I used to hunt with my brother Ray,' sounded sad, as if it would never happen again.

"Your dad, Vic, was quite a hunter in his day, as I recall," said Mr. Claussen.

"The best," said Dad, stacking the wrapped ducks in a pasteboard box. "He and our uncle Amer taught Ray and me everything we know about hunting and fishing. We used to go to all the shoots. Managed to win a few trophies on the clay pigeon circuit."

Dad carried the box of mallards upstairs to the refrigerator, to be parceled out later. When he returned to the basement, he plunked down next to me on the lopsided sofa that sat against one cement block wall of the larger room. Mr. Ryan and Mr. Claussen sank back into a pair of cushioned gray chairs that had mint-colored towels tacked over the arms. A large brown area rug covered part of the concrete floor. Snuggled next to Dad, I watched the smoke curl up from his pipe, picked at the lace trim of my anklets, and listened to the men talk until the deep murmuring sounds of their voices faded and I fell asleep.

After that evening, I took refuge among the men every chance I got. Instead of ordering me around in persnickety voices, with scowls or forced smiles, and fretting about their ailments, the men took me in without a word. Although I would soon learn that they had cares of their own, I was happy being with them while they cleaned fish and wild game, listened to baseball and big bands on the radio, watched the Gillette Friday night fights on television, and talked about the world. They called me Small Fry and Skeeziks and Snickelfritz and asked me how was my gizzard. They gave me pheasant feathers and empty shotgun shells (like Grandad's), fishing lures and cuss words. And once, Mr. Claussen offered me a chaw of sweet, moist plug tobacco.

From then on, Dad called me Cal.

Three

The Ring

"CAL, SEND UP THE EMPTY PAIL," Dad calls down from his perch near the roof of Gram's cottage.

With a blue sky for a backdrop, he leans against the top rungs of an extension ladder propped at the second story, scraping rotten leaves from the gutter with his bare hands.

Our day at the lake has started, as always, with work before fishing. This time, it's fall cleanup and closing the cottage for winter. Ever since Grandad died and Gram became too old to stay on by herself, it's been up to us to take care of the place.

As soon as we turned into the driveway, the smell of dead carp hit us through the open car windows. Ripening in the morning sun, it was most likely dragged into the yard by a mink. Flies buzzed around as Dad scooped up the stinky mess and buried the works deep in the ground, next to a volunteer tomato plant.

"Won't the tomatoes taste fishy?"

"Could be," he said, patting down the dirt with the back of his shovel. "But we'll take our fish however we can get 'em."

"Yuck."

"Good for what ails you, Cal."

He's always saying that. That and "How's the world treating you?" and "How's your gizzard?"

While he fishes leaf soup out of the gutters, it's my job to see that the ladder doesn't slip, hand up an empty pail, and dump the full one. It doesn't take long for the oozy black gunk from rotten oak and birch leaves to make a heap in the ditch near the lane.

It's hot out for October, a time we call Indian Summer. Grownups, especially, cling to these days. Now that I'm ten, I understand why. Dad calls them bonus days, extra warm in a month that can turn on you, and full of smells so strong they pop into your head in the dead of a long winter: leftover summer algae and marshweed stewing on the sandy shore and stinky carp carcasses wedged in the rocks with patches of thick scales and maggoty meat on mostly white bones. And then there's the hot unsettling wind that pushes waves ahead of it, along with the smells of everything in that gray-green water. Those smells find their way right up your nose: lake weeds and fish and turtles and bloodsuckers and waterfowl dung. Last winter, when we came out to check on Gram, I flopped down in the deep, powdery snow to make an angel. When I was finished, I lay there for a minute, staring up through stick trees and snowflakes, remembering those smells of our last Indian Summer.

"The lake sure is beautiful from up here!" Dad lowers another pail to the ground with a long rope. "If your mother could see this view, she might consent to a boat ride one day."

"Hah! Don't bet on it."

As much as we wish Mom would join us, we know she won't. She mostly stays in town, says she prefers housecleaning to fishing. But that isn't the real reason. Ever since she was a little girl, she's been afraid of the water. I'm pretty sure it has to do with somebody drowning, but whenever I ask, she chokes up and changes the subject to stuff like, "Now, Callie, with Liz away at college, it's up to you to help your dad with the lake chores. Heaven knows Ray never comes around to do his share. Just be careful when you're out on the water."

The end of summer, we moved Gram into a little house in Masterton. After two years at the lake without Grandad, she'd started acting weird, muttering to herself, forgetting where she put things. She called Dad one night from Mr. Johnson's cottage, complaining that she couldn't find her coin purse.

"I just know someone stole it," she said, sounding on the verge of tears. As Dad was getting ready to drive the twenty-five miles back to the lake, she called again, giggling this time.

"Silly me. I found my little purse in the icebox. And the pound of butter was on my dresser. Imagine that!"

Dad had a talk with Mr. and Mrs. Johnson, who agreed that Gram was acting stranger than usual. She needed their help finding her spectacles, wore her aprons inside out, and talked to the squirrels, which doesn't seem strange to me. Dad always speaks to animals during our walks. The turning point was when Gram started leaving burners on and scorching empty pans. One day, she fell off the dock in spite of the safety rope Dad had tied around the posts.

"We've got to consider your age, Mother," he'd told her, "and the fact that you're getting to be quite forgetful."

Finally, he was able to convince Gram to make the move so we could look after her in winter without driving miles through snowdrifts.

"As long as you promise to take care of things, Willie," she said. "Open up the cottage first thing in April so Ray and his family can come for a visit. We'll have a big fish fry then."

She was constantly talking about Ray—the son who never came to see her.

Now, climbing halfway up the ladder with an empty pail and thinking about Gram's fish fries, I hear tires crunch gravel. Turning into the driveway is the longest, most beautiful car I've ever seen—a brand new 1954 powder-blue Cadillac with fins. And it's pulling a trailer with a fancy fishing boat.

Dad grins at first, then frowns. "Well, I'll be damned," he says, clutching a fistful of soggy leaves.

I inch down the ladder and stand off to one side, surprised by the car, doubly surprised by the boat on a trailer, unusual in these parts.

Dripping with muck and sweat, Dad steps down and stands for a minute, wiping his hands on his shirttail before rushing over to the car.

"Look who's here, Cal! It's your Uncle Ray."

I can tell that my dad's trying to be enthusiastic about this unexpected visit, trying to act as if there's nothing wrong. But he can't fool me. Just last week, I overheard Mom say, "You and your brother! If the two of you ever get together again, you'll be facing off before anyone can slap at a mosquito."

Dad and Uncle Ray, who is older by eleven months, grew up best friends, hunting and fishing, even traveling together as young men. All of that ended the night they met Eloise.

I edge toward the car where my uncle and another man sit, taking their own sweet time, in no hurry to get out. They fiddle with their pipes and hats and car keys while Dad stands waiting and wiping his hands, the look on his face changing from a worried grin to irritation.

Finally, the two men open their doors, ease themselves from the ivory-colored leather seats, stand and stretch as if they're alone at a campground, pipes clamped between their teeth, in no hurry to greet us.

If they were kids, my mother would say, "With that attitude, you can just turn right around and go home."

Uncle Ray, who's treating us like strangers he doesn't care to know, looks nothing like my dad except for the lively blue eyes behind wire glasses. He's shorter by a couple of inches. His thin hair, the color of yellow clay, is trimmed just so. With a sweep of their hands, the newcomers smooth back imaginary out-of-place hairs before adjusting their new sports hats.

"You look like you're going on safari," I mutter.

They glance at me without so much as a smile and turn away. I start to add, "or some hot-shot fishing expedition," but Dad gives me the eye and I stop after the word "shot."

Uncle Ray's friend reminds me of a ballet dancer the way he turns on the balls of his feet and raises one hand to shade his eyes. He bends backwards to scan the trees and sky, ending with a quick glance at our brown box of a cottage.

Both men wear rust-colored vests with a ton of pockets. Their porkpie hats are loaded with yellow, red and green casting flies. They could have stepped out of Grandma's *National Geographic* magazines, except their khaki pants and plaid shirts are too clean and hold sharp creases.

I've seen men like these before—up from Chicago or down from Minneapolis. They stand out from the locals in ragged shirts and overalls, who wave big and have a friendly way of calling out to one another above the putt-putt of their motors, "Havin' any luck?" Then they hold up their stringers, filled or not, and trade tips on bait and location until they're out of earshot.

It's easy to spot a city man. Just motoring by, he sticks out like an oversized bobber. He might give you half a smile or none at all. He might wave a business-like finger, but he won't say anything. And he'll never show you his stringer unless he's off to see the taxidermist.

"How the hell are ya?" Dad holds out his hand.

Why doesn't he say what's really on his mind?—"Where the hell have you been? We sure could use some help around here, damn it!"

Instead, it's, "Nice car, Ray. A real beaut!"

I want to gag.

I count five pumps when they finally shake hands. (I'm in the habit of counting things: ducks and geese on the fly, the number of steps down to the dock, how many times our neighbor, Mr. Johnson, says "so on and so forth," and how often our preacher pounds the pulpit on a Sunday morning when he's angry about something, like "those loose women in Paris, France."

Ray's friend saunters over to admire the Cadillac, as if he's never seen it before.

"Say, Will, I'd like you to meet a friend of mine," says Ray. "He works with me at Fidelity. Barber, my little brother, William—Maywood County Auditor."

"I didn't know Ray had a brother until just last week," says Barber.

Dad looks startled as he shakes hands with the guy (three pumps). He puts his arm around my shoulder.

"This is my daughter, Cal. She just started fifth . . ."

But Uncle Ray and Barber have already turned away. Moving toward the boat trailer, they leave behind the fragrant smell of cherry-blend tobacco.

Dad looks at me apologetically and shrugs. I don't care. Little kids are used to being invisible around grownups. Besides, I'm busy noticing how pale and clean these men are and without a wrinkle in their clothes, even after driving all the way from Sioux City, Iowa.

Dad says it helps to have air conditioning in a car.

Uncle Ray peels the boat cover back part way.

"Say, you've sure got yourself a nice outfit here." Dad runs his hand along the gunwale. "One of those new aluminum rigs."

"Yup. Alumacraft Model K, sixteen-footer. Bought her a few weeks ago."

Uncle Ray walks around to the stern and lifts part of the cover to show off his new Johnson fifty-horsepower motor. (Ours is a ten-horse.) "Took her out on the river a couple of times. She only weighs a hundred ninety-five pounds. A real cinch. No more wooden boats for me."

When my uncle says that, I feel like kicking his tiny tires. It's as much the tone of his voice as the words that get under my skin.

"It trailed all right on the highway?" asks Dad, frowning slightly.

"No trouble. Of course, I held the speed down."

"Did you stop in town to see Mother?"

"Nope. We came straight out. Didn't know if you'd be around or not."

Dad steps back and glares at Ray who returns the look, as Mom once said, "with the confidence of a man who has just sold a big insurance policy."

"So how've you been, Will?"

"Busy." He motions toward the cottage. "Not much time to fish or hunt since Dad died."

A flush of color rises in his cheeks and I know why. He and Mom talk about how hard it is to keep up three places: this cottage, our house, and Gram's house in town. Wasn't easy getting her settled in a new place.

"Well, Barber and I are going after some big ones. There's plenty of room in my boat if you want to come along."

"Say, that'd be fine. We'd like that, wouldn't we, Cal?"

Dad turns to me and winks. I roll my eyes. Fishing with my uncle might be okay if he was alone, but a dose of two city slickers in a boat is like one playmate too many.

"Let's go then," says Ray.

"What's the rush? You just got here. Besides, I need to finish up a few things."

"We haven't got all day."

Dad's jaw muscles ripple and I hear him let out a deep breath. "You might want to look at the lake. It's been choppy this morning, blowing pretty hard."

I run ahead, past the protection of the cottage, into a blast of hot wind blowing across Tepeeotah Bay. It fills my ears with the noise of a big seashell. The wind tries to pull my hair out by the roots and shakes up the last dry oak leaves still hooked to their branches. Other than my favorite birch tree, there's nothing but old oaks in the front yard—no sugar maples, no ash, no color. I stop short of the steep hill and look down at the whitecaps rolling in. They slap against the huge boulder and crash with bellowing sounds inside the hollowed-out clay cove. The wind and waves churn my insides.

Thirty-six steps lead down to the dock—long, thick planks that Dad laid out on cross pieces nailed to heavy posts driven into the lake bottom with a sledgehammer. Waves wash over the end sections. Our small wooden boat, beige with faded green trim, tugs at its ropes and slams against tire bumpers.

The three men stand at the edge of the hill. Dad's thin shirt and pants cling to him in the wind. "It's rough out there," he says.

Ray smirks. "My boat can handle it."

"Well, all right then. I just have a short stretch of gutter left to clean and we can get our gear lined up. Maybe by then the wind'll die down a bit."

As the men start toward the back yard, Dad says, "I could sure use a little help, Ray. Suppose you move the ladder for me, carry a few things back to the garage."

"Hell," says my uncle, "I didn't come all this way to work. I came to fish!"

Dad stops short and swings his whole body around. In spite of the wind, I can hear him suck in a loud breath through his nose. Then, in a voice higher than usual, he shouts, "Who the hell do you think you are?"

Ray doesn't answer. And he doesn't look away. He just stares at Dad with the same I-dare-you look I've seen among boys on the playground. Finally, he says, "Aw, hell, you're just sore about my new rig."

"Like hell I am! You've never once helped out around here. That's the problem!"

Dad's voice gets louder and louder. Spit gathers at the corners of his mouth like soap bubbles.

"First time you come back since the funeral and you can't even stop to see Mother! What the hell's the matter with you?"

"I don't have time. You live here. It's easier for you to take care of things."
A wild mean mask comes down over Dad's gentle face. His hands turn to fists.
"God damn it!" he roars, "I'll knock your Goddamn block off!"

I freeze for a second before backing away from the men and colliding with
the big birch tree. I feel my eyes go wide. My heart is pounding. I swear I can
hear the bell at Madison Square Garden, like when Dad and I watch the fights
on television. Except this boxing ring is under open sky, on grass littered with
acorns, our cottage on one side, the hill on the other—a steep hill that pitches
straight down to the lake.

The wind blows harder across the bay, carrying smells of fish and rotting
algae. The hot sun pokes through the leaves and spots the men as they circle
each other with their dukes up.

My temples throb and the birch bark scratches at my arms. Even though
I'm scared, something inside me itches to see a fight. What's that about? This
isn't Sugar Ray and Sonny—this is my family. What will I do if Dad and Ray
fall to the ground punching and knocking each other's teeth out, blood splat-
tering all over? Where can I find help? At least they don't have guns like when
my great-uncle Amer got killed.

Barber is tense as a deer hunter. He stands on Uncle Ray's side of the ring,
his eyebrows trussed up like little tents.

There's no one at the Johnsons' to rush out and break things up. They left
earlier, waving on their way to town. Mr. Johnson wouldn't be much good anyway—his wife has to bait his hook and take the fish off his line.

And there's no one at any of the other nearby cottages.

While the men circle each other, I hug my birch tree and think of Rocky
Marciano pounding the bejesus out of Jersey Joe Wolcott, slugging with wet
jackhammer gloves against cut lips, swelled eyes, and smashed noses until halos
of sweat and spit arc around their heads and snot and blood fly out of our television set.

All I can do now is hope that Dad has learned something from those fights.
At forty he should still be fit, having trained in yard work, dock building, and
long walks.

Yet I don't want my uncle to get hurt either. He's family, after all, and I
want to like him. But he's soft from sitting in his air-conditioned car and selling
life insurance in Iowa.

I know which man to bet on.

My heart is pounding and I feel dizzy in my head. Seeing Dad like this, with mean eyes and his face all red, like at Grandad's funeral, scares me. What if he goes down before he can throw a punch?

Over and over, they shuffle in close, then back off, moving their arms slowly, as if pushing bike pedals with hands that want boxing gloves.

Dad holds his fists tight to his face, looking like Ernest Hemingway in a book I found at the library—handsome with shiny black hair and a good build. But that's as far as it goes, because my dad is no fighter. Everyone in town knows that.

Uncle Ray looks nervous—no more sarcastic grin. The way he stands his ground, though, with fists high and away from his body reminds me of bare-knuckler John L. Sullivan, whose picture I saw once.

Back and forth they move, circling each other, closing in and shuffling away in a stupid dance, while the wind rattles the oak leaves and acorns crunch underfoot.

The long wait for that first punch goes on forever. And they're still wearing their glasses. I break away from my tree and run toward them.

"Dad! Stop!"

Uncle Ray's eyes flicker as he takes a step backward. Dad turns his head slightly without looking away from his brother.

"Stay out of it, Callie! Get in the house."

"No! I won't!"

Within seconds, I enter the ring, standing with my legs apart and fists up, aiming first at Uncle Ray, then at Dad, then at Barber, who backs away. The noises around me grow louder: smashing acorns are loud fans stomping their feet. Leaves applaud like crazy. The roaring waves call for blood.

"I hate you! I hate all of you!"

Dad and Uncle Ray, their lips pinched into thin lines, freeze at the edge of the hill. Dad lowers his arms and chuckles nervously, probably at the sight of his skinny girl in the middle of their boxing ring. Even though I'm bawling and wetting my shorts, I try for a mean face, with bare feet in Sugar Ray position, the way Dad taught me.

"Oh, Cal," he says softly. His shoulders slump and he lowers his arms.

At that moment, my uncle takes another step backward and loses his balance. It's like slow motion, with his one foot connected to tall weeds before he drops out of sight. A second later, splash.

Ray barely misses hitting the boulder. He surfaces, gets knocked over by a big wave, resurfaces, and manages to stand, chest deep, facing the whitecaps. Because his back is to the cove, I can't see his face.

"Ray!" shouts my dad. "Are you all right?"

No answer.

We run down the steps and onto the dock just as my uncle wades in, scowling as if he hated the lake and everything around it. Drenched, with his wire glasses hanging from one ear, he slaps the water and struggles onto the dock. Dad and Barber each offer a hand. Ray ignores them, steps up on a boulder, and rolls himself onto the planks. His clothes are wrinkled and squishy. Thin strands of moss hang from his hair and shoulders. "Fuck!" is all he says. His face turns white, his scowl replaced by an expression I've seen in the movies when a guy gets shot and the meanness disappears and all he's left with is a look of sad surprise. Uncle Ray takes the steps two at a time up the hill.

I follow the men partway and peek around the corner in time to see my uncle whip the canvas cover back over his boat. Barber tries to help, but is waved off. Dad stands to one side, looking sad and alone, as if someone else in the family has just died.

Uncle Ray yanks open the car door, flops behind the wheel, guns the engine, and jerks the car into reverse. Tires shoot gravel as he rams backwards out of the driveway. The trailer jackknifes. He pulls ahead, then launches into reverse again, lurching back and forth until he smashes into my second favorite birch tree. One of the wheels hits the long metal pipe at the edge of our property, knocking it off its cement blocks. The boat swerves into the ditch.

"Son of a bitch!" he screams.

Barber stands nearby, shouting lame directions and waving his hands.

Having seen enough, I go back to the lakeside, curl up in the Adirondack chair, and pick at the loose flecks of sun-baked green paint. Dad's words reel through my mind: "I'll knock your Goddamn block off!" Then there was that word "fuck," not to mention "son of a bitch"—words that would result in more than a bar of soap in the mouth if I ever dared repeat them.

The Cadillac engine roars, along with spitting gravel. I concentrate on the loud motor until it hums out of earshot. And then I listen still—just in case—until the wind is the only sound left.

"I'll knock your Goddamn block off!" That's what my dad said and I don't blame him.

Growing up Swedish Lutheran, I'm told never to utter God's name, except in prayers and hymns. Tons of hymns. Now, to the tune of "What a Friend We Have in Jesus," I sing-shout above the waves, "I will knock your Goddamn block off . . ."

It makes me feel a bit better, but after several choruses, thoughts of Hell and Purgatory crowd my brain. My Catholic friends warn me all the time that if I don't stop swearing, I'll go straight to Hell or end up in Purgatory until someone bails me out with prayers and a lot of money. I tell them about Aunt Hazel who converted to please her husband, and say I don't care, that our religion has no such stupid place as Purgatory. Hell concerns me, though I'll never admit it. I consider repromising God not to swear so much—at least till I get older, like my dad.

Just as I begin another verse of "I Will Knock Your Goddamn Block Off," Dad walks over from the other side of the cottage. He stands for a minute, blinking his eyes as if he's just gone through a dust storm. Without a word, he sits down next to me on the Adirondack and gives me a hug. I lean into his strong arms. We sit quietly until the wind dies down to a murmur and the oak leaves stop shaking.

"I'm sorry you had to see all this, Cal. It was no good to end that way."

"Uh-huh."

"Don't worry, sweetheart. Everything will be all right."

"I guess."

"You know, Callie girl, you looked pretty good in that ring."

With a hard grin, I try to hold back the tears, remembering how mean my dad looked just minutes ago.

He stands and smiles so that his eyes light up. He turns toward the bay, raises an arm and points. "I think there's a great northern right about there with your name on it." He looks back at me. "Okay, partner?"

I take his hand. As we walk to the rear of the cottage, I think about the day he came home after fishing alone.

"Can't say for sure," he'd said in a sad voice, "but I think I passed Ray in his boat heading in the opposite direction. It was awfully foggy, though, and . . ."

Maybe that's how it's going to be with Dad and Uncle Ray—in separate boats, floating past each other in the fog.

Victory Run

ITH MINNOWS, WORMS, TACKLE, AND A LANDING NET, we float in our wooden boat a hundred yards from shore, eyes fixed on the red-and-white bobbers dancing on small waves. Dad says he feels like still-fishing instead of trolling for a big one.

"Let's relax tonight, Cal, let the fish come to us."

It is the end of the fighting day. The wind has died down, but my insides still feel yucky.

I reel in my line to check bait. The hook is bare except for a pale, washed-out section of worm. I dig around in the Butternut coffee tin filled with dirt and nightcrawlers, choose a long fat one, thread it onto my hook, cast the line, and lean back against a folded life jacket. Dad smiles and nods. Guess he doesn't feel much like talking, either.

I gaze up at our cottage on Tepeeotah Hill, imagining how the whole thing must have looked from here—Dad and Uncle Ray circling each other like boxing bears. Uncle Ray rolling down the cliff and splashing into the lake. I'll bet that looked funny, like a Buster Keaton movie. But what if he'd been killed? Like that guy who took a running dive at the state park and cracked his skull open on a boulder. Then what?

The boat rocks gently and gives off a soft *glou-glou* sound of water lapping at the hull. I push the memory of the fight aside and daydream about the times our family used to have up on the hill: Grandad hoisting a brace of mallards; Dad grinning into a Brownie camera, showing off a stringer of northerns; Liz snuggling in the Adirondack with her boyfriend while he carves "Brian + Liz" inside a heart on the wooden arm of the chair; Mom on the dock, in her black-and-white swimsuit. I imagine her looking up from the book she's reading to wave at us.

"Whoa, Cal, wanna practice your landing skills?" Dad reels in a big bull-head and lets it hang from his line like a dark weight above the water.

We generally don't use a net for bullheads, but it's fun to pretend that I have five seconds to scoop up a great northern. I land Dad's fish and swing it into the boat.

"Our first catch of the evening," he says, untangling it from the net and removing the hook. He eases the fish into our metal bucket filled with fresh lake water.

"Need a worm?" I ask, ready to hand him the coffee can.

"No, I think I'll try a minnow."

The last bit of sun catches the tops of ripply waves. Our anchor line is taut, keeping us where we started, where we want to be.

Leaning back against my cushiony life jacket, knees bent, feet on the gunwale, I look up at the cottage once more, this time picturing Gram in her turquoise-and-white checked apron over a house dress, calling us in to supper with her shrill, "Yoo-hoo, everybody! The fish are ready! Come and eat!"

I imagine myself in shorts and a T-shirt, wandering barefoot along the shore, far from our cove, in search of driftwood and pretty stones and arrowheads. I know where to find tadpoles and where the goslings rush after their parents to hide among the cattails and which side of the point the wind blows coolest and where the tipsy-timbered boathouses threaten to collapse but never do. Around that far point, away from shore and in the middle of a hayfield, stands Lone Tree. It's been there forever, that old scrub oak with a trunk so thick my arms barely start a circle around it. One of its gnarly branches would be perfect for a rope swing, but that would ruin the wildness of it. After rounding the point, I like to dash into the north wind and across the field to touch Lone Tree for good luck.

Eight docks down from ours, in the opposite direction, a huge boulder sticks up out of the sand. It feels strange to imagine the outline of myself perched on that black rock, looking back at the "me" sitting in this boat. Thinking that way makes me realize that everything in our lives is over as soon as it happens. Every day, a thousand little acts, a thousand little deaths.

I shift my attention to the stern of the boat. Dad straddles the seat next to the motor, looking like the letter "S" with his feet tucked under and his shoulders hunched forward. His left hand rests on the throttle of the Johnson ten-horse. His right hand holds the steel Pflueger Supreme he uses for both trolling and still-fishing. It has a green-and-white handle, and I wonder how old I'll have to be to cast it as smoothly as Dad does. Once, while sitting together at the end of the dock, he let me try. The resulting backlash snarled inside the reel like a heap of spaghetti, impossible to untangle.

"No need to worry, Cal," he said, picking patiently at the mess of line. "We have all the time in the world."

I look at him now and wonder if he ever thinks about the times our family had up on that hill and how, not an hour ago, he and his brother couldn't even go one round. He acts like he's already forgotten about it. When he looks back at me with a smile, his face is kind and open, as if he hasn't a care in the world. I'm glad that the awful mask he wore inside the boxing ring is gone.

"Dad, why did Uncle Ray act that way, not wanting to help and all?"

"What happened this afternoon, Cal—try to put it out of your mind."

"Just wondering."

There is a long silence.

"Well, how come?"

Dad looks at me as if to determine how much he wants to reveal.

"I guess he thought he had to prove something. Hard to say, but it goes way back to when we were youngsters. He got by with a lot."

"Like what?"

"Oh, the usual stuff with kids."

"Like what, Dad?"

"Well, I had to do most of the chores while we were growing up. My brother got the easy jobs, like feeding the dogs and gathering cobs for the stove. Seems as though more was expected of me. I always thought Ray was Mother's favorite. He was a bit on the delicate side. Still is, in a way."

"That wasn't fair. He's older than you."

"Not by much. Anyhow, it was a long time ago. Don't you fret about what happened. You're too young to worry."

"People can worry at any age."

"Is that so?"

"Yes, that's so . . . Anyhow, I like our boat better'n that ol' tin one he's got."

"So do I, Cal. So do I."

He reaches down to pat one of the boat's wooden ribs.

Along the shoreline, October's early dusk blends the lake colors with the land. The water is like gray glass. Our boat is perfectly still, except for when we shift our weight. Off the port side, something pierces the water from beneath. I lean over the gunwale and spot the snout of a snapping turtle sipping at the air. As soon as he sees me, he slips down and away.

"A turtle, Dad! Think I can catch him?"

"Could be, Cal. You never know."

I poke the tip of my fishing pole into the water to stir it up.

"Do you have a favorite?" I ask, watching the circles widen.

"A favorite what?"

"Well, do you like me or Liz the best?"

"Your mother and I love you both the same."

I'm glad to hear him say that, even though I don't think it's true in some ways. Dad likes that I'm not afraid of worms and bloodsuckers.

"What was Billy like?"

"Your brother was a good baby, Cal. He wasn't with us for long. Only a few weeks."

"How'd he die again?"

"The doctors called it a crib death. It happens sometimes when a baby goes to sleep and doesn't wake up. No one really knows why."

"Do older kids die like that, too?"

"No, not likely."

"I'll bet that's what happened to Mrs. Swenson's babies. Mom said that she lost a lot of 'em. Enough to make her mean."

"I wouldn't know about that."

"Are you still sad about Billy?"

"Of course. We'll always feel sad, even though it happened a long time ago. Now we've got you and Liz to worry about." He chuckles. "You two can be quite a handful."

I grin and tug at my line to see if anything is on the other end besides my glob of worms.

"Oh, I've got something!" I reel in and heft up a huge bullhead.

Dad catches one at the same time.

"We'll eat tonight, kiddo," he says, slipping his fish into the pail. "Looks like yours swallowed the hook. Shall I take care of it for you?"

I hand the line over. Dad probes the fish's gullet with a long needle-nose pliers and removes the hook without pulling out the innards so the fish can stay alive on the way home.

"Almost enough for supper, Cal. As Uncle Amer used to say, 'Fry 'em up nice and crispy and eat 'em with bread, butter, and a bottle a beer. Nothing better.'"

I cast my line with a new worm, reel in enough to take up the slack, and smack my lips.

"I'll have a beer."

Dad snorts. "In ten or twelve years, maybe."

"Did Uncle Amer give you and Ray beers?"

"Mostly soda pop. We were pretty young at the time."

My line grows taut again. I tug back and reel slowly. Whatever it is coming toward the boat feels heavy and doesn't fight, as if I've caught a slug of big old lazy fish. Just then the snapping turtle rises to the surface with my hook in his mouth. He looks at me for the second time, slips the hook, and disappears.

"Did you see, Dad? I caught that turtle! He was huge!"

"A granddaddy, all right. I'd hate to have to pull a hook out of that guy."

I settle down and think some more about Billy, wondering what it would be like to have a big brother.

"It'll soon be dark, Cal. Time to go in."

"Hmm," I murmur, working my line back and forth in the water.

Neither of us budges. We always hold off until the last minute, waiting for that one big fish to strike before it gets too dark to see our bobbers.

"It was midnight on the ocean," I say, inviting Dad to recite our favorite nonsense poem.

"Not a streetcar was in sight," he continues.

"The sun was shining brightly, for it had rained all night."

"'Twas a summer's day in winter, and the rain was snowing fast, as the barefoot girl with shoes on stood sitting on the grass . . ."

Our laughter bounces back at us from the coved hill.

Tonight, we've caught only bullheads. We would rather have northerns or walleyes, but we weren't exactly going after them. Anyhow, as Dad says, "A meal is a meal."

I'm still excited about the snapping turtle. Turtles almost never take a baited hook, but when they do, it's like meeting up with a monster from the deep—a magical monster that will grant one wish never to be told to a living soul.

"Ready to pull anchor, Cal? We'd best make tracks."

Dad gives me plenty of time to haul in the anchor rope, I suppose because I'm a girl.

"Take your time, sweetheart. No rush. Easy on the arms."

He doesn't need to be concerned about my muscles. The last day of school, before summer vacation, I beat Bobby Keeler arm wrestling.

Hanging over the gunwale, I swish the anchor back and forth like a heavy pendulum, until mud and weeds fall away. My biceps strain as I heft the mud-hook and wedge it into the V of the bow. With my feet scrunched together on top of the coiled rope, I face forward in my usual position and call back over my shoulder,

"All set, Dad! Give 'er hell!"

He shakes his head and shoves the lever of the ten-horse to full throttle and takes off in the opposite direction, away from shore. We always make a victory run whether we've caught anything or not. Soaring around the bay behind a pair of low-flying mallards, I grip the gunwales and lean into the wind, feeling like a beautiful figurehead on the prow of our ship, pitching above the spray. Through tangled hair I glance back at Dad and we laugh.

It is pitch dark by the time we get back to the dock. The water, gentled down after the wake of our boat subsides, *clucks* beneath the planks and inside the clay cove. I tell Dad it sounds like old lady Swenson. He nearly chokes with laughter when I imitate her in my best witch's voice: "You were a dickens, you know . . . Your poor mother . . . Those fingernails need a good cleaning . . . A pretty dress does nothing for scabby knees."

"Just pass it off, Cal, and she'll never get the best of you."

We secure the boat and haul our gear up the steps and around to the garage. Crickets chirp in monotonous rhythm. Hordes of mosquitoes hum in the shrubs. There hasn't yet been a killing frost. A heron scream pierces the night air, startling me so that I drop the landing net.

"Something got to that one," says Dad, dumping our fish onto the grass for a final count: a half dozen bullheads. Only one is mine. He slips them back into the dented pail and fills it halfway with cold water from the spigot. "Those birds sound off as if they're announcing the end of the world."

He pauses to fill and light his pipe.

"I'll take care of the rest out here, Cal. I'd like you to go inside and check around before we lock up. Make sure all the lights are off and the doors are closed. I want to visit with the Johnsons about keeping an eye on things this winter, let them know when I can get the boat and dock out. We'll have to shut the water off and drain the pipes, too. Probably next week."

The idea of going through the place and closing it until spring makes me sad. The rooms already smell funny, kind of stale, as if no one has ever lived in them.

In the garage, where we store our tackle, Dad takes a rag from the workbench and wipes our rods and reels.

"We'll leave these here in case we get out fishing another time or two," he says, hanging the rods between clips on a wooden fish plaque nailed to a wall stud. "But we'd better take the worms and minnows back to town with us."

Dad heads toward the open door and turns around.

"Guess that does it for tonight, kiddo. Don't forget to check the stove. I'll be back shortly."

"Shortly" to Dad means at least a half hour, once he starts visiting with the Johnsons.

Tobacco smoke lingers inside the garage. Propped near the workbench are the matching blue-and-white Schwinns Grandad bought for us to use at the lake. The bike I ride is clean and its tires are still inflated. The other one looks new, although its seat is dusty and the handlebars have grown cobwebs. Its tires are nearly flat, which reminds me of the summer's day when my cousin Jenny and I rode out to Slaughter Slough.

Five

Mudflats and Ghosts

ENNY WAS LIKE ANOTHER SISTER to me the summer she was eight and I had just turned seven. We rode our bikes to Bloody Lake, past the haunted house, the Gypsy camp, and on to Slaughter Slough. Afterward, we pedaled to Belle's Tavern for a drink. By the time Jen had to go back to Sioux City, we'd planned our next adventure and promised to write every week and exchange school pictures in the fall. Just before she left Tepeeotah, we held hands, balancing together one last time on the long pipe above the "alligator pit."

Jenny was taller than I was, more like a twelve-year-old, which is how old she'd be now. I'll be eleven next June. She had long dark hair, high cheekbones, like her dad's, and eyes the same color as Elizabeth Taylor's. But she didn't look like her the way my sister does. Jen's eyes turned up at the corners, as if she might get into mischief. She had deep dimples like Uncle Ray. Like my dad and Liz, too. Sometimes, while doing homework, I try to make dimples of my own by poking the eraser end of a pencil into my cheeks.

On a day in August, Liz and Mom had gone shopping. Aunt Eloise, as always, stayed in Sioux City. The rest of the grown-ups were sitting around the kitchen table after a fish fry. Gram got up to make a pot of coffee, while Dad and Uncle Ray argued about politics and Russia. Grandad stayed mostly quiet.

"Just wait and see," said Uncle Ray. "Communism will take over if we don't put a stop to it."

Dad shook his head. "A buncha hooey. I don't believe they can do any real damage to the good old U. S. of A."

"Thanks to McCarthy," said Gram. "Why, if it weren't for him . . ."

"McCarthy is dangerous, Mother!" Dad exclaimed. "He's on a witch hunt. They've got us all so scared, we're building bomb shelters in our back yards."

I didn't know what Dad meant. I watched Charlie McCarthy on television. How could a puppet be dangerous? And what did he have to do with bomb shelters and our teachers making us crawl under desks at school? They said it was in case of an air raid, whatever that was.

"Charlie McCarthy?" I said, leaning against Dad's shoulder. "He's funny."

"No, Cal, we're talking about a senator—*Joe* McCarthy."

Grandad chuckled and said he liked Charlie McCarthy, too. Preferred him over the senator. "I wonder who's pulling *his* strings," he said in his slow voice.

After more arguing between our dads, which sounded like preaching, Jen and I rolled our eyes and began to fidget. Gram gave us each a whole Popsicle and told us to go outside and play.

The screen door slammed behind us as we skipped down the steps. Sitting on the ground with our backs against the birch tree, we sucked and munched our cherry Popsicles before the heat could melt them. In between bites, we took turns imitating a mourning dove cooing in the distance.

"My friend Janet has a bomb shelter in her back yard," I mumbled through cold teeth and numb lips. "Her dad dug a big hole and lined it with cement blocks and a roof flat to the ground. We play down there sometimes."

"Is your dad going to build one?" asked Jen.

"Naw. He says what's the use. If the whole damn world goes up in smoke, he doesn't want to have to crawl out of a pit and start over. That'd be hell."

"You shouldn't swear, Callie."

"I'm just sayin'."

"We don't have a bomb shelter either."

"Hmm. Say, do you wanna go to Slaughter Slough?" I whispered through a slushy bite.

"Where's that?"

"A couple miles from here. We could ride our bikes."

"Why are you whispering, Callie?"

"Because Dad doesn't like me to go there on account of the mudflats. He worries that I might get stuck. Not like in quicksand, but it's hard to get out when you're by yourself, especially after it rains. Then you sound like 'a Texas steer trying to pull his hooves out of the mud.'"

"That's silly! How come they call it Slaughter Slough?"

"Because it's where the Indians massacred some settlers. We could hunt for arrowheads and maybe even find pieces of bone. I found an arrowhead once, but it's at home in my room. Why don't you come back to town with us tonight? I can show you."

"Is it haunted? At that slough?"

"Yes, every inch of it."

Jen's eyes lit up. "Let's go," she whispered.

We tossed our Popsicle sticks on the ground, jumped up and ran into the garage for the bikes. Both of us had on shorts and sneakers, but instead of a grubby T-shirt like mine, Jen wore a fussy pink blouse.

"How come you're all dressed up?"

"My mother won't let me wear T-shirts. I had one once, but she threw it out."

"That's weird."

As we rolled our bikes onto the driveway, I noticed how thin and white Jen's long arms and legs were compared to my own. Mine were as brown as acorns and full of scrapes and scabs from mosquito bites and climbing trees and tripping over cracks in the sidewalk on my roller skates.

"Your back tire looks flat," she said.

I squeezed each of the wide tires. "They're all low."

Jen looked puzzled. "What'll we do? Maybe we should get your dad to help us."

"Nah, I can do it. Besides, we don't want him asking questions."

My cousin crossed her arms as if she didn't believe me.

"We'll take turns, okay?" I said, bringing out a hand pump.

Jen's arms wore out after the first tire.

"Your dad is weird, Callie."

"No he's not. What do you mean?"

"He pinched the back of my neck when we got here and asked me, 'How's your gizzard?' When I told him I didn't have a gizzard, he acted surprised and said, 'You *don't*? I thought everyone had a gizzard.'"

"Aw, he just means 'how are you?' He always says that to kids."

"Oh. I still think . . ."

"Why didn't your mom come along?" I asked, plunging the tire pump handle up and down until sweat rolled off my nose.

"She's busy."

"Doin' what?"

"I don't know. Just busy. She doesn't like to go places."

"How come?"

"I don't know, Callie. Stop asking!"

Surprised by the sharpness of Jen's tone and the flash of her eyes, I didn't say another word until after I'd finished with the tires. We wheeled our bikes across the ruts in the driveway and past the "tightrope," the rusty pipe that divided part of our property from the lane leading to other cabins. Earlier in the day, I'd taught Jen how to balance on the twenty-foot-long pipe raised off the ground on cement blocks. We ended up screaming and laughing and grabbing onto each other to keep from falling into "the alligator pit."

"Let's walk 'the tightrope' when we get back," she said.

"Okay." I wiped my face with the bottom of my T-shirt, glad that Jen was no longer mad at me for asking about her mother. We pedaled out to the main road. Hot whirlwinds and dust clouds from a passing car made me sneeze. Cicadas sounded shrilly from the woods.

"What's that noise?" Jen asked, trying to keep up.

"Katydids."

"It sounds like screeching high line wires."

As we rode past Bloody Lake, a blue heron screamed and flapped his wings in a clumsy takeoff.

"He's announcing the end of the world," I said. "Oh, and there's the House of Thirteen Gables." I pointed out a huge three-story ramshackle building.

"Does anyone live there?"

"No. Not since the murder."

"What murder?"

"I don't know. Some man got killed. That's what Liz told me. I dare you to go inside when it gets dark."

"Have you ever?"

"No, but Liz did once, with Brian. That's her boyfriend. They said it's haunted."

I noticed that Jen was lagging behind, as if she was already tired.

"Don't you ride bikes at home?" I called out over my shoulder.

"Sometimes," she panted. "Not very often. Don't worry, I can keep up."

"Over there is Belle's tavern," I said, pointing out the low building with faded blue paint, a short distance off the main road between the end of our bay and a field. "Belle Kittleson. We'll stop on our way back."

Just before the Sunrise Schoolhouse, I pedaled backwards to set the brake and held out my arm as a signal to stop.

"There's a Gypsy camp across the road." I nodded toward several tents and a big wagon like the ones at the circus, painted red and yellow in wavy shapes. "Gram says to stay far away from the Gypsies 'cause they steal children. Dad says that's a bunch of malarkey but to be careful all the same because you never know."

We kept to the opposite side of the road and pedaled hard past a bunch of scrawny dogs nosing around the ditch. A dark-skinned man with oily black hair watched us speed by.

"Did you see his face? He looked scary!"

"Go as fast as you can!" I shouted. "Or he'll get you!"

Jen shrieked and pedaled so fast her legs were a blur as she passed me.

"Oh," smiling to myself, "we're lucky we didn't get stolen right off our bikes."

Jen slowed down and scooted her feet on the gravel.

I locked my pedals and skidded to a stop.

"Don't worry," I said, breathing hard. "We're safe."

"I'm not *worried*, Callie. Besides, I saw you smirking."

"I don't know what you're talking about."

"Oh, never mind."

We caught our breath and settled into a steady pace, riding side by side down the middle of the road.

"Tell me more about what happened at Slaughter Slough," said Jen.

"It had something to do with the government. The Indians got mad and shot the settlers, including little kids."

"With bows and arrows?"

"Mostly guns. The families hid in the marsh and the Indians flushed 'em out and killed them."

"They killed whole families?"

"Yup. Not only little kids but babies, too. Clubbed them to death right in front of their mothers."

Jen looked at me with narrowed eyes. "I don't believe you."

"It's true."

"That's awful! Why would anyone kill a baby?"

"They wanted revenge because their own babies were dying from starvation. They shot the mothers after they killed their babies."

"What about the dads?"

"Killed, too. But some went for help and some ran away."

"They ran away?"

"Yup."

"I don't want to hear any more, Callie. Besides, you're just making it all up."

"No, I'm not. I've got a book to prove it. And when we stop at Belle's, she'll tell you."

Jen and I had to stand and pump hard to make the last hill before the slough. We were out of breath again, and soaking wet by the time we got to the top.

"To this day," I panted, "if you listen real hard, you can hear them crying."

"Who?"

"The babies and their mothers. Who else?"

"Well, which ones? The Indian babies or the white babies?"

I thought for a second and shrugged.

Jen frowned. "You're just making up stories again."

"No lie!" I shouted, leaving Jen behind and coasting fast down hill. "My dad knows! He and Grandad hunt out here all the time!"

Hot and thirsty from the long ride, we jammed on our brakes next to the slough and let our bikes fall to the ground. The mudflats were dried up at the edges and mucky toward the center. We stepped into the tall sweet-grass, found a spot where it was dry, and flopped down to rest.

"This is how they tried to hide from the Indians," I said in a hushed voice. "You don't dare move or the grass will give you away."

"It's so quiet," said Jen. "Like in a church."

"Better than inside a church. That's what my dad says. Out here there's nothing between you and heaven."

On our backs, gazing up through a tangle of long grass at the blue sky, we lay very still, except to slap at mosquitoes whining into our damp hair and ears, and a bee that circled our lips for the last of the sticky Popsicle juice. A soft breeze ruffled the tops of the sweetgrass. Meadowlarks sang nearby, then from a distance. In between all those sounds, I began to hear something else.

"Listen, Jen. Shh. Hear that?"

"What?"

"Those strange noises."

"I hear birds. And the wind in the grass."

"No, not that. Listen harder."

Jen was quiet for a moment. "Yes," she said. "I hear it. It sounds like the wind with eerie voices behind it."

"Babies crying," I whispered. "And the mothers, too."

"Do you think so?"

"Could be."

"Aren't you scared, Callie?"

"No. Are you?"

"A little."

"Well, I'm not."

After a while, I couldn't move. The strange sounds seemed to be coming closer to our hideout.

"Callie, do you think your dad would have run away when the Indians came?"

"No. How about yours?"

"I don't think so . . . I hope not."

Jen rolled over suddenly and jumped up. "Let's go look for arrowheads."

I jumped up just as quickly, glad to get away from that spot.

We left our bikes where they were and wandered around with our heads down in search of anything interesting. By late afternoon, we were very thirsty. We hadn't found any arrowheads. Instead, we loaded our pockets with tiny snail shells and pretty stones.

Pedaling slowly back toward Tepeeotah Hill, we could smell roasting game before we even reached the Gypsy camp.

"I'm hungry," said Jen.

"Me, too," I chimed, feeling saliva trickle down the insides of my cheeks.

As we passed the camp, a little boy, filthy with matted hair and gnawing on a chunk of brown meat, waved at us. We gave him a quick wave back, then pedaled hard toward Belle's Tavern.

"I'm so thirsty I could spit cotton," I groaned.

"Me, too," said Jen.

"Wait'll you meet Belle. She's real nice. She'll give us some water for sure, maybe even a bottle of pop."

We rode down a lane overgrown on both sides with brown weeds, razor grass, and scrub oaks. Heat rose up from the gravel in the empty parking lot. In front of the building was a rusty gas pump with a chalky black hose crumbling away from its nozzle.

Jen hung back next to her bike, looking as if she'd just smelled something rotten.

"What's the matter?" I asked.

"Are you sure we should go in?"

"Of course. I've been here lots of times. Belle's parents used to run this tavern, but they're dead. Now it's just Belle." I punted my bike's kickstand down and waited for Jen to do the same.

"Be sure to notice her toes," I said in a low voice as we shuffled up the wooden steps.

"How come?"

"You'll see."

I opened the flimsy screen door and smelled stale beer.

With her elbows resting on the bar, Belle stood in front of a fan, peeling an apple with a filet knife. Her long yellow-gray hair was blowing straight back, like in a speedboat. Her tanned face was deeply lined, especially at the corners of her eyes. She never used makeup like the town women who wore tons of it. I could tell by the sparkle in Belle's brown eyes and her warm smile that she was glad to see us.

"Well, hello, girls. I was needing some company this afternoon." She set aside the apple and knife, switched the fan to low, and stood up straight, open for business. "What'll it be?"

"Just water, Mrs. Kittleson. We don't have any money with us."

"Well, now, you two look like you've been working pretty hard today. How's about a soda pop?"

Belle reached into the cooler, lifted out two bottles dripping with icy water, and wiped them off with a rag. "Go ahead, belly up to the bar. And by the way, you can call me Belle."

Jen and I laughed and hopped onto metal stools. The red plastic cover felt smooth and cool to my skin. But before my feet could find a rung, the sharp edges of cracked piping dug into the backs of my knees.

"Here you go, ladies. On the house."

Belle set our root beers on the bar, then smoothed her hair back and adjusted a couple of bobby pins as she walked across the room to latch the screen door. We gulped down half of the cold sweet brew, our eyes on Belle.

Tall and big-boned, she wore baggy trousers and a faded green-checkered shirt with the sleeves cut off at the shoulders. Her biceps were so large that I'd bet on her against any arm-wrestler that came in for a challenge. Her eyes were soft, the color of our root beer—the same brown color as my Sparkle Plenty doll after I'd left her too long in the sun.

Jen's eyes went wide as she looked at Belle's toes. Although I'd seen them lots of times, I was always surprised that Belle could walk, even with the ends cut out of her large Oxfords. She had the biggest cocked toes in the world. They aimed straight up—as Dad described them—like prairie dogs standing at attention. Mom said that Belle should cover them with socks or pieces of cloth while minding the store. Of course, by her admission, Mom was self-conscious about her own big feet and always sat with them tucked beneath her chair. I thought it was cool that Belle didn't care.

"Callie, aren't you going to introduce your friend?" she asked, returning to her spot behind the bar.

"This is Jenny," I said. "She's my cousin, from Iowa."

"Jenny what?"

"Lindstrom. Same as Callie. Her dad and my dad are brothers."

"Oh?" Belle looked surprised. "That would be Ray. I didn't know he . . ." Belle cleared her throat. "Yes, he's spoken of you." She offered a large weathered hand. "I am very glad to know you, Jenny Lindstrom. Welcome to Tepeeotah."

Jen gave Belle a big smile, shook her hand, and settled in next to me at the bar as if she'd been there often.

"Any sisters or brothers?"

"Nope. Just me."

"Is your whole family at the cabin this weekend, Callie?"

"No, my mom stayed in town. She and Liz are sewing school clothes."

"How old is Liz now?"

"Going on sixteen."

"Already! Won't be long before she heads off to college. I'll bet you're going to miss her."

"I guess." I shrugged and thought about the bedroom I shared with my sister and what a mess it was with piles of clothes and books and games and bowls, crusty with dried milk and bits of *Rice Krispies*, shoved under the bed. There'd be a place for all my stuff after she went away to school.

"Just think, little Sis," Liz had said, "in a couple of years, you'll have this room all to yourself."

Her saying that gave me a funny feeling. To think there'd be no more waking up in the middle of the night to suck on *Tootsie Pops* while Liz talked about the double feature at the drive-in and roller-skating at Valhalla and how much she loved Brian.

I was especially glad my cousin was here to play with me.

"And how about your mother, Jenny? Did she come along?"

"No." Jen swirled the last of her root beer around in the bottle. "She never goes anywhere. I usually have to stay at home with her."

Frowning slightly, Belle stared at Jen. Then, in a cheerful voice, she said, "Well now, girls, tell me what you've been up to today."

Jenny and I practically fell over each other, giggling and interrupting one another as we told about our adventures.

"We went to Bloody Lake and saw the haunted house. Only from outside."

"And the Gypsy camp."

"Callie and I are going to sneak into the House of Thirteen Gables when it gets dark."

"And we explored Slaughter Slough." I drained the last of my pop. "But we didn't find any arrowheads."

Jen asked Belle if my story about the Indian Massacre was true.

"I'm afraid so," she answered. "That's exactly how it was ninety years ago."

"See! I told you so!"

Jen stuck her tongue out at me.

Belle continued. "It was in 1862 and known as the Sioux Uprising."

"The name of my town! Sioux City!"

"That's true, Jenny. There's Sioux City, Sioux Center, Sioux Falls. A great and proud people before the government messed everything up for them."

"What did they do?"

"Bought tribal land, then held off paying them for it. Crops failed and many of the Indians starved. Government money came too late."

"Even the babies and little kids, like Callie said?"

Belle nodded her head slowly. "It doesn't excuse them for killing the settlers, but the Indians were angry and desperate, losing their people, their land, their way of life."

Belle turned and disappeared into her private rooms through a faded blue-and-orange curtain hanging from a rod in the doorway. When she returned, she held a fist out to each of us.

"Open your hands and close your eyes."

We did as we were told. My eyes popped open as soon as I felt a stone drop onto the palm of my hand. Belle had given us each an arrowhead. Mine was caramel-colored, small and delicate, sharp at the point.

"That's where it was tied to the end of an arrow with sinew," explained Belle, pointing at the flared end. "But I guess you already know that."

Jen's arrowhead was black and half again as large. Both were chiseled into perfect shapes, smooth and shiny with age.

We were so thrilled, we didn't know what to say, except, "Thank you."

Then Belle took something from her shirt pocket. "Look at this treasure," she said, holding a little bracelet.

Jenny and I examined the tiny circle of blue and yellow and white beads.

"It belonged to an Indian baby," said Belle. "I found it near the slough a long time ago, when I was about your age."

I held the bracelet for a long moment before giving it back. Seeing those pretty beads made me think about the babies and little kids and how they must have cried out.

"Belle?"

"Yes, Callie?"

"Oh . . . nothing."

"It's lovely, isn't it?"

I handed her the bracelet. "Uh-huh."

Then, because Belle had grown up on this land, she told us about her own adventures, searching for arrowheads and driftwood along the shores of Lake Shetek, pitching a tent in the woods where she'd slept all one summer, making pets out of raccoons and rabbits and garter snakes, hunting ducks and fishing for pike with her father. She described how they'd nearly drowned in a sudden storm.

"In a typhoon, you have to go by your own instincts and hope for the best," she said, teetering back and forth behind the bar. "All we could do was drag anchor and lie flat along the bottom of our boat. Pitching around on those enormous waves was like riding a bucking bronco."

"Weren't you afraid, Belle?" asked Jen.

"A little, but I trusted my father to know what to do."

"That sounds exciting," I said. "Better not tell my mom, though, or she'll never let me go out on the lake again. She's such an old scaredy cat."

"I'm sure she has her reasons." Belle patted my hand and then turned to Jenny. "I hope your mother can come up sometime. This is such a beautiful place."

"No, she doesn't ever . . . she, she's in a hospital."

Surprised, I shot Jen a look. I didn't know that. If she's telling Belle, why didn't she tell *me?*

"What's wrong with her?" I asked.

Jen frowned and began running her fingers over some initials carved into the bar.

Belle reached across and gave Jen's hand a happy little shake. "Well, I'm glad you and Callie are having fun together. And I'm glad you came to visit me."

Jen looked embarrassed.

"Now let me give you some more stories," Belle continued. "I love that the Gypsies return every year. Just like the ducks and geese, you can set your calendars by them. They're friendly enough, but you have to watch out or they'll steal you blind."

Belle looked sad when she told us how times were bound to change. There was talk of draining the slough for corn planting. Sunrise School would be boarded up at the end of next year.

"The children will have to go to town school then," she sighed. "At least the Gypsies keep coming back. They know where to find good hunting."

"Belle," said Jenny, "do they really steal children?"

"No, dear, I don't think you need to worry. But then again, you never know. It's best to be watchful."

Jen and I looked at each other with raised eyebrows.

"We better get going," I said, "or our dads will wonder where we are."

"Be sure to greet them for me. Vic and Julia, too."

"We will." Jen and I giggled at having answered together and at hearing our grandparents called by their first names.

"Thanks for the root beer," I said, "and thanks for the arrowheads."

"Thank you, Belle," said Jenny.

With strong arms, Belle gave us each a hug. The warm softness of her body felt like my mother's.

Outside, I turned and asked Belle if she ever heard sounds out at Slaughter Slough. "I don't mean the songbirds or the wind in the grass. But the other . . ."

"It's been awhile since I went there to listen. Mostly I go to hunt." She paused for a moment. "I remember one time, though."

"You heard something?"

"I might have. Whatever it was gave me an uneasy feeling. I left before I could flush a mallard."

I gave Belle another quick hug before skipping down the steps to my bike. She stood at the open screen door and watched us pedal away. We waved.

During our ride back to the cottage, Jen and I talked about how kind Belle was. Jenny said she wished she could have a mother like her. We wondered how her toes got that way and why grown-ups never gave a straight answer to anything.

"Could be. Maybe so," I mimicked. "Anything's possible. Might have. You never know."

"Be careful," Jen giggled. "Watch for cars." She jerked her handlebars from side to side to make her bike wobble. "I guess no one knows anything for sure."

I fishtailed my bike, and we shouted and laughed. I was glad that Jen was happy again and the shadow of her mother was gone. I wasn't going to ask her any more questions. But later on, when Dad and I left the cottage to go back home, I planned to ask him about Aunt Eloise.

As Jen and I rode along together, I cupped my hand around the sharp edges of Belle's gift and wondered what it had killed long ago. I thought about the tiny beaded bracelet and decided the next time I went to Slaughter Slough, I'd look for beads. And I would be extra quiet. Would I be able to hear the crying of Indian babies? Would they sound different from the white babies?

After supper, while Grandad wound new line onto his reel and Gram sang her opera songs and played the piano with her usual flourish, Jen and I snuggled together on the couch between our dads who sat at opposite ends looking at *National Geographic* magazines. We were safe from the Gypsies and far from the mudflats and ghosts of Slaughter Slough.

My cousin and I wrote to each other a couple of times after she returned to Sioux City. And we exchanged school pictures in the fall. I wonder if we'll ever have another day like the one that summer.

Six

The Alligator Pit

THE MEMORY OF THAT SUMMER'S DAY with Jenny fades and I wonder what she would have done this afternoon when our dads were fighting—not a real fight, but awful just the same.

I leave the garage, shivering at the idea of being alone inside the cottage. I will avoid the basement. Nothing down there but Lydia Pinkham bottles, dusty canning jars with dried bugs crusted on the lids, dead plants in cracked clay pots, a scurrying mouse, and tons of spiders and cobwebs.

It seems as if Grandad, Liz, Dad, and Mom should be sitting at the kitchen table playing pinochle or popping corn, while Gram and I plink the yellowed ivories, pronouncing the Italian words printed on her sheet music—*O Mio Babbino Caro, mi piace è bello bello* . . . When Gram sings, the gold trim on her front teeth sparkles in the lamplight. And the sounds of those words and the way the notes rise and fall make the others stop talking and look a little sad.

It's strange to wander through the dark and empty house. With no one frying fish or cleaning and oiling a shotgun or lighting a fire, it even smells empty. It's been a long time since anyone called out, "Hey, Callie! Time to put your Girl Scout skills to some use."

That would mean gathering twigs, sticks, and logs, and building a tepee around a wad of paper inside the big stone fireplace. The cottage warmed up fast, especially inside the staircase with an open wedge for looking down into the living room. With the door closed to the upstairs hallway, the space around the top step became an oven. Leaning against the warm pine paneling, I could watch Grandad checker a gunstock. And I could keep a sharp ear for conversations I wasn't supposed to hear.

Now the cottage is filled with ghosts, which are friendly enough, except for an echo of Gram hollering at my mother for no good reason. I wander through the rooms, taking my time, certain that Dad won't have to wait for me. Once he sets foot inside the Johnsons' cabin, he'll be there for a while.

I remember moving day. I was three when Gram and Grandad sold their farm near Hadley, west of Masterton, and bought this cottage on Lake Shetek. While the grown-ups hauled in boxes and furniture, I straddled the long rolled-up carpet, pretending it was a pony.

Neither Dad nor Uncle Ray wanted to take over the land where they'd grown up. Grandad didn't seem to mind. If he did, he wouldn't have said so. Mom says he's like a poker player—never gives away his hand, keeps his thoughts to himself.

"That man is happiest," she said, "tramping around out of doors all day and sitting by the fire at night, carving lures and polishing his guns."

Now that Grandad's gone, I've been thinking about how quiet he always was. "Words," said the little fox in a story I read at school, "are the source of misunderstandings."

I think Grandad was smart to stay quiet. I tried it once.

Since Gram's move into town, Dad has hinted at selling the cottage. I've begged him not to. I plan to warn whoever noses around that the property is haunted and only our family knows how to live here.

The smell of mothballs has me ducking in and out of rooms. One bedroom was decorated with a 1952 calendar tacked on the wall—the year Grandad died—and here it is 1954. The next room Gram fixed up for Liz and me with a wide bed and two pictures overhead; the first is of a little girl in her long nightgown, praying with her white Spitz dog for *Good Night*; in the second picture, they are awake and stretching for *Good Morning*. There's a prissy vanity with a pink stool where I used to sit and stare at myself making silly faces. Gram stitched together a wad of pink ruffles and arranged miniature perfume bottles. Most of the stuff inside the bottles has gone dry or turned oozy brown. They smelled yucky without the stoppers, like the sweet stink behind Uncle Warren's barn the time I discovered a bunch of dead baby pigs. I could understand one or two dead piglets, but a whole heap of them? I never did find out what happened. Related to Mom's side of the family, Uncle Warren was quiet, too—sort of like Grandad—except I never trusted him. Didn't like his eyes.

I run into the narrow bathroom, raise the window, and stick my head out for some air. Down below is where Uncle Ray had parked his Cadillac and boat. Now it's just our black Pontiac off to one side, and the long pipe where

Liz taught me and I taught Jen to walk *the tightrope*. We had to wear sneakers, though. Gliding barefoot on sun-hot rusty metal two feet off the ground taught us where the sharp places are.

"Don't lose your balance," Liz warned, "or you'll fall into the alligator pit."

I can still hear our screams and laughter.

Even though it's nice to have our bedroom all to myself, I miss Liz.

On Saturdays, we used to mix chocolate chip cookie dough, stand ten feet apart in the kitchen, and toss little balls of it into each other's mouth. That is, until Brian came over. Then they didn't want me around. I told Mom and Dad on them whenever I saw them kissing. I told on them a lot. Then Dad had a serious talk with her. I guess that's why Liz signed her high school graduation picture, "To my dear, sweet sister who sees all, knows all and tells all." At least she signed it, "*Love, Liz.*"

My sis is a lot prettier than I am. It was Aunt Hazel who said so. I overheard her. "Of the two girls," she said to Uncle Cecil, "Liz got all the looks." I guess I don't mind. Anyhow, I'm proud of her, because she looks like Elizabeth Taylor, my favorite movie star. Senior year, Liz's classmates voted her Homecoming queen. The day she was crowned, I got two desserts in the lunch line.

"An extra slice of chocolate cake," said the cook, "for the queen's sister." Too bad she wasn't crowned every day.

Now Liz is away at college and almost never comes home or out to the lake. She spends all her free time with Brian. Mom says nothing can stay the same forever. Belle Kittleson was right. It's kind of lonesome without Liz's stuff stacked in our bedroom. She wants me to come to Mankato to stay in the dormitory with her and her roommates for a weekend. I can hardly wait.

Rid of my yucky feeling from smelling the dried perfume and the memory of dead pigs, I open the medicine cabinet to check on the eye wash cup still in its place next to a gummy tube of orange Tangee lipstick. When I suction the cold glass cup against my eye, the oval fits better than the last time I tried it. Still, the thought of keeping my eye open in a globe of water gives me the creeps. I put it back, close the cabinet, and peel a dried sliver of Tea Rose soap from next to the faucet. The pink shard still holds its scent. Reminds me of Gram.

The lake looks huge from the wall of cobwebby windows in my grand-parents' bedroom. Hundreds of dead ladybugs cover the sills. One big puff sends them floating to the floor. This room feels more than empty since Grandad died. His second-best suit hangs from a wire hook on the open closet door: gray tweed trousers, vest, and coat—a suit he'd worn for their fiftieth wedding anniversary party two and a half years ago. I was going on eight, and had to pass around glass teacups filled with punch, which was a hell of a lot better than handing out tallies to the women at 500 Club.

Inside one of the dresser drawers I find bits of wine-colored yarn and Gram's tiny wooden loom with a half-finished blanket square.

"For your Sparkle Plenty doll," she'd said, "so you can get her out of the yard and tuck her in at night."

She never finished the blanket. Doesn't matter. I don't play with dolls anymore.

The mothball smell in this room is enough to gag a maggot. I slam the drawer shut and go to the storeroom, my favorite place in the whole cottage, besides the piano room. It's large and musty, but doesn't stink. Winding around straight-back chairs and end tables and a treadle sewing machine, I stop for my usual look at grumpy old German and Swedish relatives glaring at me from inside their picture frames. Did they ever smile in their lives?

Next is a large steamer trunk filled with strange old things: spooky-eyed porcelain dolls with stained cloth bodies; an ivory hairbrush and comb set, turned yellow; a brown moth-eaten pouch with a sharp razor inside that opens up like a switchblade, a wide leather strop for sharpening the razor, and a curling iron heated by sticking it inside the chimney of a burning oil lamp. Dad says I can nose around all I want, but to be careful and not take anything.

Some stuff isn't where it's supposed to be—probably because of moving Gram to town. And some things, blocked by boxes and chairs in the far cor-ner, I never noticed before. Like the horsehide blanket with a violin on top. That violin is worth some climbing to see.

The wood is nicked and dull with all but one of its strings broken. I tuck the instrument under my chin like Jack Benny on television. Stringy shreds hang from one end of the long bow, leaving just enough to work across the single string. When another shred breaks, I pluck the string with one finger until it sounds irritating. How can anyone make decent music on such a thing?

I set the violin down and turn back to stroke the brown-and-white hair blanket, wondering what Pinto pony of long ago had to give up its hide. Beneath the bristly robe is another trunk. Where did this stuff come from? How could I have missed it?

I shove aside the heavy blanket and find a treasure chest. Its curved top, bleached in spots, is decorated with dark wooden strips and a fancy metal latch. It could be the chest from *Treasure Island*, filled with silver, gold doubloons, strands of diamonds, emeralds, pearls, rubies. My heart beats fast as I lift the lid.

On top is a faded blue work shirt wrapped around a shaving mug with a stubbly brush stuck to dried yellow gunk. There are stacks of books and heavy vinyl records with labels that read *Gramophone and Typewriter Company* and Enrico Caruso.

It would take hours to read any one of these books. Their hard gray and dark-green and blue-black covers are worn and faded. I've never heard of most of the authors: Cervantes, Jonathan Swift, Willa Cather. But Charles Dickens and William Shakespeare—I've heard of those guys. The print is small and there are no pictures, except for one inside a front cover, under a thin sheet of tissue paper.

I dig to the bottom of the trunk to see if I've missed anything and find a large Manila envelope with the name "Amer Lindstrom" written across it. And all this time, I thought his name was spelled "Aimer." That's how Dad pronounces it. So these things belonged to my great-uncle, a man who loved books and music and got killed out West. I've always wondered why.

I make a little clearing on the floor and dump out newspaper clippings, official-looking documents, and a bundle of letters tied with old string. Most of the letters are from Forsyth, Montana, dated 1919, and addressed to Mr. and Mrs. Victor Lindstrom, Will and Ray. Here it is 1954 and I'm looking at something from that long ago—personal things. Gram must have organized all this stuff years ago, then put them away.

Sitting with my back against the trunk, I read the first letter, written with pen and ink on large paper. The ink has faded to brown and there are lots of curlicues, like in the old ledgers in Dad's office at the courthouse, especially in the vault which smells like the inside of our town library.

March the 30th, 1919
Miles City, Montana

Dear Family,

> *I trust this letter finds you well. I am the same, except bursting with eagerness to get started cultivating some land now that I've reached my destination. The train trip was remarkable. From Fergus Falls, we crossed the Red River and headed toward Valley City, North Dakota. The terrain begins to roll where the great Missouri River marked our passage and welcomed us into western country—Mandan and Custer land. Small buttes thrust themselves up in western North Dakota and grow massive near Miles City, Montana.*
> *I like Miles City. It's in a beautiful valley surrounded by buttes colored with sunshine and shadows, many shades of rose and ochre above sagebrush and laurel. All along the Yellowstone are groves of trees and winding crevices. It's a mighty river . . .*

I've never read such fancy words, not even in the books at school. Suddenly, Amer isn't just a name from long ago. These things in the trunk were in Montana with him. He'd read these books and played this violin. He sounded educated, excited to be traveling. I want to read more, but there isn't time. Dad is probably back from the Johnsons' by now, eager to get home and clean fish.

I stuff everything back into the envelope, replace the books, records, and shaving mug, lower the trunk lid, drape the horsehair blanket back on top and pet its coat once more. I tuck the packet under my arm, shut off the light, and close the storeroom door. Who will know if this envelope goes missing? After all, it was at the bottom of the trunk.

It's chilly downstairs. Old ashes in the fireplace smell like crushed green olives. The mantel's long slab of pipestone looks bare without Gram's knick-knacks and the black-and-gold chiming clock. I slip Amer's letters into my beach bag and take a last look around, remembering the anniversary party, the decorated table, the guests in their suits and pretty dresses—one of our happier times when Gram wasn't hollering at my mom and Grandad made an effort to enjoy the afternoon when he probably would rather have gone fishing. Uncle Ray even showed up, although he came alone and left early. Probably a good thing considering how Aunt Eloise behaved at Grandad's funeral the following year. But I'd hoped Jen would come.

I switch off the last light in the kitchen and return to the garage. Dad isn't back yet, so I pick through cigar boxes filled with old tackle: rusty hooks, lures, lead sinkers, pitted cork bobbers, wads of useless line. The shelf that held Grandad's shotgun shells is empty.

"All set, kiddo?" Dad calls from the driveway. "We've got fish to clean."

Alone with my thoughts too long, I jump at the sound of his voice.

"We'd better get-a-goin' or your mother will think we've drowned."

"Oh, she's such a scaredy cat." I toss my bag onto the back seat of our Pontiac while Dad lowers the garage door.

"She's got good reason."

"I know, afraid of the water. But that doesn't mean we should be."

"Go easy on her, Cal."

"What makes her so scared of a lake, anyway? Whatever drowning she won't talk about was a long time ago."

But Dad has hustled away to check the locks on the cottage doors. Circling back, he picks up the pail of fish and sets it on my side of the car.

"Make sure it doesn't tip, Cal. See that they don't jump out on the way home."

"I know, I know. You don't need to tell me every time. I've had the same job since I was five."

"So you have." Dad gives the back of my neck its usual little squeeze. "Hard to realize you're growing up."

With a foot on either side of the bucket, I lean over to watch the cluster of wide mouths open and close in their swirling water nest, bobbing around as we bounce backward over ruts and stones onto Tepeeotah Road. A gentler sound than my uncle's car earlier that afternoon, peeling gravel as it sped away.

Sluggish bullheads live a long time crowded together in their little bit of water, quietly working their gills and enormous mouths, like strange birds hungry for air. Their feelers remind me of the tapered ends of a handlebar mustache.

I don't have to be very watchful tonight. Bullheads aren't bound to flop around like sunfish and crappies. Those spend the last of their energy shooting straight up and out of the bucket to the freedom of the car floor. Then you have to guess where they'll land, pin their tails under a shoe, scoop them up and slip them back into the pail. Most of them die after thrashing around like that.

The bullheads live all the way to the cleaning room. And who knows how long after that, if you don't gut them right away.

Dad and I are quiet for the first few minutes of our ride back home. Guess we both have a lot on our minds. I know I do: the fight with Uncle Ray, wishing I could see my cousin again, finding Uncle Amer's stuff. The books looked interesting, even though there weren't any pictures. And I wanted to play those records—*Un Bel Di* and *Mio Babbino Caro*—songs Gram plays on the piano. Songs Dad tries to sing and I tease him: "You're messing it up, Papa."

"Ah, but I sound Eye-talian, don't you think?"

"Maybe, but you can't carry a tune."

"Doesn't matter. As long as you feel the music, let it out. Sour notes and all. Whoever doesn't like it need not listen."

To think these songs are among our favorites, all because of a man who lived way back in 1919.

Finally, I have to ask. "Dad, tell me some more about Amer Lindstrom."

"A good man. My favorite uncle. Why?"

"Oh, I dunno. What did he do again?"

"He went to Montana. Got in on a land rush out there. What makes you ask?"

"Just wondering." I lean over to check on the bullheads. "What exactly happened to him?"

"He died before his claim went through. Wasn't very old, only thirty-eight."

"He got shot, didn't he?"

"That's right."

"How come? Who did it?"

"Some fellows, name of Carmichael, jumped his claim. But I think there was more to it."

"Like what?"

"It's pretty involved, Cal. I'll go into the particulars another time."

For some reason, Dad isn't giving me the full story. If he's worried about upsetting me, that's stupid. From what I can figure out, the whole thing sounds like a Western. And I've grown up with those. Friday night boxing, Saturday matinee cowboy shows: Roy Rogers and Dale Evans, the Lone Ranger and Tonto, Gene Autry, Hopalong Cassidy, and my personal favorite, Rex Allen, who sings only to me. I'm going to marry him when I grow up.

As we drive along, Dad and I talk boxing instead: how Floyd and Sugar Ray own the ring and there's no one more fearsome than Sonny. We discuss some of the boxers who died after their matches: Dick Miller and Robert Lee and Jesus Morales who got pummeled by Roy Hernandez last September.

"Nineteen-fifty-three was a bad year," says Dad. "They were just young fellas."

"I wonder why nobody stopped those fights, when they could see what was happening."

"That's for sure. They were brutal."

Dad turns onto Owanka Road from the Eastlick Trail near Bloody Lake, named for the color of the water after the 1862 massacre. The Eastlicks were one of the families slaughtered.

We stop for a minute to watch a huge flock of Canada geese take off. Their cheek bands, white against black necks and heads look like helmet chinstraps. Alarmed, they stretch their necks, honk in fifty different keys, and arch their powerful wings. Feathers, like long fingers, flare, then close for flight. In a running start, a hundred webbed feet, the size of lily pads, pound puddles across the surface of Bloody Lake.

"Airborne, at last," says Dad, swinging an imaginary lead out of his open window. "Gearing up to head south."

The command goose barks an order. The wedge climbs higher and aims for the horizon.

"Isn't that some sight, Cal? Don't they look sharp the way they cut the air in perfect V formation?"

The Gillette jingle that plays between boxing matches pops into my head: *Look sharp! Feel sharp! Be sharp!*

Dad puts the car in gear and drives away from Bloody Lake. The water in our pail of bullheads sloshes around, but not onto the floor. We head for home, singing:

To look sharp and feel sharp, too,
choose a razor that is built for you.
Light and regular and heavy, Hey!
Decent shaves for any beard, Olé!

Mom doesn't like me to watch the fights.

"Little girls, of all people, should not be exposed to this stuff," she announced one night, standing infront of the television set. Dad turned to stare into my face, "searching for signs of trauma," he said. I crossed my eyes and let my tongue hang out of the corner of my mouth. Mom just shook her head and went back to her sewing.

I've seen the greatest boxers in the world: Sugar Ray Robinson, Floyd Patterson, Sonny Liston, Rocky Marciano. I tried to imitate them when I fought Danny last year. He's my next-door neighbor. His dad bought him a pair of boxing gloves for his birthday. Danny used the right one (first dibs). I got the left and ended up with a bloody nose. I knocked one of Danny's teeth loose, which made his mom really mad at me. But she got over it.

Now, after a long, tiring day, I lean back against the seat and listen to the droning engine and the ticking sounds of the bullheads sucking air. With the lakes behind us, I watch for the landmarks we've passed hundreds of times: the big dark house with thirteen gables not far from Bloody Lake, the turn-off to Belle's Tavern, the Gypsy campsite with its little fires dotting a black ravine, the road leading to Slaughter Slough. Although the night air is chilly, I crank open the window and let my arm bob and float like a wing on the wind. How would it feel to fly like a Canada honker? How would it feel to swim through Lake Shetek like a northern pike? Or like these bullheads when they're free and feeding along the lake bottom? Although they're trapped in this crowded pail filled with warm tap water, they never give up trying to live.

I close my window and glance at Dad. Lost in his own thoughts, he drives with one hand on the wheel, the other against the side of his head.

After passing long stretches of fields spiked with broken corn stalks and farmyards protected by thick, dark groves, our headlights catch the green sign announcing MASTERTON, POPULATION 2,438.

I'm glad to be home.

Seven

Still Mouth, Fixed Eyes

OM GREETS US AS SOON as she hears Dad raise the garage door. Her cheeks are flushed from the warmth of the day and from baking bread to go with our fried fish.

"I was getting concerned. You've been gone quite a while."

"Dad and Ray got into a fight," I tell her, excited all over again. "And Ray fell down the hill and landed in the lake and nearly got killed by the big rock."

Frowning, Mom looked from me to Dad.

"Now you're fighting? And in front of Callie?

"It didn't amount to much, Em. We'll talk later."

"No, tell me now. What happened?"

And I pour out the whole story, with interruptions from Dad, who seems determined to spoil its flow. Or, as he puts it, to set the record straight.

"It isn't enough that Callie watches the fights on television? Now she has to see her father fight, too?"

"Nobody got hurt, Emily."

"I wouldn't be so sure."

"Anyway, we got a nice mess of bullheads for supper."

"Always changing the subject!"

Mom gives us each a quick hug and returns to the kitchen. She smells good, like the bread dough she's been kneading and the rhubarb sauce with sugar for dessert.

I tuck my beach bag safely away in my room. Uncle Amer's letters will have to wait while I help Dad clean the fish. On my way to the basement, I stop to lift the lid on a kettle of simmering potatoes and carrots. The bread is rising in two large loaf pans.

"I'm starving, Mom. I need a tide-over."

She pulls a chunk of raw potato from the kettle and sprinkles a little salt on it. Cupping my chin in one hand, she gently wedges the potato in between my teeth.

"Tastes better than Ivory soap," I mumble around the starchy, crisp piece.

"As your papa says, 'It's good for what ails you.' Now get going on those fish." She gives me a swat on the behind.

The seven o'clock hour in the basement is cool and dim, especially on hot summer nights when my face burns from the afternoon sun reflecting off the lake. This October day feels like summer.

Minnows scatter like buckshot as my arms plunge into the long green pop-and-beer cooler Dad has turned into a live-bait tank. Sam Cat leaps onto the edge, eyes a shiner swimming too close to the surface and strikes. He turns his gray paw to show off the minnow impaled on a needle claw and crunches it down with sharp teeth.

I leave Sam to his fishing and set up the cleaning board on top of a low table between the two empty crates Dad and I use for seats. Nearby are the workbench and vise where I blew up my shotgun shell two years ago. Each time we're down the basement together, Dad notices me looking at the shot pits and rusty pockmarks in Mom's washing machine, but he never says anything.

He tamps his pipe full of tobacco from a pocket-shaped can of Union Leader—red with an eagle on the front—and strikes a match on the little ridges at the bottom of the tin.

"Holy smoke, the preacher shouted!" I yell as soon as he starts puffing.

"And lard was rendered by the choir!" he thunders back.

Sweet-smelling clouds drift toward the bare light bulb as Dad adjusts the radio dial. Static clears and Benny Goodman's orchestra fills the room with "Oh Lady Be Good."

After performing a little soft shoe, he prepares the whetstone, a thick block of slate kept in a neat box he made from narrow pine strips, tiny nails, and a bronze flip at one end. The box is dark with age and smells of linseed oil and fish. The entire cleaning room smells like fish and oil, singed birds, innards, and pipe smoke.

He squeezes a few drops of oil onto the whetstone. With easy circular motions, he sharpens two filet knives and hands one to me. I raise my eyebrows.

"You've watched me clean bullheads long enough, Cal. It's time for you to take care of your own catch."

The wooden handle feels light in my hand. Its long thin blade ends in a dangerous point. I've begged Dad to let me clean a big fish all summer. Now that I hold the sleek knife, I'm not so sure.

"My brother and I used to have races to see who could clean a bullhead the fastest."

"Who won?"

"I did. Eight seconds flat was my best time."

"Didn't Uncle Ray ever beat you?"

"I don't recall. Seems like he was always running off some place to sulk."

"Maybe you should've let him win once in a while."

Dad peers at me over his wire-rim glasses and draws on his pipe. "Maybe so."

He reaches into the pail. "There's only one slick way to skin a bullhead, Cal. Shouldn't even have to use the pliers."

The first fish is so big it covers the board. Lying on that slab of wood with its creamy belly spread out, the fish works its gills hard. A faint squeak comes from its yellow-and-brown mouth. I can gently run my fingers over the fish's miniature razor-like teeth and not get cut.

"Just remember, Cal, the only harmful parts of a bullhead are these spikes: this one just behind his head and these on the sides, behind the gills."

He points the knife tip at each of the three spears camouflaged by sheaths of flesh.

"There's a mild poison if you get stung. It might hurt for a while, but it won't kill you."

"I know all that, Dad. 'It takes a careless or ignorant fisherman to impale his own hand on those stingers.'"

"Did I say that?"

"Yup. That's what you always say."

"Well then, you'll want to get a good grip on his head before you start cutting. Keep this dorsal spine against the web of skin between your thumb and finger, like this."

Balancing my knife in the palm of my hand, I watch Dad cut into the first bullhead.

I was eight or nine the first time I saw him kill an animal. He raised his shotgun over harvested cornrows, swung a smooth lead, and fired. It scared me when a beautiful pheasant fluttered to the ground, still alive. Dad picked the bird up by the head, twisted its neck with a sharp crunching turn of the wrist, and stuffed the limp body into the back pouch of his hunting vest.

"Quick and painless," he said, taking up his shotgun and leading the way through another row of corn stalks. I was too shocked to speak. The rest of the afternoon, tagging along after Dad, I had some thinking to do. Until then, I'd always eaten my share of birds and fish without paying much attention to how they died. Roasted and smelling delicious, our ducks and geese and grouse and pheasants were served on platters placed in the center of our table. Since that day pheasant hunting, I've seen a lot of wild game and fish killed. I still cry a little when the animals die.

"They go to feed us, Cal," Dad reminds me. "That's why you must never waste a bit of them."

That's why he always sits at the supper table long after the rest of us have finished eating. All that's left on his plate are tiny bones without a speck of flesh.

While Dad cleans his next bullhead, I tease Sam Cat with a piece of fish skin. On hind legs he stretches in a long backward curve, bats at the dark skin, hooks it with a claw, and hunkers over his treat with half-closed eyes.

"What's the biggest animal you ever killed, Dad?"

"A fox—used to trap 'em with my brother in Bear Lake woods. There was a bounty on red fox in those days. We needed the money."

Dad's pipe rattles with spit each time he draws on it.

"Did you ever shoot a deer?"

"Nope. Came close, but I couldn't do it."

"How come?"

"Buck fever."

"What's that?"

"It happens sometimes when a hunter gets close enough to see into a deer's eyes and the deer looks back, kind of trusting like. It happened to me and I couldn't shoot."

"I had buck fever once. Remember? Mom had to take me home from the show when Bambi's mother got killed."

"Uh-huh. I remember."

Dad facing a deer, not able to shoot, doesn't surprise me. He couldn't even slug Uncle Ray a few hours ago.

By this time, he's cleaned four bullheads. He reaches into the pail for the last two and slides one across the slimy board.

"Here you go, kiddo. This one's yours."

My fish, all yellow and green and brown, squeaks through little bubbles seeping from its mouth. He's a lot bigger than the sunnies I've handled.

Some people say that a bullhead, which has no scales, is an ugly fish. But I don't think so. To me, it looks like one of the prehistoric animals in the *Wildlife Book of Knowledge* Mom got for me at the grocery store.

Holding my fish down against the board, I'm not sure I can kill him. His skin is smooth and silky against my own. Compared to the sunnies, bullheads just lie there, helpless. Panfish fight the hand and the cutting board. I know, because Dad let me clean one with a little knife last summer and it kept slapping the board until I got a firm grip on it, then shivered when the knife cut off its head. Its tiny scales fell away like little pieces of armor.

"Delicate armor," Dad calls them, especially when he scales a big fish for baking and the little pieces end up all over the place, even in our hair. He says that has to happen with people, too. You must scrape away the outer layer if you ever want to get at the heart of something.

Bullheads, except for their spines locked straight out, won't fight. Every time Dad cleans one, only its tail works back and forth in a kind of graceful wave as if it were trying to get back into the water.

Dad carves into the black band of skin on his last fish. The band grows wider as the knife comes up on the tall spike and plunges deep at an angle toward the head. Then comes the awful muffled crack as he breaks the spine and flips the band of skin away from the cut.

"See, Cal?" he says, his teeth gripping the stem of his pipe. "Think you can do that? Make sure to increase the width of skin as you near the head or it won't peel away. Then you *will* have to use the pliers."

The gray-pink flesh beads up with blood. Dad holds the blade edge against the main part of the body and slowly pulls it from its skin as if he were turning a sock inside out.

The white air sac has popped in all five of his fish—a sign of mercy, I think.

"As long as they get air, they're alive, aren't they?"

"Just barely, Cal, when they're out of water."

Cradling the meat in his left hand, Dad scoops out a bit of coagulated blood from its cavity with thumb against knife (he never even cuts himself), places the chunk no longer resembling a fish back on the board, slices off its tail, and slips the remains into the pail. Sam Cat rears up on his hind legs and reaches over the rim to paw at the limp shred of skin and the head with its still mouth and fixed eyes.

The music on the radio changes tempo. Dad hitches his shoulder in rhythm. "'String of Pearls.' That was popular during the war."

He finishes his pipe with a final low rattle and sets it aside. Bitter smoke has replaced the smell of fresh tobacco.

"Were you ever in a war?" I ask, still holding my fish whose gills aren't working so hard as before.

"No. I was too young for the first World War and too old for the second."

"Could you shoot a man if you were in a war?"

"I wouldn't want to, but if I found myself in a situation where it was him or me, why yes, I guess I would."

"How could you shoot a man if you can't shoot a deer?"

"Because the deer doesn't wish me any harm."

"But neither does a fox or a pheasant or . . ."

"Just clean your fish, Cal, if you want to have supper tonight. Your mother has been very patient. I'm sure she's hungry, too."

Imitating Dad's steps, I carve away at my bullhead, but the black band doesn't grow wider and we have to use the pliers. The fish can't be tugged out of his skin. The air sac won't pop. Finally, after poking the knife tip into the milky balloon, it deflates.

"I don't want him to suffer any longer than he has to."

"A swift cleaning doesn't hurt them, Cal. They can't really feel pain. It just tickles a little bit."

"Are you sure, Dad?"

"Could be."

He always says that. *Could be.*

Mom calls down from the kitchen. "Are you two finished yet?"

"Almost, Em."

"I'm cleaning my own bullhead, Mom!"

"With what?"

"One of Dad's knives!"

"You're letting her use a filet knife, Will?"

"A spoon won't do, Emily. Don't worry, she still has a couple of fingers left."

"Oh, for heaven's sake. It's getting late. Don't forget it's a school night."

"Start heating the lard. We're just finishing up."

As I scrape the marrow from its cavity, what is left of the fish suddenly bends in my hand. I drop it, jump up from my crate, and yell.

"Don't let that scare you," Dad says in a calm voice. "It's just a reflex—nerves and muscles remembering when it was a whole fish swimming in Lake Shetek."

Holding the lump down with my fingertips, I slice off its square tail, place my catch in the pan of fresh water alongside the other fish, and look up at Dad with a strange feeling that is at once happy and a little sad. And lonely.

Grandad should have been out fishing with us. Uncle Ray is probably gone for good. So is Liz, maybe. Billy died alone in his crib before he even had a chance. I wish I could see Jenny again. And what about Uncle Amer? All that's left of *him* is a pack of old letters.

Dad rinses his hands in the washtub, but they still smell of bullheads as he squeezes the back of my neck.

"Good work, kiddo. You're a full-fledged fisherman now."

With proud tears burning my eyes, I help to scrub away the blood and slime from the cutting boards. Sam Cat drags one last shred of skin out of the pail before Dad can pick it up. He will bury the remains in the garden after supper.

He hands me the pan of cleaned fish.

"Take these up to the fry cook, Cal. Tell her I'll be right along."

"Dad?" My voice sounds shaky to my own ears.

"What is it?"

"I'm glad you don't shoot deer."

He grins and tousles my hair. When he gives me a hug, all the smells of the day come together: pipe tobacco, oil on whetstone, lake water, bullheads, and the sweat on my dad's shirt.

A Zillion Stars

*I*T'S A CURIOUS THOUGHT—those bullheads swimming in Lake Shetek, hooked and bobbing around in a pail of water, then carved up, fried to a crispy brown, and "gone down our gullets," as Dad says, "to keep us a-goin'."

After eating my share, along with whipped potatoes and carrots from our garden, and slices of warm bread and butter, followed by rhubarb sauce on vanilla ice cream, lying on my stomach is uncomfortable, even with a pillow.

Dad is taking a "clearing-of-the-mind-constitutional." I figure he has plenty to sort through tonight. Mom says she doesn't mind cleaning up in the kitchen.

"You're exempt from dishes, Callie, if you'll do your homework."

I thought I'd never get back to Uncle Amer. With a tablet and opened math book off to one side, I sprawl on the floor with another of his letters. This one, dated "April the 2nd, 1919," has a little blob of ink at the beginning of the D in Dear Vic, Julia and boys,

> I made it to Forsyth, Montana, population five hundred, and signed the necessary papers at the land office. The acreage that I'll prove up in exhange for my labor is near a couple of little burgs called Edwards and Jordan, north of Forsyth.
>
> I had to spend some time and money lining up supplies. I am now the proud owner of a buckboard, four draft horses, some field equipment, and tools for building my sod house and digging a well. I purchased a good rifle and a pistol.
>
> Imagine me sitting on the bench of my loaded buckboard, giddyuppin' a new team across the Forsyth-Yellowstone river bridge and onto a long open trail. It is like an endless black ribbon cutting across the land for as far as you can see. Nothing like it back in Minnesota . . .

I grab another pillow from my bed and flop back down on the floor holding Amer's letter overhead, imagining Rex Allen riding under the stars, then strumming his guitar next to a campfire. Roy Rogers' song starts up in my mind. Clip clop, clip clop: "Happy Trails to you, until we meet again . . ." Amer seems like these cowboys and ranchers in the movies. That is, until I read the rest of his letter:

Toward evening of the first day out, the sky turned a deep violet. It was a backdrop for the thousands of cattle grazing in the distance, so still along the hillcrest and lower buttes that they seemed like cardboard cutouts. A lot of mule deer forage on the dried up creek beds, but they skittered as soon as I got near. What unsettled me was the sight of so many animal carcasses: dogs, cattle, mule deer, most likely done in by starvation during the harsh winters and finished off by coyotes and wolves. Nothing left but a few bones and tufts of hide. That gives you an idea of how rugged it is out here. I have never seen such vast country nor felt so alone. You should see the sky! It is wide open and goes on forever. And the stars are the brightest I have ever seen. By comparison, Minnesota is closed in, especially in winter, as if a canopy were drawn over it, whereas, in this part of Montana, the sky is broad and never-ending, just like the land.

It took me two long days to cover the distance to Jordan and Edwards. I was all in that first night. It was late by the time I found a place off the trail where I could water and graze my horses and camp . . .

An uneasy feeling starts up inside me. Rex Allen and Roy Rogers always smile a lot and their eyes twinkle, as if everything they do is so much fun. Now, the idea of Amer, tired and alone and surrounded by all those dead animals, searching for water and a place to sleep with only the stars for light, bothers me. I tuck that letter back into its envelope and unfold the next one:

The McKammans have a place across the trail and down a quarter of a mile. They appear to be in their fifties and talk with a thick Irish brogue. They like to tease and call me "Swede." John is helping me get started and Mary frets about how thin I am. She bakes good pies.

A stray shepherd dog found his way to my place. Looks to be about two or three years old. I named him Radge. He is a fine one, even-

tempered, makes for good company. I call the horses Rounder and Sam, Johnny and Skeeky. Does that ring a bell, Julia? Gianni Schicchi. Thought you'd like that. The horses are not anything like Bessie and Fanny, but they will come around in due time. By the way, I miss our duets and hearing you play. Missing all of you . . .

Lucky Amer. He got to have four horses and a dog. I've been begging for a horse for years—a Shetland pony, even—one that we can keep in our back yard or inside the screened-in porch.

"We could turn the porch into a little barn," I'd once suggested.

Mom and Dad just looked at each other and laughed. "You have Sam Cat," she said. "You can do as you please when you're on your own."

Amer missed my grandmother and her music. It's strange to think of her as a young woman, as Julia—a pretty name—but no one ever calls her that, except her friends. Mom called her Julia before they started avoiding each other. To me, she's Gram, old and hunched-over. Would have been fun to hear the music she and Uncle Amer played together. On second thought, I'd be an old lady by now if I had. Or maybe dead. Or not right in the head, like Gram and Aunt Eloise. Gram almost never plays piano anymore, ever since she started acting funny.

She wrote this next letter, dated April 12, 1919, from Hadley, Minnesota:

> *. . . Vic and the boys have been out hunting. They brought back three prairie chickens and I roasted them. After chores on Saturday, Willy and Ray hiked to Lake Summit and caught a mess of bullheads. They wished you were with them.*
>
> *We miss you at the table and talk about how you always like your fish fried up nice and crispy. Can't you just smell them? Are there any lakes where you are?*
>
> *We have had good weather; the crops are coming along fine. We wonder how you are doing out there . . . such hard work for one . . .*

UNABLE TO FIGHT MY DROWSINESS ANY LONGER, I get into my pajamas, and hide the packet of letters on my closet shelf. Mom taps at the door and comes in, carrying my good blue jeans—the ones that upset me when I scorched a big spot above one knee with the iron. Mom solved the problem by stitching an appliqué over it with a piece of fabric she'd clipped from left-over skirt material: a green and blue jungle scene with a tiger in it.

"Good as new," she says, holding the jeans up to show off her handiwork.

"I guess."

I don't want to hurt Mom's feelings, but I can't help thinking of the re-marks I'm sure to hear at school tomorrow, especially from the boys.

She hangs the jeans in the closet. I hold my breath when she straightens my stack of comic books on the shelf. Without asking about my homework, she tucks me in with a kiss.

"Sweet dreams, Callie. You and your papa have had a long day.

"Night, Mom."

Dad, back from his walk, calls out from the living room, "Good night, Cal. Sleep tight. Don't let the bedbugs bite."

Staring into the dark, I think about Dad and Uncle Ray. And I think about how brave Amer had to be in such a wild land filled with coyotes and wolves and all those open spaces and sad old bones.

My eyes close, but it all seems too real to be just a dream. All night long cowboys shoot each other on the outskirts of Masterton. One after another, men fall off their horses into Cemetery Creek, splitting their heads open on boulders. Grant Van Vulsa, our drayman, drives his team out to the creek and pulls the lifeless bodies from mossy water packed with bullheads. He hauls the bodies to Mr. Kimmel's funeral parlor where Grandad is sitting up in his casket. And all the while, under a zillion stars, Uncle Amer's four big work-horses plod along a thin black trail, past animal carcasses hidden under brown-and-white horsehide blankets.

Nine

Opium, Craps, and a Brothel

A VOICE AND A FAINT TAPPING SOUND—Grandad trying to get out of his coffin—grows louder until it becomes Mom knocking at my door, chirping her usual wake-up song: *It's time to get up, time to get up, time to get up in the morn-iiiing.*

"I'm awake, Mama."

Last night's dream hovers, making me feel frightened and heavy in my bed. I turn over and burrow beneath the blankets. Mom calls twice more.

Certain that someone will make fun of my patched jeans, yet not wanting to disappoint Mom—although she wouldn't say anything if she saw me at the breakfast table in a different pair—I hesitate over my choice. Then, at random, pull a blouse off its hanger. What a coincidence; it's the one patterned with sketches of the forty-eight state license plates: Montana on one shoulder and Minnesota on the pocket.

Mom sets out oatmeal, peanut butter-grape jelly toast (made from last night's bread), and orange juice, then fishes lunch money from her coin purse and ties the two quarters in a corner of my hanky.

After breakfast, I go to my room and slip a few of Amer's letters into my book bag.

"All set, kiddo?" Dad calls out.

Because the courthouse is next door to the school, Dad and I often walk together. This morning, he seems preoccupied, probably still worried about Uncle Ray or Gram or stuff at work. I decide not to tell him about the letters.

"Would you like me to carry that book bag for you, Cal?"

"Naw, that's all right. It's not heavy."

"Did you get your homework done? It got to be a late night."

"Uh-huh."

We walk the rest of the way with our own thoughts.

During math class, Miss Thompson uses the eyes in the back of her head and whips around from the blackboard.

"Callandra Mae!" she shouts in front of the whole class, "Put away whatever doesn't apply to math or it'll go in the wastebasket."

I quickly stuff the letter and its envelope back into my book bag and try to concentrate on multiplication. Staring at the pages in my math book is like drowning in numbers, so I end up writing words instead of problems on a blank sheet of paper. Words and names, beginning with August.

When Liz was home from college one weekend and we were sitting around the breakfast table, Dad told us about his Swedish grandfather.

"Back in 1898, August lit out for who-knows-where, leaving Grandma Ernestina and their six children, including your Grandad Vic and Uncle Amer. They were all just youngsters at the time."

Of course, my dad, Will, hadn't been born yet and when I asked him how he knew these things, he said he'd overheard talk when he was a boy. (No doubt eavesdropping, same as me when it comes to Uncle Ray and Aunt Eloise.)

"Where do you think he went?" Liz asked.

"Well, I'm not sure." Dad looked puzzled and took a moment to spread liver sausage on his pancakes. "At first Grandma thought he'd left Rockford to return to the Old Country. Others thought he might have come back here to Southern Minnesota, where he'd been linked to another lady. Apparently, he was quite a womanizer."

Mom turned from the stove, holding the spatula the way Miss Thompson points her ruler at the class. "Will," she said, "I don't think Callie needs to hear such details."

I groaned. "But Liz can? It's history, Mom. Anyhow, I've heard about things like that before."

"What things?"

"Just...stuff."

"All right, Woman of the World."

Liz snickered and reached across the table to push me off balance. Dad chuckled and took a big bite of pancake and liver sausage.

"Grandma was sure he was in Sweden," he said around a mouthful, "but a few years later, he was spotted north of here, up near Skandia and Ellsborough—in the company of a second wife and three young children. Imagine that!"

"He had two wives?"

"Apparently so." Dad wiped the corners of his mouth with the back of his hand, and then shook his head, as if Grandpa August had just been found out.

"That would be called bigamy," said Liz.

"Big of me?" I screwed up my nose. "That doesn't make sense."

"No, no," Liz giggled and wrote "bigamy" on a scrap of paper from the junk drawer. "Here." She tossed the scrap onto my plate. "Use your dictionary."

"Yuk! You threw it into the maple syrup!"

"Dear Lord," said Mom. At first, I thought she was referring to what Liz had just done. "That must have thrown the whole family for a loop. It would have been easier on everyone if August *had* gone back to Sweden. They would never have had to know the truth."

"What happened to your grandmother?" asked Liz.

"Within a year, Grandma Ernestina died. Most likely of a broken heart."

A valentine with a jagged crack running down the middle popped into my mind and I thought about old Mr. and Mrs. Samuelson who lived on a farm north of Masterton. She passed in January and Mr. Sam died in February. Mom said that some folks live together for so long and get to be so tight, it's as if they're one person, which is why one dies on the heels of the other.

"There are people," she said, "who can only take so much in life and wear out early, like your Grandma Ernestina. Life keeps beating them down until they can't rise again and so they just give up."

"I've seen that sort of thing happen with animals, too," said Dad. "When I was a boy, we had a shepherd dog named Sport who died for no reason other than some old mongrel he ran with got hit by a car. Those two roamed the fields together every day for years. Sport moped around for a long time after that. We couldn't bring him out of it. One morning, Ray and I found him half way down the lane at the edge of the alfalfa field, still warm. I don't think there was a thing wrong with him other than missing that old mutt pal of his."

"What about Gram?" I asked, still thinking about Sport, a dog I never knew, but would have cared for if I had. "Doesn't she miss Grandad?"

"Of course, Cal, but she's a tough old bird. Something deep inside keeps her a-rowin'."

I looked from Dad to Mom in the kitchen that day, wondering which one would miss the other most. I hated that thought and couldn't imagine living without either one of my parents.

And how about Uncle Ray? Would he lie down one day like Sport if something happened to Aunt Eloise? But how could he even love her the way she acted? What if he died first?

I dawdled with the syrup on my plate, stuck my finger to Liz's slip of paper, and waved it under her nose.

"What about Grandad and Amer and the others?" I asked. "What happened to them?"

"Edna, the only girl in the family," said Dad, "was left in charge of the boys. Then she died."

"What? How old was she?"

"Seventeen. Died of the influenza."

Dying at seventeen! That was only six years older than me. Two years younger than Liz. Mrs. Swenson's girl died at age eight—Strange how often I thought about *that* girl. And I never even knew her.

Having finished frying pancakes, Mom joined us at the table. "Edna most likely suffered from exhaustion, as well," she said between sips of steaming coffee. "I can't imagine keeping house and cooking for five strapping boys. That would have been rough."

"Probably so," Dad agreed. "After she died, that was the end of the family. The boys drifted away like tumbleweeds. My dad used to say, 'We all left home, drifted away like sagebrush before the wind.'"

"Sounds like a poem," said Liz.

"Like sagebrush before the wind," I whispered. "Sagebrush before the wind." I'd never heard Grandad talk that way.

"Two of the brothers," said Dad, "Uncle Frank and Uncle Ed, wandered around the West for a few years before settling on farms outside of Rockford. Did pretty well for themselves. They were sure close with their purses, though. We saw that at Amer's funeral. Tight as ticks on a dog. We never knew much about Uncle Reno, but rumor had it that he shot craps and went for the ladies in San Francisco. As Uncle Frank put it, 'Reno frequented brothels and languished in opium dens in the back streets of Chinatown.'"

"Now there's a story that needs no further telling at this table," Mom announced.

"What's a brothel? And craps?"

"Never you mind, Callie."

"Well then, what's an opium den?" I persisted, making a mental note to look up "craps" and "brothel."

Mom said that it was a place for smoking. Because that explanation sounded suspiciously ordinary, "opium" got added to my list.

"Okay," said Liz. "So now we have Reno, Ed, Frank, and Grandad."

"That leaves Uncle Amer."

"The fifth brother," said Dad. "He was like another pa to Ray and me. Came to live with us on the farm, worked alongside my dad until he decided to try his luck out west." Dad finished his coffee and let out a long sigh. "If only things had gone right for him in Montana."

THE SCHOOL BELL CLAMORS, signaling recess, and I jump out of my daydream.

"Callandra Mae, remain at your desk!" Miss Thompson calls out. "I want to talk to you." She stands near the classroom door while the other kids file out, and then leaves. Bobby Keeler shoots me a stupid look with a twisted grin and knocks my pencil to the floor as he passes my desk.

"Your new glasses are just as ugly as the ones you broke crashing into Mr. Paulson's car," I hiss.

He crosses his eyes and sticks out his tongue. "Ha! You're in for it, Callie."

While Miss Thompson was tiptoeing up and down the rows, she must have noticed that my tablet was empty, except for seven large words: August, Ernestina, Amer, bigamy, opium, craps, brothel.

I pass the minutes poking my pencil into the cork bulletin board next to my desk. Mr. Olson, the principal, peeks in, sees the damage I'm doing, and orders me outside.

"But Miss Thompson said that I . . ."

"You're defacing school property, young lady! I have a good mind to call your parents right now. Outside, to the playground! We'll see about this later."

"But . . ."

"Don't argue. I said out!"

Mr. Olson rushes over to me, grabs my arm, and yanks me into the empty hallway where the nauseating smell of lunch drifts up the stairway from the basement cafeteria: macaroni and cheese. That means bread pudding for dessert. I feel like vomiting, which is exactly what happened last year in fourth grade when Mr. Olson made me sit at the teachers' table until every last spoonful of the watery bread pudding on my tray had gone down my gullet.

"Bread pudding makes me vomit," I'd warned him. "I can't eat this . . ."

"You'll do as I say, young lady." Mr. Olson gripped my shoulder until it burned. "Now you sit there until it's gone. Until I dismiss you."

That's when I puked and all the teachers scooted back in their chairs to avoid the slimy mess dotted with raisins flooding around their trays.

"I told you I couldn't eat this damn slop," I blubbered through the froth around my mouth.

Mr. Olson slapped the back of my head, sent me to the washroom, and called my parents. Because I had cussed and insulted the cook's dessert, Mom made me apologize to everyone who'd sat at the table that day. From then on, the principal was on the lookout for the littlest thing.

Out of doors and glad to be rid of Mr. Olson, I find a private corner of the building where the bricks are warm from the morning sunshine. Cross-legged on the dirt, I feast my eyes once more on the brown ink and fancy writing of Uncle Amer's next letter, dated April the 14th, 1919, Jordan, Montana.

While reading his words, I imagine myself traipsing through the fields behind Amer's horses, running with Radge, and building a soddy. Filthy dirty from a day's work, I watch the night come down under a big sky while Uncle Amer plays Puccini on his violin.

The last paragraph, about a man named Carmichael, makes me scared for my great-uncle. What does this guy have against him, anyhow?

Before these letters turned up, Amer was just another name on an old photo. But now his words make him real and I like him. I don't want him to die. In the movies, it's the bad guys that get killed. Uncle Amer is a good guy. Whenever the good guys get shot, they always recover, don't they?

The school bell signals the end of recess. I pack away the letters and brush myself off. Janet and Judy race over, out of breath.

"Where've you been, Callie?" Sweat has turned Janet's fresh *Toni* permanent into a cap of tight red curls. "We took the Giant Strides away from the boys just before the bell rang. You should've been there."

"I really like your jeans," says Judy, pointing at the jungle appliqué Mom stitched over the burned spot. "How come you sat out recess?"

"Forgot to do some homework," I mutter, still offended by my treatment in math class and how rough Mr. Olson had been, grabbing my arm and pushing me out the door. I decide not to tell my friends about any of that.

And as for Amer? His story belongs to me. At least for now.

Ten

Tea and Cinnamon Toast

LOCK AFTER BLOCK, we trudge through deep snow, alone in the dark arctic winter. Our neighbors, snug in their warm houses, appear to us through the television screens of their picture windows. Children run in and out of rooms, men relax in easy chairs, turning the pages of newspapers, puffing on cigarettes or pipes, and the women stand before their kitchen sinks, gazing out into the night, looking tired or pleased, irritable or sad.

"Come along, Cal," says Dad. "Mustn't stare."

He points out the Big Dipper and how its handle forms the tail for the Great Bear called Ursa Major. I can see the ladle, but not the bear.

We stop midway to check on Tequila, our new chihuahua. (Mom said I could choose from the litter of pups at Mrs. Evan's house if I stopped begging for a horse.) Tucked inside Dad's coat, the tiny dog gently bounces along without a whimper.

As we turn onto Gram's street, I remember the summer sounds of her piano and scratchy voice pouring out through an open window: *O Mio Babbino Caro*, first slowly and deliberately, then as a fast waltz. Dad took my hands and we shuffled through the long grass in front of Gram's house—one two three, one two three—*mi piace è bello, bello*.

Now it's December, the town is glutted with snow, and our weekly visits with Gram aren't fun anymore—haven't been since Thanksgiving. The only one excited to go is Tequila.

Dad gets worn down from trying to steer Gram into pleasant conversation. My reports about school and Girl Scouts don't seem to interest her any longer. She listens for a few seconds, gets a distant look on her face, and starts complaining about the neighbors and relatives. It makes me especially angry when she starts in about my mother. My breath catches in my throat and

Dad sits up ramrod straight, trying to coax her away from what he calls "her tirades" or "the little storm brewing in her shanty." When nothing he says makes any difference, he clams up and sinks further down in his chair.

I tell Gram, "Stop talking about my mother that way!" and mutter "Shut up" under my breath when she doesn't stop. "Shut up," in my parents' estimation are rude words that fall into the category of "hell, damn, shit." When Gram won't stop yammering, I say, "Shut up" in a louder voice, figuring that Dad will ignore it at times like this. He does.

It makes me feel mean to holler at my grandmother, but I can't hold it in. She jerks her head around and nails me with eyes made large by magnifier bifocals. Sometimes I feel like crying. But now that I'm going on eleven, I figure crying is for babies. Except, that didn't exactly hold Thanksgiving night.

Because I've put off reading the rest of my great-uncle Amer's letters, he is still alive and happy in my mind. Maybe, if we avoid Gram, she might settle down, be nicer to us, get back to how she used to be.

"Why don't we stay away from her for a while?" I'd suggest. "Then maybe she'll stop being so ornery."

"Can't do that, Cal. She's my mother. I have to help her get turned around."

Dad's been saying that a lot lately—She's my mother—as if we don't know it.

Ever since Grandad died, nearly three years ago (May tenth, nineteen fifty-two, as recorded in the family Bible) and Gram moved into town, we visit her every Tuesday night. Mom used to go along. But the morning after Thanksgiving, she told Dad, "I refuse to endure any more of Julia's wrath, at least until Christmas. And maybe not even then."

With Liz away at college, that leaves me to make sure Dad doesn't have to walk the mile alone.

Last Tuesday after supper, he stood in front of the entry mirror, adjusting his hat. "All set, Callie girl? Time to go see Gram."

I told him I didn't feel like going, because I was still upset over what had happened Thanksgiving night.

He stopped shaping and smoothing the velvety brim of his hat.

"Well, I'd like you to go along, but I'll understand if you decide not to. I promise that if Mother goes off on another one of her tangents, I'll bring you right home."

The sight of Dad going through our little ritual by himself, a race to see who could bundle up first, made me decide to stick with him. By the time I pulled my snowsuit from the closet, he'd already tucked Tequila inside his storm coat, wrapped a scarf around his neck, and worked his hands into the fur-lined black leather gloves Mom gave him last year for Christmas. At the last minute, he switched hats, choosing the one with earflaps instead of his dress hat.

We linked arms that night, as if going to the theatre, and stepped out of doors. The icy wind took my breath away. Snow crystals from the blue spruce hooked themselves to Dad's nubby wool coat. Half way down the sidewalk, we turned to look back at Mom shivering under the bright porch light, her arms tightly folded across the light green bib of her apron. The folds of her housedress rippled around her legs.

"Are you sure you don't want to come along, Em?" Dad called out.

"Yes, I'm sure," she said with a determined edge to her voice.

"Maybe next time?"

"We'll see."

Their words hit the cold air like puffs of smoke.

Mom lifted her chin and waved. I ran back and kissed her before starting down the sidewalk alongside Dad and Tequila.

Even before the big blowup, Dad seemed troubled by how distant Mom was becoming. Whenever he gave her a playful pat on the butt or tickled her neck, she backed away, irritated. She used to giggle and nuzzle up to him when he did that. Now it made her mad, especially when he kept asking her to try harder to get along with Gram. They even started arguing in front of me, something they tried never to do before.

"She's my mother, Emily," he'd shout, "I can't give up on her. Be more patient, can't you? She's getting old."

"I have, for heaven's sake," Mom would holler back, "every way I know how! For years I've tried with that woman."

"Well, try harder, dammit! I'm pulled in two directions here."

During these arguments, Tequila would run to the bathroom and peel toilet paper off the roll, stringing it through the house. Sam Cat hid in the basement, on a pile of dirty laundry dropped down the clothes chute. And I sat rigid at the kitchen table, watching my parents' furrowed faces, listening to their angry words. Would they get a divorce? What would happen to me and to Liz? She was almost grown up. I could go live with her at college.

But after Gram went really crazy, things changed in our house. Dad stopped pressuring Mom to try harder. I was relieved to hear him say, "We have to make life smoother for Cal."

But he also started doing more for Gram, as if the more he did, the nicer she'd be to us: he bought her groceries, balanced her checkbook, replaced light bulbs, ran the vacuum, and shoveled snow, which, by itself, was a full-time job in our corner of the state. We set a record in November 1952, when thirty-six inches fell in forty-eight hours. Weathermen called us "The Snow Belt." Anyhow, nothing Dad did for his mother seemed to work. She just stayed mean.

"Do you love Gram?" I asked him one day while we were in the basement singeing ducks over a small fire Dad had set in an old metal pail.

He looked surprised. "Well, sure, Cal. Of course."

"As cruel as she is, how can anyone love her?"

"She wasn't always like this. We have to remember her good times. She saw to it that Ray and I had a comfortable upbringing."

"Yeah, especially Uncle Ray. She spoiled him rotten. That's what you said."

"Now, now. Gram kept us clothed and fed. Sometimes, she fished and hunted with us, told us stories, taught us music. She loved us very much." Dad paused, and his eyes glistened as he looked up toward the bare light bulb above the workbench. He shook his head. "Mother used to laugh a lot. Now I can't remember the last time she was happy."

"What's happening to her?"

"It's hard to say, Cal. I talked to Doc Grimm about her condition. He said there was nothing to be done for hardening of the arteries. That comes with old age. But I don't believe it. I still think I can turn her around."

"Stubborn man," said Mom, checking to see if the drakes were ready for the roasting pan. "You heard Doc. Why can't you accept that you'll never get through to her?"

"She's my . . ."

"Yes, dear, we know. She's your mother."

"Well, I have to keep trying, don't I?" He shrugged. "I don't know what else to do."

Mom rubbed the back of Dad's neck. "No such thing as defeat for Will Lindstrom. Ever the politician."

Dad grinned and held up his two gutted, featherless mallards for Mom to take upstairs.

She was right. Dad was always coming up with fresh ideas on how to solve a problem.

Like tonight—once again, on our way to Gram's house, he tells me of his new plan:

"If things get bad, Cal, we could pretend to listen while we think of other things."

"Like what?"

"Oh, summer vacation, setting the hook on a big fish, a summer hike through the countryside. Just watch me. If Mother goes off the beam, I'll look at her and nod, but I'll really be thinking of something else."

"Like what else, Dad?"

"I'll be planting our spring garden or trying out the new fly rod I hope to get for Christmas. I might even think up something to make her laugh. How about that?"

Dad chuckles, sounding a little like Grandad when he used to play tricks on me—like the time he cut off a dead goose's foot and, by pulling its tendons, made the toes claw at the air in front of my face; and the time he baited my Christmas stocking. Expecting a Hershey bar, I peeled away the paper and found, instead, a chunk of wood cut to size. There came that same low chuckle. Grandad eventually gave me the candy, but I never saw the humor in that trick. Mom said it was probably a remnant of old Swedish amusement that made him joke around like that.

"Who knows?" Dad repeats, in case I haven't heard him, "maybe tonight I'll even make Mother laugh."

"Hope you're right, Pa."

With the houses buttoned up against winter, there is only silence. Not even a loud argument from the Ryan's house. I hum a few bars of *Babbino Caro*. Dad joins in, off key, as usual.

Gram stands in front of the picture window, watching for us. She moves quickly away, flicks on the porch light, and tugs open the door just as we reach the first step.

"Hello, hello," she says, giving us each a hug. We stomp the snow off our boots onto the entry carpet. Dad lifts our pup from inside his coat and hefts her high above his head.

"Say hi to Gram, Tequila." She wags her tail, and then tenses as Dad lowers her suddenly to the floor.

"Tequila! Honestly, Will, I don't know why you picked that name."

"Callie's choice."

"I don't care. People might think you've taken to drink. And you in public office."

"Well, I have been known to toss back a shot or two after my visits with *you*, Mother dear." Dad grins and kisses her cheek. "Just kidding."

Uh-uh! He's not kidding. Lately, he's been pouring shots from a bottle that usually lasts from one New Year's Eve to the next. He calls it "medicine" or "a physic," and says it calms his nerves after a hard day at the office. He also reaches into the small cupboard high above the kitchen sink after trying to put a call through to Uncle Ray and Aunt Eloise. They always hang up on him whenever he tries to let them know about Gram's condition.

"You've been difficult from the moment I went into labor with you," Gram says out of the blue. She's been doing that a lot lately, bringing up stuff that has nothing to do with what anyone else is talking about.

Dad and I exchange looks. Is it time to pull out my own thoughts? We just got here and already Dad's staring at the carpet, probably rigging up a fly rod.

Gram's chin puckers and trembles. It doesn't take much to get her going these days. This time, though, she surprises us by turning the pucker into a smile. She must have sensed that we knew what she was about to say. Or maybe she caught me crossing my eyes at her as I sprawl on the floor to play with Tequila.

Still in his coat, Dad slumps into the armchair, silent and frowning, while Grandma Julia drones on about the gristly cut of beef Mr. Hager "pawned off" on her at the market and how Mrs. Erickson snubbed her on the street that very same morning and how disgusted she is with the bushel of potatoes purchased from a friend—"puny, wee ones" beneath a deceiving first layer of lovely specimens.

Dad sighs and picks at the ecru doilies tacked over the chair arms. The way he slouches reminds me of the teenaged boys at school, bored, with glazed-over eyes. Gram complains about everyone she knows in Masterton, ending with a story we've heard a million times.

"...And I nearly died giving birth to you. Why, the doctor had to resort to the forceps."

"Is that why he has those marks on his head, Gram?" I ask out of routine.

"Yes," she says, "to this day."

Once, while Dad was inspecting his face in a mirror, I leaned over his shoulder for a closer look. Sure enough, there was an indentation above each temple, especially noticeable since his hairline had receded.

"Like the eyes on a coconut, right Gram?"

She looks startled for a moment, then shakes her head in agreement.

"An ordeal! It's a wonder either one of us is normal after what I went through bringing your father into the world."

"That's for sure," I chime. "Nobody's normal in this family. A hell of a mess!"

Gram's scowl reminds me of Hulda Swenson's when I used to pass out tallies at 500 club.

"Why do you let Callie sound off that way, Will? She's acting more like a juvenile delinquent every week! The way she crosses her eyes. And those cuss words. Why, if I'd spoken to my elders in such a manner, I'd have taken a good beating! All I went through for you."

I glance at Dad, wondering if he'll scold me. Instead, he rises and slowly bows—a deep, exaggerated bow, as if on stage.

"Thank you, Mother. I'm grateful for the trouble you took bringing me into this world. I thank you. Cal thanks you. Tequila thanks you. Now let's have tea."

We laugh. Tequila prances around the living room. Even Gram's stern expression gives way to a high-pitched cackle.

"You actually got her to laugh, Dad," I whisper.

He grins. "I told you so."

For a while, Gram acts happy and normal as we sit around the kitchen table. I hold my hands above a cup of steaming orange-spice tea until droplets of moisture gather on my palms. Then I help myself to slices from a tall stack of toast oozing with melted butter, sugar, and cinnamon.

In the middle of a quiet moment, Gram blurts, "She ought to dress more respectably."

"Who?" asks Dad, a puzzled look creeping back into his eyes.

"For church. I said she ought to dress more respectably."

"Who're you talking about, Mother?"

"Why, Mrs. Benton, of course. She looks like a woman of ill repute, sitting there in the front row, brazen as you please while her man preaches away at the rest of us. My Lord, the way she dresses! No collar, just a bare neck. And that awful red lipstick. Imagine—a Methodist minister's wife carrying on like that. She ought to know better."

"Mother, you need fresh material. Even Jack Benny gets new stuff every week."

"Oh," says Gram, "I like Jack Benny. He puts on such a good show."

As we sip tea and eat our toast, I think of asking her about Uncle Amer. But then I decide not to, because I still haven't confessed to taking the letters. Besides, the way Gram carries on, she might not have anything good to say about *him*, either.

"Would you like to hear about my bike ride out to Cemetery Ridge?"

"Oh? When was that?"

"End of October. The last nice Saturday before the snow came. Janet, Judy, and I had a picnic down by the creek."

I tell about the sunny, crispy cool day when my friends and I nosed around the graveyard on our way to the creek. We pored over the dates and names on tall monuments and sunken stones, wondering why so many babies had died and been buried in the same corner under the giant oak tree.

"Most likely the flu epidemic of 1918," says Dad. "I remember seeing all those little stones."

"Most of them just say, 'Baby Boy' or 'Baby Girl.' Why don't they have names? And dates?"

"Maybe they did have names, Cal, but the families couldn't afford detailed stones or separate plots."

"Oh. We visited Grandad's grave, too."

"That's nice." Dad helps himself to another wedge of cinnamon toast.

I look at Gram, but she is busy stirring more sugar into her tea and munching a corner of her toast, gazing absentmindedly at the cupboards and the ceiling.

While standing with my friends next to Grandad's grave, it was easy to picture him lying in his casket with his hands folded and his head on that silky pillow. It was harder to remember him alive. Janet thought it was creepy how Grandma Julia's name was already carved into the tombstone, waiting for her final date. Here in the kitchen, I keep these thoughts to myself, remembering, instead, how quickly we'd turned away from my grandfather's grave. We ran back to our bicycles, which were propped against a granite monument, and hopped on. The picnic supplies in our handlebar baskets bounced up and down as we bumped over rough ground littered with twigs, aimed our bikes through a narrow opening in the fence, coasted and zigzagged down the hill to the creek, and arrived breathless and alive.

I grab another triangle of cinnamon toast and dip it into my tea.

"We built a great big bonfire," I explain, "and cut branches with our Girl Scout knives, for roasting wieners. We cooked beans, too. A great big can that we wedged into the coals so they'd be hot when we got through wading in the creek. It took us a while, though, because Judy slipped and fell in and almost dr . . ."

Dad sits forward in his chair, frowning.

"You never told us that. Water was high this fall. And there's a wide flow down there below the cemetery. What were you kids thinking?"

"It wasn't a big deal, Dad. We were just wading with our jeans rolled up. Everything turned out okay."

Gram, who is still glancing around the kitchen with vacant eyes, shifts in her chair to focus on us when she hears our voices rise.

"The rest of the story, Cal," says Dad, tapping his fingers on the table. "Let's hear it."

"Well, Janet found a long stick and we ran fast along the edge of the creek until Judy could grab the end and we pulled her in toward the bank. Then we roasted hotdogs and made S'mores. We would have had beans, too, but the can . . ."

Too late, I clam up.

"The can *what*, Cal?"

"Well, it kind of blew up while we were fishing Judy out of the water. I thought it was a shotgun blast. Janet said it was dynamite."

The furrows in Dad's forehead deepen. "Did anyone get hurt?"

"No, Dad. Nobody got hurt. We were nowhere near the bonfire when it happened."

"Didn't you girls realize you have to puncture the lid first?"

"Uh-uh. We do now."

"Well, you'll know better next time, I hope."

"Uh-huh."

"Did you hear what I said, Cal?"

"*Yeah*, I heard you."

"Not only with the can of beans, but also the river. Don't ever toy with a river."

"It's a creek, Dad, not a river."

"Water is water. You have to respect it . . . Callie, did you hear me? You'll know better next . . ."

"I *heard* you, Dad. Geez!"

As if someone has lit her fuse, Gram blurts, "That wife of yours should know better! I don't why she . . ."

Dad sits back, startled and still aggravated.

"*What?*"

"I said Emily should know better."

"Where did that come from?" I mutter, eager to shift Dad's focus away from me.

"Mother, I have no idea what you're . . ."

"I don't know what you see in her. Why, I wasn't . . ."

"Now hold on. Let's not start this up again."

"Why, I wasn't even talking to her at dinner and she interrupted me just like you're doing now."

Elbows on the table, I sit with my chin in my hands, eyes veering from one to the other.

Dad sighs. "What on earth are you talking about?"

"Why, Thanksgiving dinner, of course."

"We've gone over this a dozen times. Emily was only trying to help while you were talking to her mother. What you can't seem to remember is that Mrs. Dahl doesn't hear very well. My God, the way you hash this stuff over! Why do you always have to chew the rag?"

"Well, she's got no manners and she's a terrible cook. That turkey was so dry I couldn't get it down. And the cranberry sauce ran all over, into the dressing, into the potatoes, a sopping mess. Not a pretty plate. Not at all."

I jump when Dad's hand comes down hard on the table. Cups and saucers rattle. Tea slurps over the rims. Toast crumbs bounce around like tiny Mexican jumping beans.

"That's enough, Mother! What you did to Emily was uncalled for. And Callie doesn't need to hear any more of this. Keep it up and she won't be back either."

With Tequila at my heels, I run from the table to the entry and grab my jacket and snow pants. Dad follows, then Gram, coaxing us in a shrill singsong voice. "Don't go. Don't go. Here, doggie wants to stay. Come, puppy. Come. Roll over, pup."

Anticipating a treat, our little dog forgets us and gives Gram the neat, quick roll that will earn her a bit of sausage meat. She prances after my grandmother, into the kitchen.

"Come here, Cal." Dad wraps his arms around me. "Don't take it to heart. Remember, she's not well. We have to allow for that."

"I hate her! I hate Gram. She doesn't care about any of us."

"Oh, sweetheart. Come on, I'll take you home."

"What she did to Mom! She'll do it again. I know she will."

"We won't let anything happen to Mommy. Besides, Gram isn't strong enough to hurt anyone."

"Why does she keep saying those horrible things about her? They're not true!"

"Of course they're not true, Cal. Mom will be fine. And so will we."

Dad stays next to me until I calm down, gives me an extra hug before putting on his own coat.

"We have to go now, Mother," he calls from the entry.

"I can't hear you," Gram sings out as if nothing bad has happened.

Dad's shoulders sag. Our Tuesday plan melts away like the snowy footprints left on the carpet.

I peek around the corner as he walks back into the kitchen where Tequila is licking a greasy spot off the floor. Gram seems more shrunken than ever, standing next to Dad. Her back is so hunched she looks as if she were folding in on herself.

"Good night, Mother," he says. "I don't want the evening to end like this but we have to be going."

"Already?" She steps back to look up at her "boy."

Dad takes her hand. "Are you eating enough?"

"Oh, yes. I eat plenty. Still weigh ninety pounds."

Is that normal? I weigh as much. How can such a tiny old woman be so nasty? Sometimes, Dad refers to her as "a pistol" or "a firecracker," which reminds me of the pack of firecrackers that blew my neighbor Danny's shirt pocket clean off last summer and left a burn mark on his chest.

"Do you have to go?" asks Gram. "You just got here."

Dad buttons his coat with Tequila inside.

"Yes, Mother. I promised Cal a game of *Clue* before bedtime."

Gram walks to the entry and tries to give me a hug. I stand as stiff as a headstone with my hands punched deep inside my coat pockets.

When we reach the sidewalk, Dad waves. I glance back at my grandmother, but it's snowing so hard she's only a shadowy outline in the bay window.

Eleven

Purification and a Goddamn Wishbone

TRUDGING HOME THROUGH THE SWIRLING SNOW, I think about how my grandmother used to be, with her easy laughter and fancy piano playing, every chord an arpeggio. No wonder Uncle Amer wrote about how much he missed her and their musicales. I miss her, too. It wasn't so long ago that she sang with me in her old lady voice, sounding like a kazoo. Next to Gram at the piano, I buzzed the same tune through tissue paper wrapped around a comb, until my lips tingled and we laughed so hard we couldn't catch our breaths. When did she stop singing? Why can't she laugh anymore? All she does every Tuesday night is complain and act as if we aren't worth listening to.

I don't feel so shaky now that the snow and cold air sweep across my face. Deep breaths wash out my lungs. The air is sharp and smells of ozone.

"Well, what do think, Cal?" Dad asks as we plod along the snow-glutted streets. "Did we make a *little* progress tonight?"

"No! What a *question*."

"Hmm. I guess you're right. But at least we didn't storm out of the house this time. We got her settled down a bit before we left."

I kick at the crest of a drift, still angry about Gram criticizing my mother and frightened by all the yelling that has come into our own house.

Several weeks before Thanksgiving, when Dad started hollering at Mom, it was as if he and Gram were ganging up on her. And she hadn't done anything to deserve it.

"Why can't you get along with her, Em?" he shouted. "You've got to try harder. Jesus Christ! I feel like a Goddamn wishbone."

Mom was worn down then. Almost on the verge of tears. And to think that *I* was the one who made her cry.

It happened just before Thanksgiving vacation when report cards were due back at school. Mr. Langseth, my social studies teacher, had given me an "F" in deportment, which I easily turned into a "B" under a black pen. After

Dad signed the report card, I sneaked some ink eradicator and whiteout from his office at the courthouse and changed the "B" back to an "F" before returning the card to school. It was perfect, but I swear teachers have X-ray eyes, because that evening, Mr. Langseth called our house to arrange for a meeting with my mother. He said that Miss Thompson, my math teacher, also wanted to have a talk with her. I didn't sleep much that night.

Later that afternoon, my mother slammed the door when she came home after talking with the teachers. Slamming a door was completely unlike her.

"Tampering with school records is serious business, Callie," she scolded, brushing her hair away with the back of her wrist. "And why did you leave the classroom when Miss Thompson ordered you to stay?"

"Mom, Mr. Olson *told* me to leave. He's the principal, not Miss Thompson."

"He caught you damaging the bulletin board. What's the matter with you? We never taught you to behave that way. And all this sassing and vulgarity! Don't you realize your actions reflect on us? And your dad in public office?"

Mom's chin trembled and there was a hurt in her eyes I'd never seen before.

"What's 'vulgarity?'"

"Miss Thompson said you were writing lists of unacceptable words in your notebook."

"Mom, I was just . . ."

"At the rate you're going, missy, you are well on your way to reform school. Your teachers will not put up with a juvenile delinquent. I'll say this only once, Callie, if you don't change your behavior, your father and I will have no choice but to send you to the School for Wayward Girls in Minneapolis. And that'll be the last straw with everything else that's going on. Might as well haul me off to the loony bin right now, because I can't take anymore."

Still wearing her good red dress, Mom switched her ample hips from side to side as she marched into the kitchen to start supper.

"Nobody ever listens to my side!" I shouted after her.

The silverware drawer jangled open and closed, and a lid clanged down on a pan. She'd never acted like *this* before. When was she going to stop banging things around? Liz and I had always been able to count on her to stay calm. What if she was turning into another Aunt Eloise? Or getting to be like Gram?

And things hadn't improved by Thanksgiving—the first time one of our holidays wasn't any fun. Any fun? It was nothing but evil. Maybe if I tell what happened, it won't keep boiling around inside me:

Dad had just hauled the folding chairs down the basement when Gram started in, first in a low voice, then with a rage that snatched away the quiet—that special quiet time inside a house after the company has left.

Our family had grown used to Gram's criticism and invitations to argue, but this was different. At first, I didn't know what to do. There was no one to help, just like when Dad and Uncle Ray got into that fight out at the lake nearly four years ago—no one to help as the arguing got worse and worse. Wishing my big sister would come home from her date, I hugged and rocked myself on a straight chair until the legs bumped along the floor.

"I said I wasn't talking to you, Emily!" Gram croaked, lashing out at Mom with her fists. "I was talking to your mother and you interrupted! You're always interrupting! Willy should have listened to me. I warned him about you!"

Gram pushed Mom hard against the door jam and slapped at her face. Mom ducked and ran from the kitchen with Gram right behind, chasing her through the dining room, into the living room, and all the way to the bedroom. I jumped up and raced after Gram, screaming, "Leave my mother alone, God damn it! Leave her alone!"

Backed into a far corner, Mom stood behind the large potted fern that's been in my parents' bedroom for as long as I can remember. Full and green, it sits on a tall oak pedestal that Dad built.

Gram was slashing away at the fern, trying to hit Mom.

"I warned him about you! I warned him. He wouldn't listen!"

The blue of Mom's eyes was mostly black and the skin of her upper arms shook as she fended off the blows. "You," she said in a strong, low voice. "You have no right to be in this room."

I could hear Dad bolting up the basement steps, shouting something as I jumped around the big fronds and stood next to Mom, wailing my head off at Gram and slapping back at her. "Shut up! Get out of our house!"

I choked on my breath and thought I was going to die. This was my parents' bedroom, their private place. Without a word, Mom put an arm around me and gripped my forehead the way she did when I was little and got sick and had to throw up. I could feel her soft body trembling. Gram backed off for a minute, looking at us with wild eyes.

"Mother! What the hell are you doing?" Dad shouted as he caught up with her. "This is insane! Stop it right now!"

"She's no good!" Gram hollered, stabbing a gnarled finger at my mother. Witch's claws reached across the plant and grabbed at Mom's dress. More pieces of fern broke and fluttered to the floor.

"I said that's enough, God damn it!" Dad took Gram by the shoulders, jerked her around, and pushed her from the room. Gram didn't resist. She shuffled away without looking back at us.

Mom and I stood there for a minute, shaking and staring at each other. The blood was pumping so hard inside my temples, I thought my head would burst. Mom took me in her arms for a little while. Then we sat down on the bed and she rocked me back and forth like when I was little.

"There, there, Callie," she crooned. "We'll be all right. Everything will be all right."

Seeing the broken fern fronds and the mess on the floor, I wasn't sure about that.

The last thing we heard before the door to the garage slammed shut was Dad shouting, "No more, damn it! Not another word!"

I could only imagine how red in the face he was—like the day he fought with Uncle Ray. Or at the funeral, holding on to Grandad like he'd never let go.

"Why didn't you fight back, Mom?" I sobbed. "She was trying to kill you!"

"Hush, Callie." Mom brushed damp hair away from my forehead. "One person screaming and hitting is enough. She can't hurt me—she's old and sick. We'll be fine, you and Liz and Daddy and I. We just have to get through this rough time with Gram."

I finally quieted down. It helped to focus on the leafy brown and gold pattern of Mom's dress while she held me in her arms.

Later, as we sat propped up in my bed, taking turns reading aloud from a Nancy Drew book, *The Mystery of the Brass-Bound Trunk* (which got me thinking about Uncle Amer), Dad rushed in, looking as wounded as Bobby Keeler did after he crashed his bike into the rear end of Mr. Paulson's Buick.

Dad must have noticed a funny expression on my face, too, because he suddenly looked very sad. And kind of old. After hugging Mom and making sure that she wasn't badly hurt, he gathered me up and held me as if I were six instead of eleven. That night, as I smelled the sweat on his neck and felt his moist face against my cheek, I *felt* six.

He eased me back against my pillow and stood with his arms at his sides, looking first at Mom, then at me. For a little while, no one said anything.

Finally, I asked, "Why does Gram get like that?"

"It's an illness, Cal. She gets all mixed up and angry feeling. We have to try and straighten her out."

"That's not possible, Will," Mom said quietly. She closed the Nancy Drew book, edged herself off the bed, and tugged the covers up around me. "What Julia did tonight will never happen again. I won't have it." Her hand brushed over my cheek like soft snow falling.

"I agree. But, Em, as awful as it was, I have to keep trying. She misses Dad, feels lost without him. He always knew how to settle her down when she'd start fussing. She's taking her frustrations out on us."

"I wonder, Will, if you saw the worst of it."

"And why does she only holler at Mama and not at you?" I asked.

Dad looked at Mom who, with a sassy expression, raised her shoulders and eyebrows at the same time.

"Maybe it's because I'm her boy and she never got over my growing up and away from her."

"Bingo," said Mom.

"That's weird," I said. "You're not a boy. You're an old man."

"Thanks a lot, Skeezicks." Dad ruffled my hair and laughed nervously, as if he were trying to lighten our mood and didn't exactly feel like it. Or, didn't know how. "Even though it was bad tonight, we don't want you to worry. Mom and I will work it out."

He kissed my forehead, snugged the covers up under my chin, and turned to switch off the light. Mom blew me a kiss and went out ahead of him.

"You're a fine girl, Cal," he said. "Now sleep tight and don't let the bedbugs bite."

"Leave my door open a little."

"I will, sweetheart. Good night now."

My room was dark, except for a narrow glow from the hallway light. I got out of bed and opened the door a little more.

The murmur of my parents' voices came from their bedroom. They had closed the door, but it hadn't clicked shut. I tiptoed over and listened long enough to hear them talking things out in a good way. I heard them say my name a few times. In a louder voice, Mom talked about Gram getting worse with the hitting and that she could really pack a wallop. Then it got quiet. I tiptoed back to my room, crawled under the covers, and tried to sleep.

And that's how Thanksgiving Day ended.

Two good things came of it, though: Dad finally understood that the situation with Gram wasn't Mom's fault. And Mom, instead of fighting back with fists and cuss words, defended herself by staying calm while everyone else was shouting.

The next morning, Liz and I sat down to breakfast with Dad, who was taking longer than usual to spoon up his oatmeal.

Mom stood at the counter, sipping coffee and buttering a stack of toast. Liz was surprised at the scratches on Mom's arms, although I'd already told her what had happened as soon as she returned home from her date with Brian. It was after midnight and we sat up in bed, whispering about Gram, wondering what would happen next.

"Mom, how could you let her do that to you and not shove her back?"

"She didn't hurt me, Liz. The way she was going at it, I was afraid she might break a bone. Grandma is liable to be pretty brittle at her age."

"That's for sure," I said. "Pea*nut* brittle."

Liz nudged me.

"If only I could reason with her," said Dad. "Get through to her somehow."

"I've said it before, Will. You've got to stop trying so hard."

"And I've told you I can't do that, Em. She's . . ."

"You're letting her lead you around by the nose. Ray isn't the only son she spoiled. Difference is you're the appreciative one, to the point of feeling beholden, guilty if you don't keep doing for her. Overdoing, really. There's such a thing as too much mothering, you know! Look at the result. There. I've said it."

Dad forced a smile. "Could be."

It surprised me that he took what Mom said so good-naturedly, especially when he launched into an old story that seemed to prove her point—one I'd heard nearly as often as the story about Gram's brush with death while giving birth to Dad.

". . . And your Grandad Vic would say, 'Mother! You are so-motherin' those boys! It's about time they combed their own hair. And you don't have to be ironing our socks and underwear. We're just going out to check the traps, and . . .'"

"And," I blurted, "she sent you off to school with a pail of lard sandwiches and a great big sugar cookie and spit-combed your hair and warned you about guns and girls."

"Well, now, I guess you know my story as well as I do. Maybe *you* should tell it."

"Callie," said Mom, "don't interrupt. Let your father have his say."

"Sorry."

Dad scraped the last bits of oatmeal from his bowl and sopped up the gummy milk with a corner of toast.

"Yes," he continued, smacking his lips, "your grandad compensated by teaching Ray and me how to fish and hunt and get along in the world."

"Hmm," I said, pondering a word: "So-mother . . . Smother!"

Nodding his head, Dad bit his lower lip and grinned.

"Who would have guessed that your papa had been fawned over like that?" Mom teased.

"Nothing like Ray, though," Dad protested. "Mother treated him as if he were a girl."

"You mean he was a sissy?" I asked.

"Oh, I wouldn't go so far as to say that. But she sure catered to him."

"Callie, do you even know what a sissy is?" asked Liz.

"Of course. A boy who's afraid of worms and walks like a girl."

"Truth be told, Will" continued Mom, "Julia catered to the both of you." Then with a wink, she said, "Now, girls, *I* have a story about your father."

Dad gave us the kind of smirk that said he enjoyed being the center of attention.

"One evening, shortly after we got married, I served squash for supper. Your papa wondered why I hadn't scooped it from the shell or mashed it with butter and salt and a little brown sugar—the way his mother always did—until all the lumps were gone. I told him I wasn't his mother and since he was a strong man, he could just as well mash it himself." Mom snapped her dishtowel at Dad. "That was the end of that!"

We laughed, and Liz said, "Oh, poor Daddy-O!" and gave him a hug.

And before I could remember that I no longer liked my grandmother, I shouted, "The next time we see Gram, I'm gonna ask her about the squash!"

DAD AND I STILL HAVE A COUPLE of blocks to go before we get home from Gram's house. I force Thanksgiving night from my mind and hope for a fun Christmas, like when I was little.

With falling temperatures, the snow has stopped. Sidewalks, fire hydrants, trees, shrubs, roofs, parked cars—everything is covered with soft, thick coats of glittering crystal. We stand still for a minute to take it all in. Tequila pushes her nose out, sniffs at the air, then burrows deeper inside Dad's coat.

When we get to the sidewalks without drifts, where the neighbors have already shoveled down to an older layer, a dry, brittle snow creaks under our overshoes. In spite of heavy woolen mittens, my fingers grow as stiff as pulled taffy. My ears ache down to the jawbones. The whole world feels like the inside of the meat locker on Main Street. I used to imagine that thick, heavy door slamming shut and Dad and I freezing to death before anyone could find us. That's how it feels walking home from Gram's house.

"If only I could reason with Mother," Dad says, picking up the pace of his even stride. He seems to be talking more to himself than to me, so I just scoot alongside him through the bone-chilling cold, feeling the insides of my nostrils freeze, listening to the steady rhythm of our boots squeaking against old snow.

"Doc Grimm says not to expect much. He says reason takes a powder when hardening of the arteries comes to call."

I don't feel like talking, not even to ask what he means by "takes a powder." And what exactly is hardening of the arteries, anyway? How the hell can hard arteries make a person so mean? Why does everything have to be so damned hard?

Dad plows on ahead, alone with a purpose. I lag behind a few steps and watch him work his way through a deep drift at the corner of our street. Soft mounds of snow along the boulevard sparkle under street lamps like diamond down quilts. I try to step in Dad's tracks, but miss a few until I take giant strides, as if I were playing *Captain, May I?*

The sky, loaded with a zillion stars, makes me think of Uncle Amer driving his team of horses under the wide Montana sky. I soon feel the strange calm that Dad calls "a purification of the soul that comes from being out-of-doors." He often says that living with nature makes him feel bigger than himself, distances him from "the petty, foolish bickering that goes on in the world of people."

By the time we reach home, he's straightened his shoulders and takes the front steps two at a bound.

Mom greets us with hugs. "How did it go?" she asks.

"Same as usual. But the walk was wonderful, wasn't it, Cal?"

I nod half-heartedly. My teeth are chattering so hard I think they'll chip. The bridge of my nose aches and my lungs hurt from breathing too much cold air.

"Ullr would certainly approve of Minnesota tonight," says Mom looking out at the fresh snow.

"Who's Ullr?"

"An ancient Norwegian god on skis. He loved the snow, brought it here from the old country, you know."

She giggles and stretches her arms forward, as if holding ski poles, ready to launch herself over the threshold.

My laughter sounds brittle to my ears in the nippy air.

"Here, Em," says Dad, "step outside for a minute. Those trees, the blue spruce, all flocked—aren't they beautiful? And look at that sky! It's so clear, you can see all the way to heaven."

Mom shivers in her cotton housedress and cardigan. "Oh, it is lovely, Will. Cold, but lovely."

I watch their words take to the air.

Late that night, low sweet sounds come from my parents' room—playful, murmuring sounds that make things seem right with the world.

Twelve

IP-IP-IP

TEQUILA BOUNCES UP AND DOWN ON STIFF LEGS, excited for her Tuesday outing. Although I don't feel much like going back to Gram's house, I slip into my winter clothes, easily beating Dad who stands for the longest time in front of the hallway mirror, carefully fitting his black dress hat at just the right angle. He flashes a dimpled grin at himself, turns and catches our little dog in mid-air.

"Tequila loves Tuesdays," sings Mom, buttoning her up inside Dad's coat and planting a kiss on all three of our noses.

"You might have kissed Tequila last," says Dad, wiping his own nose. "Sure wish you'd go with us tonight, Em."

"No need for *me* to be there." Her voice is calm but firm. "Just more aggravation."

"I know. I suppose it's best to let a little more time go by."

"You two go on now. I want to work on some Christmas presents."

Dad acts relieved that Mom has finally gotten over her hard feelings. I know I am. That things are finally quiet makes it easier to concentrate on my homework and have more fun with my friends. Even the teachers and Principal Olson have stopped picking on me, at least for the time being. And old lady Swenson doesn't whisper mean things to me during 500 Club, probably because I'm older and no longer have to pass out the tallies. Now, when I walk through the living room, I'm taller than the women seated around the card tables. If Mrs. Swenson looks up at me, I simply smile and look straight ahead on the way to my room.

I overheard Dad tell Mom to go easy on me, that he thought I'd be fine now that a little time has passed since Gram went on the attack. "Doc Grimm assures me," he said, "that children are quite resilient."

Although I knew its meaning, I looked up "resilient" to verify its spelling and thought it might be true, because I still like to play leapfrog with the neighbor kids and bounce around on the trampoline at school.

Dad walks with a spring in his step as we march off to Gram's house for the second time since the big blow up.

"I think tonight should go pretty well." He skips over an icy patch on the sidewalk and gives Tequila a little jog.

"Hope you're right, Pa. Maybe we can get her to play a tune this time."

"Maybe so. Sing us a song, even."

We wave at Birdie Crowley who looks out from her kitchen window.

"Still doing the dishes," says Dad.

"She has such a down-turned mouth you can see it from here."

Halfway into our walk, Dad says he regrets wearing his dress hat and leans into the bitter wind, clapping a gloved hand against one ear at a time while holding Tequila in place with the other hand. Sleet stings my face like needles. What was he thinking, not wearing his cap with the earflaps? Spring is a long way off.

"I don't understand why the hell we can't drive the car once in a while, especially when it's so damned cold outside."

"You shouldn't swear, Cal. Your mother doesn't like it. Doesn't sound lady-like."

"If men can swear, why can't ladies?"

"I dunno. It's just the way it is. Guess we expect better from the womenfolk."

"Well, then, why the *heck* can't we take the car in this weather?"

"Constitutionals are good for a body, gives us a chance to think and talk."

"Can't we think and talk in the car?" I squint against the sleet, which feels like pins pricking my eyeballs. The wind gusts force my words back into my throat: "Summer . . . constitutionals . . . make . . . more . . . sense."

Along the boulevards, pine branches bend and sway under heavy snow. Sagging telephone lines bounce in the wind. Although I feel more grown up, more sure of myself since Thanksgiving, a tightness settles in my chest and stomach as we approach Gram's house. She stands, as usual, in front of the picture window. Through my frozen eyelashes, the brown of her dress and the blue and white of her apron run together like a smeared painting. Something else about her looks strange. She waves and hurries to open the door.

The clean cold air we carry in on our coats is soon smothered by the acrid, metallic odor of Gram's house in winter—a combination of the gas stove and a furnace that cranks out eighty-five degrees around the clock.

"Hello, hello." Gram hugs me. "Brrr, come in quick."

"Gee, Mother, you're looking particularly lovely this evening."

He sets Tequila on the floor, places his hands on his hips, and shakes his head. "You've been at it again, haven't you? I've told you to stop or you'll asphyxiate yourself."

"Never mind. I know what I'm doing."

Gram's hair springs from her head like a tangle of live wires.

Every so often, she washes her coarse, permed hair in the kitchen sink, turns on the gas, perches on a low stool, leans forward with her head inside the oven, and brushes that gray mass until it gives up every ounce of moisture. Gram always comes out of the oven looking like a crazy woman. Reminds me of Aunt Eloise.

"Mother, one of these days you'll go up in flames. And by the way, you need to lower the thermostat, especially at night before you go to bed. It's not good for the furnace to run that hot without a break. I can smell it. Smelled it last week, but it's worse tonight."

"Talk, talk, talk. Never you mind."

While Dad follows Gram into the kitchen, still warning her about the oil furnace, I nose around the living room, looking at the things she brought with her from Tepeeotah: Grandad's gray armchair, too large for this room; the fancy gold and black mantel clock with no mantel to set it on; a large faded picture of geese flying in V-formation over a marsh, out of place here.

Taking up much of the space is the traveling upright, from Chicago to the farmhouse in Hadley to the lake cottage to this little pink house in town. The wood is dark, nearly black in places where the varnish has turned gummy. Many of the yellowed ivory keys are chipped with dirty brown lines running along the cracks. How many musicales took place around this big box of a piano? I sit down on the long, narrow bench and softly play "Heart and Soul" with one hand, while listening for changes in conversation coming from the kitchen. Gram's voice is getting louder, but it's only about the pastor's wife—for the zillionth time: "... Mrs. Benton's red lipstick and those flouncy dresses and the way she sashays down the aisle at church ... Why, she looks like a . . . a . . . I just don't know what this world is coming to."

It sounds like Dad still has things under control, so I turn to the Vincello cigar box on the end table next to the armchair, where Gram keeps old photographs. Tequila prances over to play as soon as I kneel down on the floor to sort through faded tintypes of suspicious-looking men, sober wedding portraits, and cardboard photos of grim-faced Yankee soldiers posing with their rifles. They are all so somber and unhappy-looking, except Grandad in a snapshot with Docky, his hunting dog, and Dad and Uncle Ray as babies in long white christening dresses. They are bright-eyed and alert. Dad is grinning—even then.

While I gather up the pictures, a black-and-white snapshot of Uncle Amer catches my eye. On the back is written, "Amer Lindstrom, Montana, 1919." Standing in front of his sod house with Radge next to him, he looks like a skinny boy with wind-blown hair, baggy trousers, and wrists dangling like broomsticks from the cuffs of his work shirt. Could that be the same shirt I found inside the trunk along with the letters? The soddy looks small, maybe because the land and sky are so huge.

Gram's magnifying glass shows Amer's forehead to be pale compared to the rest of his face. He's smiling, but he looks worn out. Who snapped this? Staring at it for a long time brings me into the picture—where that Carmichael guy galloped up and down the fence line, whipping his horse because he didn't like Amer's music. Thinking about what is going to happen to my great-uncle is like reading a book or watching a show when you get the first clue that the good guy is in danger and there's nothing you can do about it. I haven't read any more of Uncle Amer's letters since that day at school, when Miss Thompson told me to put them away or she'd throw them in the garbage. And here it is nearly Christmas.

Dad still hasn't told me exactly how or why Amer was killed. All I know is that it had something to do with his land and a man named Carmichael. Dad prefers to talk about Amer's stories:

"Did I ever tell you, Cal, about how your uncle Ray and I came to be born?" he asked one day while we were down the basement, dressing out pheasants.

"Yes, but tell it again."

"We weren't very old, only about five and six when Amer told us that baby Ray was found in a slough, hanging around a flock of mallards. Vic tried to get that bunch to fly, he said, so he could shoot one for supper. Just as he raised his shotgun, he saw your brother amongst them. He lowered his gun fast. That's why you must never shoot a bird on the set. What about me, Uncle Amer, I asked. How did I get to be born? You, Will? he said, why, you swam all the way through Lake Summit to your mother and dad on the tail of a great northern pike. And that's why you must never take a fish that's longer than your arm. When I told Uncle Ed that Ray and I came into this world on a duck and a fish, he stared at us as if we really did."

"That's a good story, Dad. Do ya think it's true?" I asked teasingly.

"Could be, Callie girl. Of course, you know how *you* came to be born, don't you?"

"Oh, *yes*. Flying around a marsh, dangling from a stork's beak."

"And don't forget all that good fish it took to fatten you up!"

HERE ON THE FLOOR AT GRAM'S HOUSE, I laugh out loud at the memory of Dad's stories and reach for Tequila to keep her tiny paws from scattering the pictures. I gather them up and put them back inside the wooden cigar box.

"I wish I'd known you, Uncle Amer," I whisper, placing his snapshot on top of the rest and closing the lid.

"What's all the laughter about, Cal?" Dad calls out.

"Oh, I just thought of something. And Tequila's being funny."

In the kitchen, her hair still on end, Gram rummages through a drawer for light bulbs while Dad balances on a stool, holding the cover away from the ceiling fixture. Brittle bugs float to the floor when the milk glass globe nearly slips from his hands.

"Be careful, Willy!" Gram shrieks. "What a mess." She grabs a broom and sweeps the dead insects into a dustpan.

When she bends over, the hem of her brown dress rises above the backs of her knees, revealing white skin at the top edges of thick beige cotton stockings. She always looks so old-fashioned, especially in those clunky black old lady shoes.

Dad lowers the blackened bulb from its socket.

"Hand me the good one, Mother . . . there, where you set it, near the sink. And a little cloth so I can wipe out the dust."

Gram stretches up to trade light bulbs and hands him a towel.

She lifts the teakettle from the stove, rinses and fills it with cold water from the tap, places it on the front burner, and turns the flame high.

"I don't know why Ray can't come to see me," she sighs, pulling bread slices from a waxed paper bag.

"I do," I blurt. Guess I shouldn't have said that 'cause Dad gives me a stern look and shakes his head. As far as I'm concerned, too many stern looks have been coming my way lately. They should look at Uncle Ray like that, not me.

"When is Liz coming back? I haven't seen her in such a long time."

"I don't know, Mother. During Christmas vacation, I guess. She isn't home much, you know. College keeps her pretty busy."

"Her boyfriend keeps her busy, too," I add.

"You mean her husband," says Gram.

"What?"

"Liz's husband. We went to her wedding."

Dad stops dusting the light fixture. We exchange glances.

"No, Mother. You're thinking of Nancy, the girls' cousin on Emily's side. Nancy got married last spring, remember? They stopped by our house Thanksgiving day."

"Hmphh! Thanksgiving." Gram's next words come out like buckshot: "What's that wife of yours doing tonight?"

I freeze, sensing that we are in for it again. Just like that. All it takes is one word to set her off.

Dad's voice rises to a higher pitch. "Oh," he replies, twisting in the new bulb, "she was washing the supper dishes when we left. And then she was going to sew some Christmas gifts."

I can tell Dad is trying to ignore "the little storm brewing in her shanty." He steps down from the stool and flicks on the switch. "There you go, Mother. Let there be light!"

"Well, for the life of me, I'll never understand why you stay with her!"

Dad's expression turns hard.

"Stop it!" I holler.

Then Gram gets angrier and angrier and begins rambling until nothing she says makes any sense. "I warned you, tromping off to the woods like that.

They have their ways, those women. Oh, they have their ways. But you would-n't hear it."

"For Christ's sake!" Dad throws the towel against the sink. "Listen to yourself! What brings this on? It just comes out of nowhere with you!" Then, in a tired voice, he says, "Mother, why do you pick a fight every time we come to visit? What has Emily ever done to you?"

"You're too good for her."

"That's ridiculous."

"My boys should never have married the . . ."

But that's as far as Gram gets, because Dad interrupts her. His voice is calm but firm. "That's it, isn't it, Mother? No one would have been good enough. You wanted to keep us at home. You hate Emily and you hate Eloise, because they took your boys away from you. It could have been Veronica Lake and Greta Garbo and you would have hated them, too. Hell, is it any wonder Ray never comes around? We're not your little boys anymore, Mother. We're grown men with families of our own. Emily is my wife and you'd damned well better be civil to her or else. God damn it!"

For the first time I don't feel hollow and sick in my stomach. And for the first time, Dad doesn't plead with her. Instead, he is giving her what for. I think Gram will go up in smoke when he swears, but what stops her short is, "We're not your little boys anymore." She grips the edge of the sink and stands with her mouth open and no words coming out.

I've never heard Dad talk to her that way. He cusses sometimes, but never around the ladies. This is more like when Uncle Ray pushed him too far.

After the "God damn it!" Dad looks at me and nods once before turning back to Gram. It's as if he has set the hook on a fish and will play it out.

Gram finally finds her voice. "Well, I never!"

"That's it, Mother. You *have* to let go. I won't allow you to do this ever again, especially in front of Cal. She has heard enough."

Wadding the folds of her apron in gnarled hands, Gram looks around the kitchen as if it were on fire. She looks little and confused, like at Grandad's funeral.

"Now we can sit for a while and be reasonable or Cal and I can leave. Which is it?"

"I'll check the tea water," she says, her voice flat.

I sit at the table in front of three empty teacups, wondering how much of Gram's meanness actually comes from hardening of the arteries or from her jealousy and failure to keep her "boys" at home. Some of each, I guess.

Dad stands next to the counter, his determined look never fading. I give him a little smile.

Gram shuffles into the living room and sits down. I follow Dad out of the kitchen to find Gram staring at the piano, her fingers laced together, twiddling her thumbs.

Dad sits in the matching brocade armchair, leans forward with his elbows on his knees and gazes at his mother.

We are quiet for a long moment.

"Will you play 'Mister Dunderback,' Gram? Like you used to?" I sit down on the piano bench and pick out the first few notes. And then I sing: "Oh, say, old Mister Dunderback, how can you be so mean? I'm sorry that you ever did invent that old machine . . ."

Gram looks at me for a minute. Then, with a wave of her hand, she turns away.

We sit there for ages. Will she ever serve the tea? And who will talk first? I am determined to stay quiet the longest and outstare the others, the way my friends and I make it a contest when we run out of things to do. Only then, we end up laughing. Tequila jumps up on my lap and looks from one to the other.

After what seems like forever, Gram says, "Did you know that your Aunt Margaret is going to the Black Hills? Isn't that ridiculous? I don't know what she's thinking. I got a letter from . . ."

Dad rests his head against the chair back, closes his eyes, and puffs out his cheeks in a long sigh.

"Did you hear me, Willy?" Gram raises her voice as if he were deaf. "I said that your Aunt Margaret is going to the Black Hills. Can you imagine? At her age? Why, I don't know what's got into her. She must be sempty-five if she's a day. And she's not at all well."

Dad opens his eyes, stares at Gram, and laughs in a weird way. "Sempty," he mutters.

"What? What's that you said?"

"Nothing. Just that you always say 'sempty.'"

"Well, that's what she is, sempty-five. She ought to stay at home near her doctor instead of traipsing off to the Black Hills. Just look at a picture, I say. My, oh my, she used to be such a pretty girl, your Aunt Margaret."

Dad closes his eyes again. I close mine, too.

What does it take to be called a pretty girl in this family? When Dad told Liz and me about bringing Mom home for the first time to meet his folks, he said, "Girls, your mother was the prettiest, smartest gal in the county."

I think about how things could be, should be. Why can't Gram act more like my friends' grandmothers? They always seem happy, hugging everybody and telling the little girls how pretty they are. My grandmother never hugs my mother. I can't even imagine it. Dad confided once that Grandma Julia had an old-school German way about her. What was that word Mom used? Adamantine. That was it. So pretty sounding, like a flower. But it's one of those words that fools you. I looked it up and found that it means "hard and unyielding."

"Adamantine," Mom said, "will have to filter through another generation before it softens."

I follow Dad when he gets up to check on the tea water. It has boiled dry and the pot is sputtering and snapping. Dad clicks the flame off and sets the teapot on a different burner.

"We have to go home now, Mother," he says, grabbing his coat from the back of a chair. I slip into my own and wait in the entry. Tequila, tight in my arms, looks up at me with her bulging brown eyes.

"Already?" says Gram. "Oh, listen to me chattering away. Can't you stay a while longer?"

"No, we really have to go."

"Wait, I have a treat for poochie."

"I'm very tired, Mother. Let me know if you need groceries next Tuesday."

"Well, all right. We'll have a good visit then."

"That would be nice."

I open the door and leave without a hug.

During our walk home, Dad and I are quiet at first. Then he says, "I remember how your grandad used to handle Mother's tantrums. If he'd been in the kitchen with us tonight, he would have fixed those blue eyes on her and chanted 'Ip-ip-ip.' That would have quieted her down."

"So that's where you got it." I dance around him on the sidewalk. "That's why you say, 'Ip-ip-ip' when you think Liz and I are misbehaving."

Dad chuckles. "Yes, but it never seems to work with you girls."

"Yup, we always end up laughing and you can never stay mad. So, ha-ha."

"Ha-ha to you, too, Skeeziks. Or shall I say, 'Double Brat.' Isn't that what Liz calls you sometimes?"

"Yeah, well, she's a Triple Brat."

"Now, now."

The rest of the way home, Dad talks about Grandad and Docky. "That Chesapeake was some dog. When we weren't hunting, we'd take him along to the trap shoots on Sundays. He'd sit on his haunches, patient and alert, watching the clay pigeons zing up. Dad was a good shot, won a lot of trophies—I can still hear him call, 'Pull!'"

"Yessir, Callie girl, I sure miss your grandad."

Thirteen

Amer's Story

RAM'S PICTURE OF UNCLE AMER reminds me that his packet of letters is still stashed on my closet shelf. For the past couple of months, I've almost forgotten about them, busy with school and friends, choir practice and piano lessons, playing with Sam Cat and Tequila, and ice fishing with Dad.

On top of all that I have to attend after-school dancing lessons for ten- to twelve-year-olds, organized by our mothers. They make the girls dance with the boys and everybody's hands get so sweaty. We waltz and foxtrot and rumba around the Catholic Church basement (rented for the occasion), something Mom says you'd never see in a Lutheran church, especially in her day.

She also makes me do the vacuuming, hang the laundry (on lines down the basement when it's too cold outside), and set the table. Her big mistake was trying to teach me how to cook.

"I'm still a little kid, Mom."

"A little kid? I thought you were practically grown up. That's what you said a few nights ago when you wanted to go down to the Silver Star with Janet and her mother."

"Just for a coke."

"A bar is no place for a child. Especially *that* bar."

"There, see? You said, 'child.'"

"Well, a young lady, then."

"I already do stuff around here—dusting on Saturdays and don't forget last summer when I weeded the garden and picked raspberries every morning before the birds got 'em. And what about the fish Dad and I catch?"

"True, you're very good at all of that. However, it's time you add to your repertoire. I was doing a woman's work when I was your age. Besides, high school and college are just around the corner."

"But I'm only eleven, Mom. Not even. High school and college are years from now."

"I have a hunch it'll take that long to teach you to do for yourself, especially in the kitchen. We're having pancakes for supper this evening, Callie, and you're in charge."

I do my best. But after spilling flour and sugar on the floor and accidentally stirring pieces of eggshell into the batter, I forget about the burner turned high under a skillet of fat. Mom shrieks as if she's seen a mouse, grabs the baking soda, dumps it on the flaming grease, throws open the back door, and orders me from the kitchen.

"You can skin a bullhead, but you can't fry a lousy pancake without burning the house down! What's the matter with you?"

"I'm sorry, Mom! I didn't mean to!"

"Dear Lord, give me strength. Now git!"

"Okay, okay!"

"You might as well practice your piano—a little serenade while I put things to right in here."

I plunk down on the bench and nimble up my fingers with a few scales. Soon, the calming notes of *"Für Elise"* fill the house.

"Sounds pretty, Callie," Mom calls out from the kitchen. Her voice sounds less frantic. Like Dad, she never stays mad for long. "Keep on playing!" she shouts.

The way I figure, if this kitchen problem gets to be a trend, then I ought to be pretty good at the piano in a couple of years.

My girlfriends and I still go to Saturday matinées. Only now, as the lights dim, each of us sits next to a boy, until the boys decide to move down to the front row so they can whistle and talk about us and make farting noises with their armpits. A few of us girls try cupping our hands under our own armpits, but can't even manage a squeak. Instead, we watch the show and the boys, crack sunflower seeds between our front teeth and spit the hulls on the floor.

I no longer believe that real life is like the movies. Gene Autrey's cowboy outfits, which start out clean and pressed, his boots shiny, his lariat stiff, stay that way to the end of every feature. *The Ten Commandments*, with Yul Brynner and Charlton Heston, is fake. Fake beards, fake talk. Fake, fake, fake. I like Edward G. Robinson, though.

After supper (Mom mixed a fresh batch of batter and fried the pancakes herself), Dad and I tune in to the Gillette Cavalcade of Sports at Madison Square Garden, but he only halfway watches the middleweight matches. He calls Mom to the living room to discuss the cottage at Tepeeotah and what to do with all the stuff inside it. This is news to me.

"How come?" I ask, surprised.

"I think we'll eventually have to put the property up for sale."

"What? You can't do that, Dad! Why would you sell our cabin?"

"Gram won't be getting any better and she needs the cash."

"Couldn't we buy it from her?"

"We don't have that kind of money. The only way we could swing it is if we went in with Ray and his family."

"That's not going to happen," says Mom, "under the circumstances."

"I keep calling Sioux City, but I can never get through."

"Par for the course."

"We've got some time yet. But with or without him, we'll need to get started. I'll write and let Ray know. He really should be here to help decide what to do with everything."

By now, the shuffle of boxers and the ringing of the bell are only background noises. Dad gets up to switch off the TV, leaving Joey Archer and Danny Jones to continue their fight without us.

While Dad and Mom discuss the unthinkable, everything I love about the lake and cabin flashes through my mind: the pipe for balancing above the alligator pit, our gnarly birch trees, the batch of kittens born at the bottom of a cream can in the tool shed, warm fireplace smells, the heat collecting at the top of the stairs, trolling for northern pike and hooking bullheads with Dad, all of that wonderful old stuff inside the storeroom.

"I thought we'd give away what's left of the furniture," he says, "if Mother and Ray agree to that. We could use some of it down the basement. And we can donate most of what's in the storeroom. The Maywood County Historical Society will likely take the antiques—those steamer trunks and the like."

"Dad! That'd be like giving away part of our family! Don't do it!"

"Oh, Callie. Your papa is just trying to figure things out. It doesn't mean any of this is going to happen tomorrow. Property doesn't sell right away. It could be a year or more, isn't that right, Will?"

"By the time we get the place ready and listed, why, yes, it could be a while."

"I'll get a job," I announce, crossing my arms, "and buy the cottage myself."

"All right, it's a deal. Now let's all just calm down. If I'd known this topic would have caused such a ruckus, I'd have saved it for another time."

"For sure, you can't give away Uncle Amer's stuff."

"What are you talking about, Cal?"

After nearly three months, I confess to taking the letters. I charge into my room for the packet which is still on the closet shelf. The three of us sit down on the couch together, with Dad in the middle.

He opens the large Manila envelope and reaches inside. "Well, I'll be darned. After all these years. Where'd you find this, Cal?"

"Inside one of the trunks in the storeroom. I know you said not to take anything. Are you mad at me?"

"No. I just wish you'd let us know sooner. I've often wondered what Mother did with Amer's things. Look at this!" He holds up a brochure. "The original broadside. And his letters to us! Oh, this is terrific, Cal."

Seeing Dad this happy and excited makes me sorry I kept my secret for so long.

Mom gets up to clear the dining room table, moving the pair of tall ceramic roosters and folded lace cloth to the buffet. We spread out Amer's letters and create separate piles for the newspaper accounts of his death, the testimonials, and trial records. With all of this before him, Dad is eager to tell us everything he knows about his uncle, including the awful parts. Question is, am I ready to hear the ending?

He pulls the first few letters from the stack. Because I've already read them, I trot into the kitchen to make cocoa while Mom and Dad catch up with the reading. Mom keeps an eye on me, calling out cooking instructions as if I were a moron.

"I know what I'm doing, Mom."

"You're always letting things boil over. I'm sick and tired of cleaning up after you. Scrubbing burners. Washing the floor."

"You won't have to this time. I promise."

"We'll see."

Tequila sits on the blue linoleum, looking up at me, her worried brown eyes following my every move.

Taking extra care not to spill, I heat and stir the milk and measure the sugar and cocoa powder, then deliver three steaming cups topped with marshmallows.

Mom stands and peeks around the corner, looking for the usual mess.

"Good job, young lady." She sounds surprised.

I grin, raise a shoulder, and flutter my eyelashes.

"Sweetness," she says with a smirk.

Dad takes a sip of his hot chocolate and calls it delicious.

"I remember all of the last times we had together with Amer," he says, setting the cup back on its saucer. "The last fishing trek to Lake Summit. The last time we mowed and raked hay and pitched it from the rack into the haymow. At night, after supper and chores, we put on musicales. Mother was always sending away to Chicago for the latest sheet music. The piano bench was full. Which reminds me, Cal, we should borrow some for you to practice."

"Won't Gram mind?"

"I shouldn't think so."

"Uncle Amer played that violin I found in the storeroom, didn't he?"

"Yes. And I had a C-melody saxophone compatible with the piano. Oh, we had a grand time."

"What about Grandad and Uncle Ray?"

"Well, my dad wasn't musical, so he clapped and danced a little."

"Can you picture him doing that, Mom? Dancing?"

She smiles doubtfully. "Not really."

"Well, he *did*," says Dad. "Kind of a slow version, but he danced. And Ray played the combs."

At last! Something in common with my uncle. I race to the linen closet for a piece of tissue paper and to the bathroom for a comb. On my way back to the dining table, I buzz my lips numb against the wrapped comb.

Mom chuckles. "Sounds like Gram's voice!"

I make a pitch for some warbly high notes at the same time that Dad starts singing, "*O mio babbino caro, mi piace `e bello, bello.*"

Mom claps her hands over her ears. "Enough!"

"Wow, Dad! You almost sang on key. Do you know what the words mean?"

"I have no idea. It's Eye-talian, that's all I know."

"I'd look up the words if I knew how to spell them. And if we had that kind of a dictionary."

"Some day," says Mom, "we'll know what they mean."

"Amer sang that song until we knew all the words by heart. Even working in the fields, he'd carry on like an opera singer. Imagine—a tenor who just happened to be a farmer."

Dad sings again, this time in a soft voice and exactly on key: "*O mio babbino caro, mi piace, è bello, bello; vo'andare in Porta Rossa a comperar l'anello...*"

He stops, as if surprised by his success.

"That was lovely, Will," Mom whispers, leaning her head against his shoulder.

He smiles and pets Mom's hair.

"As Amer used to say, 'Now there's a song that'd like to make you cry.'"

"That was the best you ever sang it, Dad."

"A song that'd like to make you cry," repeats Mom. "What an unusual way of describing it."

"Ray and I sure felt like crying when we watched Amer pack. He didn't have much. Some clothing and personal things, that old Victrola we've still got out at the lake. I'm not sure what happened to the records and his violin."

"That stuff is still there, in the storeroom! Books, too. It's all in the trunk, where I found the letters, covered with a horse hide."

"It is? I haven't been in the storeroom since we moved Gram to town. Wonder how I missed that particular trunk."

"It's way off in a corner, sort of hard to get to. Do you think I could have the violin, Dad? We could polish the wood and get it fixed up with new strings."

"I don't see why not. Golly, it's wonderful to see these letters again." Dad polishes his glasses with a handkerchief from his back pocket. "To think it's been nearly forty years."

He folds the white hanky to show off his initials, **WL**, monogrammed on a corner, one of a gift set from my sister.

"I wish Liz could be here with us," says Mom. "She'd love reading these letters. Might coincide with the history class she's taking,"

What would Mr. Paulson, *my* history teacher, have said if I'd brought these letters to his class instead of to math class?

Dad reads aloud the next letter that Amer sent. He'd been badly beaten, yet wrote about it in a matter-of-fact way.

"He didn't want to alarm the family," says Dad. "It wasn't long after that we had to bring him home."

As curious as I am about what Dad had to do in 1919, I'm not ready to hear the end of Amer's story. I want to keep him alive in my mind a while longer.

"I suddenly felt older than my sixteen years," says Dad, sensing, I think, that he should tell the details of Amer's story another time. "You see, that's when your Grandad Vic told me I was to go with him to Montana, that he would need a backup in case anything else went wrong."

"That's when Uncle Ray got mad, right?"

"Well, yes. But Dad knew that Ray couldn't have stood a trip like that. Heading into the unknown, seeing our uncle dead would probably have been more than he could handle. Besides, one of us had to look after the farm. He and Mother were close. Dad wanted to make sure that two family members survived in case something happened to us. Ray was awfully upset when he learned that Dad chose me."

"What'd he do?"

"Stormed off and didn't come back till nightfall. Mother was concerned for him, but my dad said, 'Aw, he'll get over it.'"

"But he never did, did he?"

"I don't know. We never talked about it."

Dad took a sip from his cup of hot chocolate.

"It was a hell of a thing we had to do, bringing my uncle home. I'll never forget our driver. Mr. Malloy stuck by us the whole time. Took us to see the sheriff, out to Amer's soddy, to the undertaking parlor. 'I'd like to see you through,' he said. 'I'd like to see you through.' Words like that mean everything to a fella in tough times: 'I'd like to see you through.'"

"Fate works wonders," says Mom. "Something or someone decent comes along when you need him the most. Like the time you twisted your ankle, Callie. Remember?"

When I was nine or ten, I'd been wandering around in the woods, far from our cottage at Lake Shetek, when I turned my ankle at the edge of a ravine. As if out of nowhere, an old man showed up and took me to his cabin. He rubbed some smelly ointment on my ankle and bound it up with strips from an old shirt. Then he gave me a tree root for a crutch and said, "You tell your daddy what I done."

"That was Cady Towhill who fixed you up," says Dad. "An old recluse. You were lucky, Cal. He didn't like people very much."

"See?" says Mom. "A guardian angel. And you still have that shiny stick to remember him by."

Soon after, Dad and I returned to Cady Towhill's cabin with a big bag of new potatoes from our garden.

Fourteen

Pup on a Pogo Stick

ELTWATER RUNS THROUGH THE STREETS of Masterton, trickling into its gutters. Because a December thaw has taken most of the snow, everyone in town acts as if spring has arrived. They stroll Main Street or drive around with their windows down, waving, calling out, laughing as if they were at a party.

On our way to Tepeeotah, Dad waves at Mr. Delhoff the barber, and at Judge Carlson who keeps looking over his shoulder as he rushes past the store windows like a scared rabbit.

"Oops," says Dad, "looks like Ruby has her eye on the judge again."

Ruby Ryan, Carl's wife, likes to switch her hips up and down Main Street, especially in balmy weather and on Sundays when the Silver Star is closed. Most of the women in town hate her.

The smells of fried onions and hamburgers drift from the open door of the Mint Café.

I stick my head out of the window to catch the warm breeze in my hair and to wave at Grant Van Vulsa perched on his wagon. He hails us back as we turn onto the highway, leaving behind the hollow clip-clopping sound of his draft horses.

"You'd never know it's winter, right, Dad?"

"The weather is fickle, Cal. We have to enjoy days like this while we can."

As he often says, "Minnesotans learn early in life to take a practical joke from the elements."

I wish we were going out to the lake for a fish fry instead of an inventory. Dad's convinced we need to sell the cottage.

I follow him from room to room, doing my best to interrupt his list-making.

"One kitchen table and four chairs."

"I love Lake Shetek and this cottage, don't you, Dad?"

"Uh-huh. One medium sofa, a coffee table, several dozen *National Geographic* magazines ..."

"I don't think Gram is gonna like this."

"Uh-huh." He keeps writing.

"This is where we fish, Dad. Only *our* family knows how to live here. What if Grandad's spirit comes back and he can't find us?"

"Whoa! Hold on there!" Dad turns around at the top of the stairs and laughs. "How many Cals are there in this house?"

"Just me. And I don't like this one bit."

We walk down the hall to my grandparents' room and look out at the frozen lake.

"A bird's eye view," he says. "Quite an expanse from up here."

The white bay seems longer and wider than in summer when the oaks and birch trees are thick with leaves. And the hill where my uncle Ray rolled down and into the water looks steeper. I'll bet he got hurt and didn't want us to know it.

I point to a spot on the lake, straight out from our cottage.

"There's where we caught the big bullheads and I snagged that turtle. Remember?"

He's quiet for a minute, smiling and rubbing his weekend whiskers.

"You know how to make a good case, Cal. But there's heartbreak in loving a place too much. Hard to let go when the time comes."

"Can't we figure a way to keep it?"

"We'll see. We'll see. Maybe, if I help Gram a little more with her finances, we can swing it—that is, if her taxes don't skyrocket. She can't get homestead now that she's living in town."

Dad closes the cover on his pale green stenographer's notebook and clips the fountain pen inside his shirt pocket. I race to the storeroom so I can show him Amer's violin and the horsehide blanket and everything inside the treasure chest.

"I'm so glad you found these things, Callie."

During the drive back to Masterton, I tuck the violin under my chin and scrape the shredded bow across the single string, nearly poking Dad in the temple as he directs the "music" with his right hand.

"We'll get that all fixed up for you," he says, taking several quick glances at the violin as he drives along. "I'll redo the finish tonight after supper. Next week, we should make a trip to the music store in Pipestone for new strings. Then you can learn to play."

I saw away at the string and finger the frets until the "scree-scritch" pitches higher and higher and Dad says, "That'll probably be enough for now."

Tuesday night is bitterly cold. But nature's practical joke won't keep me indoors. Hoarfrost flocks everything in sight—parked cars, porch railings, roofs, highline wires, branches etched against a star-filled sky. Prettiest of all is the giant blue spruce next to our garage, all plumped up with a coat of sparkling white. Standing water has frozen into long sheets of ice, perfect for running-slides. All in all, it's a "nice evening for a constitutional," which is one reason I agree to go back to Gram's house. That, and Dad needing help with the groceries.

"No sense driving," he says, "if we each carry a bag."

For once, I don't argue. Tinker Bell has waved her magic wand over the whole world.

I sit at the kitchen table, gorging myself on cinnamon toast and tea while Gram and Dad sort through the groceries. She seems different this time. For once she isn't saying anything mean about anybody. But she is forgetful in a weird way.

"What's this?" she asks, "rhubarb?"

"No, Mother, that's asparagus, on special. Shipped in from sunnier climes."

"Yes, of course, for pie . . . Oh, good, you got me some fish. I've been hungry for that all week."

"It's not like fresh caught, but it'll do." Dad places the vegetables in the crisper. "Can't wait to taste your asparagus pie." He winks at me, unsmiling.

"Don't be silly, Will. Did you catch this fish out at Lake Shetek?"

"No, Mother, it's from the store. See the wrapper?"

"Oh, of course." Gram taps her head with the palm of her hand. "I used to fish with your pa, you know, way back when."

"Yes, I know."

"We caught the biggest pike. Mmm, they were good. Heavens, there wasn't much else to do at Bear Lake Woods until you and your brother came along. I got to be a pretty good shot, too . . . Well, you know, I had the best teacher." She makes an effort to stand a little straighter.

"That's true, Mother. He was the best."

One of the photos in the cigar box shows her in hip boots, cradling a Remington 12-gauge, her head tossed jauntily back. She is grasping one end of a brace of mallards while Grandad holds the other end, a rare smile on his face. I might swipe that picture. And the one of Dad's christening. And the picture of Uncle Amer.

"It was a long way from Rockford, though," says Gram. "I missed my folks something fierce." Suddenly, she turns to me. "Callie, don't you ever leave your papa."

I glance at Dad, who looks the most relaxed I've ever seen him in Gram's house. For once, he isn't frowning. He stands next to the counter as if he's just danced a waltz at Valhalla.

"She will eventually, Mother. We all have to leave the nest sometime."

"Not necessarily."

"Yes, we *do*. Now tell us more about Bear Lake Woods."

"Well, that was the hinterland. Some winters we couldn't get out for days on end. I worked at my tatting—lace doilies were my specialty back then—and your dad spent the long evenings by the fire, oiling his guns and carving those lures he liked to make."

"From balsa wood?"

"Yes, you know the ones. We stayed inside many days in a row, except to take care of the livestock. When we were able to make it through the drifts, we called on the Lowes to see how they'd fared. Mrs. Lowe, you know, was none too well. Still and all, she outlived Mister. Isn't that always the way it goes?"

"Sometimes."

"Doesn't surprise me," I mumble through a mouthful of buttery, sweet toast. Either Gram doesn't hear or she's ignoring my comment, because she keeps on talking like in a dream.

"Nice people, the Lowes. We played a lot of cards together."

Dad smiles and leans casually against the counter. The kitchen feels cozy and smells good from the cinnamon toast and tea, and the lingering aroma from the roast beef supper Gram cooked in the oven.

"Yes, indeedy, those were some good years . . . Oh, before I forget." She reaches into her apron pocket. "Here's a half dollar I've been saving for you, Callie."

I take the shiny 1955 coin from Gram's gnarled fingers and, for a second, flash back to the claws that tore through our fern plant to slap at Mom. I force the thought from my mind. Thanking Gram for the coin, I turn it over and wrap my fingers around Lady Liberty. The metal grows warm inside my fist.

"I have one for Liz, too." Gram holds up a second half dollar.

"You can give it to her at Christmas, Mother. That's coming up, you know."

I shiver at the memory of my parents' conversation the night before: "Let Ray and Eloise have her this year," Mom had said. "I refuse to chance another fight in this house."

Dad frowned at that. "I don't know *what* to do. The last time we put her on a bus for Sioux City, she came home the next day in tears. Don't you remember, Em? Eloise didn't want her. She made Ray take her right back to the terminal."

"Well, *she* was probably sick of the fights, too."

"Or," I suggested, "Aunt Eloise went nuts again in order to scare Gram into leaving."

"We won't leave her alone during the holidays," said Dad. "Especially Christmas."

Now, sitting next to Gram at the table, Dad must be remembering how awful it was for her in Sioux City. He pats her shoulder and says in a gentle voice, "We'll make our plans in a day or so, Mother. We'll have a nice Christmas together."

Because Gram is in such a good mood, I decide to ask her about Uncle Amer.

"He's my brother-in-law. Works alongside Vic and the boys on the farm."

"What was he like?"

"Oh, he's smart. Reads books. And musical? Why, he sings and plays the violin."

"He's no longer living, Mother. Don't you remember?"

"Oh?" Gram looks puzzled. "Oh, that's right. We couldn't make it to his funeral."

She breaks a corner from her slice of toast and sets both pieces down on the table. "Ray had to mind the farm. He balked at first. Fit to be tied when he couldn't go. I had to do the milking that first night. He was nowhere to be found. I worried about him. He took it so hard."

She gives us a scalding look. "Ray feels awful bad being left behind."

Dad plays a little drum roll with his fingers against the table, drains the last of his tea, gathers up the toast crumbs, and tosses them into his mouth like a handful of popcorn.

"Any projects for me tonight, Mother?"

"Let me think . . . no, I guess not."

"Well then, we'll get-a-goin'." He scoots his chair back and stands up to stretch.

"So soon? You just got here. Wouldn't you like more tea and cinnamon toast? Callie, you're still hungry, aren't you?"

I'm about to say yes when Dad butts in.

"Next time, Mother. I've got some paperwork to do."

Tequila jumps around like a pup on a pogo stick. Dad scoops her up and tucks her inside his coat. As usual, her saucer eyes and chihuahua snout poking out from the wide, furry lapels make us giggle. And for the first time in weeks, Gram laughs in her old way.

Dad leans over for a hug.

"I enjoyed tonight, Mom. See ya next Tuesday."

That's strange. I can't remember ever hearing him call her "Mom" before.

I thank Gram for the half dollar and give her a quick kiss. She holds onto my arms and gives me three kisses—one on each cheek and one on the forehead.

"Good night, you two," she says, waving at us. "Thanks for all you do to help me out."

Dad turns and looks at his mother as if John Beresford Tipton has just handed him a check for a million dollars.

"You're welcome, *Mama mia.*" He skips like Fred Astaire off the last step. "Make a to-do list for next week."

"And think up some more stories," I call out from the sidewalk. "More about Bear Lake Woods!"

"And, say, while you're at it," Dad shouts, "practice a tune on the old pie-ano. We'd like that!"

In spite of the cold, Gram stands in the open door, waving her dishtowel until we reach the end of the block and turn the corner.

Halfway home, Dad works up a running slide onto a long patch of smooth ice, as free and easy as a kid. Tequila scrambles up to look back at me, her eyes nearly popping out of their sockets as she sails along with Dad. I slide after them until the ice stops dead on the concrete.

Sometimes, like tonight, I wonder about my dad. In our geography books at school, there's a picture of an Italian family having a picnic under a big tree. The table is loaded with wine bottles and platters of food and everyone is laughing and gesturing as if they're all talking at once. My dad is the spitting image of the guy at the head of the table. And even though he doesn't know what the words mean, he can sing "*O Mio Babbino Caro*" well enough to make you cry.

Once, when I heard him joking around with Mom, he said he might have been adopted, because he felt "daringly Eye-talian," and not at all Swedish and German. Then he got a sly look on his face and started chasing her around the living room. When he caught her, he bent her over backwards and gave her a big smooch smack dab on the mouth, right in front of me. I thought it was yucky and cool at the same time. But mainly, I figured they wouldn't be getting a divorce—not that they'd talked about one, but when they argued, I wasn't so sure. Finally, I decided that my dad couldn't possibly have been adopted, because Gram was always telling us about the awful difficulties surrounding his birth and the forceps dents on his head.

"At least," Dad told me after the last time we'd listened to that story, "I no longer feel responsible for her pain."

Fifteen

Livers and Lampshades

RANDMA JULIA IS SPENDING CHRISTMAS with us. Dad's plan is for Mom to stay at arm's length, for everyone to remain calm and ignore Gram's invitations to argue. "If we can't do that," he says, "we should get out of the house and go for a walk."

It helps to have Liz and Brian home from college. They could talk all day about life outside of Masterton. Also, Grandma Dahl is visiting from North Dakota and I get to make potato *lefse* with her. During Thanksgiving week, there wasn't time, because she stayed with Aunt Hazel and Uncle Cecil.

My mom's mother is nearly as wide as she is tall and has the softest cheeks of anyone I've ever kissed. Her steel gray hair is long and thin. At night, she brushes and braids it. During the day, she wears it twisted into a little bun at the back of her head and covers it with a mesh net. Grandma Dahl never uses a recipe for anything—goulash, tall loaves of bread, thick sugar cookies, and *lefse*. The whole week she stays at our house, she cooks and bakes and gives Liz and me tight hugs no matter how much flour sifts onto the floor.

Besides me, there are six others at the Christmas table: Mom, Dad, Gram, Grandma Dahl, Liz, and Brian. Except for Gram, everyone is happy and talkative, like how I imagine that Italian family in my schoolbook picture—eating and drinking wine (ours is Mogen David, because Mom likes its sweetness). Dad sits at the head of the table, nibbling bits of meat from the leg bones of roasted goose. Laughing, he asks, "How's your gizzard, Emily?" when he notices Mom at the other end of the table, flushed from the kitchen, giddy from the wine, cutting thin slices of goose gizzard.

Liz and Brian tell us about their classes and professors, new friends, quiet walks along the bluffs in Mankato, last fall's Homecoming parade, and the lavender dress Liz wore to the dance. Grandma Dahl, as rosy-cheeked as

Mom, says in a slurred voice how happy she is to be with us for Christmas this year, and "how Liz and Callie have become such lovely young ladies." And "Brian is such a handsome young man." Brian's face turns red and his wine glass isn't even empty. I excuse myself to go to the bathroom and take an extra minute to study my looks in the mirror.

Gram wishes Ray and his family could have come up from Sioux City. "Wouldn't that have been nice," she says, "if we could all have been together."

The rest of us exchange glances. Dad reaches over to touch her hand. "How about if we put a call through after dinner, wish them a Merry Christmas?"

"Why, yes," she says, "I'd like that."

It doesn't take long to realize that the bluster has gone out of Gram. As if for old times' sake, she half-heartedly picks on Mom over how long it takes to roast a goose. In the middle of her sputter, she falls quiet and glances around the table, as if she hasn't known us for long. In between bites, she forks the food around on her plate, shoving a little pile of corn here, mashed potatoes there, a piece of goose breast opposite where it has been. By the time the rest of us have finished, her plate is still half full.

When we exchange gifts (Dad gets his fly rod), Gram just sits and watches everyone else while a stack of presents grows up around her feet. We have to remind her to open them. She unwraps and sets each gift aside without a word: pink floral stationery from Liz and Brian, Jergan's hand lotion from Grandma Dahl, a mint-green nightie with matching bed jacket and slippers from Mom and Dad. As soon as she opens that box, the whole room smells of Chanel No. 5 from Marbella Kinmore's Fashionette. My gift to Gram is the latest sheet music from the store in Pipestone: "Blueberry Hill," "Banana Boat Song," and "Chances Are" with Johnny Mathis pictured on the front.

I open packages with navy stretch pants inside, and rosin and a new case for my violin—that is, Uncle Amer's violin. Grandma Dahl and Gram Julia each give me a book: *Little Women* and *Treasure Island*. Liz tosses me a big box with a red bow. Inside is a white, blue, and red sweater she knitted on extra-large needles.

I jump up to hug my sister, and then hug the bulky sweater before slipping it on.

"I love it! I love it!"

"You'll have to take up skiing, Sis. There's a hill near Mankato. We could go there next time you come to stay at the dorm."

"Who was that old guy on skis, Mom? The one you said brought tons of snow to Minnesota?"

"Oh, yes. Ullr. Our ancient Norwegian god, Ullr."

I strut around the living room, pretending to ski. Tequila shreds wrapping paper. Sam Cat bats a green-and-gold bow across the carpet, until it wedges between the piano pedals.

After clearing the table and doing the dishes, we sit next to the bubble-lit tree and sing Christmas carols. Gram plays "Silent Night" and then gets disgusted when I change the words for "We Three Kings": "We three kings of Orient are, puffing on a rubber cigar, it was loaded, it exploded. Pop! Bang! We two kings . . . Pop! Bang! We one king . . . Pop! Bang! Si-ilent Night."

Mom rolls her eyes. Dad smirks. Grandma Dahl, her eyes sparkling, turns her face to one side. Liz giggles.

"That's a cool version, Callie," says Brian.

"Shall I sing another?"

"No, that'll do." Mom gathers up the boxes and shredded wrapping paper and bows.

Before taking Gram back home, Dad calls Uncle Ray and lets it ring for a long time. There is no answer.

Although everyone's relieved to get through Christmas without a fight, I feel sad to see my grandmother losing her grit. She seems to be giving up on everything, including the fun and the laughter.

After Christmas, Dad, Tequila, and I continue our Tuesday visits with Gram. Sometimes, Mom goes along. I'm glad to have her as an ally when she insists on driving during the cold snaps.

"I wouldn't consider going if Julia were still throwing punches, but now that she's not so feisty . . ."

Most Tuesdays, Gram sits quietly in her chair while I play the tunes she has taught me on the upright: "Mr. Dunderback," "Little Old Lady Time for

Tea," "Wonderful, Wonderful Copenhagen." I also play the new songs I gave her for Christmas, feeling clever and hoping to make her laugh with my imitation of Johnny Mathis singing, "Chances Are."

Mom takes over the tasks of boiling water for tea and making the cinnamon toast. Tired from work and shoveling snow, Dad often dozes with Tequila curled up on his lap. His head bobs forth and back, until his chin drops to his chest, then snaps back against the curved padding of the green armchair. He looks startled and clears his throat, then smiles sleepily. I think he's relieved to have Mom and me take over the Tuesday nights.

For a long time, our days pass with nothing more to unsettle us—that is, until late in January 1957, when the first in a string of murders takes place in Masterton.

Two sharp blasts wake me up. I think it's an ice dam snapping along the eave outside my bedroom window. Turns out to be gunshots a block away, in front of the Catholic Church. It makes the papers, thanks to Elmore Billings, reporter for *The Maywood County Herald* and *The Black Duck Chronicle*. A Mr. Byers, no longer allowed to see his children after a divorce, shoots his wife and mother-in-law as they leave Mass.

It's impossible to shake the sounds of those gunshots. They remind me of Uncle Amer's murder, and I wonder all over again what it feels like to be hit by bullets. Of course, I know the impact of a shotgun shell's brass head blown out of a vise. It's harder to imagine the full load. Maybe it's like being punched hard by tiny fists.

Soon after the Catholic Church murders, Mr. Olson's wife dies on their farm west of town—chewed up in the power take-off hooked to the hay bale elevator. The woman's nightgown gets caught in the shaft. Pulled right in at three o'clock in the morning, ten below zero.

Mr. Olson goes free and we wonder if he has bought off the judge. Dad says that sometimes happens, especially if the judge is a close friend.

I love reading the newspapers. It's like discovering new stories by Edgar Allen Poe. The creepiest is about a man (not from Masterton) who butchers people and stores their hearts and livers in his refrigerator and uses their skin for lampshades.

Mom announces that because good fiction is better for me to read than these newspaper reports, she has arranged for an appointment with the Colliers Encyclopedia salesman, who soon delivers a set of six green-and-black volumes—short stories, not only by Edgar Allen Poe, but Kipling and Robert Louis Stevenson and Edna Ferber and O. Henry and Selma Lagerlöf and a bunch more.

One of my favorite stories is "The Slanderer," written by a guy with a very foreign name: Anton Chekhov. It's about a man who goes into the kitchen to check on the wedding feast preparation for his daughter. When the cook, Marfa, shows him the sturgeon, he's so impressed by the huge fish that he smacks his lips and snaps his fingers. Someone hears the sounds and teases him about kissing the cook. Because he worries about rumors going around, he tells everyone what really happened. No one cares until he starts making such a big deal about it. The rumor upsets his wife and he wonders who has ruined his reputation. All because of a kissing sound over "a big fat sturgeon, amid capers, olives, and carrots."

Our own Mr. Olson got away with murder. Now everyone in the county avoids him and his reputation is ruined forever. *He* deserves it.

With all the weird and scary things happening, it's a relief to look out of the window each night to see Dad coming home from work. To see him walking down our block, happy to be "among the elements," makes me feel as though nothing bad will ever happen to us.

Long famous for his walks around town, Dad takes a lot of teasing from his friends and some of the men he works with at the courthouse. Most of it is good-natured:

"There goes Mr. Will Lindstrom, Maywood County's strolling auditor."

"Is that car of yours always on the fritz, Will?"

"Day or night, no matter what the weather . . ."

"Don't it make you wonder?"

"Yessir, our Man about Town."

But some folks snicker when they see him marching down the street in his shirtsleeves on hot summer days, swinging his briefcase, his suit jacket slung over one shoulder. Or through a heavy rain in his mackintosh, water streaming off the brim of his black dress hat. Or leaning into a blizzard—a globe of swirling white—his long wool overcoat whipping at his legs.

Dad greets everyone he sees from one end of town to the other. And when they tease him, he laughs, ribs them back.

"I plan to keep on walking," he says, "while everyone else gasses up."

It isn't that he's cheap. He just can't get over the habit of rationing fuel in order to save on tire rubber. After fourteen years, a 1943 poster still hangs from a nail inside our garage: *Is this Trip Necessary?* Besides the war effort, knowing that his car is parked inside, "safe and immaculate," especially when it rains, makes Dad feel that all is right with the world.

"Exercise makes me feel good," he says. "The fresh air clears my head and settles my mind after a hectic day at the office."

It isn't enough that he walks a mile to the courthouse and back twice a day for his job as Maywood county auditor. Or to Gram's house once a week. He often takes a constitutional after supper. In all weather, he strides the streets of Masterton—a town that's changing.

Sixteen

Man about Town

TELEVISION ANTENNAS SPROUT from the neighbors' rooftops. Liz and I marvel at families who update their kitchens but eat TV dinners off TV trays in front of TV sets in their living rooms. Old men in sporty hats spring into new cars and drive them around just for the fun of it, inviting everyone they know to go for a joyride, grinning like kids in bumper cars at the fair.

After two years at college, Liz puts it this way: "Everyone in Masterton, except us, is enjoying a speedy recovery from World War II. Ours is more leisurely."

She tells me about a new show she's seen on her friend Nancy's TV, called *American Bandstand*. I really want to watch it.

Finally, after weeks of begging, we convince Dad to buy a Zenith. He's also going to replace Mom's wringer washing machine with an automatic, since the pocks from my shotgun shell have finally rusted through.

"A hell of a reason to have to replace a perfectly good machine," he grumbles.

Mom winks at Liz and me. "It will certainly make my job a lot easier."

"Anyone in need of a giant sieve," Liz teases, "just call Shotgun Callie. Ha! Maybe she should pay for the new washing machine out of her allowance."

When I tell her to "Shut up! Just shut up!" Mom switches her mood in a flash and threatens to wash my mouth out, because my words sound too much like "shit" to suit her.

"Shut, shit! Why don't you ever scold Liz for a change?"

"Because," says Liz on her way out the door. "everyone knows I'm *perfect.*"

"Shit, hell, damn!" I spout, ready to sprint.

"All right, that's it!" Mom chases me through the house, wielding a bar of Ivory over her head. Round and round we run, from the kitchen through the dining and living rooms, into the hallway, through a two-door bedroom and back to the kitchen, round and round, until Mom catches me (rare now that I'm nearly thirteen). Doubled over with laughter, she drops the soap.

Usually, I hide out in the garage, behind the wheel of our black Pontiac, inhaling its new-car smell all the way to California and New York and Florida.

Sometimes, Dad gets irritated with us girls. Once, when we were driving Liz to her summer job at the drive-in, on our way to Butterfield and Lime Creek to look over some harvested cornfields for fall hunting, Liz tuned the radio to WDGY and we sang "Peggy Sue" along with Buddy Holly. When we got to "Wake Up Little Susie" with the Everly Brothers, Dad frowned and turned the volume down.

"What do you kids want to listen to that stuff for?"

Liz got out of the car and did a little dance in her pink-and-white striped pedal pushers and matching blouse.

"Because it's cool, Daddy-O."

At first, "Daddy-O" didn't seem to know how to react. But then he laughed and said, "You're as good as Mom at the dance, but you talk like a Beatnik."

"Cool, man, cool." I turned up the volume as we drove away.

Dad made his usual little chirping sound out of the corner of his mouth and shook his head.

Back on the highway, he held the foot feed at thirty-five miles per hour, as if he were still expected to obey the 1940s speed limit.

"Doesn't this ve-hicle go any faster, Dad?"

"And waste gas? Miss all the scenery? I'm still breaking it in."

"You've been breaking it in for years. Hell, it still smells like new."

"Ip-ip-ip" he warns. "Anyhow, it's far more efficient to walk. Someday, we'll get Liz and your mother to go with us on a walking trip. There's a lot to see around these parts."

"They wouldn't."

"You never know. Once they see how beautiful the world is outside of a car, they might enjoy it."

"You can't make people do what they don't want to do. Like Uncle Ray. Where have you ever got with him?"

"Yes, well . . . *You* enjoy a good hike, don't you?"

"Yeah, but I still like to drive places."

"Well, now, think of the savings."

"I know, I know."

Some time ago, Dad figured out exactly how many miles he saved per month by not driving, then calculated his savings on gas and tires, and gathered us around to explain his math, as if he were conducting a guided tour of his museum piece, regularly polished on account of Sam Cat and summer dust, enthroned inside the garage.

"You have to consider wear and tear on the engine, ladies. My daily round trips to the courthouse equal six miles—six point three, to be exact. And on Tuesdays, I calculate another two miles when we walk over to see Mother. That makes thirty-three and a half miles per week—more if you figure in hunting season. Why, if I could strap an odometer to my leg, I'll betcha it wouldn't take long to match the three hundred and sixty-two miles on my old jalopy here."

He patted the shiny finish, rubbed off the notion of a handprint with a piece of ribbed undershirt and wiped down the chrome strips that trailed along the hood to the silver Chief Pontiac ornament.

"Save the pennies and the dollars take care of themselves," he chanted, ignoring our rolling eyes.

But if saving money by not driving means we can get that Zenith television set, then who am I to complain?

Sometimes, I run to the end of our block to meet Dad coming home from work. No matter that pounding rain or sleet pings off his glasses, he waves and calls out, "Hey, Cal! Isn't this a beautiful day?" Then we scramble into the house, shake water from our raincoats or stomp snow from our boots, "exhilarated from our meeting with the elements."

This evening Dad is so exhilarated by the elements, he acts as though he's about to take us on a walking vacation here and now. Mom puts her foot down.

"Are you right in the head, Will? Minnesota to California? That's absurd."

"Well, then, how about Iowa?"

"Oh, for heaven's sake!" Mom points at the snow melting in the entry. "Imagine trudging through that all the way to Iowa. And then you talk about walking to California? What's gotten into you?"

Lucky for him Liz is back at school or she'd take sides with Mom and make some wisecrack about our dad going through a mid-life crisis.

"Ah, but once we get there." He circles around in a little soft shoe. "Some day, dear heart." He waves his out-stretched arms like a bird in flight and croons, "Southern California, orange and lemon trees, salt sea air, a warm ocean breeze. Some day, Emily, some day we'll travel the good old U.S. of A."

"See the U.S.A. in your Chevrolet, America is asking you to call . . ."

It might be fun to walk to California, except he'd have us on slim rations. No high-off-the-hog trips when your father licks gum wrappers for the flour and acts as if Roosevelt were still president.

At a closer look, I can see the effect walking has on my dad. Fresh air and a brisk pace have kept him fit, given his complexion a high color, especially when the temperature falls below zero. Deep dimples crease his cheeks and his blue eyes show a readiness to laugh at most anything. His hair, equal parts black and gray, is usually combed straight back. On special occasions, when he keeps it in place with Brylcreem, the hair that is black shines like the finish on his '55 Pontiac. People like to be around him—their "man about town."

"Let 'em gas. I have two sound legs," he says. "Walking gives me a chance to see and hear things—and a chance to think. Folks miss out on an awful lot when they're ramming around in a car."

When I was five or six, Dad took me to a place in the country between Masterton and Heron Lake, where there was a section of uncut tallgrass called "virgin prairie land."

"My brother and I were just little shavers," he said, "when your Grandad Vic and Uncle Amer brought us here, so we could see and hear the prairie for ourselves. Smell and feel it, too—this rich soil, the brush of buffalo grass against our faces. And I've never forgotten those windsongs. Now it's your turn, Callie girl."

Unable to see above the acres of wild rye and bluestem, I jumped up again and again to catch a glimpse of where we were, hearing only my own chatter and the crunch of tough roots and stems underfoot. Once I'd settled down, I could see the clear blue sky and a hawk rising on a thermal. And I could smell the earth and hear a kind of whispering around me. While Dad rested nearby, I made a nest for myself, curled up, closed my eyes, and listened to chirping crickets, bird songs, and a steady breeze pushing through the long grass.

"Better friends than these, Callie, you'll never find," he said.

At nearly thirteen, overcoming my reluctance to be seen in public with my parents, I join Dad for an occasional stroll. During these walks, I piece together what he's been talking about all these years—that we can pay better attention to the world outside the confines of an automobile: curious cloud formations, blazing sunsets of pink, crimson, and apricot, the first sugar maples to turn, the deep burgundy of red maples, the steamy stink from the drayman's horse droppings on a frosty street, first prints—human or animal—in deep snow, lilacs and apple blossoms, mourning doves cooing from the high line wires.

Through open windows come the smells of frying steaks ("Must be payday," Dad comments) and pies cooling on the sills, boiled coffee, fried eggs and bacon. On Sundays, we can smell roasting chickens and roast beef dinners with onions, timed for the table after church.

One afternoon, a mud turtle, missing a rear leg, was struggling across the road toward Miller's pond. Dad lent a hand.

"Makes his journey a little easier," he said, carrying the turtle the rest of the way, its three legs swimming against the air.

At night, Masterton is like another world when the moon casts strange shadows over the boulevards. Voices even sound weird, like when Hazel Benson hollers for her daughter who stays out long after dark. "Su-ZEE! Su-ZEE!"

Dad chuckles. "Reminds me of Mother back on the farm, calling the pigs to slop."

Down the block, we wave at old Doc Dohms, the doctor who took care of my shotgun shell wounds. He's backing his Edsel out of the garage.

"There he goes again, on his way to reassure old Mrs. Calder."

"Why?"

"She suffers panic attacks at night."

"How come?"

"Dreadful loneliness."

On the next block is the Ryan house. Most afternoons, we can hear Ruby's shrill voice as she scolds Tommy and Doug or criticizes her husband, Carl, whose voice never rises above her own. At night, the house is dark. With Carl at work and Ruby down at the Silver Star, the boys roam the streets.

Next door to the Ryans live Thelma and Everett Christensen, the town druggist. Dad calls him "the quintessential butter-and-egg man," but not to his face. Heavy-set with great jowls, he has, as Mom says, "an eye for the ladies." Whenever my friends and I hang around the drugstore soda fountain, drinking cherry cokes, we notice how he holds a woman's hand a little too long while slipping her a receipt. He tries to make his eyes smolder like Errol Flynn's, but he's a dead ringer for Oliver Hardy. The ladies never seem to mind Mr. Christensen's huge body pressing up against their own. In fact, they titter like schoolgirls whenever he squeezes around the counter and sidles up to them while ushering them out the door.

Mom thinks it's shameful the way he acts.

"And it's shameful the way he expects Thelma to do all the work around their place. Why, the poor thing has to mow the lawn and take down storm windows and put up the screens, then take down the screens and put up the storm windows. That's heavy work—work that Everett ought to be doing. And why does he spend such long hours at the drugstore, anyhow? I thought he had a bookkeeper."

Further on, Doug and Tommy Ryan dawdle under the corner streetlight, tossing a baseball back and forth.

"Hello, boys!"

"Hi, Mr. Lindstrom," they shout back. "Hi, Callie!" They snicker and run off toward the park, braying like donkeys and catapulting the ball in high arcs impossible for anyone but boys to catch in the dark when that's all they ever do.

"Stupid boys," I mutter.

Dad laughs. "You won't think so in a few years, Cal."

We comment on the fact that ash trees grow along Maple Street while maple trees thrive on Ash, and Birch Street is lined with oaks.

As Doug and Tommy's voices dim in the distance, we come upon Marge Paulson pouring a pan of sudsy dishwater onto her petunias. Moths careen around a porch light, nearly colliding with each other in their frenzy.

"Evenin', Will. Callie."

"Hello, Marge." Dad tips his hat. "Beautiful evening."

"That it is." She sniffs at the air. "Glad Harry cut the grass before it decides to rain again."

Dad glances once more at the night sky. "We can certainly use the moisture."

By the time we turn onto Linden Avenue, the wind has picked up, pushing through a stand of tall pines. It's the kind of wind that is at first steady and calming, then surges enough to make a sleeping dog open her eyes.

Clyde Robert's Chesapeake greets us with a grin. She's liver-colored and her rear end dances the hula with the force of her wagging tail.

"Well, hullo, Queenie." Dad gives her rib cage a thumping pat. "You gonna walk with us tonight?"

Queenie lopes along to the the end of Main Street, past Don Patterson's Law Office, Delhoff's Barber Shop, Leo Thompson's furniture store, the Mint Café, and the Maywood County Library. Of course, no one is bustling in and out at this hour. The red-and-white barber pole is still. The floodlight featuring Mr. Thompson's new, celery-green living room set, on sale for $299, has been turned off. The lingering smell of greasy hamburgers with fried onions drifts around the Mint just after closing time. As we pass the library, I imagine the smells of all those books waiting to be read. The moors must smell like the pages of *Wuthering Heights* and *Jane Eyre*.

While crossing Main Street, Queenie's ears cock in response to Clyde's shrill whistle. She turns abruptly and trots home.

At the Worthmore, next to the library, Dad taps at the windowpane. Carl Ryan, night custodian, opens the door and invites us into the office, which smells of cream and ozone.

"Can't stay, Carl," says Dad. "Just wanted to stop by and say hello."

Mr. Ryan seems troubled. The tic in his eye is worse than I remember.

While the men visit, I snoop around the office and try the heavy door of the walk-in freezer where we and other town families keep our butchered beef and pork and chickens, as well as wild game. I wander through the back room, which hums with the machinery that keeps the locker plant running. Although there is a heavy cover over it, I avoid going anywhere near the cistern in the middle of the floor. Like fireplace chimneys, cisterns have scared me ever since I read *Murders in the Rue Morgue*. You never know what has been stuffed inside them.

As soon as we leave the Worthmore, I ask Dad about Mr. Ryan.

"Family troubles, Cal. He's going through a rough time."

We pass the Our Own Hardware, Buckle's Five and Dime, and peer in at Eva Robert's dusty display of rings and watches. The window case of Philcos and Zeniths in Sandi's TV and Appliance store includes a set just like, ours.

The Masterton hotel is dark, except for a dim light in the lobby and a brighter one in a room on third floor. Some woman is standing in front of the window. I step off the curb for a better look.

"Isn't that Ruby Ryan?"

Dad glances up. "No, just someone who looks like her. C'mon, kiddo, we'd best get on home."

I look back at the Mint, a block behind us, and notice a couple leaving the cafe.

"That looks like Uncle Ray."

Dad squints. "By golly, it is. Wonder what he's doing around here."

"Who's that with him?"

"I don't know. Oh, wait a minute. Now, *that* looks like Ruby."

We stand near the hotel, watching the two shake hands.

"Imagine," says Dad. "Ruby Ryan shaking hands with a man. Wonder what *that's* all about."

She flounces in our direction, then stops in front of the Silver Star, tugs the door open and disappears. Uncle Ray turns the corner off Main.

"I didn't see his car. He must have parked on a side street."

"Do you want to catch up with him, Dad?"

"No, Cal, not tonight."

It's as if the air around us suddenly grows prickly.

"What the hell is he up to with the likes of Ruby Ryan?" Dad mutters. "Wonder if he even bothered to stop and see Mother. Hell, if he doesn't have the decency to look us up, then the hell with him."

"Yeah. Hell, who needs him, anyway?"

"Probably up from Sioux City, peddling his life insurance. Wonder if he's staying at the cottage."

"The hell with him, Dad."

It feels good to cuss on my dad's behalf. And so, I repeat "The *hell* with him!" several times over, until he says, "That's enough now, Cal."

We pass the bank, a brick fortress with a cement ledge, now vacant of the four men who lean against it every day.

Besides Dad, they are the only other people who walk around Masterton. But they aren't normal. There's Hulda Lowe's son, Glen, born retarded, but not so bad that he can't talk a little and smile at everyone he sees. Although he's at least forty years old, people call him "Hulda's boy" or "that mongoloid." Some folks think he should be kept inside, the way other families hide their own. But I'm glad he hangs around town. He's always grinning and his eyes light up as he pretends to ride a bicycle whenever he sees me pedaling down the sidewalk.

Selmer and Clarence Johnson came back from the war maimed. They *have* to walk if they want to get anywhere, Selmer being too shell-shocked to drive a car and Clarence unable to work a foot-feed and a clutch with only one leg. Some German soldier shot off his right one and he couldn't afford a replacement. Mayor Thompson offered to head up a fund drive, take Clarence to the Twin Cities to get fitted for a new leg, but Clarence said, "Thanks, but no thanks."

Every day, the two brothers hobble along Main Street, Selmer in a daze and Clarence on creaky wooden crutches with ragged, gray terry towels wrapped around the tops. Every day, they head for the cement ledge in front of the Maywood County Bank where they halfway sit next to Glen.

Norman Koost joins them. A retired math teacher, Mr. Koost is so bent over with a spinal deformity that he can only study the sidewalk while shuffling along. I tried walking that way once in order to see what he sees: tufts of brown grass and tiny yellow flowers poking through cracks, a stringy wad of gray-pink bubblegum on the curb, a few pennies and cigarette butts in the gutter.

I guess Mr. Koost recognizes his friends when he spots the familiar row of scuffed shoes and crutch tips in front of the bank. He backs up against the ledge next to Selmer and Clarence and Glen, bends his knees and raises his eyebrows so he can look up a little, but never as far as the sky. All afternoon, those four friends nod to people passing by, until it's time to walk home for supper. They remind me of crippled birds lined up on a fence.

Everyone else in town rides around in some kind of conveyance, even if their destinations are only a few blocks away. Country folks drive to town on tractors, in orange buses, or trucks. Townies, with their chins jutting forward, sit behind the steering wheels of brand new cars with "good rubber tires." Kids scooter and pedal. Even old Mrs. Galles aims her electric cart down the sidewalk, weaving like a drunkard and, as Dad says, "sounding the klaxon for stray pedestrians and dogs with a purpose."

From blocks away, you can hear the slow clip-clop of Grant Van Vulsa's draft horses. Each day, Grant, the town's only remaining drayman, delivers goods from the train depot and picks up castoffs and sundries along the streets of Masterton.

"Easy there, Jack. Whoa, girl," Grant calls out to his team over the lumbering grind of wagon wheels. The sharp, rhythmic sound of hooves grows louder as the horses plod toward us. Grant wears his usual faded bib overalls and a wide-brimmed hat. With a light grip on the reins, he perches like royalty on the bench he nailed to his flatbed wagon. The two Belgians, their feet the size of spittoons tufted with long, flapping yellow hair, wear blinders decorated with faded Veteran's Day poppies.

Looking down from his wagon, Grant greets us with, "Mornin', Missy. Mornin', Will. Your car on the blink again?"

"Could be."

"What you need is a good horse."

"How much you askin' for yours?"

"Not for sale."

With a gee-up and a wink, Grant rolls on. Sometimes, my friends and I jump onto the back of the wagon to ride around town for part of a day. Grant doesn't mind.

Dad's friends crank down their car windows and slow to a crawl when they spot us.

"Mornin', Will! No gas coupons this week?"

"That's right, Gus. What are you runnin' on—fumes?"

"Hey, Will! Need a lift or are ya hoofin' it as usual? Bet Callie'd like a ride."

"Now why would we wanna hitch a lift in that old Tin Lizzie?"

Off they go, shaking their heads and grinning back at us in the rear view mirror, bending an arm in salute, cruising down the street with an elbow on the window frame, as if they're holding up the roof.

From one end of town to the other, Dad greets people like the county politician he is.

But I sometimes sense a certain caution in him.

"Masterton," he once told Mom, "is a small town where a fellow can soon find himself the topic of gossip."

One summer morning, inside the courthouse entry, we overheard Judge Carlson shooting the breeze with two of the county commissioners. The subject made Dad wonder if he might be the next brunt of a joke.

"Don't it beat all?" sneered the judge. "You never know what you're gonna see next around these parts. Isn't that right, Will?"

"No idea what you're talking about, Hjalmer." Dad reached into his coat pocket for the office key.

"You know the Kleins out there on the north edge of town? Well, they've got a cousin visiting, name of Schmidt, all the way from Germany. Seems he was walking along the township road near old man Jacobson's place, hotter'n blazes. Jacobson was heading out to his fields on that new Case tractor he bought off Al Nevis last week. Well, old Jake spots what looks like a body in the ditch near a culvert. So he pulls over, gets off his tractor and edges along the shoulder 'til he gets up good and close. Damned if he didn't near have a heart attack when the body jumps up in front of him. Seems this fella, Schmidt, was taking a nap right there, bedded down in the grass. Couldn't even speak a word of English."

"Don't that beat all!" said Mr. Erickson, one of the commissioners.

Judge Carlson and the others shook their heads and snorted. But Dad didn't laugh. He just winked at me. Although I'd never met this Mr. Schmidt, I could imagine what had drawn him to the countryside—the same things I've known all my life: sunshine and meadowlark songs, an easy wind rustling through tallgrass. I know those sounds. I know what that soft, warm breeze feels like brushing across my face. Why shouldn't he be out there if he feels like it?

"Odd duck," continued the judge, "but what can you expect, him bein' German and all. Say, Will, you go everywhere by Shank's pony. You sure you're not related to this *Herr Schmidt*?" He slapped my dad on the back and guffawed.

Dad turned away to unlock the door. "I can think of worse folk to be related to, Hjalmer."

I giggled until Judge Carlson scowled at me.

Once inside the office, I noticed furrows in Dad's forehead and hoped he wouldn't be reconsidering his own walks.

"Old fogies," he muttered, hanging our hats on a wooden rack.

"Yeah, stupid old fogies," I repeated, snooping around the office for colored pencils and paper. "You're not worried about what he said, are you?"

"Well, with elected office, some of us have to consider our constituents. Judge Carlson has a tendency to exercise his work outside the courtroom. He can make it tough for folks in a minute. This Mr. Schmidt, for instance."

"Don't let him stop you, Dad. That's what you always tell me. If you enjoy walking, you shouldn't care what other people think."

Then I told him about the story I'd read by that Chekhov guy. About how the man worried over what people would say when all he did was appreciate that big fish by making a loud smacking noise.

"That's quite a story, Cal. A good reminder."

He gave the back of my neck its usual little squeeze, then sat down at his desk and rolled a sheet of ledger paper into the typewriter.

I pulled up a chair and sat opposite, sketching and coloring lime-green palm trees, purple islands, and a turquoise ocean.

"Tell me some more about California, Dad."

"Well, now, just imagine," he said, rolling his creaky chair backward and reaching a hand toward the high ceiling, "you can saunter up to a lemon tree and pluck the biggest, fattest, bright-yellow lemon you ever saw. Then you sashay over to a different tree and grab a juicy orange the size of a grapefruit at Cooper's Grocery. Just imagine, Cal, picking your own sweet oranges and lemons."

I looked up at the crenellated ceiling and felt saliva running down the insides of my cheeks.

"What about the ocean? Tell me about the ocean, Dad. It's like Lake Shetek, isn't it? Only a zillion times bigger?"

"Yup, with salt water to help you float. Tides come and go twice a day and little birds on stick legs run so fast it's like flipping the pages of an action cartoon to see them scurry across the sand."

"When were you there?"

"I wasn't." Dad clasped his hands behind his head and gazed dreamily out of the window at the giant elm trees that mark the beginning of Main

Street. "I've never seen the ocean, but I heard about it years ago from my Uncle Ed."

I wondered what his descriptions would have been like if he'd actually seen California and the Pacific for himself.

I tossed aside my pencils and paper and took several giant strides around the office. "Let's go, Dad! I know we can make it!"

"Some day, Cal. Maybe some day."

Now, in silence, we head for home after our walk to the Worthmore and after seeing Uncle Ray with Ruby Ryan. We retrace our steps beneath the dark elms and deep-red maples whose branches shift and wave at the wind. Under each streetlight, I can see the little muscles working in Dad's clenched jaw.

"There now," he says, ushering me into the house, "isn't that better than rushing off somewhere in the car?"

"Uh-huh," I yawn.

Shrugging off the sight of Uncle Ray, I wonder when we'll ever get to taste the Pacific Ocean and stroll under all those palm trees.

Seventeen

Shank's Pony

Maywood County Herald

MAN ABOUT TOWN RESCUES NEIGHBOR
by
Elmore L. Billings

Carl Ryan is one lucky fellow, thanks to Will Lindstrom, our Man About Town.

It is a well-known fact that during his night shift at the Worthmore Dairy and Meat Locker, Carl nearly drowned after taking a blow to the head and ending up in the cistern.

"I wasn't sure how much longer I could last," said Carl. "And then I heard this voice. If it hadn't been for my good friend, Will Lindstrom, and his daughter, Callie, coming to see me by Shank's Pony, I'd have been a goner."

On the occasion of the 70th anniversary of the founding of our illustrious town of Masterton, I am pleased to announce Maywood County's choice for Contributing Citizen of 1957. Tip your hats, ladies and gents, to Will Lindstrom, winner of this year's MCC award.

ay, Dad! But what's a Shank's Pony? Can we get one? I've always wanted a horse."

"You've got two, Cal." He points at my legs. "Sometimes we say, "Ride on shank's mare." You trot along on your own two legs."

Mom laughs from the kitchen table where she clips the article about Dad and Mr. Ryan for our family scrapbook, writing "Masterton's Contributing Citizen—May 24, 1957" at the top.

"Good thing you two showed up when you did," she says, clipping a second copy for Gram.

I can't wait to tell my grandmother all about finding Mr. Ryan who was minutes from death. Maybe she'll be proud of us. I've already told all my friends at school.

"I was sure glad to have Callie with me." Dad tousles my hair. "She showed what she's made of. I only hope Carl can get over the shock. Get his life back in order."

For a while, I had only a couple of ideas about how and why Carl Ryan ended up in the well. After the Catholic Church murders and Mrs. Olson getting chopped up in the power takeoff, I wondered who would be next.

The Minneapolis paper even ran an article about the attempted murder, titled, "Love Triangle," which I couldn't wait to read:

"Love triangle suspects," I begin aloud, "in a small town southwest of the Twin Cities, will stand trial for the attempted murder of . . ."

"What kind of news is this for you to digest?" Mom snatches the *Tribune* from my hands. "First the church killings and Mrs. Olson, then all that grisly business about Ed Gein. Now this. Such stuff! When will it stop?"

"At least Carl didn't end up dead," Dad reminds her.

"Yes, thanks to you. But 'Love triangle!' Good heavens, what next?"

"What exactly is a love triangle, Mom?" I already know. I just want to hear what she says about it.

"Oh, I don't know. How would you put it, Will?"

"Umm. Two men vying for the affections of the same woman. Or two women interested in the same man, I guess."

"But Carl Ryan is married. And so is . . ."

"Yes, that's true."

"That's why it's such a hornets' nest." Mom puts the finishing touches to Dad's page in the album. "Best to forget about it."

I decide not to tell them what my friends and I saw in the alley off Main Street a couple of weeks earlier. Or what Janet and I heard while eavesdropping on her parents the night I stayed over. Satisfied that I know more than they do about this particular "love triangle," I change the subject.

"Who won MCC last year?"

"Doc Nelson."

"Whaaat? What *for?*"

Mom shrugs and looks at Dad. "I'm not sure. Do you remember, Will?"

"For being the town big-wig, I guess."

Dad seldom utters a word against another soul unless he deserves it.

Doctor Bennett Nelson is Masterton's richest, most powerful citizen. And stuck-up. Every year, he rides his huge palomino at the head of our Days of Eighty-Seven parade and flings pennies for the little kids to snatch from the gutter. He sits straight in the saddle, with a haughty look behind rimless glasses and a firm set of his jaw above jowls nearly as great as Mr. Christensen's. His fat stomach is trussed up with a giant silver buckle. Every year, I can't help thinking that he looks like a bloated toad in a white cowboy hat.

When we were little, my friends and I were scared of him, especially while riding around town on our bicycles. He'd drive his Cadillac up close behind us and honk his horn, long and loud. Startled, nearly crashing, we barely regained control of our wobbly bikes and rode home with our hearts in our throats. It was as if he wanted us injured. Or dead.

Doc Nelson is also a crook. Once, when Tequila and I were visiting Dad at the courthouse, Dr. Nelson charged in and pounded on the office counter, demanding to know why Dad hadn't adjusted his taxes the way he'd expected.

"Can't do that, Doc. I've told you before. You'll have to take it up with the assessor if you think your taxes are too high. I work according to the statutes and you know it."

Doc took one gruff look at me, hollered over his shoulder, "Aw, go to hell," and stormed out.

Tequila tensed in my arms and growled. I wondered if this was how Doc treated his patients at the clinic.

"He's always trying to pull a fast one," I overheard Dad tell Mom that evening. "Just like he did when we were serving together on the church building committee."

Doc had impressed the new Lutheran minister by announcing his own personal contribution of five thousand dollars for the building fund. Reverend Weiker praised him for his generosity. Doc laughed and said he had no intention of drawing the dollars from his own account. He'd simply raise the fees of his non-Lutheran patients.

"Too bad Mr. Billings didn't write the truth about that one," says Mom. "It would have made for quite a story."

Dad shakes his head. "Doc would've had Elmore run out of town on a rail."

"Or," I suggest, "by Shank's Pony."

Mom suddenly looks as concerned as she does when Dad and I watch the bloody boxing matches on television.

"To think Callie had to witness Carl's near-drowning." She gives me a quick hug. "You should have stayed at home with me that night."

"She did all right, Em. No need to worry about this girl. I think she'll be able to handle whatever comes her way."

"Dad, do you think Uncle Ray had anything to do with this?"

"God, I never thought about that."

Mom doesn't act surprised. Dad must have told her about seeing Ray with Carl's wife.

In honor of Dad's MCC award, Elmore Billings interviewed him and wrote the following piece for the *Black Duck Chronicle* and *The Maywood County Herald.* I was so impressed with this story that I asked Dad if I could use it for my sixth grade school report on what our fathers do for a living. Teacher told us to include interesting details about their lives and about what makes them stand out in the community.

"Oh, no," he said, "too many people got talked about, upset over what happened to Carl. Things have finally settled down. Best to let sleeping dogs lie."

I'm saving this part of the newspaper on my closet shelf:

AT THE WELL
by
E.L. Billings

Carl Ryan's voice, heard only by the mice, was barely audible. Deep inside the narrow cistern in the back room of the Worthmore, Carl struggled to keep his head above water that was too deep to stand in and impossible to climb out of. The coiled rope ladder, his only means of escape, lay tossed in a corner, far from the covered hole in the floor.

Kicking and scraping his feet along the walls, Carl searched for a toehold in the concrete blocks. His bleeding fingers grew numb as he clawed around the circular reservoir. Hour after hour he clutched at the cement seams, finding nothing more than surface chinks. Finally, his cries reduced to a whisper, he lost hope that anyone would find him.

It had been a spring of heavy rainfall in Maywood County. The farmers could relax, confident that their soybeans and corn would green up and grow tall. Folks in town fell asleep to the comforting sounds of fresh water trickling into their basement reservoirs.

At 2030 Norwood Avenue, Will Lindstrom finished his supper and went out to check on the orderly rows of his vegetable garden. He pulled weeds until dark, repaired to his garage to polish his car, then

*left with daughter Callie, for his "evening constitutional," as May-
wood's County Auditor refers to his daily walks.*

*Appearing younger than his fifty-three years, Will Lindstrom is a
popular figure on the streets of Masterton. As his friends will attest,
he takes conservation to new heights in the preservation of the automobile and the promotion of physical fitness.*

*During the evening in question, neighborhood families were going
about their usual business. A few boys and girls were playing a late-
night game of softball in the park.*

*Perhaps, as Will Lindstrom turned from Ash Street onto Maple
and headed toward Main Street, he thought about himself as a boy,
growing up, not in town, but on a farm west of Masterton. As a result,
from this journalist's perspective, Will acquired a far away look, like
that in the eyes of sailors in sea-faring pictures. After all, he'd grown
up on an endless sea of prairie with no hills or buildings to cut into
distant horizons. That look seems to be missing in the eyes of city folks,
whose horizons have been choked off.*

*Like other boys of his time, Will fished and hunted small game.
Unlike them, he wandered great distances from the farm, often without a gun or a fishing pole, spending his time listening to songbirds
and slipping in for a swim at a favorite lake.*

*After high school, he left the prairie—packed a bag and took the
train to Mankato where he enrolled in commercial college. But he soon
grew homesick, boxed in by the bluffs surrounding the river valley.
After his two years of business training, Will returned to Maywood
County and ran for auditor.*

*"That was a great year," he said. "I won the election and met Emily.
Walked into Ole Swanjord's law office one afternoon and there she
was—waiting for me to sweep her off her feet."*

*Besides his job as Maywood County Auditor, and caring for his
family, an invigorating walk is something Will Lindstrom does well.*

*You all know by now what Will did to deserve Masterton's con-
tributing citizen award for 1957. If it hadn't been for our "Man About
Town," Carl Ryan would not be among the living.*

This is a good article, but since I'm not allowed to use it, I plan to write
my own.

Besides, I was there. I know what really happened.

Eighteen

Bloated Toady Pig

*A*S SOON AS DAD SENSED TROUBLE inside the Worthmore, he tried to send me back home, but I wouldn't go.

That night, everything seemed normal: little kids playing Annie-I-Over and Hide-and-Seek, Birdie Crowley frowning at her kitchen window, Doc Dohms driving around in his Edsel with old Mrs. Calder.

The Christensens' house was dark, except for a dim light upstairs.

"That's strange." Dad stopped at the curb. "Everett's usually home by now. Especially, with Thelma so sick."

A week earlier, on our way to the Mint Café for ice cream, we ran into Everett Christensen in front of his house. He was sweeping grass clippings from his sidewalk and panting from the exertion.

"Evenin', neighbors," he said, mopping his face with a handkerchief. "A brisk walk tonight, Will?"

"Yes, sir. Good for the digestion."

"Well, then, you must be the healthiest fella in Masterton."

"One of 'em, I hope. Say, Everett," Dad teased, "it wouldn't hurt you to step out a time or two. And I don't mean on your wife."

Mr. Christensen tried to look casual by draping his wrists over the top of the broom handle. His jowls shimmied with a forced laugh.

I gulped when Dad said that about stepping out on his wife. It was obvious he had no idea what my friends and I knew from snooping around the alley off Main Street. We'd spotted Everett Christensen behind his drugstore, wedged between two lilac bushes, waving and blowing kisses.

"What on earth is he doing?" asked Judy, straddling her bike.

"Look," said Janet, pointing. "That's what he's doing."

A block away, Ruby Ryan was standing next to a tree, blowing kisses back at Mr. Christensen.

Janet, who lives next door to the Christensens, said she saw him late one night slipping into Mrs. Ryan's house by her back door.

"Tommy and Doug were staying with their grandparents," she said. "Thelma was sick, probably asleep, so Everett must have figured the coast was clear. I saw him from my bedroom window." Janet laughed. "It took him forever to squeeze through that fence opening."

I tugged at Dad's sleeve, wanting to get away from this talk about "stepping out."

"C'mon, Dad, let's go."

"Cal and I were just on our way for some ice cream, Everett, so we'll leave you to your work."

But Everett Christensen wasn't ready to let us go.

"Thelma's been suffering from a terrible nervous condition lately. Upset stomach. Some days she can't get out of her bed."

Her bed? She has her own bed? I thought married couples slept together.

"I'm sure sorry to hear that, Everett. Emily would like to have her over for coffee as soon as she's able."

"Thanks. I'll let her know. Say, Will, you didn't happen to pass by here earlier today, did you? Past the Ryans'?"

"No, only at noontime on my way home for lunch. Why?"

"Oh, they've been havin' awful trouble. Sheriff had to stop by this afternoon. A big ruckus. Thelma saw it all from her bedroom window. Since she's been ailing, she doesn't have much else to do but watch the goings-on in the neighborhood and make up a lot of nonsense."

Then maybe Janet wasn't the only one who saw you creeping into Ruby's house that night.

"Truth is, some fella from Sioux Falls has been hanging around Ruby. A jealous type from what I hear. Carl found out about it. He and Ruby had quite a row."

Or do you mean Sioux City? Is my uncle the jealous type?

"That's strange," said Dad. "It isn't like Carl to argue about anything."

"Ruby's been pushing for a divorce. Guess he finally found the courage to stand up to her. Oh, it was some quarrel, all right. She even chased him around the yard with a ..."

Dad turned to me. "Maybe you should go back home, Cal. Tell Mom I'll be right along."

"But we were going to get ice cream!"

If he thought I shouldn't hear this conversation, well . . . I knew a whole lot about the Ryans ever since last Saturday night when Janet and I eavesdropped on her parents.

Hunkered over the Ouija board in Janet's room, waiting for it to spell out the names of boys we liked, we heard Mr. Dodson's loud voice:

"I'll side with Carl any day. He's a decent, hard-working man. But since he married Ruby, he's so browbeaten and tongue-tied he can't even come into the store without breaking out in a sweat." (Mr. Dodson manages the Our Own Hardware.) "More than once, I've seen him wandering the aisles in a daze. Then he leaves, forgetting why he came in."

"That's strange," said Mrs. Dobson. "Ruby boasted that she'd finally got him to sign up for the Dale Carnegie course. Did you know that?"

"No, I didn't. A good idea, though."

Dale Carnegie programs, the latest rage, offer classes "geared to help shy adults become more confident in public and public officials become better speakers and politicians." In our town, they're held Monday evenings in the Methodist Church basement.

"Carl's been going to every one of them," said Mrs. Dobson.

"Darned if I can detect any improvement."

"That's what Alvina said down at the bowling alley."

"If anything, he's gone backwards," said Mr. Dodson. "Quieter than I've ever seen him."

"Well, you know why, don't you? Everyone in town is talking about it."

Mrs. Dodson made this last comment in such a low voice that Janet and I had to creep down several steps to the first spindle in the banister and strain our ears in order to hear what she said next.

"As we all know, Ruby likes to screw. Or haven't you noticed?"

Mr. Dodson snorted at this, then snorted again.

"Let me finish, Bob. Suffice it to say, she's increased her activities on Monday nights. Traveling salesmen, musicians, what have you. She even bragged about a one-night stand in Minneapolis. Some well-known band leader, but she wouldn't say who."

"Poor Carl. He sure got the rotten end of the deal when he married her." Mr. Dobson's voice softened while Mrs. Dobson's grew louder.

"There isn't a soul in town that hasn't seen Ruby Ryan flirting. And in broad daylight, mind you! Gyrating down Main Street toward every man she meets. Doesn't matter if they're alone or with their wives and kids. Utterly shameless! She's got a large field to choose from, apparently—plenty of local men who stray because 'their wives don't understand them.'"

This last she said in a sarcastic voice while scratching quotes in the air with her fingers, just as I peeked around the spindle.

"Believe me," she added, "Ruby doesn't let anything interfere with her plans. As soon as the weather warms up, she's out in the yard pulling her pants off the clothesline and wriggling her little fanny right into them."

Janet and I looked at each other, screwed up our noses, and stifled a laugh.

What Mrs. Dobson was talking about, my friends and I have seen for ourselves—married men rubbing up against married women, married women flirting with the men. We always know Ruby's around when the wives suddenly pinch their lips together, lift their chins, and hiss, "Here comes that tart!" It's when they grab their husbands' arms that the men change in a flash, as if they're shifting a bunch of gears and can't decide which one to drive in. One minute they're minding their own business and the next they act agitated, then surprised, then cautious, then nervous all over again. I'll bet most of those men can't tell you if it's the sight of Ruby or the sudden attention of their wives clutching at their arms that causes them to stir.

Gentlemen in town tip their hats to the ladies. So when Janet and I saw two men dart around a corner one summer afternoon just as Ruby strutted toward them, we rode our bicycles onto the same side street to see who it was. We got off our bikes and pretended to be looking at something in the gutter.

"Not worth it," Mayor Thompson said to Mr. Delhoff, the barber. "If I so much as give her the time of day, it'll get back to my wife. Then it's the dog house for me."

"You got that right, Bud. It just ain't worth it."

Janet and I watched as the two men peered back around the corner before returning to Main Street.

Even my dad wasn't exempt from Ruby's attentions.

We were standing in front of Marbella Kinmore's Fashionette, waiting for Mom to try on a new dress she'd had altered, when out stepped Ruby.

"Oh! William," she sang, "I've been wantin' to talk to you."

She dragged out the "you" and shot me a quick glance that said, "Scram." I stayed right where I was.

Ruby was wearing black capris and a snug cherry-red sweater with short sleeves. A dozen bracelets jangled from her wrists. Long red spit curls bounced around her thin face. She got so close I could smell the dress shop on her—*Chanel No. 5*—Marbella buys it by the gallon.

Dad tried stepping aside, but Ruby blocked his path with every curve she had.

A little scared, but also curious to see how Dad would handle the situation, I backed away toward the shop's entrance and peeked in to see if Mom was out of the changing room. She wasn't, so I waited next to the door and kept an eye on things.

"Now hold on, sweetheart," Ruby cooed, her voice deep and throaty.

Dad stood his ground with one hand held up as if to push a revolving door.

"Oh, Will. I'm not gonna bite." Ruby drew out the "i" of this last word before biting off the "t" and reached out to caress Dad's arm. "Has anyone ever told you you are one good lookin' man? You have the most beautiful blue eyes and . . ."

"Ruby! It's shameful the way you're acting. And in front of my daughter." He nodded at me. "Now you've got a good man in Carl. Why don't you stop this nonsense and go on home with your family where you belong? And while I'm standing here talking to you, I want you to hear this: Stay away from my brother!"

It took but a second for Ruby Ryan to go sour. "I don't know what the hell you're talkin' about. You sound like a goddamn preacher!" she snarled, turning on her heels and beating a path to the Silver Star.

Ruby never spoke to my dad again. And to this day, she turns her back whenever she sees anyone from our family.

Mom finally came out of Marbella's. I couldn't wait to tell her what had happened. Dad blushed and said he let Ruby know he wasn't interested.

"I'm not worried, my dear. At least you gave her what for. Maybe now, she'll think twice before approaching another married man."

"I wouldn't be so sure about that, Mom."

I've always been a little intrigued by Ruby. Also, embarrassed for her. Was she that unhappy at home?

"No, Callie," said Liz when I told her about the incident with our dad, "she's just over-sexed."

At first, I was shocked to hear Liz say the word "sex." But then I saw her and Brian smoking cigarettes and making out on the dock at Lake Shetek when they were home from college for the summer. You couldn't have slipped a filet knife between them.

Like the words "shut up, ass, hell, damn, shit, and fuck," the word "sex" is never uttered in our family. My little blue dictionary, *Dig These Definitions*, doesn't give any detailed or interesting notations: "hell: a place where wicked are punished after death; ass: horse-like animal with long ears; damn: condemn, curse; sex: condition of being male or female; males collectively, or females collectively." The words "shut up, shit, and fuck," (the one Uncle Ray shouted after he rolled down the hill and into the lake) aren't even listed. I have to go to the big dictionary to find "shit" and another definition of "ass." "Fuck," I guess, isn't considered to be a real word. *Then how come everybody uses it?* When Bobby Keeler said "ain't," our teacher told us, "Now class, you can't use a word, unless it's in the dictionary."

"Fuck" ain't in the dictionary.

Getting back to Ruby Ryan. In a way, I think she's brave to act as if she isn't doing anything wrong, even though the whole town talks about her. Or maybe, she's just plain stupid. Either way, she impresses me. When I'm alone in my bedroom, I sometimes practice walking the way she does, switching my hips this way and that, until a very different feeling comes over me and I wonder what that's all about.

Along with those tight capris, Ruby wears spikes and a tucked-in sleeveless white blouse "whose ample armholes," as Judy describes them, "reveal an abundance of creamy flesh bulging from the tight, black edges of a D-cup bra." My friend turned thirteen months ago.

"In other words," I say, "she's over-sexed."

"Uh-huh," says Judy. "And then some."

In place of natural eyebrows, Ruby draws thin, reddish-brown arches that might give her a look of surprise if they didn't curve downward near the bridge of her "pert little nose," as Janet describes it. She piles her long red hair up high on her head and fashions spit curls that flounce about her rouged cheeks with each click-clacking step she takes down Main Street.

Janet and I could hardly believe what her mother was telling Mr. Dodson during that Saturday I stayed over. We sat on the steps listening for so long that our butts grew numb.

"Every night," said Mrs. Dodson, "after she claims her stool at the Silver Star, Ruby loses track of time. Forgets she has a family. The woman lets her housework go, doesn't bother with decent meals. Oh, I could go on and on."

"I sure wouldn't put up with *that*," said Janet's father.

"Don't I *know*," Mrs. Dodson giggled. "Apparently, Ruby never once put supper on the table until after Dougie burned his hands."

"How'd that happen?"

"Dumping French fries into boiling fat over the gas burner. Can you imagine?"

"Poor kid. Trying to get a meal for himself."

So that's why Doug was running around with bandaged fists, holding his arms outstretched like Frankenstein and stomping through the neighborhood, scaring all the little kids.

"Ruby tells the story over and over at the bar," continued Mrs. Dodson, launching into an imitation of Ruby's voice: 'Goddamn it, I screamed at that little bastard, what the hell were you thinking, you little idiot!'"

Janet and I gasped. Fortunately, her parents didn't hear us.

"Now, I ask you, Bob, is that any way for a woman to talk to her children?"

"Absolutely not."

"After Dougie's accident with the French fries, Ruby fed the kids as soon as they got home from school. And she told Carl that he could either eat with the boys at three-thirty in the afternoon or fend for himself later on, before he left for his nine o'clock shift."

"What'd he decide?"

"Eat with the kids."

Janet and I looked at each other and shook our heads. We waited a while longer in case more was said. But Mr. and Mrs. Dodson were finished talking about Ruby.

"How does your mom know all this stuff?" I whispered to Janet.

"She goes down there a lot—to the Silver Star."

We tiptoed back to Janet's room and picked up where we'd left off with the Ouija board, screaming at what the glider spelled out when I asked it *the* question: "U LUV BOBBY."

Dad and I left Mr. Christensen that night, his wrists still draped over the top of his broom handle, and made it to the Mint Cafe just before it closed.

"Too bad you had to hear about all that foolishness, Cal."

"You mean what Mr. Christensen said about the Ryans?"

"Yes. Such a mess."

"Uh-huh." I said.

Now, a week later, the Christensens' house is as dark as the Ryans', except for a dim light upstairs.

As we turn from Ash Street onto Maple, Dad says, "We'll look in on Carl, then turn around and go home. I've been worried about him lately."

It's nearly ten-thirty by the time we reach the dark corner of Maple and Main; the streetlight in front of the Worthmore is out.

Dad taps on the window and peeks in. We wait a few minutes before trying the latch.

"That's strange. He usually keeps the door locked."

We go inside. As usual, the office smells of cream and ozone from the freezer.

"Carl?"

No answer.

"Maybe you should run on home, Cal. Something here doesn't feel right."

"No, I'm staying with you."

"Carl?" Dad calls out again.

A muffled sound comes from the next room. Dad tugs at the door. I follow him in.

"Carl, where are you?"

"Haalp," a weak voice echoes, as if from a distance.

"He's under the floor, Dad!"

We rush to the cistern. Dad pulls aside the iron cover. We peer over the edge.

"What the hell are you doing down there?"

"Will! Thank God!" Carl cries out as if he were choking. "They . . . I was about to give up."

"Grab that rope ladder, Cal! Over there in the corner!"

I run to where Dad points, then scurry back to the hole, dragging the heavy rope, which Dad loops around hooks driven into the cement. He eases the ladder down through the opening.

"Here, Carl! Grab the outside ropes and get a foot up on that first rung!"

Carl tries to heft himself onto the lower rungs, but he doesn't have the strength.

"You gotta help me, Will. I can't make it."

"Callie, girl," says Dad in a calm voice, "go to the phone. Call Sheriff Remer. Tell him what happened and ask him to bring a long rope."

I dash back to the office and pick up the receiver. "Hello, Central?"

Betty Lou Fry, the switchboard operator, says, "Number please."

"This is Callie Lindstrom. Get Sheriff Remer quick! There's been an accident at the Worthmore." I quickly tell Betty Lou what has happened and race back to the cistern.

"Hang on, Carl," Dad calls down to him. "Help is on the way."

Within minutes, the sheriff and his deputy are lowering another rope into the well.

"Put the loop over your head and under your arms, Carl. We'll get you outa there."

Inch by inch, the three men haul up Carl's dead weight, until he can find his footing. He collapses at the edge and has to be hoisted the rest of the way by the back of his belt. Lying on his side and soaked to the bones, he gasps for air like a dying carp.

"What the hell happened?" Sheriff Remer kneels next to Carl in a widening puddle of water.

Dad and Deputy Browning crouch down next to them. I stand aside, but not so far that I can't see Carl's crushed and bleeding fingers. His whole body is shaking and his teeth are chattering.

"We're taking you to the hospital, Carl."

"I don't know what to do," he cries.

It's scary to see my dad's friend go to pieces. I remember how nice he was to me, along with Dad and Mr. Claussen, the night I sat with them in the basement, after taking all I was going to take from that rotten old lady Swenson.

The sheriff and his deputy boost Carl to his feet. Dad and I follow them out to the squad car. Deputy Browning drapes a blanket around his shoulders and eases him into the back seat.

As they drive away, Carl manages a sad smile. "Thank you," he mouths through the window.

Dad and I turn out the lights and close the door to the Worthmore Meat and Dairy.

"Well," he says, on our way home, "by tomorrow morning, everyone in Masterton will have heard about this."

"I'll bet they already know, Dad."

After every crisis, our Central, Betty Lou Fry, calls her best friend, Myrna Ploot, who phones her mother, Doris Conklin, and it goes from there. All those cords plugged in at the telephone office—like a tangle of giant night-crawlers plastered against a flashing board, while Central shrills, "Number, please! Number, please! Number, please!" and her hands fly across the switch-board, making connections.

R<small>UBY</small> R<small>YAN AND</small> E<small>VERETT</small> C<small>HRISTENSEN</small> are going to trial for attempted murder. Elmore Billings interviews everyone for the newspaper. When Carl Ryan comes to our house, no one asks me to leave the room. Carl doesn't seem to care what he says in front of me.

"It was a hell of lot more than a love triangle," he says. "Ruby took out a big life insurance policy on me."

"Oh, no."

"That's right, Will. Can you believe she'd do such a thing? I knew she was no good in a lot of ways, but I didn't think she was capable of being that low-down."

"I don't know what to say, Carl, except I'm sorry. Do you know the origin of that policy?"

"Not yet. But whoever the agent was, why, what he did wasn't against the law. It was strictly Ruby and her intentions that stink."

I can imagine what Dad and Mom are thinking.

"I'm having an awful time," says Carl. "Terrible nightmares—what Ruby and Everett did to me."

"Would it help to talk it out?" Dad looks at me as if to ask if I can handle what we're about to hear.

"Well, they came to the plant just after nine, which is when my shift starts. I unlocked the door to let them in, thinking something terrible had happened to our boys. Tommy and Doug are left on their own too much. I never know what they're up to half the time. When Everett brought a two by four out from behind his back and raised it up over his head, I realized what they'd come to do. Before I could run to the backroom, he clobbered me a good one. His aim was off, but it stunned me all the same. I couldn't move."

"Good thing he's out of shape," says Dad, "or you might not be walking around today."

"It could have been a whole lot worse, I suppose. He knocked me down and I pretended to be out cold. Sure didn't want another wallop."

"How'd you end up in the cistern? Everett's barely able to rake leaves, much less haul a good-sized fellow like you."

"They did it together, Ruby and Everett. She's a bear-cat, clawing and tugging away until they'd dragged me to the edge and shoved me in. I tried to climb back out, but Ruby stomped on my fingers. Everett pushed me down with the two by four. Then they slid the cover over the cistern and it was dark."

"Thank God you're alive, Carl," says Mom.

When he buries his face in his hands, I feel so sorry for him, I blurt the first thing that comes into my mind: "At least you didn't get killed like those women in front of the Catholic Church. Or Mr. Larson's wife. Or my great-uncle Amer."

The others are quiet for a minute.

"You're right, Callie," says Mr. Ryan, his bloodshot eyes glistening in the lamplight. "I am grateful. Nobody heard me for the longest time. Nobody, until you and your dad came along." He sobs some more.

In our town, no one is more hated than Ruby Ryan.

"Reviled," Mom said earlier. "She's likely to serve a long time in the Shakopee prison for women. A very long time."

Everett Christensen is also despised. But not as much as Ruby, which I can't understand, since Everett had *more* than an equal part in the whole affair.

Turns out he was poisoning Thelma—slowly—over several months, with an arsenic concoction brewed after hours in his drugstore.

I suppose, when you consider the Fidelity Mutual life insurance policy Ruby took out on Carl, it makes their guilt about equal. Except for the way she dressed and sashayed down Main Street, hunting for men. I guess that's what makes her more despised, especially among the women.

"There was no law broken," says Dad after our visit with Carl, "but if I were Ray, I'd sure feel like hell."

"How do you know it was Ray who made the sale, dear?" asks Mom. "Is he even licensed for the state of Minnesota?"

"I don't know. Good question. It's just that Cal and I saw him with Ruby a while back. Oh, I'll soon get to the bottom of this."

Since Thelma Christensen's release from the hospital, she comes to our house every day, as if she's moved in. When I get home from school in the afternoons, she's sitting at the kitchen table, sipping coffee with Mom, and so taken up with her problems that she can't even say hello when I go to the refrigerator for a snack. I have to wait until supper to tell Mom any of *my* important stuff.

"Don't think I was blind to his flirtations," says Thelma, blind to my presence. "No siree! They say Everett will go to the prison in Stillwater."

"Oh, my dear," says Mom. "I am so sorry."

"Not me! I don't give a damn where he goes, as long as it's far, far away. I never want to see that dirty low-down bloated toady pig ever again!"

Her eyes wide, Mom covers her mouth and jumps up to pour more coffee. I run outside to laugh.

Thelma seems to have hit on a good line, because she repeats it over and over around town, until folks wonder if she took the same Dale Carnegie course as Carl Ryan.

As Carl regains his strength he, too, talks about his ordeal. Details fly around town like field dust. He ends all his speeches with the same comment: "If it hadn't been for my best friend, I'd have been a goner. Will Lindstrom and his daughter saved my life."

As for me, I still prefer driving around in the Pontiac. But ever since the Worthmore incident, I don't mind walking places.

Nineteen

Ocheyedan or Bust ❖ *June 6, 1957*

AD COMES HOME FROM WORK with a quick step and tosses his briefcase and hat on a chair. Before the party starts, I get thirteen spankings from everybody, plus one to grow on.

My gift is a Seth Thomas metronome made of a wood that glows like honey. I've never seen one before, and when I open my mouth to speak, nothing comes out.

"The sales lady at the music store said to use it at the beginning of a piece," says Mom, "but not all the way through."

"How come?"

"Something about allowing for dynamics and tempo variation, so that you can keep your own sense of flow. She said you should have a notion of time, but not let it restrict you."

"In other words," says Liz, "you don't want your songs to sound mechanical."

"Exactly."

While Mom and Liz prepare my birthday meal—beef stroganoff and asparagus, followed by chocolate cake and maple nut ice cream—Dad and I sit down at the piano with my metronome, adjusting its metal weight, listening to it tick from Largo all the way down to Presto. I prefer number 132, between Adagio and Andante, especially for *Mio Babbino Caro.*

After the cake and ice cream, Dad makes an announcement. He's been more enthusiastic than usual all through supper, I thought on account of my becoming a teenager.

"Gather 'round, family. You're going to be very surprised."

Mom looks skeptical. "Now what have you got under your hat, Will?"

"Well, I've decided to walk to California and whoever wants to go along should fill a knapsack and be ready to leave in two weeks' time."

"Yay!" I holler, jumping up and down as if I were ten again. "Finally!"

The images Dad word-painted for me in his office at the court house come flooding back: orange trees and lemon trees; an ocean meeting the sky with only a thin line for the horizon; powerful, rolling waves and the smells and taste of salty sea water and kelp; long-legged birds that skitter up and down the beaches. How he can know all this without having been there is beyond me.

Liz slouches with her elbow on the kitchen counter, her upper lip hitched in an I-don't-believe-this sneer. Mom frowns and plunks down in a chair.

"Walk to California? Are you crazy, Will?"

"Just kidding, Emily." Dad dangles the car keys in front of her before marching around the room as if the Armistice had just been declared. "We're all going on a motor trip." He glances at me. "Cal doesn't know this yet, but she and I are hiking as far as the Iowa border. Emily, you and Liz give us three days, then pick us up in Ocheyedan."

"Ocheyedan, Iowa? Why Ocheydan?"

"Why not?"

After a brief silence, the room erupts with shouts and laughter.

"We have to start packing," says Mom, bustling about the kitchen as if we are leaving that very minute. "You'll need plenty of food and water. And don't forget your hats. You don't want to get sunstroke." She turns to inspect Dad's face and feels his forehead. "Maybe that's what already ails you."

Liz runs to sift through her summer clothes.

"I might need a new swimsuit," she says over her shoulder. "And some shorts and a new halter top."

Mom suddenly stops bustling about.

"Oh, Will. What about your mother? Are you sure we should be leaving her?"

"She seems about the same to me, Em. A little more forgetful, but other than that, she's all right. Hasn't had to see the doctor lately."

"How long would we be away?"

"At least two weeks. Maybe a little longer, if I can get the time off work."

"That's quite a stretch. Anything could happen to her and then where would we be? It's not as if Ray or anyone else is available to look after her. It's all up to us."

"How about Mrs. Tofte? She already checks on her nearly every day."

"I don't think we should ask her to be any more responsible than that. She's elderly, too."

"I guess I never thought about anything happening to Mother. Everything's going along so smoothly. If it comes down to it, maybe we could just take a short vacation. I *would* like to do the walking part. Callie and I have been talking about that for a long time. It's territory that Ray and I got to know when we were boys. I'd like to show that part of the countryside to Cal and see it myself once again before it gets all built up."

"Oh, that's not going to happen, Will. What makes you think so?"

"There's talk around town, Em. Big money making big plans—housing developments, resorts, a golf course."

"That's terrible."

"I know. And darn near impossible to stop once they get rolling."

"Liz is going to be awfully disappointed."

"Me, too! I thought we were going to California."

"Yes, Callie, you, too. Maybe we should have talked this over, Will, before you came home and sprang it on us, got our hopes up. I don't know. I'm disappointed, too, but I just have a bad feeling about Julia and her condition. Maybe you and Callie should take your little jaunt and Liz and I could plan an outing to Worthington or Sioux Falls and then pick you up in Ocheydan."

"How about Sioux City, Em? We could pay a surprise visit to Ray and Eloise."

"Oh, Lord! That'll be the day."

"I'd like to find out if he was involved with that insurance policy Ruby took out on Carl."

"Better let it rest, Will, and not trouble ourselves over him. Put your walking plan to work, instead."

"How far is it to Ocheydan, Dad?"

"Forty-three miles. I have it all mapped out."

He pulls a folded sheet of paper from his shirt pocket and a road map from the kitchen junk drawer and spreads them out on the table. It strikes me that we're about to plan a tiny version of the trip Amer took out to Montana, except we'll be walking the whole distance to Iowa.

"If it's forty-three miles to Ocheyedan, Cal, how many miles do we have to make in one day in order to get there by the end of the third day?"

"I don't know," I groan. "I can't do story problems, Dad. You know that."

"Yes, you can. What's three into forty-three?"

Ever since Miss Thompson's class, math makes my brain ache and my stomach churn. "I dunno. Fourteen something?"

"That's right! Fourteen point thirty-three to be exact. Think you can make it that far each day?"

"I guess so. That's a long way, though, fourteen in one day."

"Not if we take our time. Once we get started, we'll have all the time in the world."

"Yeah, but fourteen?"

I think I will always dislike numbers. As far as I'm concerned, they are mostly useless, except for the ones on my new metronome and birthdays and for counting stuff that interests me, like finding a four-leaf clover or six wide-eyed mewers at the bottom of a rusty cream can or the number of kisses I was promised until the jump rope tripped me:

> *Down in the valley where the green grass grows,*
> *there sat Callie as sweet as a rose.*
> *She sang and she sang and she sang so sweet*
> *when along came Bobby and kissed her on the cheek*
> *How many kisses did she get that week?*
> *One, two, three, four . . .*

Now that I'm thirteen, I don't need to jump a rope in order to imagine kisses from Bobby Keeler.

Dad puts an arm around Liz's shoulders as soon as she comes back to the kitchen. "Liz, I might have jumped the gun about a trip to California."

"What do you mean?"

"Your mother thinks that Gram shouldn't be left alone for that length of time. We've got a back up plan in the works."

"That's okay, Dad. I didn't really want to leave Brian for that long, any-how. Unless he can go along."

"Not likely."

"We're practically engaged, you know."

"No. We didn't know that."

Dad looks helplessly at Mom.

"Liz," she says, "you and I'll go on a shopping trip while these two go bumming around the countryside. How's that?"

"Cool."

"Well, I guess that's it, then." Dad shrugs his shoulders. "We'll postpone California, until—who knows when?"

"When you retire, perhaps?"

They laugh and waltz around the kitchen. Though a little slower than when I was ten.

At eight o'clock in the morning on June twentieth, Mom, Liz, Brian, Aunt Hazel and Cecil McDonough, Carl Ryan, Ted Claussen, and a bunch of other neighbors gather around to see us off, clapping and shouting and honking their horns as Dad and I leave town with knapsacks on our backs. The tooting of Brian's Mercury follows us all the way to Main Street: Be-Ba, Be-Ba. I catch our reflections in the store windows. Still skinny, I at least come up to Dad's shoulder in height. We look like a couple of hayseeds in our straw hats and blue jeans with the cuffs rolled up. The outlines of our backpacks make us look like Quasimodo.

At the end of Main Street, Dad starts singing in rhythm with our stride:

> *Pack up your troubles in your old kit-bag,*
> *And smile, smile, smile,*
> *While you've a lucifer to light your fag,*
> *Smile, boys, that's the style.*
> *What's the use of worrying?*
> *It never was worth while, so*
> *Pack up your troubles in your old kit-bag,*
> *And smile, smile, smile.*

"What's a lucifer, Dad? And a fag?"

"Those are what the British soldiers called a match and a cigarette. An old World War I song. But don't you try it. It'll stunt your growth."

"Singing that song will stunt my growth?"

"No. Cigarettes."

"Oh."

A mile out of town, cars slow to a crawl. Drivers and passengers roll down their windows to gape at us. Dad waves his hat and smiles at the gawkers. Some of them stop to ask if we need a lift.

"No thanks," says Dad, "we're hoofin' it."

"We're walking to Iowa!" I boast. "By Shank's Pony!"

One woman shakes her head and murmurs, "That poor child."

It feels good to be away from home, away from Masterton and all the stuff that happens in a town. I especially feel free and easy after we leave the highway and take to the more distant country roads where I've never walked or ridden bikes with my friends. Where bean fields meet the ditches and perfect rows of corn run all the way to the blue-green horizon. Where farmsteads are acres and acres apart. Meadowlarks and redwing blackbirds call out their greetings from fences and sturdy reeds. The wind carries the smells of ditch water and moldy weeds and road dust and new crops. I carry my hat so the hot wind can blow through my damp hair. On the way to Heron Lake, Dad tells me stories about when he and Ray were boys working their way through these same fields to flush pheasants.

"Your grandad and Uncle Amer taught us how to fan out or walk abreast when there were two of us. Always be aware of the next guy over whenever you take aim. Some seasons, there were so many birds, we took turns shooting and kept a tally. Seldom missed a shot. We usually got our limit. Now it seems as though the game birds are thinning out, not as plentiful as they used to be."

As we walk along, I'm surprised by the number of small lakes that are mostly hidden, unless you're looking for them or know where they are because you live nearby. I remember what Dad said a long time ago—that you can see and appreciate a whole lot more by walking than by driving a car. There are Heron Lake and Rush and Silver Lakes, of course, but many of the little ones that suddenly sparkle through a stand of pines or oak and butternut trees aren't shown on a map. They glitter like little jewels when the sun hits them just right. As the day wears on, Dad and I pass the time naming these bodies of water: Amer Lake, Lake Victor, Lake Julia, Lake William, Raymond Lake, Lake Elizabeth, Lake Emily, Callandra Bay.

"What? I only get a bay named after me and not a whole lake?"

"Better than Callandra Pond. I thought it had a nice ring to it."

"Callandra Bay. Yeah, I guess it does."

When we reach the dirt road that turns off toward Heron Lake, Dad recalls the time when he and Ray hunted ducks and geese with Docky, their Chesapeake.

"That was some dog. He had a big heart. Why, he could retrieve anything you asked him to, even the wounded ones that hid in the marsh grass. Unless, of course, it was one of those that dive deep and don't come up again."

"What kind of a duck does that?"

"I've known bluebills to do it. Sometimes, when they're injured, they'll hold onto a reed until they drown."

"I didn't know animals committed suicide."

"It wouldn't be considered suicide to them. Just instinct."

We walk along in silence for a while. Heron Lake is in sight, but we still have about a half-mile before we reach the shoreline. I'm eager for a rest.

"And that's where we fired at a deer." Dad points out an opening in the woods where the long grass is matted down, almost in a circle. "Would you look at that. They're still coming through here. That's good to see."

I remember a little of our conversation while we were cleaning bullheads several years earlier, about deer and buck fever and *Bambi*.

"I didn't think you shot deer."

"I never did. Ray took a crack at that one. He shouldn't have, because the gun wasn't powerful enough for an animal that size. It was pretty rough. Probably not something you'd care to hear about."

"I can handle it, Dad."

"Well, I know how you feel when it comes to animals, Cal. Guess I should have kept still and not brought it up to begin with."

"Well, you did, so now you have to tell me."

As we trudge along the narrow dirt road, Dad leans forward to look me full in the face, the way he used to when we teased Mom and I pretended to go bonkers while watching the boxing matches.

He straightens up and keeps walking.

"It was a young buck. Ray got him in the shoulder. The deer jumped backwards, then just stood there, looking at us. We had more shells, but . . . It was foolish of Ray to think he could take him with anything less than a ten-gauge. He couldn't shoot again. Neither could I. We figured maybe that single shot had only grazed him and he'd run away."

"And did he?"

"No. He stayed where he was, his eyes locked on ours. Oh, he was a beautiful animal. Graceful, dignified."

"What happened?"

"He didn't move, just kept staring at us for the longest time, questioning-like. The shot went deeper than we realized, because he eventually dropped and lay there until he bled out. It took an awful long while.

Dad falls quiet. I lower my head and try to keep pace on a path that has changed to pockets of gravel—gravel that swims before my eyes and grates against the bottoms of my shoes.

"Is that why you never shot a deer?"

"That's right. Ray never shot at another one, either. As far as I know."

After a while, my knapsack grows heavy. Dad scoops it up and carries it along with his own—one in front, the other on his back.

"What did you do with him?"

"The deer?"

"Yeah."

"We talked to a farmer who lived not far from here. He was glad for the meat."

After a moment, he says, "Yessir, I'm happy to see there are still herds moving through these woods. Bedding down on that same spot."

I'm glad to reach Heron Lake. We sit on the sandy western shore and crunch down the greenings Mom packed for us from our apple crop last fall. Wrapped in tissue paper and stored in the cool fruit cellar, they last all winter and into the spring.

Dad points out the eastern side of the lake, which is edged in pondweed and bulrushes.

"We always had good duck hunting over there."

"What kind?"

"Mostly canvasbacks and teal. A few bluebills and mallards. We generally filled out."

"Didn't it bother you to shoot ducks?"

"No. I guess the bigger the animal, the less inclined I am to kill it."

I remember having this conversation, as well, and let it drop, pleased that Dad has not changed his thinking since then.

I take off my sneakers and stockings, roll my jeans up to the knees and wade in the clear, cool water while Dad stretches out on the warm sand for a snooze. I slap at the water and watch circles fan out until the rings roll far away and I can't see them any longer. My apple core makes a small splash when I fling it, sinks for a second, and then bobs back to the surface. I watch it float for a minute, wondering where it will end up. Maybe a fish or a turtle will nibble at what's left of the meat. A sudden cool breeze purls the surface and brushes across my face. I wade back to shore and flop down on a patch of grass. While picking little bloodsuckers off the bottoms of my feet, I can't help thinking about that deer.

After Heron Lake, we drop south toward Okabena. In each small town along the way, we never see another person walking, except to go into a store. Just like in Masterton, everybody drives around for the fun of it or parks in the center of Main Street, where the men lean against fenders, arms crossed over bib overalls or suit jackets, chatting with one another. Now and then, one of the men gives his tire an affectionate kick.

Three miles outside of Okabena, we stay the night with an elderly farm couple—old friends of my grandparents. Even though they live in a different county, Dad spends a little time visiting with them while campaigning for his job as auditor. Mr. and Mrs. Moline are eager to hear about our adventure, clucking and shaking their heads as if we are on our way to the moon. They feed us a supper of fried pork chops, mashed potatoes and gravy, and canned tomatoes. Mrs. Moline must notice how tired I am, because she shows me to my room early, pointing out the chamber pot beneath the bed. She carries a cloth and a pitcher of water, which she sets next to a large bowl on a low table. I'm to wash myself before crawling into bed.

The sheets are cool and tight against my damp arms and legs. I hear the murmur of voices coming up the stairwell. And then, sleep.

AﬀTER A BIG BREAKFAST, our hosts stand outside the door to see us off— Mr. Moline, tall and gaunt in his overalls and Mrs. Moline, heavy-set, with her hair in a bun like Grandma Dahl.

"Good travels!" they call out, waving us west toward Round Lake.

"Greet your mother for us, Will!"

"I'll do that! And thanks, again. Goodbye!"

"Thank you," I call back, stuffed to the gills with pancakes and eggs and ham.

After several minutes, Dad groans, "I'm so full, I can barely walk. We won't need to eat again until suppertime."

"Where do you think we'll end up tonight?"

"Who knows? Depends on how far we get. Maybe under the stars."

Now it's my turn to groan. "Dad! The mosquitoes will kill us!"

"Oops, I forgot repellent. If we can make it to Round Lake before the drugstore closes," he says in a voice designed to perk me up, "we'll get some 6-12. *And* some ice cream."

I carry my own knapsack all day, while trudging along dusty roads. Dad figures out a way to shave off a couple of miles by shortcutting across hay fields. Sometimes, we find more ponds and hidden lakes. While resting under a large oak tree, which reminds me of Lone Tree near Lake Shetek, we eat some of the cheese sandwiches Mom packed, but leave the Twinkies for later.

"Too bad we don't have our fishing poles along, Cal. We could catch our supper."

By evening, we make it to Round Lake's Main Street. The drugstore is still open for business.

The soda jerk peers at us through squinty eyes as we set our knapsacks down and take a stool.

"Two root beer floats," says Dad.

The jerk sneers. With a little snort, he says, "You sure you can pay?"

"Why not?" Dad reaches into his back pocket for his wallet.

"I've seen hobos before. They ain't got the price of a peanut."

I look closely at Dad, at the limp strands of gray-black hair pasted to his grimy forehead, at his sweaty and dust-streaked face and a two-day growth of whiskers. I glance at my own filthy clothes and hands.

"Now let these poor folks alone, Mike," says an old man from the far end of the counter. "They's in need of a little handout, that's all. Prob'ly can't afford a meal."

"No, really." Dad pulls a dollar bill from his wallet. "We have the price of ice cream. Plus a peanut or two."

The old man chuckles. The jerk's pimply face turns a fiery red.

While we savor the vanilla floats, a few people gather around to hear about our journey, including the old man *and* the soda jerk. The more questions they ask, the less tired I feel.

"Why Ocheydan?" asks one customer.

"Why not?" says Dad with a chuckle. "Actually, I'm retracing old familiar territory with my daughter, here. I wanted to show her where my brother and I used to hunt and fish when we were youngsters."

"Well, you've come a long stretch from Masterton," says the old man. "I've got to hand it to you."

"I think I could walk all the way to California, Dad."

He grins and squeezes the back of my neck.

"Cal's a good sport," he says proudly.

The others nod and smile, including the soda jerk.

The second night, we sleep under the stars, in a hay field near Round Lake.

"What about the mosquitoes? Did you remember to get the 6-12?"

"Damn! I forgot."

He snaps his fingers and pulls a small jar from his knapsack. The jar is ancient-looking, oily, and grubby.

"Never fear. This might take care of the problem."

"What is that?"

"Bear grease."

"Bear grease! Won't it *attract* insects? Where'd you get it?"

"I found it out at the lake, among your grandad's things. It should work."

I take a whiff. It smells rancid, like rotten beef tallow.

"Yuck! How old is this stuff?"

"Pretty old would be my guess. But it might help."

Because the mosquitoes have found us, I reluctantly smear a lardy chunk on my arms and neck and the backs of my hands. It helps a little, but stinks to high heaven.

Each of us gathers straw to make up our own "beds." Dad instructs me to dig a shallow hole with a stick for a latrine on the other side of the haystack. I go to the bathroom and cover it up, like Sam Cat, before settling in for the night. Dad takes his turn.

Lying there, looking up at the stars, and getting dive-bombed in the face and around the ears by mosquitoes, I wonder what Mom and Liz are doing.

"Oh," says Dad, "by now, they've likely bought out the stores in Worthington. Spent all my hard-earned cash."

I laugh and reach for the bear grease.

"Cover yourself with some hay, Cal. That'll help. And set your hat like this. See?"

Dad is blanketed in hay and wears his straw hat over his face. I follow suit.

"Have you given any thought to what you'd like to do, Cal, once you're out of school?"

His voice is a little muffled.

"Something to do with music. I for sure want to go to college, like Liz. But I don't know where."

"Oh well, it's still a long way off."

"Ha! That's not what Mom says. She thinks she has to get me ready to go out on my own right now. Probably can't wait until I'm gone."

"Naw! You know that's not true. She just wants you to be prepared for whatever comes along."

"Yeah. I guess."

"Good night now, Snicklefritz. We've got a long day ahead of us."

"Yup. Our third and last day."

"We won't soon forget this trip, will we, kiddo?"

"That's for sure. Night, Dad."

After a while, the dive-bomb buzzing around the edges of my hat dims as my brain fades and I fall asleep, but only for a few minutes at a time. I wake Dad up a couple of times on account of the strange noises and rustling movements going on around us.

"It's only field mice," he says, "and an old hooty owl."

"What about those!" My loud voice scares away a pair of yellow eyes that were moving close to the ground, in my direction.

"Just a barn cat out mousing," he says.

After a bat swoops across my face, I burrow deeper into my straw bed.

Come morning, we search our backpacks for breakfast: a Twinkie and an orange each, as well as hard-boiled eggs and packaged toast, called Rusks.

"Well, Callie-girl, this is it. Day three." Dad wipes a trickle of juice from his stubbly beard. "Do you think we'll make it?"

"Hell, yes. How far is Ocheydan from here?"

"I calculate just under fourteen miles. Maybe less if we cut across a couple of fields."

Compared to day one and in spite of the mosquitoes, I feel sad that our trip is nearly over. Because my backpack is lighter, it no longer bothers me to carry it. My legs feel stronger. And, as Dad says, "We're lucky that old Sol decided to keep us company the entire time."

Well before dark, we cross the state line and swagger into Ocheyedan, Iowa. The front doors of our black Pontiac, parked in the center row on Main Street, fling open. Mom and Liz jump out and rush toward us, calling out their hellos, throwing their arms around us as if we've been gone for years.

"Are you two all right?" asks Mom, stepping back to look at us. "Whew, a little rank."

Liz pinches her nose. She's wearing new shorts and a California-style halter-top.

"What's that awful smell?"

"Bear grease."

"Pee-U! Whew! You need a bath!"

I brush up against Liz before hopping into the back seat.

"Little creep," she says, frowning.

Dad bows to Liz with a sweeping gesture as she gets behind the wheel. "Driver, to Masterton, if you please."

"Better fill up the gas tank, Will." Mom leans forward to muss his hair and plant a kiss on his stubbly cheek. "And don't forget to check the tires. Liz and I have been driving all over creation."

"You mean 'All over hell?'"

"Is that what your papa taught you out there in the wilderness? More cussing?"

"Could be."

Laughing, Mom sits back and, while I launch into a minute-by-minute account of our adventure, draws me close to her—bear grease, filthy clothes, and all.

"Happy birthday, Callie dear," she says, kissing the top of my matted hair. Liz smiles at us from the rearview mirror. Dad reaches a hand over the seatback.

Twenty

Saws and Leeches

OW THAT I'M THIRTEEN, I get to do more stuff with my friends. Sometimes, we meet the boys we like at the movies or at the swimming pool. Once, we went out to the state park and drank beer. It tasted yucky.

It's the end of summer and Liz returns to Mankato for her senior year, majoring in accounting, which pleases Dad. I'm in seventh grade. Mom works part time in the auditor's office to begin saving for my college tuition.

"It won't be long before you're out of the nest, too, Callie."

"What's the rush?"

"The years go by awfully fast, sweetheart. We need to get you ready."

"I know, I know. Prepare me for whatever comes along, huh, Ma?"

She gives me a strange look.

For the next several months, our lives "play out according to Hoyle," until New Year's Eve 1958.

Back from my church choir program, we no sooner pull into the garage than the phone starts to ring.

"Goodness gracious, who could be calling at this hour?" Mom looks concerned. "I hope Liz is all right."

Evening phone calls usually mean bad news. We rush inside.

Mrs. Tofte, Gram's next-door neighbor, is so excited that Dad has to hold the phone away from his ear. "You'd better come quick!" she shouts. "It's your mother! She fell and I think she's broken her hip!"

"Call the hospital, Mrs. Tofte. We'll be right over!"

Mom and I jump back into the car while Dad lifts up the garage door. He gets in behind the wheel, starts the engine, backs down the driveway and onto the street faster than I thought reverse could go. Then he revs into forward and fishtails along the snow-packed road.

It gives me a start to see the ambulance in front of Gram's house, the same kind of chill that skitters down my back when I see the hearse cruising around town, which makes me think of Grandad. The idling motor of the ambulance is loud. Clouds of exhaust rise in the cold air. Mrs. Tofte, her white hair puffed up like cotton candy, stands at curbside, clasping and unclasping her hands. Here it is January and she's wearing only a shawl over her housedress.

"Oh, Will," she cries, shivering, "I'm so sorry! I found her lying on the bathroom floor. She must have slipped."

"You need to get back inside before you freeze to death, Mrs. Tofte. I can't thank you enough for looking in on Mother."

"I had a bad feeling," she says. "No lights on in her house. That's not like Julia."

Dad hopped into the rear of the ambulance where Gram lay belted onto a stretcher. A quick peek tells me that she is awake, but probably confused about what is happening to her. Mom and I follow in the Pontiac.

Because no children are allowed inside the hospital, unless they're sick (not even the entry), I have to wait in the car.

"I don't get it," I grumble. "The doctor kept me overnight when I got shot. Why the hell can't I go in with you guys now?"

"Watch the tongue, Callie. I agree, but those are the rules."

"At least you agree with me for a change!"

"I won't be long."

It soon grows so cold I pretend to smoke cigarettes, trying to click out rings with my tongue the way the men do it. But frosty breaths aren't enough. I need real smoke to make decent rings.

I check the glove compartment and find a pack of Pall Mall cigarettes and a book of matches. I didn't think Dad smoked cigarettes. Mom doesn't. Maybe they belong to Liz or Brian and one of them hid the pack there.

The lighted match slips from my fingers and lands on the car seat. With a cigarette dangling from my lips like Ruby Ryan in front of the Silver Star, I quickly smother the flame before it burns a hole in the upholstery, then lean over to strike another match, hoping no one will see the charred spot on the seat.

After inhaling once and coughing a lot, I figure out how to hold back the smoke in order to try for a ring. I click my tongue like a snake until something resembling a square pours out of my mouth. Watching the smoke drift up to the ceiling and around the windshield, I begin to feel woozy and light-headed, then sick to my stomach. Although I don't vomit, signal juices gush down the insides of my cheeks and pool in my mouth. I roll down the window and try flicking the cigarette away from me, but it only falls next to the car.

Cold and on the verge of puking, I sit with my head hanging out of the window and watch my icy breaths—small puffs and long streams—and wonder if I should go into the hospital for help. But what would I tell them? That I've taken ill from a cigarette? I roll up the window and lean back with my head against the seat, moaning, willing myself to feel better.

Instead, I imagine all sorts of awful things inside that brick building: long dull needles soaking in jars of alcohol, strange beds with saddle stirrups (like in the clinic), filet-sharp knives and long toothy saws, leeches for blood-letting, water-head babies, old men with monstrous tumors protruding from their necks.

At age six or seven, my friend Judy and I found her mother's medical book in their attic. There were tons of pictures and drawings of people with terrible skin diseases covering every inch of their bodies, deformed arms and legs, huge staring eyes from cadaverous faces, large goiters and strange tumors attached to every part of the body. The weirdest drawings were of babies inside women's stomachs. We couldn't figure out how they got there. Judy said it had to be something the women ate.

"It's like if you swallow a watermelon seed," she said, "it'll grow into a huge watermelon inside you."

Certain that it had to do with the belly button, I pointed to my own. "No, Judy, something from a man goes in through here and then into a tube connected to the stomach."

Sitting in the hospital parking lot, waiting for my nausea to disappear, and fully aware of how babies are made, I nevertheless picture women inside those walls screaming and moaning with giant watermelons or monster babies that won't come out. Just as the imagined smell of ether washes over me, like when the dentist claps an ether-soaked rag over my face before pulling a tooth, Mom comes hurrying out of the hospital. I push the car door open and run to meet her.

"The nurses are taking good care of Gram," she says, drawing me to her side with a hug. She sniffs the air. "Has someone been smoking around here? I smell cigarette smoke."

"Oh, somebody who parked next to us, but he left."

"Anyway," continues Mom, "we got her settled in for the night. Daddy'll stay with her for a while."

As soon as she gets in the car, Mom's stern eye falls on me. She reaches over to open the glove compartment.

I hold my breath and look out of the window.

"Don't you ever do this again, Callie," she says, waving the Pall Mall package in front of my face. "And don't lie! Do you understand?"

"Yes, Mom," I groan, wedging myself in the corner between the seat and the door, still feeling queasy.

She glares at me for a moment before starting the engine.

"All right, then. That'll be the end of it. Lord knows we've got enough on our hands without having to worry about *you*."

Looking at me sidewise, Mom backs out of the parking lot, stops, and holds up the pack, again.

"Where did you get these, Callie?"

"They were in the glove compartment. Liz probably hid them there. Why don't you ask her? Give her hell for once."

Mom shakes her head and starts for home.

I wait for the inevitable lecture, but it never comes, which in some ways is worse than getting it over with. Somehow, I feel more shamed than if she'd fired a round of words at me.

"What did the doctor say?" I mumble, after a long moment.

"Just as we suspected. Gram broke her right hip."

"How?"

"Trying to clear the bathtub drain with a toilet auger, of all things. The auger jammed and she fell trying to pull it out."

"That was silly. I didn't know she could do stuff like that."

"She can't. That's the trouble."

The next morning, Dad sits across from me at the breakfast table.

"Did you sleep at all?" I ask.

"A couple of hours." His hand rubs across whiskers with a light sandpaper sound. "I don't know what on earth she was thinking," he says between bites of toast and sips of black coffee. "I asked her why she didn't wait for me to do it."

"What'd she say?"

"She didn't think it'd be so hard to run that snake through the tubing. Said that if she took care of it herself, there'd be more time to visit with us on Tuesday. She'd even been practicing the piano and singing."

"Well, *that's* a good sign," says Mom, wiping up crumbs from the counter with a dishrag.

"I told her we'd have a concert as soon as she got back home, but for now, she needs to rest and mind the doctors."

I don't like that idea—minding the doctors—especially after what happened to Grandad. And what about Doc Nelson cheating his non-Lutheran patients? What else does he do to them? And the way he swore and pounded on the counter in Dad's office, angry about his taxes. Which doctors can we trust?

Because I'm still on vacation from school, I help out with meals, dishes, and laundry while Mom and Dad take turns going to the hospital. On Tuesday afternoon, the unexpected happens.

"Get your coat on, Cal," Dad says. "We're going to see Gram."

"I didn't think . . ."

"It's Tuesday, isn't it?"

"Yes, but they won't let me in."

"We'll find a way. Now put on your duds and let's go."

It's one thing to get into a hospital. It's another to have to look at all those horrid medical contraptions and freaky sick people. At first, I'm not sure I want to go. Then I do. But how is he going to get me inside?

"I'm sorry, William," says the head nurse after I tell her I'll be turning fourteen in less than six months. "You know our policy—no children under sixteen."

Sixteen. I think about what my dad went through at that age, going to Montana for Uncle Amer.

He gives the nurse a look that could charm a fish into a frying pan. "This is one time I'll have to ask you to break the rules, Maxine. You see, it's Tuesday and Callie has come to see her grandmother."

"Well, I don't know . . ."

"No Tequila tonight." Dad opens wide his overcoat.

I burst out laughing. Nurse Maxine scowls at me and presses a finger to her lips.

"I should hope not," she whispers. "After all, we have rules about that, too."

Then she surprises me by winking at Dad and waving us on.

I've never been in a hospital before, except when I was born, which doesn't count. And of course, the night I blew up Grandad's shotgun shell. But I never saw much then, because after going blind under those bright surgery lights, I got whisked away to a little room.

Now that I'm inside and walking around, I wonder what's the big deal. The hospital feels empty and is as quiet as a library. The hallway, a long stretch of scuffed green linoleum, is uncluttered except for a silver cart with stacks of white towels and silver pans. Dad points out the metal bedpans, bulb syringes, and small kidney-shaped pans, which, he explains, are for when patients have to vomit. Which makes me feel urpy all over again, just thinking of that cigarette.

The only sounds are occasional coughs or soft moans from the other sides of half-opened doors and the nurses' murmuring voices as they make their rounds. The air is heavy and warm and smells funny, like a mixture of rubbing alcohol and the stinky breath of a sick person. I peek inside several rooms on the chance of seeing a monster-head kid or an old man with a huge goiter. But there are only normal-looking people, asleep or reading or staring into space or listening to low music from a transistor radio.

The nurses step briskly along the corridor in starched white caps and uniforms, their white shoes squeaking on the linoleum. Even their stockings are white. Each one greets Dad by name—Mr. Lindstrom—and assures him that Gram is doing as well as can be expected, considering her age and her condition. They even speak to me without asking how I managed to get inside.

"Everyone seems happy to be in the black," Dad says when we're alone again.

"What does that mean?"

"It means the hospital is solvent."

"What's 'solvent'?"

"I just finished auditing their books, Cal. A few years ago, they were in the red. Now the records are as they should be and the hospital is making a profit."

"Oh. Well, that's good."

"Yes. *Very* good."

This evening, I feel like a grown-up. And the respect these nurses show Dad compensates for the meanness of Doctor Bennett Nelson.

Before we get to Gram's room, I stop short in front of a painting of a little girl tucked in bed, under a white down comforter. She is flushed with a fever that makes her look strangely pretty. Her hair, like cornsilk, is damp against her skin. In a chair, next to the bed, sits an elderly doctor in a black vest and white shirt with the sleeves rolled up. A stethoscope hangs from his neck. Leaning forward, peering at the little girl over wire glasses perched at the end of his nose, this doctor looks like Doc Adams in *Gunsmoke*. In the dimly lit background, the child's parents gaze anxiously from a half-open door, as if they aren't allowed inside the sick room. It strikes me that this child doesn't have long to live. This could have been Mrs. Swenson's daughter. Was this how she died? Here in this hospital?

"Dad, do you remember when Roberta Swenson died?"

"Oh, yes, Cal, I certainly do. It was awful."

"Mom told me how it happened."

Dad nods and stands by my side, studying the painting.

The Swensons' only child died two years before I was born. I used to think of her a lot, especially when trying to figure out why Mrs. Swenson was so nasty to me whenever I passed out tallies at card club. Now, because of this painting, I am finally able to give Roberta a face. Unlike the doctor in this picture, Doc Nelson had neglected Mrs. Swenson's daughter after a routine tonsillectomy. Mom told me he was at a party when the nurse called for him to return to the hospital. He wouldn't leave the gathering, and instead, told the nurse what he thought should be done. It didn't work. At age six, Roberta Swenson bled to death. Everyone in town was angry and upset—but, because it was Doc Nelson, no one did anything about it. He just went on leading the Days of Eighty-Seven parades, perched on his white horse, tossing pennies to the children, and taking extra money from his non-Lutheran patients.

"She was a beautiful, sweet child," said Mom the day I asked her to tell me more about Roberta. "Mrs. Swenson fixed her hair in pipe curls and bought her the prettiest little dresses at Marbella's Fashionette."

To think that Hulda Swenson had been mean to me all because of Doc Nelson. I hope I never have to look at his mug ever again.

"Doc Nelson isn't Gram's doctor, is he?"

"No, Cal. We've got Doctor Grimm. He's fairly new here, ever since old Doc Dohms retired.

"I didn't know he left. Where'd he go?"

"I believe he moved to Lakeland, Florida."

"With old Mrs. Calder, I'll bet. I haven't seen her around town for a long time and we would have heard about it if she'd died."

"I guess that's accurate, Callie. No more night terrors for Mrs. Calder."

"Who was Grandad's doctor?"

"A man by the name of Pierce, but that was in Sioux Falls."

We reach the end of the hallway and Gram's room.

It's stuffy inside with the faint smell of disinfectant. The lights are off, except for a dim lamp to the right of the window. It is so quiet I can hear myself breathe. The bed, all metal and white sheets, seems about to swallow Gram up.

"Hello, Mother," Dad says softly. "We're here." He places his hand against my back to urge me forward. He and Mom have been doing that ever since I was a kid—pushing me forward. Like at Grandad's funeral.

"Go ahead, Cal. She'd like to see you."

I edge toward the railing, which feels cool to my hands in spite of how warm it is in the room. The second I look down at my grandmother, the image of Grandad in his coffin comes rushing back. Since then, I hate to see grown-ups lying on their backs. Even on the ground while camping or making snow angels or looking up at the stars or resting on the living room floor after a game of marbles or playing with Tequila and Sam Cat. It doesn't bother *me* to do those things. I just don't like to see old people down like that.

Gram's bent fingers are laced together across her stomach. Her chest barely moves with her breathing. Without rouge or powder, her face has that same pasty look as Grandad's: sunken cheeks, thin pale lips, and eyelids like parchment.

"Hi, Gram," I whisper.

Grandma Julia opens her eyes and slowly reaches for my hand.

"Hello, hello," she mumbles. Without glasses, her eyes are a watery blue. "You came all the way from Illinois."

Confused, I glance at Dad.

"No, Mother, this is Callie, your granddaughter."

"Oh? . . . Oh, yes, I remember now. Did your papa give you that shiny half dollar I was saving for you?"

"*You* gave it to me when we came to your house one time."

"Oh?"

After a long pause when no one says anything, I reach into my bag.

"I brought a book, Gram. Shall I read to you?"

"Yes, dear, I'd like that."

"It's the book you gave me for Christmas a couple of years ago. Remember?"

Dad's eyes get watery and his chin trembles a little as he sits on one of the folding chairs next to the bed. I sit down and open my book to chapter one:

> "Christmas won't be Christmas without any presents," grumbled Jo, lying on the rug.
>
> "It's so dreadful to be poor!" sighed Meg, looking down at her old dress.
>
> "I don't think it's fair for some girls to have lots of pretty things, and other girls nothing at all," added little Amy, with an injured sniff.
>
> "We've got father and mother, and each other, anyhow," said Beth, contentedly, from her corner . . .

I read to Gram until she falls asleep.

"You're a good reader, Cal," says Dad. "I enjoyed that, too."

"Thanks, Pops. I'd like to go home now."

"Of course. I'm glad you got to see Gram."

After kissing his mother lightly on the forehead so as not to awaken her, Dad ushers me out of the room and back down the hallway.

We thank nurse Maxine. She touches my shoulder and smiles.

"You can visit your grandmother whenever you like, Callie."

All through January, Mom and Dad take turns sitting with Gram. Sometimes, I go along. Whenever Mom is there, Gram won't speak. She jerks her head this way and that, slaps her hands against the bed sheets, and stares for the longest time at her presents: a bouquet of flowers, a soft hairbrush, a small jar of Jergen's lotion, another pretty bed jacket from Marbella's Fashionette. The pink flannel still smells of *Chanel No. 5.*

The few times Liz comes home from college, she gets spooked whenever Gram asks her where her husband is and how many children she has by now.

I feel sorry for my sister because she hasn't seen this coming first-hand, especially the meanness toward our mother. I usually tell her about it, because she's never around to hear it for herself.

Doctor Grimm sets Gram's hip, but it won't mend, mainly because she keeps thrashing around and sneaking out of bed. She's so tiny that she can slip feet first through the wide end of the railings. When the nurses find her and steer her back to bed, she hits at them and swears, something she's never done before.

A couple of times a week, I go to the library after school for more books. Nurse Maxine says that Gram seems to calm down when I read to her.

This particular afternoon, just as I turn to pull out a book from my bag, Gram punches me hard in the back. Hard enough to make my book bag fly across the room.

"Ouch!" I yell, and whirl around to see my grandmother leaning over the bed railing, glaring at me with cruel eyes, as if she'd like to kill me. Tears well up in my own and roll down my cheeks. It hurts where Gram slugged me, but what's worse is the idea that my grandmother hates me, just as she hates my mother. Does she think I took her "boy" away from her, too?

Nurse Maxine rushes in to settle Gram and to examine my back after I tell her what happened. She leads me into the hallway and speaks to me as if I were a grown-up.

"Hardening of the arteries," she says, taking my hand in hers, "affects the brain. At times your grandmother may not remember you and she might do and say things that are very strange and upsetting. Hurtful, even. You're not to take it to heart."

In my mind, I hear Mom's voice saying, "Control yourself now!" But it's all I can do to stop crying.

"Do you understand, Callie?" continues Nurse Maxine. "We mustn't take it to heart when our family members get this way."

She gives me a big hug. "Now go back in there and read to her. She seems to like that. Just keep your distance."

"It's hard to imagine," says Dad, returned home after work, "that such an old, little bit of a woman can muster that much fight." He lowers his head and quickly leaves the room.

The next time I go to the hospital, I watch my back and wear a heavy sweater under my coat.

By the beginning of February, my parents are exhausted. And I'm tired of trying to be agreeable. Because there is no nursing home in Masterton, Gram has to stay in the hospital. The state mental ward and the Poor Farm are out of the question.

"We're not desperate and we're not destitute," says Dad. "Even if we were, I'd never put her in one of those places. Besides, they're not equipped to handle her physical injuries."

Sometimes, while driving north out of town, on our way to Lake Shetek, we see a down-and-outer shuffling along the shoulder or in the ditch. "Must be someone from the poor farm," Dad comments each time. I turn to look at the man's gaunt face and shabby clothes, wondering what it is that causes him to have to live at the Poor Farm. I always give a little wave and he waves back, his eyes following us as we drive on by, as if he wishes for folks of his own and some other place to live.

"As long as Mother has family that can support her," says Dad, "she'll not end up in St. Peter or at the poor farm."

Because the regular nurses have many patients to care for, Dad hires a special-duty nurse to sit with Gram through the night so he and Mom can get some rest. Unless someone keeps a close watch, she either climbs or falls out of the crib set up for her. Dad won't permit a tie-down. "What if there's an emergency? A fire?"

In spite of the extra care, Gram managed to slip over the railing and defecate in a corner of the room. She slipped and fell down in the mess, and re-broke her hip. I looked up the word "defecate" to make sure it meant what I thought it meant. It takes a long time for a picture like that to fade away.

I can't imagine anything worse happening to Gram. But it does.

Bedsores and poor circulation eventually lead to gangrene in her right foot and ankle. Doc Grimm says that he has no choice but to amputate before the poison travels upward. He cuts off Gram's leg below the knee.

For some time, now, Dad has been trying to get calls through to Uncle Ray and Aunt Eloise. They slam down the phone before he can finish shouting, "Don't hang up! It's about Mother!"

Finally, he sends a telegram.

Twenty-One

You're a Good Boy, Willy

THE JINGLING OF SPURS. Itchy trigger finger. Like a scene out of *Gunsmoke*, Dad eagle-eyes his brother who saunters toward him down the hospital corridor, wearing a smirk and juggling his car keys after driving up from Sioux City.

Dad glances at his watch. "What the hell took you so long?"

"I stopped to get a haircut." As Ray reaches up to smooth his sandy-colored hair, his diamond ring shimmers in the late afternoon sunshine like fish flies around a porch light. "And I had lunch with a prospective client in Sheldon." He drops the keys into his suit coat pocket. "A very productive meeting, I might add."

Dad's nostrils flare. "You son-of-a . . ." He turns his back on Ray and marches into the sick room. I trail after him.

Gram brightens as soon as Uncle Ray enters, reaching out to him as he leans over the railing to give her a kiss.

"What's this I hear about you not feeling so great, Mother?"

"I know. Such a bother. It's so good to see you, son. To have both my boys here with me."

"Well, you just concentrate on getting well, Mother. I'll have you out of here and dancing around in no time."

Dancing around. What the hell is he thinking? Doesn't he know what happened?

Dad mutters, "Cut the bullshit, Ray."

Uncle Ray moves into Gram's house, doesn't bother to stay in touch with us or with the doctor. He just comes and goes. Because Masterton is a small town, we know his routine, seeing him at a distance and hearing off-handed comments regarding his whereabouts. He visits Gram for a few minutes each morning, then spends a couple of hours chatting with "the fellas" in Delhoff's

Barber Shop. He eats lunch at the Mint Café before going for a drive, sometimes to Tepeeotah, according to Mr. Johnson who keeps an eye on our cottage during the winter. Late in the afternoon, Ray returns to the hospital for
another brief visit before taking his supper at the Mint. I think he spends
about as much time at Gram's house as he does visiting her in the hospital.
My friend Janet tells me that her mom sees him at the Silver Star every
night—not to drink or pick up women—but to "meet up with the fellas," and
to talk life insurance.

After a few days of this, Mayor Thompson sees fit to have a visit with
my dad.

"Your brother's a great guy, Will, almost as funny as Bob Hope. But he
gets a little pushy and up close with that insurance business. Folks are getting
sick of it, especially after what happened with Ruby and Carl."

"I'll have a chat with him."

"This is embarrassing, Em," Dad says over supper. "It's shameful, how
the guy goes around drumming up business, especially with Mother in the
hospital. Why can't he put someone else first for a change?"

"We all know the answer to that one, Will. He's like cream on milk—
rising to the top. Or at least trying to."

"Yes, well, if he isn't careful, he'll end up like cream in January."

I picture our milk bottles, delivered twice a week. If they're left too long
on the stoop in winter, their cardboard caps pop up from tubes of frozen
crystals that hang cockeyed over the bottle necks, leaving no decent cream
for morning coffee.

Although we haven't *really* seen my uncle since that fight at the lake after
Grandad died, he looks pretty much the same, except for thinner hair. During
these past several years, he's been sneaking into Maywood County without
bothering to look us up. Cecil McDonough (Aunt Hazel's husband) spotted
Ray and Barber around Masterton and out at Lake Shetek. Our neighbor,
Mr. Claussen, saw them during spring fishing opener. Carl Ryan reported
Ray stocking up on groceries at Cooper's Market during fall duck hunting. I
don't know what disturbs Dad more—a brother who avoids him, who hunts
and fishes without him, or his mother in the hospital, needing loving attention as she waits to die.

Evenings after work, Dad pours himself a shot glass full of whiskey and takes longer walks than usual. If I don't have any homework, I join him for a constitutional. Sometimes I lie about not having homework.

Only now when he walks, he takes longer strides than usual and swings his arms as if he's beating up on the bowling pins.

"I can't walk this fast, Dad. Slow down!"

"Whaaat? Can't you keep up with me?"

"Hell, no. I thought you liked to look at things."

He slows his pace, glances up at the darkening sky and its glut of snow clouds.

"Guess I forgot. Too much on my mind."

We avoid going in the direction of Gram's house. From what I gather, Dad hopes to catch a glimpse of Ray in a neutral setting on the chance of coming to terms with him.

"Some day, I'll have it out with that guy. He acts as if he's related to everyone in town but us."

"Yeah, at the barber shop, he and Mr. Delhoff act so buddy-buddy."

Dad gives me a searching look, shakes his head, and chirps from the corner of his mouth.

Maywood County is Dad's territory. As much as he wants to settle things with Uncle Ray, I can't imagine it being done in a friendly way. At the hospital, he came close to telling his brother off, but walked away at the last minute. He can't risk turning a family squabble into ammunition for gossip, especially with re-election coming up next year. It was embarrassing enough when Aunt Eloise blew her cork at Grandad's funeral. Fortunately, no one had registered that year to run against Dad.

Every four years, he has to campaign for his job as county auditor. So does the Maywood county treasurer, the clerk of court, the county assessor, the registrar of deeds, and the county sheriff. Their terms are staggered so they won't all have to seek votes at the same time.

I was nine when election time first mattered to me.

"Unless we have an income," Dad joked, "we'll end up at the Poor Farm."

That's the first time I ever heard about such a place. I tried my best at campaigning.

Liz and Mom covered Masterton that year, while I helped Dad knock on doors around Black Duck. On the way home, we stopped at every farm in between, where Dad spent long minutes visiting with the people who lived there. The looks on their faces when they said, "You've got my support, Will," and the way they shook our hands and clapped us on the back when we left, gave me a warm feeling—something I never felt around Gram or Uncle Ray or Aunt Eloise. Odd how a person is treated better by strangers and acquaintances than by some family members.

It's a good thing Dad still has a year to go, in case of a showdown with his brother. That should give people time to forget before they go to the voting booth. He only sounds off at home, no longer careful that I shouldn't hear.

"Who in hell does he think he's fooling? Why bother to come around if he's not going to spend time with Mother? I wish he'd stay the hell away from my constituents, Goddamn it!"

"And to think I was so naïve," says Mom, "as to expect him for dinner his first night in town."

Dad snorts and pours himself another whiskey, which makes me wonder if he'll turn out like my friend Judy's dad. Mr. Bergman drinks a bottle of whiskey every day and it makes him mean. He slapped Judy when she told him she was going to the Saturday matinee with Janet and me whether he liked it or not. It was an awful slap.

Sometimes, I get out of bed, hungry for a snack, and hear Mom and Dad talking in the living room—like tonight:

"Face it, Will, he's saddled with a woman who has a screw loose."

I *have* to hear this. I tiptoe into the kitchen for an apple, a banana, and a roll of *Lifesavers*. Although my parents don't seem to mind what I hear during the day, joining them now might interfere with the flow of their conversation. For old time's sake, I crawl under the dining room table and hide behind its thick pedestal, just as I did when I was little—a perfect place for eavesdropping, except too tight for me now. Sam Cat winds through the chair legs and into my dark corner, happy for a new game at his level. What if he gives me away with his loud purring? I stifle a sneeze when a tiny tuft of his hair flies up my nose. Although cramped and beginning to feel silly about my regression, I huddle there, listening to new and intriguing information.

"Eloise is crazy, Will. Why else would the doctors lock her up? Therapy in a leather-tooling ward—dear Lord." After a pause, Mom adds, "She's to be pitied, really."

"Hell, I don't feel a bit sorry for her. She's ruined it for every one of us. And Jenny? That poor girl has been caught in the middle all these years—imagine, growing up in that hellhole. As for Ray, why, it seems all Eloise has ever wanted is to drive a wedge between us."

"Your brother's a grown man, dear. He could decide things for himself."

"Not any more. He's in way too deep. And for too long. How would you feel, Em, if I threatened suicide every time you set out to do something I didn't want you to do?"

"Oh, my, Will! That's ugly."

"Well, think about it. That's how she manipulates him."

"He manages to get away on business trips, goes fishing and hunting, and she hasn't killed herself yet."

"Most likely she's bluffing, but who knows? For years, she's kept him on guard with those threats."

Mom and Dad stop their discussion for a time. They play with Tequila, asking her to speak and roll over. She's quick to please and I worry they might head to the kitchen for doggie treats. But they don't budge.

"Driving a wedge," "leather-tooling," "psychotic," "suicide." This is the first time I've heard these words used to describe what's going on with Uncle Ray and Aunt Eloise. They echo through my mind, especially the word, "suicide." Not only is Aunt Eloise sick in the head, she apparently controls her family in a strange and sick way. So that's why my cousin never returned to play with me. Dad said once if Uncle Ray ever tried to bring Jenny back to Minnesota, Eloise would raise the devil. No wonder my uncle goes away by himself, away from them, away from us. Does it trouble him to see our family happy?

I still have the arrowhead Belle gave me, safe on a wad of cotton in a little box. Does Jen still have hers? Or did her mother throw that away, too, like she did her T-shirt?

In the only picture we have of my aunt, she is young, thin and stylish with wavy black hair that brushes the collar of a fitted suit popular in the forties. Her skin is creamy white. She's beautiful, but a little snooty the way she holds her head and stands with one hand on her hip. The other hand is threaded through Uncle Ray's arm. They make a handsome couple. Except, she isn't smiling. I wonder if she ever did.

"You know," continues Dad, "this whole deal with Ray goes way back, before he met Eloise. He got by with everything when we were kids."

"I know, Will, I know. You can't seem to let that go."

"Well, it's true. I suppose it shouldn't matter now. We were just kids. But he was *never* asked to do any of the heavy chores on the farm. That is until the time Dad and I had to go out to Montana to bring Uncle Amer home."

"Why couldn't Ray go along? Or go instead of you? After all, he's the elder. Isn't that usually how important decisions are made?"

"Cal wondered the same thing. Honestly, he was too emotional, rather fragile. At least that's how he acted. My folks felt they had to protect him. Whatever was going to happen out west, Dad knew I could handle it better than Ray."

"To know that and be left behind must have hit him terribly hard."

"I suppose so. He was especially close to Amer, a lot like him in some ways. Difference was, Amer could do a full day's labor and then some. Ray threw an awful fit when Dad told him he couldn't go."

"I don't doubt that."

"Hell, he soon learned what hard work was all about. Although, the way Mother pampered him, I wouldn't be surprised if she took care of the farm all by herself while we were away."

"And possessive in later years. Didn't she try to break up his marriage at one point? Seems to me I heard words to that effect."

"Yes. There was talk. Some time ago."

What an earful I'm getting! Having already eaten my banana and sucked on a few *Lifesavers*, I take a big bite of apple.

"What was that noise, Will? I heard a crunching sound."

Then comes the squeak of a spring from Mom's easy chair. She would make a good teacher, with eyes and ears on every side of her head.

"Callie, come on out of there." She stoops over, lifts up the lace tablecloth, and begins to laugh. "This is too funny! What do you think you're doing?"

"Playing with Sam?" I offer, swallowing my chunk of apple.

"We know better than that, Cal," Dad calls from the living room. "You're far too old for this sort of thing. Better join us. You've apparently heard all we've said so far, anyhow."

I crawl out from under the table, feeling a bit sheepish, and sit on the floor with my back against the couch. Sam Cat and Tequila squirrel in next to me while I finish my apple. Cramped from sitting hunched over in a space I outgrew long ago, I stretch my legs and tilt my head back against the sofa cushion, happy to be out in the open, pleased to be treated like an adult.

Far into the night, we talk about Aunt Eloise's behavior, especially at Grandad's funeral, and how it likely has affected Jen. I tell Mom and Dad about our long-ago bike ride and the fact that Jenny refused to discuss anything that had to do with her mother.

"Except with Belle, at the tavern. Jen told her a little bit."

"Belle is a woman to be trusted," says Dad. "Children and animals gravitate to her."

Mom smiles. "I'm glad you had that time with Jen. She's had a hard life. I just hope she can come out of it all right."

We talk about what it means to be psychotic and suicidal. Mom wonders if we'll soon get a late-night phone call.

"He might not even bother to notify us, if something happens to Eloise."

"What if something happens to Ray first?" Mom shivers. "I just had an awful thought, Will—what if she harms Ray or Jen?"

"Better left unsaid, Em."

That thought sends shivers through me, too.

ALTHOUGH UNCLE RAY AVOIDS US while in Masterton, I sometimes see him at the hospital, laughing with the nurses and looking in on other patients—probably on the chance of selling them a life insurance policy. He says hello to me as if I were just some kid off the street. I can tell how full of baloney he is, but at the same time I'm drawn in by his charm and slick energy—an energy that makes sick people perk up.

"He's their Pied Piper, by God," says Dad. "He'd figure a way to lead 'em down the corridor and out into the world if he could sell them Fidelity Mutual."

The few times I saw my uncle before Grandad died, he reminded me of Montgomery Clift, my favorite actor. I loved him in *From Here to Eternity*. Uncle Ray doesn't exactly look like him and he isn't shy like Montgomery, but there is something similar in the way they move. And there is that sense of vulnerability, actions that can never quite hide a wound.

Five years ago, when I was eight, I was impressed and hung around Uncle Ray, waiting for him to notice me, waiting for the silly attention uncles are supposed to pay their nieces, like the attention my friends' uncles gave them when they were little: a pat on the head that musses the hair, a dime for my pocket, silly questions like, "Where's your nose?" "Cat got your tongue?" "Who's your boyfriend?" I waited and waited. After a while, I stopped hanging around him.

Sometimes, while I read short stories to Gram from the books Mom got from the encyclopedia salesman, Ray comes in, nods at me, walks up to the bed, and recites his usual lines: "Hello, Mother. How're we doing today? You're looking better . . . I went out to the lake this afternoon . . . Ice fishing is good . . . They're catching big crappies and some northerns . . . Well, see you tomorrow." Then, after planting a quick kiss on Gram's forehead and waving a limp hand in my direction, he leaves.

After my uncle goes, the room feels strangely empty, even though he's been in it for only a short time. I gaze for a minute at the hollow doorway, and then look back at Gram. She seems to be looking in that direction, too. And then I go on reading:

> "You say that you bought a necklace of diamonds to replace mine," said Madame Forestier.
>
> "Yes; and you never found it out! They were so much alike," and she smiled proudly.
>
> Touched to the heart, Madame Forestier took the poor, rough hands in hers, drawing her tenderly toward her, her voice filled with tears: "Oh, my poor Mathilde! But mine were false. They were not worth more than 500 francs at most."

What Doctor Grimm has been telling our family might happen, does. Shortly after the amputation, the healing stops mid-way. Gram insists that the leg is still there, that it pains her and itches a lot. Once, while the nurses were changing the bandages, I peeked at the raw, oozing stump, and felt sick. How long does it take to heal something so awful as that?

"I can walk off the pain," she says "if only those damned nurses would let me out of bed. I want to go home where I belong."

"It'll take some more time, Gram," I tell her.

"I want to get back to my piano, my music. I had a dream, you know, when I was a girl."

"What, Grandma? What was your dream?"

"If only my parents had had the money, I could have sailed to Germany, studied to be a concert pianist."

"I didn't know that, Gram."

"Why not?"

"You never told me."

Now, in spite of all the past hard feelings, I wish my grandmother's dream could have come true. It might have made her a different person. I picture her on stage at Carnegie Hall, a tiny woman sitting before a shiny black concert grand, filling the auditorium with the soulful *"Mio Babbino Caro"*—a song that would like to make you cry.

"We're your audience, Gram. We have been all along."

Propped against pillows, she looks at me.

"And I'm glad you taught me how to play."

She looks at me more closely. This time, she smiles.

For a while, during the next week, Gram seems to improve.

"Maybe she can come home," I tell Dad, "and play her old songs again."

But it doesn't last. Within a few days, she grows quiet and acts as though she doesn't care whether we visit her or not—except once, when she thought I was her sister and Dad and Uncle Ray were her brothers come all the way from Illinois. When the gangrene takes over and her kidneys start to fail, we know she is going to die.

Every day after work and again after supper, Dad sits next to her bed. He leaves the room whenever Ray swings in.

A glad moment that will forever stay with my dad is this:

While dozing in his chair, he awakened to hear Gram singing "Mister Dunderback," a song she taught to anyone willing to learn it.

"And there she was," says Dad, "singing her heart out."

I imagine Gram's high, raspy voice, only weaker now:

Oh, say, old Mister Dunderback, how can you be so mean?

I'm sorry that you ever did—invent that old machine.

Now the dogs and the cats and the bobtail rats can never more be seen,
for you've ground them up in sausage meat—in that wonderful machine . . .

"Mother was more alert than I've seen her in weeks. She looked straight at me, like when she was a young woman and had something important to say. She sang and sang, and then I joined in and when we came to the end, she whispered, 'You're a good boy, Willy.'"

Dad's voice breaks. He lurches up from the kitchen table and rushes out the back door.

Gram died in the middle of the night, February 26, 1958—during Mom's watch. When it was time, Mom called home from the nurse's station. Afterward, she told us about the trouble she had trying to reach us.

"I'm afraid I woke up the whole hospital when Betty Lou Fry came on the line—'Number please'—and I shouted, '471W—Please hurry!'"

We never heard the phone ringing, partly because of where it's cradled—in a nook between the kitchen and dining room—and partly because Dad was so tired he couldn't wake up. Uncle Ray didn't hear his call either. Liz, of course, is in Mankato. And I sleep through everything.

Things have a strange way of working out in a family. Like, at the end, Mom being alone with the woman who hated her and wanted her gone. She told us how she stroked Gram's arm to help ease her out and that Gram lay very still with her muscles relaxed and her body sinking deeper into the bed.

"Julia opened her eyes for a minute and looked at me," said Mom. "Even lifted her hand a little as if to reach out. But it fell back onto the sheets. All I could do was watch those blue veins pulse out. She left without a fight."

At first, I think it's sad that Dad and Uncle Ray couldn't be at Gram's bedside. But, on second thought, they did say goodbye in their own way. Especially Dad, singing with Gram like that and what she said to him at the end. Her last words were a gift.

As for me—I guess I said goodbye, but I'm not sure. All I know is that Gram lost her music a long time ago. I don't feel quite as sad as when Grandad died. And as Liz says, "You can only build so much on what might have been."

Twenty-Two

Babbino Caro

THE MORNING AFTER GRAM DIED, Uncle Ray left for Sioux City, saying he'd return with Aunt Eloise and Jen. My parents met with Reverend Weiker and Mr. Kimmel, in order to finalize the funeral arrangements. Then they spent the rest of the day calling friends and relatives.

Jenny—I can't wait to see her. I wonder what she looks like at fourteen. Does she have a boyfriend? Maybe she can stay with us for a few days and we could do stuff together, go to a show, meet up with my friends.

The day before the funeral, Liz and Brian came home from Mankato. While Dad and Brian take Tequila for a walk, the rest of us spend the afternoon making ham sandwiches and gluey fruit salad with miniature marshmallows, fancy-cut carrot sticks and radish florets.

"When are Ray and his family coming?" asks Liz. "I haven't seen those people in ages—since Grandad died."

"Hard to say." Mom's voice is edgy. "Five minutes before the service is my best guess."

"Especially if he stops for a haircut. And to see a client."

"What do you mean, Callie?"

"That's what he did after Dad called to let him know how sick Gram was. He just took his own sweet time driving up from Sioux City."

"That doesn't surprise me. He's always been egocentric."

For once, I don't need to run for the dictionary.

"Wouldn't you think he'd like to see Hannah and Nellie?" asks Mom. "Those cousins are making the trip from Rockford—the last of the Lindstroms still living in Illinois."

"Well, I can't wait to see Jenny! I wish she lived closer."

"Oh, sweetheart, so do I. For her sake, as well as yours. After all, you and Liz are the only cousins she has."

Liz puts an arm around my neck and playfully rubs her knuckles against the side of my head. "When things settle down, brat, you'll have to spend another weekend with me on campus. It's my last year there, so we'd better do it soon. We could go to that ski hill."

"Yippee, that'll be fun! I'll wear that sweater you made!" I hug Liz. "When can I?"

"Next month. Okay, Mom?"

"Just say when and we'll drive her to Mankato. She can stand to get away for a few days."

"Whew! That's for damn sure."

"Oh, Callie." Mom heaves a sigh. "So elegantly stated, as usual."

Last October, my sis and her roommates took me to a college football game and out for pizza. We stayed up all night in their dorm room, eating popcorn and chocolate chip cookies and drinking cokes with salted peanuts poured inside the bottles. They talked about cute guys, sock-hops, and beer-busts down by the river.

I can hardly wait for this funeral day to be over.

After a light kick at the door and a "Yoo-hoo!" Aunt Hazel, out of breath, staggers in with a huge coffee maker.

"Oh, here," says Mom, tossing her dishcloth onto the counter, "let me help you with that."

"It's from the Catholic church basement, don't you know," she whispers loudly, glancing over her shoulder as if someone from Saint Therese has followed her. "Sixty-four cups! I don't think they'll notice. Besides, it's for a good cause."

"What's good about it?" I mutter.

Aunt Hazel scowls at me just like Mrs. Swenson did when I passed out tallies.

It's serious business whenever things Catholic and Protestant intermingle. The priests and nuns don't like it when their Catholics date Protestants. They throw them out of the Church if their parishioners marry non-Catholics (unless they convert, like Aunt Hazel). The nuns scold us kids for dipping our grubby Protestant fingers in their "holy water." So, I guess it stands to reason that Aunt Hazel will likely go to hell if she's caught sneaking the Catholic coffee maker into a Protestant house. I wonder what happens when a really serious sin is committed by one of their own.

Several Lutheran church ladies and members of Mom's 500 Club stop by with dessert bars and gallons of lemonade. Dad and Brian, returned from their constitutional, set up card tables, chairs, and TV trays.

Everything is ready for the after-funeral luncheon.

Around a hundred people take up the pews inside the Lutheran Church. Before the service begins, Mrs. Claussen plays the organ at full stop, triple forte, full speed ahead—somewhere between allegro and presto—a new protestant idea about an "upbeat celebration of eternal life after death." Rather than drag everyone down with a dirge-like largo, Mrs. Claussen goes at it until her butt dances on the bench.

Dad keeps turning around to look for Uncle Ray, and then sighs as he focuses again on Gram. I look for Jen, then back at Gram lying in her pale bronze casket just a few feet from us. Seeing her gray-white hair looking like straw doesn't upset me the way Grandad's did. Probably because Gram looked far worse than this each time she came out of the oven after washing that hair. Her eyebrows, though, seem bushier and her nose larger than I remember. And her face is plumper than when she lay dying in the hospital.

Reverand Weiker sits on a chair against the wall of the chancel, clutching his Bible and shifting his feet. Reminds me of when he sat on the dock at Bible Camp, swishing his legs in the water alongside Mrs. Ecklund, the church secretary. I miss Pastor Gullsvig ever since he transferred to the church in Black Duck.

Just as Mrs. Claussen launches her last bombastic chords up to the rafters and slides off the bench, Reverand Weiker approaches the pulpit in his white robe with the green and gold shawl. Everyone rises like cornstalks as he extends his hands and arms toward the crowd, like Jesus blessing the multitudes.

At that moment, Uncle Ray, Aunt Eloise, and Jen file into the front pew opposite us. I lean forward with a big smile and wave at Jen, surprised at how tall she's gotten since the last time I saw her. She looks at me once, without returning the smile, without a little wave even, then tosses her long dark hair and sits down next to her mother.

"Mom," I whisper, "why'd she snub me like that?"

Silent and facing straight ahead, Mom puts her arm around my shoulders and draws me to her side.

At the end of the service, Mr. Kimmel oozes forward to lower the lid on Gram. He hasn't changed much since Grandad's funeral, except for being more stooped over. And his eyes still have that weird look from working over too many dead bodies. Anyhow, that's what I think. Finally, everyone rises with a noisy *kerchunk* and we follow the pallbearers as they wheel Gram down the aisle and out to the idling hearse.

About half as many people as at Grandad's funeral come to our house after the graveside service. They eat standing next to the piano or at the buffet, or sit huddled around the dining table and at card tables set up in the living room. Some perch on the sofa, balancing plates and coffee cups on their knees. The luckier ones use end tables and TV trays.

I wander around, watching Dad smile through his sadness, listening to what people have to say about Grandma Julia, wondering, at first, if they're talking about *my* grandmother.

"She was the nicest lady," says one woman. "We think of her each time we use that beautiful silver tray she gave us as a wedding gift."

"And could she play the piano! Right along with the orchestras on the radio."

"I remember the twinkle in her eyes. She was always such a lot of fun, a real storyteller."

"What I remember are the fish fries out at Lake Shetek. She sure could catch those northerns, right alongside Vic."

"And clean and fry 'em."

"She wasn't a bad shot either. Yes, sir, she kept right up with Vic in her day."

"A lovely woman. Very generous."

"Yep. Julia and Vic. Quite a pair. Raised two fine boys . . ."

"By the way, Will, where *is* that brother of yours? I haven't had a chance to talk with him yet."

"He should be along any minute."

Liz and Dad and I have been keeping a lookout, wondering what could be holding them up. After an hour, they still haven't arrived.

"Probably went back to Sioux City," whispers Liz, making the rounds with another platter of sandwiches.

"I rather hope they did," says Mom. "Eloise made it through the service without calling attention to herself and managed to keep still at the cemetery. How she'll behave here is anyone's guess."

Just as I reach for a pumpkin bar from a large tray on the dining room table, the phone rings right next to my ear. It's Mrs. Tofte and she sounds upset.

"Callie, I need to speak to your father right away."

Mrs. Tofte had gone directly home after the funeral, said she wasn't feeling well.

I find Dad in the living room, visiting with his cousins, Hannah and Nellie, who, in their Swedish brogues, have just extended an invitation to visit them in Rockford.

"Any time, Will," says Hannah.

"And bring the family," Nellie adds.

When I tell Dad who is on the line, he looks worried. He follows me to the dining room, picks up the phone, and stretches the cord around the wall as far as it will reach into the kitchen.

"Uh-huh—Is that so?—I'll be right over—Thanks for letting me know."

"Cal," he says, hanging up the phone, "ask Mom to come in here. Liz, too."

When the three of us have assembled, he tells us in a strained voice, "Mrs. Tofte just called. Ray and Eloise are ransacking Mother's house."

"Oh, for heaven's sake." Mom's shoulders droop.

The four of us move toward the basement entry for more privacy.

"He can't get by with this," Dad says through clenched teeth. "I'm going over there now."

"Try to stay calm, Will. It's not worth getting into a fight over."

"What do you want us to do?" asks Liz.

"Keep this quiet around the company. I'll be back as soon as I can."

I follow Dad out the back door and around to the garage.

"You stay here, Cal. I'll handle this."

"Dad, I've been in on it *all* since the beginning. I'm going with you."

He nods. I jump in the car.

As we drive the cold streets we've walked together nearly every Tuesday night for years, it strikes me how often Dad has been driving lately—to the hospital, to work, everywhere.

We turn the corner and pull up behind Uncle Ray's black Cadillac parked in front of Gram's house. The trunk is open, already loaded with the good silverware, pots and pans, boxes of dishes, and a stack of piano music. I spot the Vincello cigar box off to one side.

Mrs. Tofte is peeking through her kitchen blinds.

Just as Dad and I get out of the car and start up the sidewalk, Uncle Ray, Aunt Eloise, and Jen come out of the house, each carrying an armload of blankets, pillows, sheets, and towels.

"Hold it right there!" Dad stands his ground as if he were wearing a pair of six-shooters.

I edge up next to him and glare at Jen, who stays close to her mother. It has been nearly five years since I've seen my cousin, since her face had that frantic look in the church basement after Grandad's funeral—a look that said she'd rather stay with us than go back to Sioux City with her crazy mother. And it's been six years since that day at the lake when we had such fun biking around Tepeeotah and Slaughter Slough, searching for arrowheads and visiting with Belle at her tavern. Now, with barely a hint of the playful look she once had, she seems hard and much older than fourteen. I can tell she doesn't like us anymore.

"Put everything back," Dad orders, "back where it came from."

"Aw, go to hell," snarls my aunt, her voice low and husky from cigarettes.

"Yes sir, true to form." Dad laughs sarcastically and his voice rises an octave. "You sure know how to pick 'em, Ray. A real treasure, that one."

Uncle Ray looks nervous, caught red-handed, but Aunt Eloise brushes past us with a pile of sheets and towels, which she tosses into the back seat of their car. She plunks down on the passenger side, makes a big production of locking her door, and lights a cigarette. Jen gets into the back seat without another glance in my direction.

"Mother and Dad never brought us up to act this way," says Dad, his voice starting low and growing louder. "What the hell's the *matter* with you?"

"This town's all yours," says Uncle Ray with a sarcastic drawl. "We won't be coming back. I'm taking our share now."

Dad's hands turn to fists and I'm afraid they're going to fight. Again.

"You're even a bigger jackass than I thought!" he shouts.

I look around and spot more neighbors peeking at us through curtains and from doorways. Dad must notice, too, because he unclenches his fists and switches to a lower voice: "Drop those things and get the hell out of here."

Ray lets the pile of folded blankets fall from his arms into the snow, then stands with his hands on his hips, facing Dad. I scurry around to the trunk of their car, grab a stack of sheet music and snatch up the cigar box. My heart pounds as I take back as much as I can carry in the crook of my arm. Out of breath, I jump into our car before anyone sees me and roll down the window in case there's a big blowup. But there are no more words.

My uncle steps around to the rear of his car and carefully lowers the trunk lid. Then he gets in next to Eloise and guns the big engine. This time, tires don't spit gravel. Uncle Ray simply drives away—slowly. I watch the back of Jen's head until they are out of sight, hoping she'll at least turn around for one last look at us. She never does.

Dad stands gazing after them, the determined expression still on his face.

"I'll be right back, Cal," he says, scooping the blankets from the snow. "I'm going to check on things in the house and lock up—have a word with Mrs. Tofte."

I wait in the passenger's seat, wishing that Tequila and Sam Cat were with me. They know how to make a person feel better.

After a few minutes, Dad returns to our car, still calm. But that changes as soon as he gets in behind the wheel and I show him the things I saved from Uncle Ray's trunk.

"See?" I open the box filled with pictures. On top are Dad and Ray's christening portraits and the photo of Uncle Amer in front of his soddy in Montana. "And I saved a bunch of Gram's music! Look!" I shuffle through the stack, calling out titles: "Beautiful Dreamer," "Madama Butterfly," "The Lost Chord," "*Mio Babbino Caro.*"

I look up, expecting Dad to be pleased. Instead, he sits clutching the steering wheel while tears roll down his cheeks. I feel scared, unsure what to do. I've never seen my dad cry before. I mean, really cry. He starts the engine. I take his arm and lean my head against his shoulder, keeping it there until we reach home.

After the company leaves and it is dark out and very quiet, the four of us sit together in the living room.

Dad breaks the silence.

"Now I am an orphan," he says abruptly.

We look at him, at his sadness and at our own.

"I thought orphans were little kids," I whisper.

"No," he says. "When the second parent dies, you're an orphan, no matter how old you are."

Twenty-Three

When Hope Yells "Sucker"

O N A TUESDAY NIGHT IN MAY, several months after the funeral, Dad asks me to join him for a constitutional. I tell him I don't care to check on Gram's house again and see the FOR SALE sign still posted in front. He says that this time we'll go in the opposite direction—to the Mint Café for maple nut ice cream. Tequila, too. I invite Mom, but she says, "No, this is your time with Papa. I'm going to work on your birthday present. It'll be a surprise."

I've already found several balls of blue and cream yarn in the back of a closet, along with a half-finished Norwegian cardigan.

"Oh, give me a hint, Ma."

"No, now off you go."

As we head toward Main Street, Dad and I talk about the old scandal and wonder how Everett Christensen and Ruby Ryan are doing in prison. Everett's wife, Thelma, makes quilts with the ladies' church guild. Carl Ryan works days at the Worthmore, and spends evenings and weekends with his two boys.

"Who was that jealous boyfriend from Sioux Falls, Dad? The one Everett Christensen told us about?"

"I don't know that he existed. Everett most likely fabricated the idea. But I'm still wondering who sold Ruby that life insurance policy."

We reach the Mint Cafe and sit in a booth with Tequila between us.

"What a *darling* little dog!" cries Shirley Olson, one of the newer waitresses. "Cute, cute!" she squeals with an exaggerated fluttering of her hands.

"Mushy, mushy," I mutter under my breath.

"She *is* adorable. How much does she weigh?"

"Not sure," Dad says, stroking Tequo's beige coat.

"Here, let me put her on the meat scale. I'll bring her right back."

"See that you do." Dad winks at Shirley in a friendly way.

She laughs over her shoulder on the way to the kitchen. I follow her, ready to rescue Tequila shivering in a silver pan chained to the arm of a large scale.

"Three pounds." Shirley hands her over to me. "Exactly three pounds," she repeats loudly, following us back to our booth.

"Almost enough for a good stew," says Dad.

I frown and slide in beside him, clasping our little dog to my chest.

Shirley carries on as if Dad were George Gobel.

"Between you and your brother, I don't know who's more of a riot," she gasps. "How *is* Raymond, by the way? We miss him around here."

She grins at me as if I must have the greatest uncle in the world.

How will Dad answer that?

"Ray's in Sioux City," he says, with a faint smile. "After Mother's funeral, it was back to business, as usual."

"My sympathy, Will. Be sure to greet Raymond for me. His friend, too. Tell him we miss his jokes. Such a breath of fresh air around here."

"I'll do that, next time we see him. Now, Cal, all set to order?"

I talk Dad into banana splits—the size served in glass boats.

"I could go for that," he says.

As we spoon down our chocolate, vanilla, and strawberry ice cream (feeding Tequila lumps of frozen strawberries and bits of banana), I glance around the cafe, wondering where my uncle sat for his meals, imagining the laughter between him and the waitresses and whoever else came in. I ask myself the same question that has troubled me for a long time: Why would anyone treat strangers better than his own family? By now, I've collected a ton of information about my aunt and uncle, but none of it gives me the answer.

Recently, Dad has been getting mail from relatives who hear from Uncle Ray. And because they know about the estrangement, these same relatives forward Ray's letters to Dad:

From his cousin Millie, in La Jolla:

> "...Eloise has been diagnosed with psychotic disorders called para-noid-schizophrenia and manic-depression and she is driving Ray crazy! He says that because she imagines no one likes her and that everyone is her enemy, she makes it come true. For example, anyone criticizing President Eisenhower is really attacking her. And she thinks Senator Joe McCarthy should go down as an American hero. Can you imagine?!!!"

After reading that letter aloud, Dad tosses it onto the table. "She's more tetched than I thought."

According to another relative, Eloise trusts only one person: her neighbor, Myra Sturbridge. Best friends, they get together every morning for martinis and Lucky Strikes. From the sounds of things, Myra Sturbridge never disagrees with Eloise.

As for my uncle, I feel a little sorry for him living in that mess, wondering if he would have been friendlier all these years had I teased and pestered him when I was little. What if I'd tugged at his hand and said, "C'mon, Uncle Ray, let's go fishing." Mom always says, "Everyone needs a little encouragement now and again."

As time passes, however, I become less concerned about my uncle and more worried about Dad. Especially whenever the cubby door above the kitchen sink slams shut and the whiskey goes "glou-glou-glou" into a glass. In the middle of the first drink, he swears he'll knock some sense into Ray if he ever sees the "S.O.B." again. After his second round, the irritability disappears and angry words give over to reminiscences about hunting and fishing and traveling with his brother when they were young and single and enjoying life.

"We drove to all the big dance halls in our 1927 Ford Model T," he says, dreamy-eyed, "in search of pretty girls and swing music—The Hollyhock in Hatfield, Valhalla at Lake Shetek, the Arkota in Sioux Falls. Crowds packed the ballrooms in those days." Dad hitches a shoulder in rhythm to an imagined tune. "Remember Lawrence Welk, Emily?"

"And Guy Lombardo." Mom sets her own rhythm, slapping chunks of hamburger into thin patties, my signal to set the table.

"And don't forget Tiny Little and his Toe Teasers," chimes Dad, sliding into a fancy dance step.

"You're kidding!" I burst out laughing. "Tiny Little and his Toe Teasers?"

It's fun to say the words and I keep repeating them until my giggles become uncontrollable.

"Oh, Callie," says Mom. "You're just like Liz when she was your age. Titter, titter over everything."

"Was he really tiny or . . . ?"

"Portly." Mom begins to giggle, too.

"Tee-hee, tee-hee," mimics Dad. "I don't care what anyone says. Tiny Little was great."

"Oh, he was *great*, all right!"

Dad leans against the kitchen counter and raises his glass in a toast: "Here's to the big bands!" He gulps down the whiskey.

"And his was a big one!" Mom laughs.

After a few minutes our giggles subside.

"I especially like Paul Whiteman," Dad says, wiping his lips with the back of his hand and slurring his words like Dean Martin. "Matter of fact, his orchestra was playing in Dell Rapids, South Dakota when . . ." He frowns suddenly. "Hell, that was the night Ray met Eloise—the night he got *smitten*."

Dad's sudden flare up startles me. The way he spits out the word "smitten" reminds me of all the times Gram talked mean about my mother.

"I warned him. Tried to reason with him, but he was *stubborn*. He's the most stubborn guy I know. 'What the hell's the matter with you?' I told him, 'You don't even know the woman.'"

"What was Eloise like back then?" I'm curious about Dad's lazy river of words. Mom casts an eye on him as she dishes up the corn for supper.

"Oh, she was a looker, Eloise was. I have to admit. And a good dancer." With glass in hand, he holds his arms aloft, and does his routine soft shoe number. "Yes, she sure could swing."

"Better than me?" asks Mom, pretending a slight and likely trying to change the drift of this conversation.

"Of course not, sweetheart. No one dances better than you."

Dad sets his glass down on the counter and plucks my mother away from the stove, twirling her around the kitchen, through the dining room and into the living room, high stepping, gliding, hitching a shoulder. In spite of the whiskey, they dance like Marge and Gower Champion. Mom spins round and round, her arms floating like gauze in a breeze.

Suddenly, there is smoke and a sizzling sound.

"Oh!" she cries, running back to the kitchen, "the hamburgers are burning!"

After a few waltz steps of my own, I sit down at the table, dreaming of the swirl of life inside that ballroom—beautiful women, handsome men all dressed in finery.

In my mind's eye, Uncle Ray wears a black pinstripe suit, white and black wingtips, his hair brilliantined. He stands on tiptoe, gazing over the crowd until he sees her—the woman who will change his life—elegant and seductive in a deep purple gown. The folds ripple as she sways in rhythm, watching this man, my uncle, threading his way through the crowd, drawn to her like an ant to sweet poison. They lock eyes. Like my Prince Charming and Cinderella wind-up dolls, the two circle and glide around the dance floor beneath a sparkling glass ball that twists slowly overhead, throwing flecks of light all over the room.

Mom interrupts my daydream, just as I imagine Rock Hudson taking me in his arms.

"Then what happened, Will?" She places a bowl of steaming whipped potatoes on the table next to me. A dollop of butter melts in its crater.

I scowl at Mom for ruining my dream, but she is looking at Dad.

"Within three days, he proposed, the damned fool! Wouldn't even come back home to Minnesota at the end of our vacation. When the folks saw me driving up the lane by myself, they rushed out into the yard, wondering what had happened. Dad didn't say a word, but Mother cried and carried on, blamed me for leaving Ray behind. Good thing he returned the following week to collect his things. Then she could see and hear all about it for herself. He drove Eloise's car, but *she* never bothered to come with him."

"Off to a good start." Mom sets a bottle of ketchup and the platter of crispy hamburgers with fried onions in the center of the table.

"There he was, twenty-five years old and Mother still babying him, begging him to stay at home, bawling her head off. I gave up. Dad stayed out of it. After a couple of days, Ray drove back to Dell Rapids and that's the last we saw of him. Until two weeks later when we went to the wedding—Ray asked me to be Best Man."

"That's a surprise, Dad."

"Not really. We were still getting along back then."

"My, what a whirlwind." Mom shakes her head. "Hardly time enough for Eloise to get to know the family."

"And vice versa. My folks hadn't been properly introduced. Eloise never did come to the farm, even after the wedding. In fact, I don't believe she ever saw the place before the folks sold it and moved out to the lake. Mother and Dad tried to make the best of it, but they felt awkward, especially at the reception. What a disaster that was!"

"Why? What happened?"

"Eloise acted nutty all afternoon, hanging onto her father's arm, calling him 'Daddy' this and 'Daddy' that. 'Why cain't I, Daddy? Huh? Why cain't I?' she kept repeating in some kind of childish, phony accent, as if she were from Georgia. I have *no* idea what that was about."

"What about her mother?"

"She always seemed to be in the background. Like a maid."

"Eloise was an only child, wasn't she?" asks Mom.

"Yes, and she behaved like a spoiled brat, miffed if the attention wasn't focused on her. I can still see her sitting on her folks' patio, pounding at the billows in her wedding gown, pouting and glaring at everybody. She was a completely different woman from the one we'd met at the dance."

"Didn't Ray realize his mistake?"

"If he did, he never let on. He'd had a few drinks by then, laughed it off. I suppose he thought it was cute. But then how do you dump someone on the same day you marry her? Eloise was sick, all right. Should have been in the loony bin all along. At first I figured she was jealous."

"Of what?"

"Well, when I asked Ray if he was going to make it home for duck hunting in the fall, you'd have thought I was hatching a plot. The look on her face—it's hard to explain—it'd turned ugly."

"I take it," says Mom with a smirk, "that she never cared to hunt or fish."

Dad chuckles and reaches down to stroke Sam Cat who is smoothing his whiskers against a chair leg.

A big supper, a tall glass of milk, and time have shored up Dad's slurred words.

He musses my hair, kisses Mom on the cheek, and thanks her for a "delicious supper. Delicious, Emily," he lilts, "in spite of the charred hamburgers—through no fault of your own, of course. Now, ladies, it's time for my evening constitutional. Be back shortly."

I'm relieved that Dad is back to his old self, grateful that he doesn't get mean and stay that way all night, like my friend's dad.

After the dishes and piano practice, I plunk down next to Tequila curled up on the sofa. All around the living room are our family pictures—on the end tables, on the walls above the piano and sofa and easy chairs: Liz and me at various ages, both sets of grandparents, and Mom and Dad holding hands in front of the stone fireplace at the lake when they were young. What do the walls look like in my uncle's house? Are there pictures of Jenny?

At first, it surprises me that Dad is only now telling us these details about how Uncle Ray and Aunt Eloise met and about their wedding. But on second thought, from my observations of men during my nearly fourteen years, I've come to the conclusion that they usually don't elaborate about such things. At least, not until something triggers it—like the letter delivered this afternoon; one that Mom refers to as *The Dispatch*. After the initial reading, she tucked it into a dresser drawer, only to pull it out after the dishes were put away.

Dad, returned from his walk, sits down with us in the living room, as soon as he sees Mom reading the letter again.

I have a hunch that *The Dispatch* will remain close for a long time, ready to be trotted out whenever we need proof positive that Aunt Eloise is way off the beam.

"She's to be pitied, really," says Mom, folding and unfolding the single sheet of light beige stationery. (She always says that about people—that they're to be pitied.) "But this letter. How could anyone in her right mind send something like this?"

"She's *not* in her right mind," I mumble around a fresh stick of Black Jack chewing gum. "That's the whole point. How come you won't let me read it?" I lick the licorice-flavored juice from my lips. "What does it say?"

Mom unfolds *The Dispatch* for the third time and looks at Dad. "What do you think, Will? Should Callie hear this?"

"Might as well. She's been in on all our business since she was born. Besides, she'll likely "discover" the letter for herself, no matter where you hide it."

I grin at Dad.

"What's more," he says peering at me over his new horn-rimmed glasses, "by the looks of those black teeth, I'd say there's a pirate in our midst."

After a burst of laughter, I settle back to enjoy my cud, ready for *The Dispatch*.

With shock and indignation in her voice, Mom slowly reads each sentence aloud, emphasizing certain words:

> *The last time we saw you was a* nightmare. *Ray and I do* not *agree with your* politics *or your* religion *or how to* raise a child *or anything else for that matter. We're a* happy, tight *little family and we* want *nothing* more to do with you. Don't *ever* call or darken our doorstep again . . .

I nearly choke on my gum. No one has ever spoken to my parents that way. Even when my sister and I quarrel, we never think of telling one another to buzz off forever.

True, Dad told them off when we caught them taking all those things from Gram's house after the funeral. And he likes to talk religion and politics. He loves to debate, even argue at times. But to be punished for his opinions? That's crazy. Besides, when was the last time they'd even *had* a conversation with my dad?

Mom folds *The Dispatch*. Dad slumps on the couch, round-shouldered, looking sad and defeated. But by the time Mom sticks the letter back into its envelope and gets up to put it away, and before I can start to worry, he unfolds his arms, throws back his shoulders, and straightens up like an inflatable. The familiar tight set of his lips and the glint in his eyes remind me of an election year.

This very night, he begins plotting a campaign—not for county office, but to win back his brother.

"I have a plan," he announces.

Mom and I exchange glances.

"We've been down this pike before, Will."

"No, this is a new one. I'll begin by writing a letter back. But only to *Ray*."

"It'll just end up in the garbage, unopened."

"Or returned to sender, Dad."

"We'll travel to Sioux City. Stop at their house."

"You'd dare darken their doorstep? What if she shoots you?"

"I'll try phoning first. Soften them up. Every week, if that's what it takes."

"Your calls will go unanswered, or the usual slam in your ear."

Eloise always hangs up on him. If Ray answers, there's a minute or two for the trading of accusations before the final click: "You'd better return the things you took from Mother's house: her good dishes and silverware, pots and pans, bedding. Do the right thing, Ray. Bring it all back!"

"You should talk, Will! You've got Dad's guns and decoys! All his tools!"

"You never wanted any of his things after he died. Said you had enough of your own."

Slam. Click.

Dad's plan seems foolish, unhealthy, even—just more of the same. Except for the idea of traveling to Sioux City for a confrontation. That part is new. With so little reward and a lot of anger, how long will he be able to stay the course before hope yells *Sucker!*?

"Oh, Will," says my mother in a tired voice, "here you go again."

"God damn it! I'll get that guy if it's the last thing I do."

"Who's the crazy one *now*?"

Dad gets up from the davenport and goes to the kitchen. After a moment, the cubby door slams shut.

Sometimes, I wonder how things might have been if Dad and Uncle Ray had really fought it out that time at the lake—like my neighbor Danny and me flailing at one another with one boxing glove each. I ran home crying with a bloody nose—something, at least, to show for our differences. What would have happened if I hadn't entered the ring that day and Uncle Ray hadn't rolled down the hill and into the lake? What if they'd talked things out instead? Just the two of them. What if there'd never been a crazy Aunt Eloise to poison everything?

The family grapevine grows with stories of heavy drinking, screaming fits, fights, and suicide attempts, mostly on account of petty disagreements and frustration over how to deal with their daughter.

"Jenny's not the problem," says Mom. "That poor girl's behavior is the result."

"Eloise swallowed another fistful of sleeping pills," writes Cousin Millie, "and Ray had to rush her back to the hospital."

"Eloise has been committed for the umpteenth time," writes Cousin Leona. "Jenny has finally had enough. She ran off with an exchange student from England. Ray travels more than ever for Fidelity Mutual."

"Holy Cow! I didn't think she was old enough to get married."

"I don't think marriage was the point, Cal," says Dad.

The one big question among the relatives is, "Will Ray remain faithful to his sick wife?"

"Well, he's still living with her," says Mom.

Dad snorts and rolls his eyes. "What a life!"

His side of the family is loaded with spies: Millie in La Jolla: Aunt Grace and Uncle Wayne in Pasadena: Leona in Lakeland, Florida: Hannah and Nellie Lindstrom in Rockford, Illinois. All of them hear regularly from Uncle Ray and forward his letters, notes, Christmas cards, and photos to us, along with their own interpretations and judgments.

Aunt Grace: "I let Ray know that the Lord is testing him. 'In God's name,' I wrote, 'remember your wedding vows—for better or for worse.'"

"I wouldn't blame him if he got out," writes Millie. "'Go ahead,' I told him, 'have a fling! Nothing better than a fling, believe you me!'"

In my estimation, that note confirms what it means to be unfaithful. I've heard that's what people do if they aren't happy at home. And sometimes even if they *are* happy. Last summer at Lutheran Bible camp, I spied our minister (who seems to care for his wife) sitting at the end of the dock playing footsies with Mrs. Ecklund, the church secretary. He kept looking at her with an idiot grin plastered across his face. This, after preaching the Ten Commandments and telling our class that all unbaptized people go to hell, including babies. I'm sure the minister and his secretary were baptized, but what about all that other crap they yammered about? Shouldn't Reverend Weiker have been playing footsies with his wife?

Now, after months of guesswork, not one relative can determine if Ray is being faithful or not. His letters never give them the satisfaction. *What's it to them, anyhow?*

This next letter, however, troubles us:

Dear Leona,

Things are about the same here. I'm nearly at the end of my rope. This morning, Eloise threw a fit over a burned pancake and runny eggs and ended up slapping me harder than usual. Threatened to run into traffic, said she'd sooner die than stay with me. If I don't humor her, she's bound to follow through and I don't think I could live with that.

She's only been out of the hospital a couple of weeks since her last attempt, more angry and resentful than ever. Some days I just don't know what to do. It's been especially hard on Jenny all these years. Now she's gone. I wondered how long she could take it. Sorry to write this—had to get it off my chest . . .

On a happier note, I hear the fish are biting in Lake Shetek. Soon time for fall hunting, too. I plan to drive up with my pal, Barber, for the opener. Let's hope there are plenty of mallards to go around . . . Love Ray

Dad studies the letter, the handwriting. "I sure don't like the sound of this. He's got to get out of there."

"What can *we* do about it, Will?"

"I don't know. Not sure."

He turns the page over and around and over again as if looking for a line with his name in it.

"Why can't he come fishing and hunting with *me*? She wouldn't have to know."

"Oh, Will. You sound like a sick calf. I have no idea—he's brainwashed or scared. Who knows? I think we should just let it go. You don't need this upset."

But letting go is not something Dad can do. The tougher the contest, the harder he fights. Uncle Ray becomes the challenge of the century. For the next thirty years, much of the time collecting dust, Dad's hat will lie in the center of the ring, while our lives go on around it.

"Time is the stream we go a-floating in."

~William Kloefkorn, *This Death by Drowning*

Part Two

Twenty-Four

Hugged by Cornfields ❖ *1981*

HE SELLING OF GRAM'S LITTLE PINK HOUSE, nearly a year after her death, was the first of those losses that erased my sense of belonging to Masterton and to my childhood. Dad contacted Mr. Reese, "an honest lawyer from Black Duck," to work out the details and function as go-between. He saw to it that Uncle Ray signed the necessary papers and received his share of the proceeds.

Although it stood empty much of the time, the cottage at Tepeeotah remained in the family for several more years—until the summer after my college graduation in 1966. Some folks refuse to let a place get under their skin. I'm not one of those. I didn't go back to see it sold. And I never returned to Lake Shetek.

"Perhaps," I told Liz, "when I'm a bit older."

Now, in September of 1981, our house in Masterton is the last of our dwellings to go. I have to return for that.

After thirty-five years as Maywood County auditor, Will Lindstrom is ready to leave for good.

"Too many changes," he says. "Time to fly when the country roads get outfitted with street signs. The moneybags finally got their way."

Much of the land where he used to hunt has been turned into grids of blacktop, sprouting subdivisions instead of wildwoods, and recreational facilities with fancy brick monuments paying abject homage to what has been replaced: Cottonwood Courts, Prairie Palisades, Willow Creek Golf Course.

"Hell, they look like tombstones to me," says Dad. "And the houses are so damned close together, I'll bet you could hear your neighbors sneeze in the middle of winter."

There are other changes along the way: Selmer and Clarence Johnson failed to show up on Main Street one morning to occupy their end of the cement ledge in front of the Maywood County Bank. They died within a week of each other, felled by old age and complications from the war. That left Norman Kust and Glen Lowe to hold down the fort for the time remaining to them.

Grant Van Vulsa and his team of draft horses are long gone. "Just sort of disappeared, when no one was looking. So, this is it, kids. Your mother and I are heading south with the geese and we'll follow them home in the spring."

While helping them pack up, Liz and I run across a few old toys, a tiny snowsuit, and little girl dresses Mom had sewn for us. I look for my Sparkle Plenty doll, but she's nowhere to be found. The large metal dollhouse that Santa brought when I was six, now dented and missing most of its pink plastic furniture, goes on the sale.

After the auction, we wagon-train out of town, Dad and Mom in their 1982 white Cadillac, followed by Liz and Brian in their green station wagon, and me in my red Dodge. We look like the last of Christmas leaving Masterton.

I focus on the rearview mirror as if it were a tiny television screen rolling fade-outs: our white rambler house with the green awnings, the apple trees, Dad's garden, the weeping willow, where I read books in summer, the giant blue spruce. Driving the length of Main Street, I say a silent goodbye to Marbella Kinmore's Fashionette (under new ownership), the Silver Star, the Mint Café, the library, and the Worthmore Meat and Dairy. Last to recede, at the distant beginning of Main Street, is the stately, red-brick courthouse. The final fade-out is the tall window near the arched entrance: Dad's office. Turning north onto the old highway hugged by cornfields, we pass Cemetery Creek and a sign that reads, "You are now leaving Masterton. Come again."

I left Masterton long ago, turning my attention to textbooks and teachers who spoke of things beyond my dreams. But the Southwest prairie never left me. Memories of this land are like reliable friends—the rushing creek that warbled and toyed with us kids in springtime, the black and caramel railroad trestle, smelling of sun-burnt creosote, offered up its timbers for climbing. The whispering tallgrass.

I will return in mind to broad pastures where cows crowd against barb-wired posts, snuffling at the right moments through moist, ringed nostrils while I recite *My Last Duchess*. I'll gallop down the slope to the gray-green inlets of Lake Shetek, where it is sometimes tranquil, sometimes cacophonous with geese and ducks, and its bays are teeming with pike and bullheads and the old snapping turtle who once paid me a visit. Time and again, Dad will pilot the ten-horse ride around the bay before docking our wooden boat. With a stringer of fish, we'll climb the steps to our cottage on Tepeeotah hill, shouting, "We're back!"

Twenty-Five

Apple Blossom Time

THE FOUR-HOUR JOURNEY FROM MASTERTON to Liz and Brian's house in Eau Claire, Wisconsin, gives me plenty of time to consider the changes in our lives. I think of the lines spoken by Emily in *Our Town*, when she says her final goodbyes to Grovers Corners. "Do any human beings ever realize life while they live it? Every every minute?"

As I, still among the living, remember some of our family minutes, I keep coming back to the same notion—that not going "home" again, to the house I'd grown up in, is like a death.

It's not as though I went back often. But when I did go home for happy occasions, and later on, for refuge, that place and old Tequila and the constancy of family gave me the strength I needed to battle a relentless storm. Warm meals served on Mom's good china and the quiet sorting of fishing tackle with Dad became references for survival, for when I had to return to my own home—where rage awaited me. Those tiny, delicate African violets painted on white china and the balsa lures Grandad had carved were among the talismans that kept me grounded.

"Won't you miss Masterton? Your friends? Our house?"

Mom's answer seemed geared toward easing the change for all of us.

"Of course, Callie. But keep in mind, once you turn your back on a place, you have no choice but to look forward. That is, unless you want to stew in your own juices, pining for a past that's impossible to hold onto."

"NO MORE LONG FACES," says Mom during a break from hauling boxes. "Your papa and I are off on a new adventure. This is our time now."

"Guess we'll have to take a cue from them." Liz sips her coffee. "Wherever you *go*, there you *are*."

"'Here and now, boys! Here and now!'" Brian raises his cup in a toast. "How does it feel to be retired, Will?"

"Well, I don't plan on being idle, I can tell you that."

"Did they throw you a big party at the court house?"

"Complete with banner above his office door." Mom traces her hand through the air. "Farewell to Our Man About Town."

"It was a wonderful send-off," Dad says wistfully.

Although I'm happy for them, I stew in my own juices for a while—nearly as much as when they sold the cottage at Tepeeotah, which prompted me to study the listings of lake property near the Twin Cities.

"I'm not surprised," Mom said at the time. "It's how your papa brought you up. Anyone living in Minnesota has to have her own lake. I'm happy for you, sweetheart."

"This is a fine spot, Cal," said Dad after a thorough inspection. He shaded his eyes for a good look at the bay. "Why, if I were twenty years younger, this is the kind of property I'd choose."

To celebrate, he bought me a little rowboat. "So you can get out there and catch a few when I'm not around."

He must have sensed my sudden feeling of aloneness then, because he quickly added, "You'll get things figured out, Cal. I'm not worried."

"Now that you're on your own," said Mom, "that is, not having to answer to old what's-his-name, you can do as you please. Come see us any time."

"Anytime," she says once again, skirting the boxes stacked in Liz and Brian's family room, deciding which items to leave and which to take with them on the road. "That goes for all of you."

"Because, you see," says Dad for the umpteenth time, "We're heading south . . ."

"With the geese!" we shout in chorus. "And you'll follow them home in the spring!"

Looking younger than his seventy-eight years, Dad sits down on a hassock and picks through his silver tackle box. "Now here's the plan."

"I think we already know the plan, Dad," says Liz.

"Yes, yes, but hear me out. By the way, where'd the kids go?"

"Down the basement, clearing a corner for your stuff."

"Oh, good . . . now for our plan."

As he enthuses about soaking up the California sunshine, dining on seafood, juicing his own oranges, walking barefoot on the beach, I feel left behind, curiously abandoned.

Mom pretend-shivers. "No more snow and cold for us. Brrr."

Her comment brings to mind the long, drawn-out Snow Belt winters, when we kids measured our annual growth according to the snowplow cuts through deep drifts along the streets of Masterton, and Tequila rode inside Dad's coat to Gram's house every Tuesday night. It seemed always to be winter, with our giant spruce towering above the rooftop, loaded with snow and swaying in a blizzard—the blue spruce that Dad planted when I was seven and could leapfrog over.

I glance at Liz, who gazes back at me with a sad smile.

"One thing, Will," says Mom, examining the left side of his face. "While we're in California, you should have that mole looked at. You've had it for so long, we kind of forget about it. I think it's getting larger."

"There are bound to be some specialists in San Diego," says Liz. "You'll have to stay out of the sun, though."

"Right. I might do that. Now, then, we'll get our things settled here, pack the car, and be on our way in a day or two."

"Do you have your route planned, Will?" asks Brian. Then he laughs. "Of course, you do. What a question. Where will you be stopping along the way?"

"Well, as I told Carl when he asked me that same question—'Here, there, and everywhere.'"

"*Here, there, and everywhere,*" Liz and I sing a few lines from the Beatles' tune.

Dad grins and sets his tidy tackle box aside, keeping out one of the lures.

"I'm sure going to miss that guy. Carl and the others. Hard to leave old friends."

"At least Carl's happy now." Mom opens another box. "He's got a very nice wife the second time around."

"Whatever happened to Ruby? And Everett Christensen?"

"Everett died in prison. He got to be so obese his heart couldn't take it. Thelma still lives in the same house, busy with her quilting and Ladies' Aid. As for Ruby, no one knows where she went after her sentence was up."

"We thought she'd come back to Masterton," says Dad. "At least to see her boys. But she never did. Of course they were all grown up by then."

He shows us the old lure he's been holding: a piece of balsa wood, shaped and fitted with scraps of tin for little fins and a bit of lead for weight. "Your grandad made this."

"I know. Are you ever going to fish with it?"

"Oh, I'd hate to lose the thing. Some day, I'll check out the action and then keep it for show."

Mom unwraps a gold-and-green vase and tosses the newspaper aside. Its front page catches my eye.

"What's this? I didn't know Doc Nelson died."

This section of *The Masterton Herald* contains columns of praise and two large photos of Bennett Nelson—in his doctor clothes at the clinic and in his cowboy outfit, leading a parade down Main Street atop his white horse. All I can hear is the noise he made pounding the counter at the courthouse and blasting his horn behind us kids on our bikes. At age seventy-five, Doctor Bennett Nelson was dead of a heart attack, and I'm no more sorry about him than he was when little Roberta Swenson died.

Dad puts the balsa lure back inside his tackle box and closes the lid. "It was pretty quiet around there after Doc passed. Especially in the assessor's office."

Mom sets the small vase on her old buffet in Liz's family room. "My, this piece of furniture looks good here. I never thought of using it to display pictures." She gazes for a time at the family photos, and then wanders into the dining room to check on her white oak table and chairs. "Everything fits nicely in your home, Liz.

"And, Callie, you've got the piano and Gram's curio cabinet."

"Plus the drop-leaf desk."

"I hope you girls are all right with how we divided things between you. Your father and I have always tried to treat you equally, you know."

"Of course, Mom. I plan to get the piano tuned as soon as I get home."

"Definitely." Liz gives Mom a hug. "How long are you going to be out west?"

"Ask your father."

"Well, now." Dad shifts a toothpick to the opposite corner of his mouth and stands up. "You can look for us at apple blossom time."

"*I'll be with you in apple blossom time . . .*" sings Mom.

"*I'll be with you to change your name to mine.*" Dad invites her to dance among the boxes.

"Oh, geez." I grin at Liz and Brian. "Here we go again. The Lawrence Welk hour."

They finish their waltz. Still humming the tune, Dad rests his hands on Mom's shoulders and kisses the top of her head.

"We'll bring our champagne music to Callie's house when we get back, then stay with you kids for a few days, if you'll have us."

"Of course," says Liz. "Silly man."

"After that, we'll head north. I put some cash down on a Hi-Lo camper. It'll be just the ticket—our home for the summer months."

With a hopeful look, he leans over Mom's shoulder in time to see her hint of a scowl.

"Your mother is keen on the California trip, but I might have to sell her on the second part of the deal."

"Living in a tiny camper all summer isn't my idea of fun, Will. Especially if I have to worry about you every day while you're out on the water by yourself. I don't mind leaving Masterton and spending our winters in a warm climate, but . . ."

"Why don't you camp for a couple of weeks," suggests Liz, "then stay with us the rest of the summer?"

"Nope. I've got a lot of fishing to do."

Just then, Brent and Josey dash into the kitchen.

Brent, fourteen, is taller than his father. Josey, age twelve, is a close copy of Liz as a teenager—dark-haired and pretty without being aware of it. She's also spunky—like the daughter I'd have welcomed. Trained early to thread worms and clean bullheads, Josey has graduated to hooking, netting, and dressing out northern pike, alongside her "gramps" and me.

"Hey, Snicklefritz." Dad holds out an arm. "How's my girl?"

"Fine, Gramps." She sidles over to him. "How's the world treating you?"

He laughs and squeezes the back of her neck. "Capital. With a capital C."

"Did you kids get that section of basement cleared out?" asks Liz.

"Yup," says Brent, in his deepening voice. "I hope there's nothin' else, cuz I'm goin' to shoot some hoops with the guys."

"Just a second there, Champ." Dad extends his hand. "Thanks for all your help." He looks up. "Boy, you are one tall drink of water."

Brent smirks and playfully punches Dad on the shoulder before rushing off.

Liz starts supper while the rest of us sit down at the kitchen table, glad for a break from the packing boxes. Josie hoists herself up onto the counter, long legs dangling, heels bouncing against a lower cupboard, the way Liz and I used to do back home.

"What's going on?" she asks around a wad of chewing gum.

"We were just talking about California. It was our dream to go there when I was thirteen. And now, they're finally going."

"Your granny and I will let you know what it's like."

"Once we find a place to rent," says Mom, "you kids will have to come see us."

"Oh, boy! California!" shouts Josey, hopping down from her perch. "Can we, Mom? Dad?"

"We'll see," says Liz. "It would be nice."

"I'm ready!" shouts Josey.

"Me, too." Brian rubs his hands together as if he were set to go this instant. "I should be able to get away for a week or so."

"We've got to get there first." Dad laughs. "When you come out, make sure it's before the first of May. We'll be on our way back to God's country by then."

"You've got a camper lined up," says Liz, "but you haven't told us where you're going to put it."

"How about some place around here," suggests Brian. "Wisconsin has plenty of good fishing lakes."

"True, you've got your share, but I have a place picked out on Leech. There's a sandy shoreline and I can keep my boat at one of the docks. Go out every day if I want."

"Knowing this guy," says Brian, nodding at Dad, "he won't have any trouble finding a good fishing hole."

"By golly! Just think of it—up north, a cozy camper, all the fish we can eat—it'll be the perfect life, won't it, Emily?"

He reaches over to pat Mom's hand.

"Oh, dandy, Will. Just dandy."

"Aw, it sounds like fun, Gran!" Josey jumps up and down, as if on a pogo stick, reminding me of Tequila, excited, long ago, for the march over to Gram's house. "First California, then I'll come visit you and Gramps as soon as school's out in June. I can't wait to go camping!"

"Camping? You sound like your Aunt Callie." Mom hugs Josey around her narrow waist. "I guess I can do that if it'll make you and your gramps happy. But you'd better not ask me to go out in that boat!"

Dad winks. "Maybe we ought to spend our winters up north, Em. Ice fishing. Then you could walk on the water."

"You old coot. Still trying to get a rise out of me."

We laugh, and then sit quietly for a moment.

Mom smiles impishly and jolts everyone to attention with a robust "*California here we come, right back where we started from . . .*"

Twenty-Six

The Lure

*D*URING OUR PARENTS' ANNUAL PILGRIMAGES to California, Liz and I call each other for updates on Mom's detailed reports, narratives for what Josie calls, "Our family soap opera."

It's been a long time—Largo number 40 on my metronome—since Dad has tried to contact his brother.

In October 1981, he resurrects an old plan:

En route to San Diego, they drive to Sioux City, Iowa, turn off the Interstate, head for Oak Street, and park in front of Uncle Ray's house.

In 1983, after the third attempt, Mom writes:

> *I always wait in the car while your dad saunters up to the door. I figure if he can't get in, then how could I? So, I just stay put.*
>
> *After knocking and peeking through a crack in the curtains, then knocking some more, he wanders along the boulevard and circles the house. Sometimes, he visits with Ray's neighbor, who usually comes outside during these fiascos. At first, Mr. Hagen wondered who we were and why your pa was snooping around. Now that he knows us, he offers up whatever tidbits he can about Ray and Eloise, which isn't much, just that they're still alive and ornery. Your dad tries the door one more time before we drive away. Then he jams on the brakes, because he swears he sees a curtain move.*
>
> *I tell him this is nuts. We should bypass Sioux City next time.*
>
> *He stays quiet for a while, just drives along and shakes his head. Then he gets angry and we end up rehashing all this tomfoolery half way to California.*
>
> *After so many years I've had enough. Your father is nothing but a stubborn Swede, torturing himself and me with this ridiculous pipe dream. I'm beginning to wonder if he wants to get back with Ray or just give him hell. I've told him over and over it's time we forget about these people and get on with our own lives . . .*

Liz and I sense that our mother is worrying more than usual and has grown quite irritable. We also agree that in spite of her carping, she will hang in there for a hundred seasons if that's what Dad wants.

The fourth year of their journey, I place my sheltie in Canine Camp and take several days leave from my teaching duties, plus weekends. Dad says that he can use some help driving and will pay for my flight back to Minneapolis from San Diego.

"Besides," he says, "your mother is getting to be hard to travel with. She constantly yells at me to slack up and announces every damn stop sign as if I don't know how to read."

After I accidentally back his Cadillac onto a center island, Dad takes over.

"I'll get us as far as Santa Fe. That ought to give you enough time to figure out how to drive this car."

"So there!" Mom laughs as I relinquish the helm.

"Titter, titter!" Dad buckles his seatbelt and announces, "First stop—Sioux City."

I feel like a kid awakening from my nap in the back seat as he pulls up in front of 2214 Oak Street and shuts down the engine. When he taps three short beeps on the horn I sit bolt upright.

"What are you doing?"

He grins. "That's to let them know we're here again."

"Our little routine," Mom mutters over her shoulder.

The three of us sit in the car, immobile, gazing out of the opened windows at the two-story white house with red trim. I imagine my cousin running out to greet us. But Jen, who would be forty-one by now, is long gone.

What might it have been like to come here as a girl? Did she have a swing set? A wading pool? A neighborhood candy store? Did she ever have a contest with her friends to see who could jam the most bubble gum into their mouths and still be able to chew? Did she like paint-by-numbers and modeling clay? Did she ever have a pet? Learn to play piano? Sing songs? Go fishing with her dad?

As it turned out, we'd only had that one summer's day together, when we were children riding bikes near Lake Shetek, searching for arrowheads, ending up at Belle Kittleson's tavern.

"They must be doing all right, Dad. The yard looks good and there's a garden off to the side."

But then I notice there are no flowers or trees, only a few shrubs and some spoiled vegetables hanging from their vines.

Dad cranes his neck. "I swear I saw that curtain move. Damn it, he sees us. Why the hell can't he come out?"

"You know why, Will," snaps my mother. "What does it take for you to learn your lesson?" She throws her hands up and strains to look back at me. "Year after year, Callie, this is what we do."

I have a hunch Mom is holding nothing back since I'm in the car, trying to recruit me, win me over, needing an ally.

Dad's face grows red. "That's enough, Emily."

"No. This is nonsense. Pulling up in front of their house every year and sitting here like idiots. We're nothing but gluttons for punishment!"

"I said enough chewing the rag, damn it!" Dad slaps at the steering wheel, but hits the horn instead. "We're here, now keep still!"

"I will not!"

But Mom does grow quiet. And the aggravated look on her face soon fades. In a low voice, she says, "This is killing you, Will. Comes a time when you have to stop."

Dad leans his head against the seat back and puffs out his cheeks, the way he used to sigh when we visited Gram and he could never get through to her.

"Did you hear me, Will? The time has come when you have to give up this business with Ray."

"I can't. He's all I have left."

"Oh, Dad." I lean forward and pat his shoulder. Mom's chin trembles as she rests her hand on top of Dad's and stares at him for a long moment.

I begin to wish I'd stayed at home with my dog. There's plenty to do around the place: fall clean-up, pulling the dock and rowboat, preparing lesson plans for my middle-school music students. This is going to be a long, hot trip. We haven't come that far from Minneapolis and already the inside of the car smells like old people upset and in need of a bath, myself included. But after a few minutes, Dad perks up like a prizefighter sitting in his corner between rounds, primed and sensing the bell is about to ring again.

He gets out of the car, stretches as if reaching for the sky, then hitches up his fawn-colored dress trousers and re-tucks his shirttail before ambling along the narrow walkway and up the steps. He knocks on the door and waits, brushing his feet repeatedly on the thick mat before knocking again. After several minutes, he turns toward us, shrugs, retraces his steps part way, and veers off in the direction of the garden.

"Here we go, again." Mom reclines her seat back and tells me that Dad has grown bolder during these stopovers, adding variations to a drawn-out routine, and that, at least on the surface, he manages to ignore not only the insult of not being admitted to his brother's house, but the even greater insult of never being acknowledged.

He reminds me of an aging actor revisiting an old stage set, long since abandoned.

"Mom." I rest my arms and chin on the seat back. "He's gonna do what he has to do. Relax and let him be."

"Always sticking up for him. Just once, I'd like to go straight to California." She glances out of the window. "Go see what's holding your father up this time."

"Okay, Ma. Enjoy the show."

It pleases Dad when I leave the car to join him in his stroll around the premises. He points out shutters in need of paint, sagging clotheslines, and weeds that want pulling, as though this were his property and he's been re-miss. Until we're out of sight, Mom watches our every move.

When the next-door neighbor walks over to meet us, the two men shake hands like old friends. Dad introduces me. Chuckling at the irony, he says, "Ben and I have a good visit here in the yard most every year."

Ben Hagen, somewhat younger than Dad, is tall and portly with hair the color of a pale carrot. His large hand grips my own and he gives me a warm smile.

"What's the news from this place?" Dad nods toward his brother's house.

"Not much since you were here last year, Will. We don't see anything of Eloise, but we sure can hear her, especially in summer when their windows are open. Ray still potters about in his garden, as you can see. But I don't think he feels well. Moves pretty slow."

Dad shakes his head and makes a chirping sound out of the corner of his mouth.

"He must be in his eighties by now," says Mr. Hagen.

"Eighty-three. And I'll soon be celebrating my eighty-second."

"You don't look more than seventy. What's your secret?"

Dad holds his arms aloft and three-steps around on the grass. "A wonderful wife, two fine daughters, and a good attitude."

Mr. Hagen laughs and claps Dad on the back. "You're a lucky man, Will. Keep on dancing and you'll do all right."

After a little more small talk, we say our goodbyes and head into the garden, where Dad admires how Uncle Ray has tied the strings in double half hitches around wooden stakes and stretched them to make long, straight rows—the way they were taught back on the farm. Even though the vegetables are done for, Dad reties the loosened knots, rights tilting stakes, and props up a droopy vine loaded with tomatoes. Some are mushy. Others are tough and white-green, tinged by a pomegranate blush. Wax beans, grown fat and dry, bulge with seeds. Carrot tops lie scattered and wilting on the hard-packed dirt. The fresh smell of soil and spring vegetables is gone, given over to the musky fall odor of decay.

A sharp rapping sound comes from a second floor window. We look up to see the silhouette of a face next to the opening.

"Get away from here or I'll call the police!" shrieks a high-pitched voice.

"Oh, God," I mutter, edging closer to Dad.

"I just want to see Ray," he says calmly.

"He's not here! Now get the hell out of our yard and don't come back!"

"C'mon, Dad." I clutch his arm. "Let's go."

"When I'm good and ready." He stands up straighter than I thought he could and, like a schoolyard bully, lets Aunt Eloise have it: "C'mon outside, you crazy old bat! You don't scare me! "

High color floods his cheeks. His eyes come alive. Taking my cue from him and still angry about how Jen was mistreated by this woman now screaming at us, I holler, "Yeah! Take a flying leap, you old witch!"

Dad breathes deeply and grins at me. "I've been wanting to tell her that for forty years."

Trying to act casual, reluctant to show fright, we linger in the garden, which gives Aunt Eloise time to remove herself from the second floor window. She flings open the back door, barges out like a bull with flared nostrils, and stands clutching a long-handled spatula in her left hand. She keeps the right one behind her, as if holding a surprise. Bulging in a gingham dress of large blue-and-white checks, she has the same wild-eyed features and unruly hair (now gray) that I remember as a girl. There isn't a pretty thing left about the woman.

"By God," says Dad, none too quietly. "Just look at her. She's gone to seed!"

Before we can take a step, Aunt Eloise raises her right arm up over her head and hurls an iron skillet at us. It falls with a heavy thud next to the first row of wilted string bean vines. My heart beats double time as I turn to hustle back to the car.

"Let's not run, Cal. We don't want her to think she's won."

"Jesus Christ, Dad!" I shout, not caring that Aunt Eloise might hear. "Why isn't she in a straight jacket?"

"Beats me! She sure as hell's got an arm on her for an old biddy!"

As we edge toward the street, the spatula lands in the grass a foot away from us.

"Guess we'd better high-tail it out of here," says Dad, "or she might throw a knife next." He scoots across the lawn as fast as his old legs will carry him. "I'll drive!"

I make it to our get-away car and jump into the back seat just as Dad sprints in behind the wheel. Our doors slam shut simultaneously.

"What was *that* all about?" Mom frowns. "I heard hollering. And why were you running?"

"Nothing much." Dad turns and winks at me, then sits for a moment to catch his breath and peer at the house.

"You old fool. You've been pushing for a showdown and you finally got one."

"It's a game, Mom." I lean forward, still panting. "For as long as it takes, let him play it out."

"I don't have much choice now, do I? Tell me what happened."

Dad puts the engine in gear and slowly drives away from the curb.

After our blow-by-blow account, Mom's lengthy criticism, and loud exchanges between my parents, I lean back and helplessly watch Dad's jaw muscles clench and unclench as we ride along in silence.

What kind of game *is* this? How much more can they take? And where was Uncle Ray while Aunt Eloise was on the attack? Had she done him in?

With the initial rush of surviving her onslaught behind me, I feel like going back to kick in her door. That Dad has been treated this way, and for such a long, long time, makes me want to grab my uncle by the shoulders and shake him up. It makes me want to give Aunt Eloise the boot. This treatment is too damaging, not good for the health. I always encouraged Dad in his efforts to stay in touch with his brother. Now I'm not so sure.

"Ben mentioned one time that he thought Eloise was a recovering alcoholic," says Dad.

Mom snorts and readjusts her seatbelt. "Well, she'd better go back into the sauce."

OCTOBER 1985: This is to be the last time my parents drive to California. Liz and I make them promise to take an extra day or two, and to temper the arguments after their annual disappointment in Sioux City—if, in fact, they plan to stop there again.

They do. And this time, things turn out in a way they never imagined. Mom writes:

> Do you remember those old fishing lures? The ones that look like strange minnows? You girls used to play with them when you were little.
>
> Your dad rang the doorbell, as usual, and when nobody answered (what's new?), he set one of those lures on the doorstep and came back to the car.
>
> It was painful to watch. He delivered that thing as if it were a May basket, except he never ran from the stoop. Not that he'd have to! Lord knows there's no one in that house bound to rush out after him to plant a kiss!
>
> Anyhow, as your pa shifted into gear and we rolled ahead, he glanced back at the house, the way he always does, and I nearly got a whiplash when he stomped on the brakes. You see, the front door had opened a crack, then slowly opened wider, and out stepped a very old, very bent man with wispy, white hair. Girls, you wouldn't have known him. He was so hunched over. I don't think I'd have recognized him if we'd passed each other on the street. The way he walked, I could see a little of Grandad in him, with those baggy khaki pants that drooped in the seat.
>
> He slowly turned this way and that, then stood on the steps staring at our car and down at his feet.

Your dad backed up fast, switched off the engine, and struggled to get out from behind the wheel, forgetting that his seat belt was still fastened.

Ray had spotted the fishing lure and stooped to pick it up. Then he gripped that iron railing and inched his way down the steps to the sidewalk.

Imagine! After all these many years. He came to meet us at the curb, shuffling along in old slippers. This time, I got out of the car and joined your dad for the occasion—or to protect him, because I couldn't be sure what would happen after that business with Eloise. Anyhow, there stood your pa, leaning against the fender, arms folded, and blinking hard. "Well, I'll be damned!" was all he could say.

It took Ray a while to close the gap. He stopped for a minute and called out, "Did you ever catch anything on this?" He was holding that old lure up like a prize fish.

"Not until now," said your dad.

The two shook hands, not knowing what to say next. They just stood there, looking each other up and down.

Finally, Ray said, "I'd invite you in, but . . ." He nodded toward the house, where Eloise stood framed in the picture window, glaring out at us.

"There'll be hell to pay," he said. "Nothing I'm not used to."

Then he quickly changed the subject.

"Say, I like your new car," he said, brushing his fingers along the finish. "I like this pearl-white color better'n that dark-blue Caddy you were driving a couple of years ago. The beige one before that was nice. I'd like to . . . that is to say . . . do you have time to go some place for lunch? It's on me."

And would you believe, girls, we had lunch with your Uncle Ray? Imagine! After all this time and effort! Your dad had to pay, though, because Ray didn't have any money on him. Guess he wasn't up to going back inside for his wallet. Not much starch left in the old guy. I had to kick your dad under the table a couple of times when he started in about the stuff Ray took from their mother's house after the funeral.

I guess there was a little pay-off after all, even though it took forever. I'm relieved and happy for your dad. This winter, he walks along the beach with a spring in his step.

We'll see all of you at apple blossom time.

Love, Mom

Twenty-Seven

Lake Mother ✧ 1986

"I CAN'T BELIEVE I KEEP AGREEING TO THIS." The rosy color has faded from Mom's cheeks. "It's a mistake, don't you think, Callie?" she asks, followed by, "Oh, never mind. When have you ever taken my side on anything when it comes to your pa?"

"Just have fun, Mom. Don't worry so much." I give her a hug and check the street for traffic. "You've enjoyed the last several summers camping, haven't you?"

"Well, yes, but not really."

"That's right, Em, listen to your daughter." Dad secures the tie-downs on his new fishing boat lashed to the top of their Hi-Lo camper. "You should be used to this by now. No better way to spend these warm months—breathing in all that fresh air, the smell of pines, good eats, plenty of fish, falling asleep to the cry of loons."

"Ah yes, the loons. You fit right in, Will."

She takes me aside. "I'm worried, Callie. I've already talked to Liz about this. Ever since he had that surgery on his face last fall, your dad can't do things like he used to. I wish he'd had that thing removed earlier."

"The doctors got it all, didn't they? That's what Dad said."

"I hope so. With melanoma, who knows? Anyhow, he had an awful time hitching the camper to the car. And don't ask me how we shoved that boat up there. I told him, 'I can't do it. Don't expect any help from me.' But there I am, trying to hold the blamed thing steady while he figures out how to thread the ropes and hook the bungee cords. I'm surprised the whole kit and caboodle didn't come crashing down on us. We could have been killed. Or paralyzed—spend the rest of our lives in wheelchairs, in a nursing home. Heaven forbid!"

"Why didn't you let us know when you were ready to pack up? We would have come to help."

"Your father still wants to be in charge. I have a feeling that'll soon come to a halt."

"Know what, Mom? You'll be fine once you get settled. You always get this way when you're not sure what to expect."

"Well, I'm worried about your papa, Callie."

"I know. But we're not going to coddle him. He wouldn't like that."

At age eighty-three, Dad has decided to return to Minnesota for good, says he has some serious fishing to do. And that's what I'd like to believe.

They're renting an apartment midway between Eau Claire and Minneapolis.

"I might even try out a Wisconsin lake with Brian sometime," he says, "before heading back up to Leech."

"Our western days are over," Mom whispers. "Your Dad may have some 'serious fishing' to do, but it's his mortality he's feeling. He's the one that made the decision. 'It's time to go home, Emily,' he said. 'No more detours.'"

No more phone calls and letters from California, no more stopovers in Iowa.

Dad's triumph in Sioux City that autumn day brought the brothers to anchor for only a short while. After intermittent attempts, Uncle Ray has drifted away again. As far as we know, he's still among the living—ever since that lucky lure afternoon.

"I wish they could settle things before it's too late, Mom. What a shame if old age and illness trump Dad's efforts."

"Which reminds me, he has no business going off into the wilderness this summer in his condition. What if he needs a doctor?"

I marvel at how skilled Dad has become at ignoring Mom's fretful lingo—unless it goes on too long. Then he tells her to "Keep still. Stop chewing the rag. I know what I'm doing, damn it!"

Several weeks ago, he traded his old wooden fishing boat—the one we used on Lake Shetek, out of Tepeeotah—for a much lighter aluminum one. He kept the '50 Johnson ten-horse. Said he knew that motor so well it was like an old friend.

"I'm not trading in the camper, either," he says, patting the silver siding. "She's served us well. Plenty of room for the whole family, if we pitch a tent nearby."

The first year he hooked the Hi-Lo to his one luxury—a Cadillac Brougham, champagne with faun-colored leather interior—we raised our glasses in a toast. His plan delighted me, but not Mom and Liz. Nothing new. It's always been two against two in these matters, with no tie-breaker.

Each summer, before driving north, they swing by my house on Cook's Bay for a day or two. This time, Dad moves gingerly as he double-checks the trailer hitch and the tie-downs that will keep his new boat from flying off on the freeway.

He eases himself in behind the wheel. Mom straightens her shoulders and marches to her place on the passenger side.

"Well," she announces with a sigh and a half smile, "I guess I'm as ready as I'll ever be."

I blow them kisses as they inch away from the curb. "Come see us," they call out, rolling slowly down the street, each waving broadly from an open window as if they're flapping their wings to get off the ground. They'll join the migration of boats and campers on I-94 and Minnesota 10, all flocking to lake country.

> *June 13, 1986*
> *Dear Callie,*
>
> *We set up camp at our old site here at Federal Dam. The Hi-Lo (once we got it up) is home to us once again. As usual, since we'll be here all summer and into the fall, you should send your letters in care of the post office. Come any time...soon, I hope. I'd feel better knowing your dad has someone to fish with...*

Settled in at the campground on the southeast shore of Leech Lake, an area belonging to a band of Ojibwe, Mom writes,

> *...Your dad's in his element here, couldn't be happier now that we're back. He met some of the Indians who belong to the Loon Clan (no joke). You know how he loves to visit. Yesterday they invited him to smoke the peace pipe. There they sat, six men in a circle next to the lake, passing the pipe around, each taking long puffs. Your pa felt very honored. He thought it was regular tobacco, but I don't think so...*
>
> *Just a minute, your dad's reading over my shoulder and wants to write a few lines.*
>
> *Dear Family,*
>
> *I'll add my two cents worth to what your mother has already written. As she told you, I had the distinct honor of smoking the peace pipe with a half dozen men from the Leech Lake Band of Ojibwe.*
>
> *We paid tribute first to the four directions, and then to Mother Earth, Father sky, and the Great Spirit they call Wakan Tanka. The men sprinkled a little tobacco on the ground before placing some in the pipe. That means we must give back to Mother Earth a part of what we take.*

Several of the men spoke and gave colors to the directions. East is red for the rising sun. South is yellow for the spring bounty, black is for West, after the sun goes down and the spirit world gathers, and white stands for the North where blankets of snow cover the land. I especially liked what was said about the East, thanking the Great Spirit for each new day that we're allowed to live upon Mother Earth. I hope your mother and I have many more.

Afterward, when I stood up, I happened to stagger a little, which caused Emily to question what I'd smoked. It's just that the tobacco they use is strong and pure. I inhaled plenty before I noticed that some of the others did not. That is why I got a little tipsy on my way back to the camper.

Now that you know all about my experience, I'll turn pen and paper back over to your mother.

With Love, Papa

P.S. Well, I guess your Dad set the record straight! That'll be all for now. Come any time. Soon I hope.

Love, Mom.

On summer break from teaching, I water the tomato and green pepper plants, take Piper to the dog sitter, button up the house, and drive to Federal Dam for a week of camping. It has been a long time since I've fished with Dad.

During my college and married years, we managed to get in a few trips. I wedged myself into the bow, facing forward, the way I rode as a kid, but it was a tight fit. I yelled "Give 'er hell" for old time's sake, to make Dad laugh, and we made our victory turns around the bays whether or not we'd caught anything. But none of it felt the same.

While driving north, my mind latches onto another memory that, for some reason, hasn't lodged with me until now: it was sometime in late July, shortly after I'd turned fourteen. I was sitting at the white enamel kitchen table in our house in Masterton. Dad came in to get a drink of water.

"What are you doing? What is that awful smell?"

"Nail polish. I'm painting my nails." I waved my hands around to show off the raspberry-red color.

Dad set his filled water glass on the counter. "What for? How're you gonna catch fish with that goop on your fingers?"

I told him that I couldn't go out to the lake with him that day. A bunch of us were going to see *Gunfight at the O.K. Corral*, starring Burt Lancaster. Bobby Keeler would be there.

Dad stared at me for a minute, looking confused. He jammed his hands in his pockets, then took them out again. With a strange smile, he turned and walked out of the kitchen, his hands clasped behind him, like one of the old men walking down Main Street, going nowhere in particular. Oh, I thought, I've hurt his feelings. But I really wanted to go with Bobby.

When we were sixteen, Bob brought me home from a triple feature at the drive-in. The headlights of his Chevy convertible caught Mom sitting on the front stoop in her pink nightie and white bed jacket with Sam Cat huddled next to her.

She looked embarrassed and said she was getting some fresh air. Just then Dad stepped out from the shadows in his pajamas, carrying the lower half of a cane pole.

"What's going on?" I asked.

"Just checking the flowers."

"At three in the morning, with a fishing pole?"

"Well," he grinned, "I don't golf."

Bob and I guffawed until the neighbor's porch light flicked on.

In high school, I'd found an English translation of Puccini's aria, "*O Mio Babbino Caro*," the piece we'd grown to love because of Uncle Amer and Gram. Dad didn't seem interested when I told him that Babbino Caro meant "Daddy Dear" and that the character of Lauretta is asking her father, Gianni Schicchi, for permission to pursue a love, that she will throw herself off the bridge—Ponte Vecchio—and into the Arno River if she finds that it is useless to continue pining after the man she loves. When I read the words to Dad, he said, "Oh?" and turned away. I guess when you've unlocked the secret to some things, it takes away the mystery of your own illusion. Like the time Mom revealed her true weight after years of our trying to trick her into telling us. Once we knew, the guessing game ended and the fun was over.

The campground at Federal Dam isn't crowded. I turn in next to the silver Hi-Lo camper and park alongside Dad's car. It feels good to be "home." The three of us soon fall into a comfortable routine:

Midmornings, while Dad tinkers with the ten-horse, reorganizes his tackle box, and sops up water from the bottom of the boat, Mom and I traipse along a path layered with pine needles to the Camp Café for warm cherry pie à la mode and coffee.

Afterward, we walk the short street of Federal Dam and hike along the train tracks outside of town. I applaud my mother's efforts as she dawdles and balances with me on the shiny rails in the noon heat. Did she ever walk the tightrope above the "alligator pit" at Tepeeotah when we weren't looking? She teaches me a song from the Depression: *Hallelujah, I'm a bum, hallelujah, bummin' again, hallelujah, give us a handout to revive us again.* Insects and dandelion fluff float up from ditches where we gather yellow and lavender-blue wildflowers for the camper table.

On our way back to town and to the post office, Mom tells me, once again, how her parents lost everything during the Great Depression, yet gave water and what food they could spare to the tattered men who jumped from slow-moving box cars at the crossing near Lake Wilson.

"It was mostly men," she says, "who found their way to our house below the tracks."

"Where were the women? And the children?"

"They generally didn't take to the rails."

"I would have."

"Yes, Callie, I believe you would do that. I can picture you scrambling down from a box car and knocking at our door for a hand-out."

"What would you have fed me?"

"Bread and canned tomatoes. And maybe, if we had any, a teaspoon of sugar."

I kiss my mother on the cheek. "Thank you, Mom."

"You're welcome, sugar."

The tiny post office in Federal Dam is hot and stuffy and smells of old glue and musty paper. With a smudged rubber tip fitted to one finger, Myrna the postmistress flips through the mail. The fleshy pads on the rest of her fingers are black with ink-stain. Her face is the color of envelopes.

"How're you doin', Emily?" she asks, bundling letters with a wide, soiled rubber band. "Catchin' plenty of fish?" She hands the packet to Mom who introduces me.

"Oh, my yes. Callie and her dad get enough to fry every evening."

"Good for you." Myrna smiles. "Wish I had more time to get out on the lake."

As we turn to leave, she says, "Don't forget the pow-wow this weekend. The fancy dancers are really good."

"We'll be there."

We return to camp and lunch on buttered bread and cold northern fillets left over from supper.

Afternoons and early evenings are for fishing. Nearly every day, Dad and I catch our limit of three northern pike each, plus a walleye or two. We clean and fry them over an open fire. Spitting grease and hot flames add layers of char to the black iron skillet. The conversation is usually the same:

"I wish your mother liked to fish," he'd say, slipping a spatula under the sizzling fillets and sliding them onto a platter.

"At least she eats them." I set the pan of hot oil flecked with seared corn meal on a flat rock.

"Who wouldn't?" He admires the heap of crispy goldens. Then we step up into the camper and the three of us sit down to our meal.

Midafternoon, we walk down to the shore. Dad's shiny aluminum boat is loaded and ready to go.

No matter how often we invite her to come with us, Mom refuses. We understand why, yet we never stop asking. To get me to stop badgering her when I was little, she told me an abbreviated version of what had happened long ago, but saved the full story until I was old enough to handle it.

Our exchange this day is scripted, ritualistic, respectful, ending with, "Don't you pester me, Callie. I'll do as I feel and you do what you want. Just be careful."

Now that I have arrived in North Country, she is relieved to know that Dad has a fishing partner, yet fears the loss of us both. After motoring around the bays each day, we keep still about the sudden squalls and high waves, the ever-changing conditions of Leech, a lake that has claimed its share of victims over the years. But Mom knows. She hears talk around the campground.

I can only imagine her launching litany when I'm not here:

"Why don't you fish from the dock, Will? Or below the dam. You're too old to be going out in the boat by yourself. You're not well. You say you know what you're doing, but no one is beyond trouble. Even the most experienced . . . Will, are you listening to me?"

I imagine her admonitions falling on deaf ears, the only response, the sound of the motor as Dad rounds tall rice beds and disappears into the channel where he turns the volume back up on his hearing aids.

Mom's even keel this week is tested by a hauntingly good storyteller. John Delmore, around seventy, has staked out the site next to us. A friendly guy, he talks constantly, especially about his younger years as a lumberjack and fishing guide. He wears the same thing every day, even in this summer heat: a plaid flannel shirt, khakis, and hard-used hiking boots. His furrowed skin is as tanned as a dried oak leaf. Long bushy eyebrows curl upward. I think he combs them that way.

Some evenings around the fire pit, John tells us stories about the West. This particular night, he talks about Lake Tahoe and how he used to dive for lost boats and motors—and bodies.

Uneasy, I jump at the snap of burning logs. Sparks shoot straight up and fly with the wind, beyond our circle, into the darkened trees.

Dad wears a grim expression—rare for him. I glance at Mom.

"John, I think you'd better reserve these tales for a different audience. My mother . . ."

"Oh, but wait," he says, "You've got to hear this one. Two couples from New Jersey, in their forties, were staying at the South Lake Tahoe Lodge. I remember they were from the East Coast on account of their accents. The men, of course, were there to fish while their wives shopped and haunted the casinos.

"Early one morning, we got a call to search for these guys. They hadn't docked their rental boat the night before. Sheriff had already talked to the wives, but they weren't overly concerned. They thought their husbands had stayed out night-fishing. Or worse, gone off to the bars to pick up floozies. Apparently, the men weren't beyond that sort of behavior.

"By daybreak, we'd located the empty boat rammed up on shore near Carnelian Bay, out of gas with the throttle wide open."

"Well," interrupts Dad, "that's quite a story, John." He is looking at Mom whose stoic expression hasn't changed, except for deepened frown lines between her eyebrows. "Time for us to turn in, wouldn't you say, Emily?"

"Wait, there's more." John raises a hand. "We had to tell the women that their husbands had most likely drowned and that we would organize a dive-search."

"I don't think my mother should hear this." I stand, but Mom stays put, waving away my words. She's either curious or too polite to leave in the middle of a story—probably both.

"Well, now, what do you suppose was the first thing those women said?" John pauses for effect and pitches his voice up an octave. "'What are we going to do? They have the car keys!'"

He laughs. "Can you beat that? First concern: their husbands have the car keys! Funny how people react to bad news. Anyhow, the ladies stuck around for a few days, then got another set made and drove home."

I try to imagine what it must have felt like for those women, on vacation with their husbands one day, then driving home without them the next—gone, just like that.

"Hell, like any lake, you don't fool with Tahoe." John tosses another log on the fire, causing more sparks to fly into the black woods. "Now, I understand that Leech is shallow, which can be dangerous in a high wind. But Tahoe runs deep, anywhere from 900 to 1,600 feet, and it doesn't like to give up its dead. When the bodies do surface, *if* they surface, they're unrecognizable. All of the soft tissue is gone. Oh, the fish and turtles do have a feast."

With that, Mom quickly gets up and rushes into the camper. Dad and I follow, leaving John Delmore to finish his endless stories alone.

"Those two men never did show up," he calls after us, "even months later—not unusual, but it makes you wonder, doesn't it?"

Inside the camper, Mom bustles around, heating a pan of water for tea, her lips pinched together. She says nothing, but I can tell she is primed, unable to fend off evil lake spirits, her mind filled with awful notions.

We sit at the small table where the wildflowers we'd picked that morning droop over the lip of the vase. We talk about my drive home day after tomorrow. We talk about when Liz and Brian and the kids plan to come up for a visit. We wonder if my garden will yield enough tomatoes for us to can in the fall.

But before we go to sleep, Mom makes us listen to her admonitions: *Don't stand up in the boat. Don't go out so far that you can't get back right away. Don't stay out too long. Watch the weather.*

I lie awake, remembering what has made her this way. I'll never forget the night when she finally told me what happened:

"As young girls," she said, "my sister Lilly and I used to skate on Lake Wilson, near our home. Early one evening . . . oh, it was a beautiful night, but cold, and the sky was filled with stars. The ice was so smooth; we glided all over the lake, pretending to be Sonja Henie. It was foolish of us to . . ." She shook her head and her chin trembled. "We should never have gone so close to that bridge, because that's where water currents thin the ice. We went down into that frigid water at the same time, several yards apart. It took my breath away, but all I could think was I had to get out of that hole so I could help Lilly. I was younger and lighter than my sister, and I kicked and broke ice with my elbows until it bore my weight and I was able to hoist myself out of the water. I lay prone and slid over the stretch of ice next to where Lilly had gone down. She was kicking, too, and trying to hoist herself up, but the edges of the ice kept breaking. I grabbed her wrists. "Keep trying!" I screamed. "Kick! Don't give up!"

Mom lowered her head and cried for a moment. "But Lilly wore out," she whispered, "and gave in to the cold. Her mittens came off in my hands as she slipped beneath the ice."

We sat close together, Mom and I. And stayed quiet for a long time.

The drowning happened more than sixty-five years ago. Mom still wants nothing to do with the water. And she encourages everyone else to avoid it as well. That she'd married into a family of hunters and fishermen who knew how to observe the rules of nature meant nothing to her. No reassurance ever eased her mind. It doesn't to this day.

Tomorrow afternoon, when Dad and I head out onto Leech, I know that our lake mother will repeat the only words she knows for what we're about to do:

Watch the weather, she will warn. *Watch the weather!*

Twenty-Eight

Never Swear at a Lake

IT LOW IN THE BOAT!" Dad shouts, gripping the throttle with one hand while struggling to haul our stringer of northerns into the boat with the other. The pike flop about, trying to swim in lake water rising beneath the seats.

"Stay low and start bailing, Cal!"

Even at age forty-two, I still rarely do as I'm told without first pondering the situation for myself. I've been in storms where shorelines disappear into a steely gray wash and the sky becomes another lake. This one is different— more like the typhoon Belle Kittleson went through with her father. I slip to the floor of the boat. Water soaks through my shorts, climbs to my waist.

Facing a fierce wind and rain that stings my eyes like sand, I stay close to the forward seat, swaying from side to side in an effort to counterbalance the tipsy boat. Rollers break over the stern, slap Dad on the back and whirlpool toward me. Tackle boxes, lunch pail, landing net, rods and reels bob around, then slam against the metal of our fourteen-foot Crestliner. The cut plastic milk jug we use as a scoop dances forward and I grab it.

John Delmore's campfire story about the drowned men of Lake Tahoe takes shape in my mind. Desperately wishing for land, I shove that story aside and replace it with a scene from earlier this afternoon: Dad and I, lining up our gear, ready to set out from shore.

With an extra-serious look of concern, Mom escorts us and stands watch as we load and push our boat part way off the beach. The sound of metal against sand reminds me of Sam Cat's hiss whenever he confronted any dog but old Tequila. Strange to be thinking of these little beasts from my childhood: Sam, who made it to fifteen and Tequo, eighteen—old for a dog. Dad had set aside a plot of ground at Tepeeotah for pets and dead wildlife. I was there for Sam's burial, but I couldn't make it back home for Tequila's.

Stepping into the boat, Dad doesn't seem as lively or jovial as yesterday. The surgical scar on the left side of his face is nearly as white as his hair.

"You're getting to be too old for this, Will. Why don't you and Callie fish from the bridge today? Some place where I can see you."

"Not the same, Emily. Sure you don't want to come along?" Dad winks at me and takes his seat before the motor. "You'd be safe with two experienced fishermen."

"You know the answer to that. Good luck, now. Be careful. And for heaven's sake, watch the weather!"

I step into the bow and, with one foot, push against the sand to get us afloat. Then I take my usual place forward, next to the anchor. I know Mom will stay where she is, watching and waving, until we disappear around the first stand of wild rice. Most likely she'll be there for several minutes after that. And she will keep a vigil until we return.

Hot, still air clamps down on us. Blue-green damselflies cling to the monofilament lines of our fishing rods, arching together in the shape of a heart.

Dad lowers the prop, adjusts the motor's lean-rich dials, and yanks the cord until a spark connects. He eases us through the first bend of the channel into a series of gentle curves, past lily pads and mud turtles sunning themselves on half-submerged logs. Red-winged blackbirds, perched on sturdy reeds, sing the air electric. A soft, cool breeze picks up as we take the final bend and are borne again onto the big water.

I reach for my rod and reel. "Mom's really nervous about our going out today."

"She'll be all right."

"John Delmore doesn't know when to stop with those grim stories. Like last night. Mom didn't need to hear that shit."

"Your mother's more resilient than you think, Cal." Dad slows the boat at the edge of a weed bed and pays out his trolling line. "Besides, we can't protect her from everything. She'll be all right once she sees us motoring back safe and sound."

"I hope so."

"Just as we couldn't turn the tide when you ended up with what's-his-name."

"Jim . . . that was a *long* time ago, Dad. Why bring that up?"

"We saw through him," he says in a quiet voice, "but there was nothing we could do or say to stop you from marrying the guy, short of intervening. You were of age. You had to find out for yourself, I guess."

"No need to rehash all that. I'm fine now." Peering over the gunwale, I catch my rippled reflection in the slow-moving wake.

"I know you are, Cal. We were sure worried, though. Didn't know what he'd do."

"It was mostly words, Dad."

"We were privy to some of those words—the kind that chip away at a person over time. Kill the spirit."

"Well, they didn't kill mine. I got through it."

"Yes, you did. And we couldn't have been more relieved. It was hard to stand by and not be able to protect you."

"Well, as you said, we can't protect everybody from everything."

"We can only do our best." He lets go the throttle to brush back a few strands of thinning white hair. "There's so much out of our control."

"Dad, what I went through with Jim made me tough."

"Only as tough as you need to be, I hope. Your mother and I always had a feeling that we never knew the full story."

"He's long gone and I'm fine now."

Dad's right. They don't know the full story. And they won't, either. If he ever found out about the kick when I was down, the kick that ended my pregnancy, he'd do more than knock Jim's block off. There was a time when I could have easily pushed my husband down the stairs when he was drunk and vicious. But he wasn't worth spending the rest of my life in prison.

Over time, there'd been plenty of other people Dad hadn't been able to protect. Baby Billy, for instance. Or Uncle Amer getting shot. And how could he have saved Grandad from the wrong blood? Or kept Gram on this side of sanity? Not to mention Aunt Eloise. Then there was Uncle Ray.

My thoughts must have been on the same wave as Dad's, because he said, "I couldn't help a one of 'em. Not a one."

"You did what you could, Dad. Don't forget how hard you tried with Ray."

"Oh, *that* guy. He never could see straight around Eloise."

"Are you going to look him up again?"

"No plans. Your mother and I had lunch with him way back when. I guess that'll be it."

We make another pass, keeping our lures toward the deep side, yet visible to a fish lazing in the shallows.

"I never thought I'd see the day when you'd turn your back on a fight, Dad."

"It isn't much of a fight anymore. Comes a time when you accept things as they are and move on."

"What about Liz? Did she ever give you and Mom any trouble?"

Dad chuckles. "Not a speck, unless you count that shopping spree when she was in college, with no means to pay for it. Your mother and I put the skids on that. Made her return everything."

"Oh, yeah, I remember. There was some yelling and crying, as I recall, when she came home for the weekend."

I smile and gaze out at the smooth surface of the lake, feeling a certain calm. Just beyond the weed bed, I snag our first fish.

"Grab the net, Dad! He's coming in fast!"

"Take your time, Callie-girl. Don't horse him. Let him run if he wants to."

The line zings out again and I struggle to keep it from getting tangled in the weeds where the fish will certainly take cover and act as if it were a stone. Keeping the line taut, I wind my reel, inch by inch, until we can see the long, dark form rising from the deep.

"Whoa," says Dad. "Look at that! An axe handle!"

The fish barely moves as I ease him toward the net.

In a single motion, Dad scoops up my catch and holds it aloft. The pike curves double against the mesh of the net.

"It's a beauty, Cal. Good job!"

All afternoon, we troll the northeast finger of Leech, catching more northerns on red-and-white Dardevles. We keep an eye on rainsqualls working themselves up in the distance. Each seems threatening at first, only to veer off and disappear beyond the horizon.

During the lulls, I glance often at Dad in order to memorize him, the way he sits in his boat, the way he holds his Pflueger Supreme, the way he looks at peace with the world—just as he did when I was a kid and we fished together on Lake Shetek.

These days, it's my turn to worry.

"How's that part of your face doing, Dad? Does it hurt at all?"

"No." He touches the long scar that has changed the contour of his cheek. "I don't have much feeling left." He rubs his nose and forehead, then runs his hand down along the jaw line. "None on this side."

"It can take a long time after surgery to get the feeling back. That's what the doctors said. They had to cut through several layers, you know. Nerves and muscle."

"That's true. But it's already been a couple of years."

"It'll get better, Dad."

"Yes. Of course it will."

When we run out of serious things to talk about, we recite our ritual nonsense rhyme from decades ago, alternating lines, laughing until the end:

It was midnight on the ocean, not a streetcar was in sight.
The sun was shining brightly, for it had rained all night.
'Twas a summer's day in winter, and the rain was snowing fast,
as the barefoot girl with shoes on stood sitting in the grass . . .
It was evening and the sunrise was setting in the west,
and the fishes in the treetops were cuddled in their nests.
As the wind was blowing bubbles, lightning shot from left to right.
Everything that you could see had been hidden out of sight . . .
While the organ peeled potatoes, lard was rendered by the choir.
When the sexton rang the dishrag, someone set the church on fire.
"Holy Smokes!" the preacher shouted, as he madly tore his hair.
Now his head resembles heaven, for there is no parting there.
Glory, glory, what a shiny dome!
Glory, glory, get that man a comb!
Glory, glory, that's the end of my poem!
Now his head resembles heaven, for there is no parting there.

While chanting those silly words, we fail to notice a gray-green and yellow mass, the color of pea soup, positioning itself above the trees across Waboose bay.

Dad grows uneasy, sniffs at the still air, and nods at a slant of rain.

"We'd better go in, Cal."

"Aw, let's stay out awhile longer. I'm not afraid of a little rain."

"I don't know. Could be a heavy wind behind it."

"We'll be fine."

Sensing that our outings together are numbered, I want to draw from this one as long as possible. Anything to delay dry-docking the boat behind their apartment building and clamping the Johnson onto the two-by-four nailed in a corner of the garage where it will, soon enough, gather dust.

"All the other systems went around us. This one will, too."

"I don't think so, Cal. This storm looks different. I can feel it."

"Look, Dad, right over there." I point toward a stand of rushes where we'd snagged a big northern earlier in the week. "I have a hunch there's another lunker just waiting to strike. One more and we've got our limit."

Dad shakes his head, but obliges and slowly motors us farther from shore.

Within minutes, the smooth lake surface scuds over with cats' paws. Then, quick as the strike of cold-water pike, a powerful wind knocks us sideways. The wall of water lingering on the horizon charges from across the bay. Frozen to my seat, I watch the storm march straight at us. Whitecaps rise up and pound our little boat. Steely gray water splashes over the gunwales.

I've read about lake spirits. "Never doubt them," say the Indians. "Never insult or swear at a lake or it might get angry and tip you over."

"Keep bailing, Cal! Don't stop!"

Off balance, I say nothing, think nothing but soothing words, as if this giant lake were a fierce dog ready to mangle us. Good lake. Pretty lake.

My arms ache with each gallon scooped up and dumped overboard. I squint through the rain at Dad. If we capsize, he might not be able to hold on, even with a life jacket. His jaw is set, though, as if during an argument when he knows he's right. Instead of hunkering down, he squares his old narrow shoulders and takes hit after hit, fending off every wave the lake pitches at him.

Our five fish slosh from side to side, each one hooked through the lips with a link in the metal stringer. The links tear through the mouths on two of them and the northerns break free. As the boat seesaws and fills with more water, the long pike wriggle up the side and swim overboard.

"Dad, we're losing our fish!"

"It's all right! Let 'em go!"

This from a man who never threw a fish back in his life, no matter what the size. Each one's a mouthful in lean times, he'd say.

After minutes that seem like hours, the boat teeters dangerously sideways. Whitecaps broadside us and gush over the gunwales, replacing the gallons and gallons of water I've dumped out. Has the wind changed directions or is Dad confused? Why has he stopped knifing the waves? Why is he letting us get broadsided?

Scooping water like a maniac, I feel drunk sick, tossed about, as if riding a Tilt-a-Whirl. Images from John Delmore's story fill my head again: empty boat, open-throttle, no more gas, deep-water drownings, turtles and fish having at us.

Native Americans say, *Listen to your Elders*. So do the Swedes. I should have listened to Dad. Now it's too late.

"Turn into the waves!" I scream. "You'll swamp the boat!"

Staying his course, Dad begins to laugh.

I stop bailing and stare at him. Thin strands of paper-white hair lie pasted to his forehead. Rain courses down his horn-rimmed glasses and streams off his chin. He is relaxed, his left hand easy on the throttle.

Either he doesn't care anymore or something addles his judgment. All I know is that we'll drown, capsized with the next wave. Or the next. I don't know this man, the way he laughs and points at something behind me. *Why does he look so happy?*

Just as I turn to see what he's pointing at, marsh grass skims the bow and brushes my face and hands. Lily pad greens pierce the gray. Trees, like specters in the milky distance, take shape. The pounding waves subside, their energy taken by the marsh. We have entered the channel. The old man has piloted us to safety.

I struggle onto my seat, calf-deep in water, and hold tight the gunwales. Ashamed of my doubts, I feel like crying, but let out a whoop instead. Dad, still grinning, stomps his feet on the flooded boat bottom like a boy marching through a puddle. He brings us the rest of the way through the turns he knows by heart, shuts down the engine, and lets the boat's momentum slide us onto shore, onto the sand that greets us with a wet hiss.

The sky, emptied of its rage, clears as suddenly as it boiled over. Red-winged blackbirds return to their reeds, calling, "Thweeee!" Everything brightens, freshly whitewashed. The world smells clean.

As I rise to step out of the boat, my legs feel like fishing lines gone limp. Dad struggles to stand and takes his time stepping over the center seat toward the bow. I lend him a hand and feel a slight tremble.

We tug our craft further up onto the beach, pull the plug, and let the water drain out. Dad gives his boat a pat on the prow. I do the same. Before unloading our gear, I flop down on the rain-soaked grass and clutch the long, slippery blades with both hands. My heart thumps against my rib cage.

Only then, as we direct our attention away from the lake, do we notice downed tree limbs. And the ground littered with broken twigs and leaves.

Dad is wide-eyed and speaks in a low voice. "That was some wind."

We gather our gear and head for the fish-cleaning hut to begin dressing out our remaining northerns. Mom rushes toward us, wildly waving a white dishtowel, a frantic look on her face.

"Play it down, Cal," whispers Dad. "Don't tell your mother or she'll never let me go out again."

"Okay," I whisper back.

"Are you two all right? *Are* you?"

"Sure," says Dad without the quiver in his voice. "Do you want to take a look at our fish before we start cleaning them?" He holds up the three pike on our stringer. "Callie caught the prize. Must weight a good eight pounds."

"Where've you been? Didn't you get caught in the storm? It was just awful here in the campground. A deluge. Radio said everyone should stay off the lake. I've been frantic, running down here every ten minutes to look for your boat!"

I hug Mom and give her a kiss as she struggles to hold back the tears.

"I didn't know what to do! Everyone came in except you!"

"I'm sorry, Mom. We didn't mean to make you worry."

Dad drops the stringer and wraps his arms around her for a long moment.

"We're fine, Emily," he says, stepping back. "Oh, we had a little wind. A few waves. Nothing we couldn't handle."

With a steady look, he nods at me, and then pulls his pipe, matches, and tobacco from vest pockets. Each is sealed in a zipped sandwich bag.

"Thank God you're safe!" Mom wipes her eyes with the end of her pink-and-white checked apron and looks closely at each of us. "Well, then," she says in a calmer voice, "I'll go on back and finish setting the table."

We watch Mom slowly climb the low hill to the campground. She turns to look at us several times, as if to make sure we're not an illusion.

Dad places an arm around my shoulders as we enter the cleaning hut. While we filet our northerns, he says not a word about my insisting we remain on the lake to catch one more. He doesn't bemoan the fact that we lost two of them. And he doesn't bring up my second-guessing the way he piloted his boat. Instead, he tousles my hair the way he did when I was a kid.

"You'll get things figured out," he says. "I'm not worried about you."

Like the time, long ago, when I cleaned my first bullhead, I smile at Dad, but feel like crying.

"You'll remember this day for the rest of your life, won't you, Cal?"

"You got that right."

"So will I. And every time we think about it, we'll feel more alive than ever." He gestures toward the channel as if extending a blessing, the way he did all those years ago at Lake Shetek. "It's what an adventure like that does to a fella. Makes him feel *alive*."

Although Dad and I keep the details to ourselves, Mom knows from our demeanor that the time we spent on Leech has not been ordinary. Subdued over dinner, we bless the fish that didn't wash overboard. We admire the golden fillets on our plates, then devour their firm, white offering.

The following Saturday, the three of us attend the Native American celebration. As we enter the gate, we can feel in our chests the deep rhythm of the drums.

Munching on fry bread, we watch those seated around the large drum, its taut head brown with age and use. The older men wear their gray hair in long braids. The younger ones sport baseball caps. All are confident and strong. Over and over again, their voices start high, descend to a lower pitch, and hover there for a long moment. These tones are as mesmerizing to me as "The Lord's Prayer" was when I was a kid. And the lyrics for "*Babbino Caro.*"

The sound of jingle dresses fills the air as young girls and women perform their dances, and then move among the crowds.

We happen upon a group of tireless dancers who look like enormous, ravishing birds in feather bustles and headdresses of green, blue, yellow, red, and white. Wearing fringed buckskin and breastplates of bone and beaded moccasins, they leap and whirl, their plumage fanning the air above flattened grass. Brass ankle bells toll their rhythm.

The power of that dance reminds me of the force and frenzy of the lake— the mighty waters of Leech Lake that clutched at our little boat and wave-tossed us into its troughs.

I turn to look at my parents. They, too, seem energized by the powerful dancers linked through generations to the deep, strong heartbeat of the drum.

"I have some unfinished business to attend to," Dad says abruptly.

"Oh? What's that?" Mom casts me a look, confused. "What are you talking about, Will?"

"My brother. I need to go home."

Twenty-Nine

A Flimsy Thread and That Little Thing Called Hope ❖ *May 1986*

*W*ILL! IS THAT YOU?"

"Who's this?"

"Your brother Ray!"

"Well, I'll be damned. Where the hell have you been?"

Uncle Ray and Dad are of the school that the further away the origin of a phone call, the louder they have to talk—in this case, Sioux City to Minneapolis. The excitement engendered by this unexpected call, plus the distance of time increase the volume. Mom and I can hear Ray's voice from the living room. We rush to listen in on portable phones.

"I'm in this here Jail House Number Two. Can you come and help me out?"

"So that's why I haven't been able to reach you. The phone just rings and rings at your house. How the hell did you land in jail?"

"Well, I'll tell ya, but I can't talk long. They might catch me. I ducked behind this filing cabinet. So far, so good."

Ray had commandeered an office telephone in the Grand View Nursing Home and was talking so fast through his dentures he sounded like someone trying to speak the Dewey Decimal system.

"I got clipped by a motorcycle."

"What?"

"I said I got hit by a motorcycle! Crossing the street in front of my house."

"For Pete's sake. When did that happen?"

"Remember the time you stopped by and we went out for lunch? Well, it was a few months after that. I've been here ever since."

"That was two years ago. You've been in the nursing home all this time and nobody notified us?"

"It wasn't serious. Bunged up my hip and twisted an ankle. Had trouble with my elbow. It took a while for the swelling to go down."

"No broken bones?"

"Nope."

"Golly, that's a miracle for someone your age, Ray."

"Yep. Eighty-three when it happened."

"Somebody should have let us know."

"Eloise got the best of me on this one. Used it as an excuse to clear me out. 'I'm not up to taking care of you,' she said."

"She's a devil!"

"Imagine! Clearing me out of my own house. Probably getting back at me for having her committed all those times. So, I guess I'm in this here Jail House Number Two for life, unless I can figure a way out."

"A rotter," whispers Mom. "A real rotter!"

I nod and snicker at the strong language she uses to describe Eloise.

"She sold everything—my car, all my fishing and hunting gear, spare boat motor. Boxes of gadgets from way back, when we lived on the farm. She told the neighbor lady I wouldn't be coming home again. 'Why wait?' she said. Imagine, Will. That's what she said! 'Why wait?'"

"She took it too far this time, Ray. I can't tell you how sorry I am. But I have to say, it doesn't surprise me."

"Good thing she didn't know where to find my boat or she'd have sold *that*, too. I overheard her tell the neighbor lady, 'I'd sell that old tub of his if I knew where to find the damned thing.' All she knew was that it's in an old barn near Lake Shetek. I never did tell her exactly where."

"Well, that's good. At least you didn't lose *that*."

I shift my eavesdropping phone to the other ear, wondering if the boat he's talking about is the Alumacraft Model K with the big Johnson motor he towed to the lake when I was a kid.

"I'm better now," he says. "Sure like to get out of this place."

"What about Eloise? Does she ever come to see you?"

"She's dead."

"Whaaat?"

"I said she died. What's the matter? Can't you hear so good?"

Mom and I look at each other, our jaws dropping.

"Are you there, Will? Hello? Hello!"

"Yes, I'm still here." He turns to us with a hint of a smile. "My goodness, that's a shock about Eloise."

"Surprised me, too."

"What happened? When did she die?"

"About six months ago. It was all those cigarettes and booze. Anyhoo! Listen, Will, I'd like to see you. You up to making the trip?"

Mom frowns and shakes her head, covers the mouthpiece on her phone. "How can he even think of visiting Ray in his condition?" she whispers.

I nod in agreement, then turn to look out the window at the tulips and daffodils clustered along the boulevard. Sparrows flit among the new maple leaves. Gray squirrels chase each other up the trunks and across branches.

It has only been a year since Dad and I survived the storm on Leech Lake. Now he's exhausted from the drive to hospital for medical tests.

"By golly, we'll be there, Ray. I'll check with Liz. She's in Eau Claire. That's where she lives with her hubby and two kids. I'm pretty sure Cal can make it." His eyes dance as he hangs up and soft-shoes into the living room.

"I don't know, Will. Are you sure you're up to this?"

"Why not? The tests are over with. It's just a matter of waiting for the results."

Picturing Dad's camper and his boat and motor stored in the garage for the first summer ever, I give him a quick hug and say, "Fine by me."

Within a week, we're on our way to visit Uncle Ray at the Grand View Nursing Home in Sioux City. Mom tries to call off the trip at the last minute because of the medical report, but Dad won't hear of it. Since his surgery in San Diego five years earlier, these tests reveal an aggressive recurrence of malignant melanoma.

"We're going to see my brother," he says. "I'll start the treatments as soon as we get back."

Of the four of us piling into the car, Dad is the only upbeat passenger.

T WO LONG CORRIDORS LINED WITH PATIENTS in wheelchairs branch off from the nurses' station. The heavy odor of disinfectant is nauseating. Some patients are draped in their chairs, heads lolling to one side. Others seem to be waiting for something to happen. Their drowsy eyes lift and stare through us. Others focus, their faces suddenly bright and expectant, only to cloud over when they realize we have not come to see them. The place reminds me of a dog shelter I once visited, where packs of excited canines gathered round, wagging their tails, offering kisses. In a moment, all but one turned away with heads lowered and tails stilled when they sensed that I'd made my choice.

From the opposite end of a hallway, Uncle Ray races toward us in his chair, slapping the wheels, leaning forward, a big grin on his face. He's wearing a clean white shirt under a Kelly green cardigan. Brown gabardine slacks do little to hide thin legs and bony knees. The knot in his necktie has come undone or hasn't yet been tied. Wispy white hair, clean and combed, loses its part as he flies down the corridor.

"Halloo!" he calls out, thick lenses magnifying his eyes.

His skin, still tight over high cheekbones, holds a hint of color. Dimples, hidden in the past by a down-turned mouth, deepen as he wheels up to us. He reminds me of a freshly scrubbed schoolboy.

"Halloo!" he yells again, although we are standing next to him. He shakes hands with Dad and reaches up for hugs from Mom, Liz, and me.

"This is my family," he says to the nurse behind the desk, "come all the way from Minnenapolis." He takes the lead and heads for the lounge.

The nurse whispers, "He's been waiting for you all morning. Kept telling everybody, 'I've got family coming. My people are coming to see me today.'"

"Has he had many visitors?" asks Liz.

"His daughter, once or twice. Otherwise, no."

"He must be terribly lonely," says Mom.

"Not really." The nurse smiles and cocks her head. "He's quite social. Somewhat of a Romeo. We have to keep an eye on him."

The lounge, airy and light, is filled with brightly colored sofas and armchairs. A massive entertainment center fills one wall. Opposite, a large window looks out onto a section of grass filled with potted pansies and lilac shrubs blooming in every shade of lavender.

Like conspirators, we gather around Ray to hear of his latest scheme to spring himself from 'Jail House Number Two.' It goes without saying what has been 'Jail House Number One.'

"I've got a lead on a pretty good lawyer," he says. "Main thing is to retrieve my lost possessions and make sure all my remaining assets don't get into the hands of my daughter and her man."

"Oh, Ray," says Mom. "That is so sad."

"How *is* Jen?" I ask. "We were only girls the alst time I saw her."

"No idea. I don't trust that Eye-talian she married." Uncle Ray's loose-fitting dentures clack with each word.

"I thought she married an Englishman," says Liz.

"This is Hubby Number Two. They both turned my daughter against me. I don't trust any of 'em. I'll get out of here, all right. It's just a matter of time."

Liz and I exchange glances, likely wondering the same thing: how can a wheelchair-bound octogenarian make anything happen from inside a nursing home? Who on the outside would believe a doped-up senior? But the longer I listen to his plot, the more I believe he can do it. He's a salesman at heart.

"I've got a girlfriend," he says with a wink, "but the most we do is hold hands and smooch when no one's looking. We sit together during the programs. Last week there was a funeral service for one of the inmates and a young fella came in from some church and sang "Amazing Grace." Real pretty. Not a dry seat in the house."

Ray grins. Like a stand-up playing to the entire room, he casts about to see if everyone has picked up on his joke.

Then, as quickly as a sky can fill with dark clouds, he turns somber and his lips quiver. "She sold all my stuff, did you know that?"

"Yes," says Dad. "You told us when you called."

"Jen took me over to the house after the funeral. There was nothing left—my car, trolling motor, guns, tools, everything—gone."

"Ray," Dad says after a long pause, "why didn't you ever leave Eloise?"

"Good question." He chews on his dentures for a minute. "Well, now, I'd say there was that little thing called hope. You fish with live bait as long as you've got it, and then you go to artificial. After that . . ." Ray shrugs, palms up.

"An empty hook," I mutter, crossing over to the window. More visitors are arriving, some with spring bouquets and boxes of candy.

Ray wheels up next to me, talking with a trace of the old familiar drawl I remember as a girl.

"Saay, I've still got my fishing boat down there by Lake Shetek. It's in that old barn not far from Belle Kittleson's Tavern. How's about if you get me out of here right now and we go down and get it?"

He glances at my dad who is dozing at one end of the sofa. Mom sits next to him, paging through a magazine. Liz visits with the nurse.

"Your dad's not lookin' so good. Suppose you could help me out? We could wet a line while we're down there."

He starts to rise from his wheelchair in an effort to grab a walker left near the window. I hold the walker steady, directly in front of him.

I stare at my uncle. *This* is our last chance.

The idea of plotting a breakout excites me—victory over death-by-nursing-home. I'll sneak Uncle Ray into my car, drive to southern Minnesota and find the old barn near Belle's place. I can picture my uncle growing younger with each mile closer to his boat. And my dad, once again robust, will take the wheel and I'll be a kid again, leaning forward, elbows on the seat backs, catching every word, every joke, every look between brothers.

While I steady the walker, Ray grabs at it, misses, and with a groan, crashes back onto the seat of his wheelchair.

The flimsy thread of my dream snaps and drifts away.

"Cake and coffee," announces an aide, "now being served in the dining room. Everyone welcome."

Thirty

Liverwurst and Crackers ❖ Late Fall, *1987*

"I DON'T CARE TO DISCUSS THE DETAILS, Will, but I thought you should know. I escaped from that there Jailhouse Number Two." "You sly devil. How'd you manage to do that?"

As the phone conversation continues, Uncle Ray provides hints enough to tell us that he was kicked out for bad behavior—taking over the Grandview Nursing Home office, among other things:

"They got mad at me for locking the door and making a few phone calls to relatives in Illinois and California. And Minnesota, of course. I tried to put in a call to Italy, but they caught me before it went through. Just wanted to find out what sort of family my daughter married into. They could be Mafia for all I know."

Ray had also been cited for rifling through files, mocking the staff, laughing during memorial services, engaging in myriad flirtations, and barging late at night into rooms occupied by persons he called "the willing."

"I'm pretty lonely now. Not much doin' around here. The ladies I hire to help me out never stay very long. I'm just being friendly. Guess they're not interested. I thought they'd like a little attention, especially the single ones. The last old gal ran out so fast she left her pocketbook behind."

"I wonder if the courts had to get involved," Dad says, once he's off the phone. "It was Eloise who put him there."

"Highly unusual for a man his age to do all that on his own," says Mom. "I have to say, though, I admire his spirit."

As for me, a bit proud of the old guy, I feel strangely disappointed at not having been involved in springing him from the nursing home.

"He wants us to come for a visit, Emily."

This time, Mom doesn't balk; Dad has rallied since completing treatments for his melanoma.

"One more trip to Sioux City, Callie, while your papa is still up to traveling."

On the road, we listen to jazz and opera and speculate about Uncle Ray's state of mind.

Finally, we arrive at 2214 Oak Street. The house, still white with red trim, is clearly weather-worn.

Dad unclips his seatbelt but doesn't move to get out. "I wonder what the inside looks like."

"Do you think the door will open for us today?" asks Mom.

"Why not?" He sweeps a black comb through his sparse white hair. "This time, I should only have to knock once."

For some reason, we're in no hurry to leave the car.

Mom belches nervously. "Every fall for how many years and never once invited in. All that upset, season after season."

"That's enough, Emily. Leave it to the past. Isn't that your motto?"

"I suppose so."

As if it were a great effort, we open the doors and step out of the car.

Dad ambles up the sidewalk ahead of us and slowly takes the four concrete steps, pausing on each one. He wipes his feet on the brittle mat and raps at the storm door. Then he turns toward us and raises his eyebrows, as if to say, "Well, this is it."

Seeing him like this, after so many years of effort, puts a lump in my throat. I wonder if there'll be another argument. Or has he gotten that out of his system, having spent half of our trip talking about Ray and his foibles?

"At least Aunt Eloise isn't here to throw skillets at us," I mutter.

Mom chuckles nervously.

We can hear Uncle Ray's metal walker banging against the entry wall. The doorknob twists around and around, as if a child were teasing us from the other side.

Finally, the lock clicks and the door swings open.

With one hand on his walker, Uncle Ray tries to stand up straight in greeting. The front of his white dress shirt is stained and his brown cardigan has slipped off one shoulder.

"Haloo, haloo, c'mon in," he says in his old drawl. "Did ya have a good trip?"

Mom and I get hugs. He is clean-shaven, but I think he hasn't bathed or brushed his teeth in a while. His breath reminds me of a marsh in August.

Dad looks evenly at Ray while shaking his hand, then peers into the darkened living room. "Well, here we are, after all these years."

It's apparent that Ray hasn't found another cleaning lady in some time. The dark brown carpet is littered with crumbs and lint. Stacks of newspapers have toppled over next to a soiled recliner with deep depressions in its cushions. Sticky plates and cups teeter on a TV tray. The furniture, upholstered in dark burgundy and brown, reminds me of a seedy funeral home, where only a hint of sunshine can find its way in through tilted blinds.

Decorating the walls are large prints of dark velvety roses in ornate gold frames, ceramic plates with flower motifs, and a pair of beige sconces without candles on either side of a lavabo dripping with faded plastic ivy.

"Yes, sir, Ray," says Dad, "I'm sure glad to see your place. After all these years."

Mom stands stiffly in the middle of the room for a moment, then wanders over to a large curio cabinet. "Eloise had some lovely dishes."

I look over her shoulder at the clouded crystal on dusty glass shelves.

"This piece looks familiar," she says. "Didn't Julia have one like it?"

Too late, she covers her mouth.

"Let me see that." Dad scoots over to inspect the pink cut-glass candy dish. "This *is* Mother's! She meant for Liz to have it." He turns abruptly, loses his balance, and grabs hold of the cabinet, which begins to teeter and rattle.

I steady the curio case while Mom steadies Dad.

"What about all that stuff you took, Ray?" His voice is husky. "Where is it?"

"Don't have anything! Never did."

"That's a damned lie and you know it!"

"Oh, Will, please don't start up." Mom blanches. "I thought you weren't going to do this. We just got here, for heaven's sake."

"You're calling me a liar?" Ray bellows. "In my own house?"

"That's right. You're a damned liar and a thief! If you think you can get away with . . ."

I rush over to the spinet. "How about a concert?" But when I plunk down on the round stool, it wobbles so crazily that I fall to the floor.

Silenced for a moment, the others stare at me while I pick myself up and figure out how to balance on the bucking stool.

I place my fingers on gritty, yellow keys. Some are cracked and chipped. The strings, hopelessly out of tune, create a unique compositional discord as I hammer away at "Wonderful, Wonderful Copenhagen" in *forte possibile*.

"Mother's sheet music!" Dad shouts over the cacophony of sour notes. "How about that?"

"What about it?" Ray roars back. He clutches his walker by the handles and bumps it up and down in frustration.

"Well, where *is* it? Bring out everything you took. Line it up!"

"Dad!" I call out above the concert, "I saved most of Gram's music. Remember?"

"This is insane!" Mom grabs Dad's sleeve and gives it a jerk. "I will not stay here another minute and listen to this poppycock. It's not why we came."

"That's right." Ray backs into his recliner and flops down. "Listen to your wife. She's got a heck of a lot more sense than you ever had. Why do you keep harping? I didn't take anything. Anyhoo, Eloise got rid of all my stuff."

"It was thirty years ago!" Mom shouts above the piano. "I'm sick and tired of this rehash!" She turns abruptly. "Callie, that's enough!"

Without stopping, I tone "the music" down to *forte-piano.*

"I don't care how long ago it was," Dad persists. "It wasn't right. Why can't he own up to it?"

"You took the guns, Will. And Dad's fishing gear. And from what I heard, you got Uncle Amer's belongings."

"You didn't want any of it. Besides, you were never around to divvy things up. Hell, you got your share of the proceeds from what I kept, plus everything on the sale, plus the cottage and the house in town. It was all done on the up-and-up. You didn't even bother to come and help us out, God damn it! Now you need to make good on what you stole!"

Although I agree with Dad, I, too, have grown sick of the same old litany. As I punch away at the keys, I feel as though I'm entertaining at an insane asylum. I finish with a thundering arpeggio across all eighty-eight keys and nearly fall off the stool again. Dad and Ray chuckle as if I had performed a vaudeville act.

Mom grabs my arm, muttering, "This is outrageous. A nuthouse."

We look at each other and begin to laugh. The men glance at us with concern, as if this shouldn't be part of the act.

Still chuckling, I go to the bathroom which is as grimy as a backwoods oil station.

From there I can hear Ray shifting the argument by listing his current grievances: Number one: cheats for a daughter and son-in-law—"That Wop turned her against me! They don't care about my welfare, only my money!" Number two: corrupt lawyers—"A bunch of thieves! Slicko crooks! Can't trust 'em as far as you can throw 'em!"

After exiting the bathroom, I hear Number three: personal possessions gone forever—"Eloise sold all my stuff, didn't think I'd be coming back," and

Number four: revisionist memories of his marriage—"She wasn't so bad. My wife was a good cook. We were pretty happy together."

What? He must really be losing it. Where is Jen in all this? Are she and the lawyers really trying to lock up his assets? What is the truth?

Propelling himself from chair to walker, my uncle skitters across the carpet like a water bug on a pond. "There's a letter here somewhere I want you to read," he says, scooting from table to kitchen counter. "Oh, and something to eat." He points out a snack he has set out hours (or maybe days) earlier. We line up at the counter to nibble on crusty liverwurst and stale crackers.

I look around the kitchen at the dust-laden treasures that once belonged to my aunt: a stained yellow-and-blue recipe box, faded nosegays of artificial violets in tiny vases, a grimy oilcloth table covering, large copper Jell-O molds, sticky with grease and dust, hanging on hooks above the stove. On a back burner, a rusty iron skillet seems to be lying in wait.

Mom looks tense, as if waiting for another squall.

"What was that letter you wanted to show us?" asks Dad. His voice carries an edge and he still looks miffed about the pink candy dish and what it represents.

"Oh, that's right." Ray disappears and returns several minutes later, waving an envelope. "An old letter from Mother, written thirty-seven years ago. See here? September 1950."

Ray passes the envelope to Dad. He and Mom stand shoulder-to-shoulder at the counter, silently reading. Afterward, they look at each other and shake their heads.

"Why Eloise saved this one," says Ray, "I'll never know. Thought you might like to read it."

"She saved it out of meanness," says Mom. "That's why. And now you're showing it to us out of that same meanness. Shame on you, Ray."

I take the faded yellow pages from her hand. The first few paragraphs are about the good fishing on Lake Shetek and how their neighbor, Mr. Johnson, got splattered on his bald pate by a low-flying gull. Then I get to page two and the paragraph that has shocked my parents into momentary silence:

> *Will and Emily are having their spats. I told Vic that I wished Willy would leave her and come back home. He said to keep my nose out of it. I can't tell him anything. Sure wish*

*your brother would file for a divorce. Don't know what would
happen to the girls. Suppose they'd go with Emily. Anyway,
we can only hope . . .*

Now it's my turn to feel her punch from the grave. So it wasn't entirely
about hardening of the arteries after all. In a flash, these written words cancel
much of the affection I had managed to reserve for my grandmother.

"Why did you show us this letter, Uncle Ray? It was a lousy thing to do."

"Ancient history," he says with a toss of his hand. "Something out of our
past."

Dad regains his composure. "I suppose you know Mother wished the
same for you."

"Sure, I know it. She was working on us, too."

"She would have been happy if neither one of us had married," says Dad.
"She just wanted to keep us on the farm."

"Jesus Christ," I say, "some mother-in-law."

Ray looks at me, appalled.

"What's that language?"

"Nothing worse than all this family bullshit. Moreover, Uncle Ray, I recall
the day when you got drenched and hollered a few choice words of your own.
Shall I repeat them?"

Looking embarrassed, Uncle Ray grabs his walker and turns away. "Is
that what you teach your girls, Will? Gutter talk?"

Mustering a sarcastic grin, Dad snorts and nods at me in salute.

"You bet, when the occasion calls for it, Goddamn it!"

Mom sighs deeply.

"Oh, Will. Callie, I do wish you wouldn't swear. It isn't . . ."

"Ladylike? I really don't care, Mom. This whole thing is exactly as I've
called it: Bullshit! The stupid games they've been playing all these years. And
for what?"

Mom seems to ponder my words and looks back at Uncle Ray.

"I have to agree with Callie," she says softly. "This is one *shitty* letter. And
it isn't the first *shitty* thing to come out of this house."

I sidle over next to her until I can smell her perfume—*L'Air du Temps*.

"It hasn't been easy living among the Lindstroms," she murmurs, her
voice a faint vibrato.

I put an arm around her shoulders. "I know, Mom. But you've managed all these years. And you've done it well."

With pinched lips, her chin puckers in an effort to maintain control. For as long as I can remember, this is how she wards off tears and showing weakness—letting her chin do all the work. Grateful for my acknowledgement, but unwilling to bask in it, she quickly says, "I'm worried about your papa."

"Me, too. We'll do all we can—you and Liz and I."

Mom squeezes my hand.

Before tucking the letter back into its envelope, I study Gram's fancy scrawl. Her flourishing capital letters and the small, angular script remind me of the messages she wrote in my birthday cards and on the inside covers of the books she gave me when I was a girl. I toss the letter onto the counter, hoping to file this memory where it belongs.

"Well, Mother," trumpets Dad, proffering his glass of iced tea to the empty space between ceiling and wall, "you never got your wish. Emily and I are still going strong—fifty-two years of wedded bliss."

He sets the glass down, wraps his arms around Mom, and kisses her for a long moment.

Bent over his walker, Uncle Ray stares up at them with wide, refracted eyes. His lips twitch for a remembered kiss.

Then, as if a signal has sounded, the three amble back to the living room where they settle in to read the Sunday paper.

Seeing them absorbed by inconsequential local news, I am overcome by the absurdity of driving two hundred and thirty miles just to read the damned newspaper. What about the family history? The good stories? A little fun-loving exchange between brothers. Isn't that why we came?

A sob rises in my throat, which I try to cover with a nervous giggle, which makes me sound like someone not right in the head. I imagine Aunt Eloise carrying on in this house, weaving from room to room, bouncing off the door jams, yammering like a mad woman.

Curious at my strange outburst, the others glance up to see me leaning on the counter, staring at them. They turn back to their newspapers. *How can they?*

Finally, the silence of the hollow afternoon and the emptiness of wasted years stir my insides, until I can no longer hold back. I pick up a knife in one hand and a fork in the other, hold them aloft and open my mouth, ready to shout, "What about this silverware?"

But I don't say it. Instead, I drop the knife and fork in the sink and wander back to the living room.

Mom lowers her paper and smiles at me. Ray looks up for a second and resumes reading. Dad tosses his paper aside, looks as if he's about to say something, then rests his head against the chair back and stares at the ceiling.

Finally, he says, "Ray, do you remember Ruby Ryan from Masterton? The one who tried to kill her husband some years ago?"

"Who could forget a woman like that? Why?"

"Did you sell her that life insurance policy she took out on Carl?"

"No. She asked me about it when I saw her at the Mint Cafe. I told her I wasn't licensed for the state of Minnesota."

Dad lets out a sigh of relief. But he isn't finished.

"Now, about Mother's things—"

"Oh, no-o-o-o," Mom and I drone in unison.

"I don't want to argue anymore, Ray. Just own up to it. That's all I ask."

Uncle Ray is quiet for a moment. Then, in a sarcastic voice, he says, "Well, I might have taken a few things, but I don't see why you have to get so worked up about it." He reaches for something on his TV tray.

Dad looks at each of us and nods once. "More than a few things," he mutters.

Mom frowns and shakes her head as if they are in church and he should pipe down.

Uncle Ray fumbles through a stack of legal papers and picks out a sepia-colored photo of himself with Dad and Grandad dressed in their hunting gear, holding their shotguns with the barrels pointed skyward. It is autumn. Their duck boat rests on a small trailer. A half dozen geese hang from a line attached to their hunting shack.

That picture, as arbitrator, allows us to part on halfway decent terms. Sent on our way with hugs and a handshake, we leave the house at 2214 Oak Street.

Our trip back to Minnesota is not a silent one.

"Couldn't you have let it go, Will?" Mom scolds. "Why can't you just put it to rest, be at ease with him? You're old men, for heaven's sake. Enough is enough. Material things shouldn't matter any more."

"He can't get away with lying about what he took."

I aim the Cadillac onto the Interstate. "At least he apologized, Dad."

"Not much of one, far as I'm concerned."

"Do you realize the bulk of our visit was spent arguing and reading the damned paper?"

Mom leans forward from the back seat. "Callie, I saw you in the kitchen wielding that knife and fork, ready to sound off."

"Ah, but I didn't."

"Good for you." She pats my shoulder. "You're making headway. But I know what you were thinking. After all, I *am* your mother. You must realize we can't stay young forever. Can't always be as lively as you'd like us to be."

"I don't know, Mom. For a while, those were a couple of pretty lively guys back there. It's just too bad they use up their energy on all the wrong stuff."

With the lightest touch, Mom reaches over to smooth back a hank of Dad's hair. Exhausted by the day's events, he has dozed off.

"You've never been able to stand seeing anyone go down, Callie. I guess we should just let things be. We'll know your pa is alive and kicking as long as he can argue with his brother."

"A hell of thing to look forward to every time they get together. He's always so excited to see Ray, but once he does, he goes ballistic. Why can't he let the past go?"

Mom settles back in her seat.

"He's stuck, Callie. And he can't stand a liar."

Over the next several months, Mom keeps Ray informed about Dad's illness. Uncle Ray answers with long, encouraging letters peppered with epithets: ". . . Those crooked lawyers instigated the sale of my possessions and the disappearance of my will. I met with a Mr. Dickerson and gave him what for. He left with his head between his tail. Ha Ha!"

Another letter, written on legal-sized typing paper in shaky longhand, and taking up every inch of white space, is a jumble. We have to turn the pages in circles in order to read the hilly sentences crammed into every margin. The letter ends:

"If you can make this out, I will hire you. Take good care of yourself, Will. You could make it to a hundred, easy."

And that's the last we hear from Uncle Ray—until the following year, when I receive a phone call from a stranger.

Thirty-One

Delicate Armor ❖ November, 1988

"I DON'T KNOW ANY DETAILS, MA'AM. I just put him on a plane bound for Minneapolis." It's the voice of a young man on the phone—pleasant, with an Iowa accent. "This *is* Callie Lindstrom?"

"Yes," I answer cautiously. "Who are you? A friend?"

"No, never saw him before today. I was parked on Oak Street this afternoon and this old guy started waving his cane and calling out, panicky-like. Said he had to get to the airport right away. Something about an emergency. I couldn't turn him down."

"Is he all right?"

"I think so. But he kept saying, 'I've got to see my brother, I've got to see my brother.' He's pretty old to be traveling alone, if you ask me."

"After all these years," I mutter.

"What's that, ma'am?"

"Nothing. Just that no one was expecting him."

I glance out the window at Cook's Bay. The lake was open and rolling yesterday. Now, at dusk, a thin skin of ice has formed along the shoreline. A sudden gust of wind scatters fallen maple leaves, chasing their crisp, brown shapes across the slick surface. It begins to snow.

"He'll be on Northwest flight 165 from Sioux City," continues the young man. "Should be landing in Minneapolis around seven tonight. At first he couldn't remember which city he wanted to go to. Had to go back inside and look for his address book. He kept turning the pages until he recognized your name. You'll meet him then?"

"Yes, of course. Thank you for your help, Mr. . . ."

"I'm Jake. Hey, no problem. By the way, he'll have a small suitcase—one of those old blue antiquey things."

SINCE OCTOBER, Dad has been receiving radiation treatments against two persistent tumors—one under his left eye, the other inside his brain, blocking the fifth cranial nerve. The first has shrunk a little, but the second, according to a recent MRI, continues to grow.

During our appointment, Liz asks if the new tumors might be the result of maverick cells spinning off into the blood stream.

"He had that surgery five years ago," she says. "Five years..."

"It couldn't possibly have anything to do with surgical techniques," the doctor insists, lecturing us on metastasizing cells.

"Bull," I mutter.

"Oh, Callie," sighs Mom, "just once in a blue moon, I wish you wouldn't ..."

"*Blue Moon*," I sing quietly, "*you saw me standing alone...*"

The oncologist ignores our exchange. "It's the trigeminal nerve," he says, tracing a leadless pencil around a sheet of paper filled with the outline of a brain divided into sections with little rivers running through them. "There are twelve cranial nerves—the fifth being the largest."

Sitting before this emotionless man, I wish for a fifth of anything at that moment: a fifth of whiskey, the fifth grade, any old fifth symphony, except Beethoven's.

"Here we have the major branches making up the trigeminal," continues the doctor, as if addressing a medical convention. "V-1 is the ophthalmic nerve, controlling the eye movements, V-2 is maxillary, and V-3 is mandibular. All three are responsible for the various sensations of the face: blinking, chewing, swallowing, smiling. It's the third most common tumor of the twelve cranial nerves, the acoustic nerve being the first."

I don't care what the second one is. Wouldn't make any difference anyhow. The doctor's dose of information makes me angry.

"The carotid artery controls the blood supply to the brain," he says. "This has been a slow-growing tumor—five years."

"Five years! That's what my sister is trying to tell you."

Liz and I look at each other, knowing what the other is thinking.

That's why Dad started to grit his teeth. And it wasn't because Mom was harping at him to slack up or be careful in the boat. It happened at the oddest times—while we were out fishing or playing cards or sitting at the dinner table. And sometimes while driving. He said that the shocks inside his head felt like electric jolts. We thought he was having mini-strokes, typical for his age, nothing serious, still functioning.

"So, get it out of there."

The doctor looks at me and slowly shakes his head. "We don't have the technology. At his age, surgery would likely be fatal."

For a moment, no one speaks.

I want to shout, You're telling us that it can't be done? That you don't have the technology to take care of him? I know just the guy who could carve that sucker out of there—except he's the one with the tumor. My dad can clean a bullhead in eight seconds flat—with the precision of a surgeon.

But I don't say any of that. Instead, I grasp Dad's arm and search his face. For the first time ever, my next words no longer describe him. I say them anyway: "He's not one to give up. There must be something you can do."

"I'm sorry. These treatments should lend quality to his remaining months."

"But he's a fighter!"

"Oh, Callie." Mom reaches over to touch my face.

Liz wipes her eyes.

Dad sits up straight and looks at each of us.

"Well, then," he says, making his usual chirping sound. "I guess it's my time." At that moment, he reminds me of Grandad.

I can't believe the end is near. He still dances in front of the television, grinning and hitching a shoulder in rhythm with Lawrence Welk and his orchestra. It's just the left side of his face that can't smile anymore.

"Dad!" I shout into the phone, "you'll never guess who's coming to see you."

"You were just here, Cal."

"Not me. Someone else."

"Who's that?"

"Your brother, that's who."

"Wha-at? I can't believe it. You know, he's never once paid us a visit. Wait. I'll put your mother on. She can get the particulars."

"Callie? Is that you, dear?" Mom's voice sounds weary.

"Hi, Mom. Guess who's on a plane coming here."

"I think I know. I've been writing Ray an occasional note about your Dad, but I didn't think he'd come."

"Well, he sure as hell didn't give us much notice. If it hadn't been for some guy off the street, Uncle Ray'd be living out the rest of his life at the Minneapolis airport. What if I'd been gone when this Jake guy phoned?"

"I wonder why Ray didn't call us."

"Who knows?"

"My goodness, I'd better get the spare room ready. It's too bad Liz had to go back home."

"I know."

"Well, drive carefully, dear."

"Wouldn't do it any other way, Ma. See you in a couple of hours."

While the engine warms up, I brush thick snow from the windshield and side mirrors. The headlights and taillights need clearing, too.

It's a pity my nagging thoughts can't be brushed away as easily as this dry fluffy snow. Dad and I haven't had any good talks in a long time. He's preoccupied, working hard on his own preparations for what's to come, hunting the courage and strength he'll need for letting go. There isn't even standing room for me at the entrance to his new world. How he will get through that gate is anybody's guess. He never talks about it.

My two cats fought their deaths: Pola urinated on the metal table and scrambled back into my arms; Topaz hissed and bit the veterinarian's hand. Mom says that dealing with all that will help prepare me for what's to come. Could be.

Meanwhile, I talk to Piper. But my dog isn't much of a listener.

Cruising along the freeway at nightfall, lulled by the drone of the heater-defroster, and hypnotized by a zillion snowflakes pelting the windshield, I realize the importance of this little journey: I am on my way to find Uncle Ray and bring him home to Dad.

Was there ever a time when my uncle was truly a part of our family? For as far back as I can remember, he only played bit parts: occasional walk-ons, cameos, a line or two, quick exits. Mom used to call him a Steppenwolf, linked to no one.

I remember how he glided in and out of the hospital in wingtips and a long winter coat over a three-piece suit, hair perfectly trimmed, gold crowns gleaming under the bright lights. Chill air, carried in on his overcoat, freshened the sick room where Gram lay dying. Uncle Ray teased the nurses until they giggled like schoolgirls and continued their rounds with a quicker step.

A young girl then, I was impressed by how handsome he was, how debonair and polished. But I never liked him because of how he treated the family, especially my father.

At the turn-off from Highway 494 toward the Minneapolis-Saint Paul airport, it is snowing hard and the snow spins around curved street lamps. A wild flurry of flakes catches in the high beams of airplanes taking off and landing.

A parking space in the ramp opens up near the terminal skyway. It is seven-thirty. My uncle will likely be near the baggage claim. I walk across to the lower level and check each of the luggage carrousels. But he's nowhere to be seen. After riding the escalator up to the next level, I ask a cart driver to look for an elderly, possibly confused man at gate D 19.

"I'll wait by this door," I tell him.

Fifteen minutes later, the driver weaves toward me through clusters of travelers trailing their luggage. Ray is seated in the rear with his walker next to him. A brown dress hat sits low on his head. He sees me standing alone, watching for him, and waves his cane as if it were a scepter.

"Halloo! Who are you?" he calls out jokingly.

"I'm Callie. Who are you?"

"Last I knew I was Raymond V. Lindstrom—V for Victor. At least I got his name." He gives me a shaky hug after I help him down from the cart. I file away his comment for future consideration.

"This *is* a surprise, Uncle Ray. We didn't know you were coming."

"Your Ma wrote that Will isn't any too good. I figured I should see him before . . . well, you know. I can stay a week."

I want to ask, *Why now, when all you can do is sit around and stare at each other or read the damned newspaper?* Instead, I look at this old man in his rumpled black suit a couple of sizes too large, bent over a walker, hanks of white hair poking out from beneath a tired old hat, his white shirt cuffs and collar yellowed and frayed, his fancy paisley-green-and-brown tie spotted with greasy food stains, and I say, "Well, we're glad you're here. Jake called to let me know. Good thing you had my phone number."

"Who's Jake?"

"The guy who gave you a ride to the airport in Sioux City. Remember?"

"Oh, that fella with the souped-up car. He drives too fast. Looks like a tramp with that beard and long hair. Wears it in a ponytail. Men shouldn't wear ponytails."

Ray turns to stare at a young woman in a mini skirt. She is tall and thin with long, straight legs.

"C'mon, Uncle Ray, let's catch the elevator. Do you want to hold onto my arm?"

"Not necessary."

He takes off behind his walker rigged with a set of wheels and a pair of chartreuse tennis balls on the front, and scoots along the corridor as if he were skating behind a chair.

"How was your flight?" I ask, trying to keep up.

"No fight. Don't know what you're talking about."

"I said 'flight.' How was your *flight?*"

"Oh. The stewardesses aren't as cute as they used to be. Too old."

At baggage claim, Ray turns to wink at a middle-aged woman standing next to him.

"This here is my niece come to get me."

"That's nice," says the woman, quickly edging toward the carrousel.

In the parking ramp, I open my hatchback and place Ray's luggage inside. Considering its age and how scuffed up it is, the suitcase is solid and intact. And very light. Is there anything in it? I stow the walker, then help my uncle into the passenger side.

"Where's your hubby?" he asks, as soon as I slip in behind the wheel. "Don't you have a man?"

"Not any more . . . Be sure to buckle up. It's nasty out there."

"What happened? Is he dead?"

"No, Uncle Ray, we're divorced. Have been for a long time."

"Everybody gets a divorce these days. Easy way out."

"Not necessarily." I exit the ramp and pull up to the window to pay the parking fee. "Let's just say Jim is happier without me criticizing his international efforts to support the scotch industry. And his local contributions in aiding young damsels in distress."

"Oh, one of those—a two-timer."

"Yup, one of those." I rev the engine, crank up the heater, and merge onto the highway, unsure why I'm confiding in Uncle Ray. Maybe because I've never told anyone about Jim and it has to come out. "Silly of us women, isn't it, to assume that the men we marry are going to be like our fathers?"

"I wouldn't know. What line of work is he in?"

"Teaches English at a community college. He's smart. Maybe too smart."

"How so?"

"He enjoys using words to put people down. Thinks he's being clever, but all it does is hurt. He calls it 'one-upmanship.'"

"Such as?"

"Let's see. One of his favorites was, 'I think I know what you think you're trying to say.'"

"I don't get it. Too many words. What else?"

"For one thing, he hates Puccini."

"Puccini! That rings a bell. What else?"

"Soon after we got married, he told everyone he was going to reel me in, whip me into shape."

A flashback blips through my brain—me in a fetal position on the living room floor, two months pregnant.

"And did he? Whip you into shape?"

I sit up straight behind the wheel and jut my chin out. "What do you think?"

Shifting sideways for a closer look, Uncle Ray strings out his next words.

"Hard to saay. You seem pretty capable, but then I don't know you very well."

"No, I guess you don't. Anyhow, I should have gotten out sooner. Should have married Bobby Keeler. We could have had a family."

"Who's that?"

"A boy I knew a long time ago, back in Masterton. He lived down the block from Gram."

"You know," says Ray, after a lull in the conversation, "I never took those things from Mother's house the way your pa says. We can't ever talk without him accusing me."

"Well, you *did*, Uncle Ray. We *saw* you."

"Only a few dishes and towels, maybe a little silverware; I don't even know where any of it is. I think Eloise sold it all."

"It's ancient history. I think you should just forget about it. Dad isn't up to the fight anymore."

"He's the one starts it!"

I glance at my uncle in time to see his gray cheeks flush. Liver spots dot his skin, which is otherwise smooth for a man of eighty-six. He removes his hat, leaving strands of yellow-white hair flat against his scalp. I expect to see him run a hand through it, as he did years ago. But he sits quietly, holding the misshapen brown fedora in his lap. A song my mother taught me when we used to walk the train tracks together near Federal Dam comes to mind: *Hallelujah, I'm a bum, hallelujah, bummin' again . . .*

Snow drifts across the highway as the wind picks up. Back home in May-wood County, with its open fields and acres of prairie land, there is little to stop the snow, except fence lines and jagged cornstalks, small cover for pheasants and snowshoe rabbits. Here, the drifts pile up against concrete abutments and woven fences, in culverts and strip mall parking lots.

Without warning, I hit a patch of black ice. My stomach flip-flops as I let up on the gas, grip the steering wheel, and hold it in the direction of the skid. The car fishtails. Uncle Ray reaches for the handle above the glove compartment and leans forward, shooting me a look that questions my driving ability.

The words, "Slack up!" echo in my mind—Mom directing Dad during his last years behind the wheel.

"Whew!" I take a deep breath. "At least there were no other cars next to us."

"That was quite a ride," says Uncle Ray, settling back, his face drained of color.

I decelerate to forty-five the rest of the way. It takes longer for my heart rate to slow down.

With the heater running full blast, the inside of the car smells stuffy. Beads of sweat trickle from my armpits. I want to ditch my heavy jacket and sweater, but there's no place to pull over.

"Been in any good fights lately?" I ask, in an effort to lessen the tension.

"Why, yes, as a matter of fact, I have."

I cast him a quick look and wait for an explanation.

"You maybe know that I've been through quite a few housekeepers in the past, but not a one of 'em stayed around very long. Well, this last old crow flew out so fast she left her pocketbook behind."

"Yes, you mentioned that."

"I don't believe I told you about her hubby, though. He came by the next day—thought he could beat me up."

"No kidding."

"I must've scared him plenty 'cause he told me he didn't want to fight. Just wanted to get his wife's purse back. I ran him off the place, told him to get out, and threw the old bag's bag after him."

I start to laugh, then notice that he's serious.

"Guess I can't blame you for trying, Uncle Ray."

"Didn't know she was married. Kinda pretty, but a little on the hefty side. Old, too.

As we drive the rest of the way in silence, I wonder what my uncle considers young.

It is nearly ten o'clock by the time we pull up in front of the apartment building in Long Lake, where my parents moved in order to be closer to Dad's doctors.

We unload the car and make our way to the entry through fresh snow.

Mom opens wide the door and gives us each a hug. I can smell the coffee brewing.

"Will is asleep," she says, ushering Ray into the spare room. I set his suitcase down next to the bed. While he gets settled, I help Mom with the cups and saucers and arrange a plate of Little Debbie fig bars.

"Listen," I say, cocking an ear. "Do you hear that?"

It's the sound of dresser drawers and metal filing cabinet drawers opening and closing, one after the other.

"He won't find anything," says Mom. "I removed all our personal papers."

THE NEXT AFTERNOON, I find my mother worn out by the commotion of Dad and Ray beating a path behind their walkers from living room to bathroom and back.

"They can't seem to light," she whispers.

I wrap an arm around her thin shoulders and rest my head against hers before going into the living room.

"Hi, guys," I call out. They stand up to greet me. I kiss each one on the cheek and they beam for a moment. Dad reaches out for a hug.

The apartment is as stuffy as a nursing home and smells like one. I open the patio door for some fresh air. The sun is shining, but the November drafts make the men shiver and tug at their cardigans. They launch themselves away from their metal contraptions and fall back onto easy chairs.

I join Mom in the kitchen. We soon hear snatches of conversation coming from the other room: ". . . those things you took from Mother's house . . . responsibility to the family . . . my share . . . when you were a kid . . . Mother's pet . . . Eloise called the shots . . ."

"Listen to that, Mom. They're at it again."

"I swear. Those two will go to their graves arguing. At least they're not shouting at each other any more."

She turns the burner off under the teakettle and prepares the tea. We place cups and cookies on a large tray and carry them to the living room.

Slightly agitated, Dad stretches out his legs and draws them back in. Ray sucks loudly on his dentures.

"You two were getting along just fine this morning," says Mom, setting the tray on the coffee table. "What happened? It's as if you have to put on a show for Callie."

"Mom's right. Every time we get together, this is what you do. What will it take for you guys to settle your differences?"

"It's not so much the things he took," Dad says in a tired voice, "but how he went about it."

"I told you, Will," says Ray, "Eloise . . ."

"Can't you ever talk about something pleasant?" I pluck a few fig bars from the platter. "All this other stuff is in the past. *Let it go!*"

"No," says Ray, "we can't let it go. Some things still need to be said."

I sit down on the sofa next to Mom, curious about the change in my uncle's voice. Calm and low, it has lost its sarcastic edge, its drawl and pretense.

Dad leans forward in his chair. "I still say we should have gone through Mother's house together, Ray, divided everything evenly."

"I took what I thought Jen could use when she went out on her own."

"That's a lot of bunk. I have daughters, too—girls who spent *time* with their grandparents. *Time*, Ray! That's something you never gave."

Ray is quiet for a long moment.

"The folks could always count on you, Will. You were always there, never let 'em down."

Dad nails his brother with his good eye.

"Yes, and Mother took me for granted because of it. But you, she had to keep working on you, paying extra attention, always trying to get you to come for a visit, a family holiday. Mother never gave up trying to get you to come home."

"Eloise wouldn't go and she wouldn't let me take Jen. There was hell enough to pay whenever I drove up by myself."

"That was no way to live, Ray. You should have gotten out."

"Wasn't easy. I kept hoping things would change. Sometimes they did, but not for long. There were a few years, though, when I . . ."

Uncle Ray loses his strained look. Gazing out of the window, he seems to be remembering some long ago time in his life when he was happy.

"Let's just say I was faithful in my own way," he says, turning back to us.

"Well, it doesn't matter any more. Everything's done with. We start from scratch."

The right corner of Dad's mouth turns up in a smile as he looks at Mom and me. He still has a dimple on that side of his face.

"You're here now, and I'm glad you made the trip."

Quiet for a moment, Uncle Ray seems to be struggling with what to say next.

"Well, I apologize," he says. "It wasn't right of me to take those things without talking it over with you first."

Dad looks as if he's about to weep.

"I appreciate that, Ray." He chokes up with his next words. "Thank you. Now we can call it 'case closed.'"

Mom and I exchange wide-eyed looks.

Uncle Ray fidgets in his chair. "There's one other thing."

"I thought we were done."

"No, we're not. I've never said any of this before. It needs saying now."

"What's that?"

"Anytime Dad needed help with something important, he turned to you."

"What the hell are you talking about?"

"He chose you to go to Montana with him. You got to see the land, Will. It was you brought Uncle Amer back."

"I wondered if that was on your mind all these years."

"I couldn't even attend his funeral. Never had the chance to see him one last time, say a proper goodbye."

"Somebody had to keep the farm going. Mother couldn't do it alone. Besides, we might not have made it back ourselves. Dad counted on you to do a good job at home."

"I never heard that from him."

"He was proud of us both, Ray. He just never said it. If you'd ever noticed the look on his face when you brought down a duck or a pheasant or hauled in a great northern, you'd have known. He never used words to tell us how he felt. You know that."

My uncle sat silent for a moment, picking at a piece of thread on his sweater. So that's why he made that comment when I met him at the airport: ". . . V for Victor. At least I got his name."

"What happened out there, Will? In Montana. I never really knew."

"You never wanted to know."

"Well, I'd like to hear it now."

And Dad tells the story of Amer one last time, ending with, "Now folks traveling out that way are disappointed if they can't find a motel with a swimming pool."

The sun settles low, behind a cluster of linden trees across the way.

"Will, do you remember when we fished with Uncle Amer?"

"Yah, the three of us together at Lake Summit."

"And when he lined us up at the edge of a field with those icy soda pops and told us to stay there until we saw the corn shoot up?"

Dad chuckles. "There you go, boys," he imitated, "just sit back and watch 'em grow."

"Finally," I lean over and whisper to Mom, "common ground."

She smiles and pats my knee as I curl up in my corner of the sofa.

"We were just little tykes," says Ray, "when Dad and Amer had us stalking game through Bear Lake woods."

"Hah! They took us fishing before we could walk."

"Lake Summit, Lake Sara, Lake Shetek," Ray says with a kind of reverence. "Season after season. Remember when we'd stretch out on the ice and pretend to swim? And those frozen fish just under the surface?"

"Uh-huh. We always wondered about that as kids—those little fish that couldn't stay deep."

"Their eyes. It was as if they were staring up at us."

What the men are talking about happens every winter—small fish that sluggishly fantail upward in search of oxygen, caught in the crystal of a freezing lake, their mouths agape, eyes fixed on the sky and on anyone sprawling above them.

"Will," says Ray with a wink, "do you remember the time we harvested frogs' legs?"

Dad grins. "How could I forget?"

"When your dad and I were boys, Callie, it froze so hard and so fast on Big Bear Lake . . ."

"Why, it froze so fast," says Dad, "that five hundred frogs diving into the water at the same time got stuck in the ice."

"With their legs sticking straight up in the air."

"Just imagine—a huge garden filled with two thousand meaty frogs' legs."

"Well, now, you can't let an opportunity like that go by. No siree." Ray chuckles and hands off the last line to Dad.

"So my brother and I ran back to the farm and grabbed the lawn mower!"

Everyone laughs, Uncle Ray the loudest.

"Oh, Dad," I ask out of tradition, "is that true?"

"Could be," he says. "Could be."

After the laughter, a dream-like shift comes over the room. The men's words wrap around me like warm currents, a release of all things good locked away too long—the kind of talk I've always longed for. I am with them in the wooden boat, learning how to fish, laughing at their jokes and stories. Walking next to them through windrows and cornrows, I sense the stealth of confident hunters. Crouching on the frozen lake, we hold our ears to the ice and listen to the bay expand with sounds like ricocheting bullets. We stare back at the sunfish encased in clear ice, their perfect scales of orange and gold, crimson and silver—such delicate armor—gleaming in the late afternoon sunshine.

Dusk moves in. Too soon the ice and sky leave off as mates in blue. I imagine the boys, cozy between feather-stuffed ticking, talking to one another about what they saw and heard on that cold, hard bay.

And now the boys are gone to old men, quiet in their easy chairs.

"Cal," says Dad after a time, "go get my shotguns from the closet. They're in the corner.

"The Ithaca 37," he says to Ray, "and the model 12 Winchester. You remember those guns."

Mom looks concerned, her eyes questioning, as I return to the living
room carrying a gun in each hand. "Shall I take them out of the cases for
you, Dad?"

"No, we'll manage."

The men fumble with the zippers, and then slowly pull the shotguns out,
letting the cases slip to the floor. The sleek blue barrels lie heavy and cum-
bersome across their laps.

Dad reaches into a back pocket for his white handkerchief and slowly
polishes the gunstock checkered long ago by my grandfather. He passes the
handkerchief to Ray, then tips slightly in his chair as he shoulders the Winchester and aims it at a wall.

"Pull!" He swings a lead on an imaginary clay pigeon. He grins at us and
lowers the butt of the gun to his knee, barrel pointed at the ceiling.

I remember the robust voice he once had. How smartly he used to snap the
sight to his eye. "Pull!" he'd shout. "Pull!"—Twenty-five out of twenty-five.

"Did I ever tell you, Ray, about the time I brought down two pheasants with
one shot? Or maybe you were with me out there in Alec Lowe's cornfield."

"I don't remember that, but we sure got plenty of mallards off Bear Lake
slough. Filled out every time. Remember?"

Dad nods. "Sure wish you could've shot grouse with me up by Itasca.
Some of the best hunting I ever had. When was that, Emily?"

"Around 1965."

"Those were the days," Dad says.

"Yes, sir," says Ray, "those were the days."

Thirty-One

A Dandy Place for a Grave ❖ 1989

OVEMBER, THAT NORTHERN KILLER of the spirit, steps forward, cold and dreary—and too quiet after the loons have left and the white pelicans and ducks and geese have flown south, each flock in its turn, until one evening at dusk, a single duck plies the cold choppy waters, his head and neck thrust forward as he paddles hard against the wind and waves the color of gunmetal. When he is out of sight, all that remains is stillness. And silence.

When the silence of November becomes deafening, I dream of the warm weather thrashing of carp in the shallows, the arguing of geese clustered near the shoreline at five in the morning, the easy rhythm of spring rains washing away winter's gray loneliness. It will be many months before the mucky lake bottom squishes between my toes and the friendly taps of sunfish noses bump against my legs. As if extending me courage, under the last full moon of October, a gaggle of wild cackling geese partied in the middle of the bay.

Piper, quiet and alert, sits on the steps next to me, keeping an eye on my changing face. Hours before daybreak, I am bundled up against the cold, surrounded by the dwindling pile of firewood Dad cut two summers ago near Pine River—enough to keep you warm, Cal, he'd said, pinching the back of my neck, when the winter winds do blow.

Last night's quiet waters have given over to heavy waves rolling against the shore like tired old things. The faint tinkling of ice shards portends an ice-blocked lake. Soon, on a very cold night when the air is still, it will freeze over and not break up until April.

The phone has only to ring once before I jump up and run back into the house with Piper at my heels. It's Mom calling to let me know that the maverick cells boating along the sanguine rivers of Dad's brain, leaving half a smile in their wake, have finally won.

"Callie, sweetheart," says Mom, her soft voice cracking. "He's gone."

For a few seconds, I try to breathe while unseen fists punch me in the stomach. My throat clenches and I sob into the phone. "Oh, Mom."

"He's at rest now," she whispers. "No more suffering. We couldn't wish him to stay with us if he couldn't get better."

"Is Liz there?"

"Not yet. She's on her way. Drive carefully, dear Callie."

At that, I hang up the phone. Feeling empty and numb to my fingertips, I grab the car keys. I must get to Dad before his spirit goes a-wandering.

"No hurry," he used to say. "We have all the time in the world."

And I believed him. If only I could have folded the hands of every clock in the world, one over the other, in order to stop the passage of time.

Yesterday had been my last with him, although I didn't know it. Well, I did and didn't. He'd been sick for so long it seemed like just another day. And when I said goodbye, I thought there'd be another day and yet another after that. I knew better, of course, because the last time he said, "Take your time, Cal. We have all the . . ." But he stopped in mid-sentence and said, "Do what you enjoy. Time is short. We have only one enemy in the whole world, Cal. And *that* is time."

Dad knew the truth, though he never put any more words to it. And I didn't know what to say. My family never discussed death. It was just there— always around us: Grandad dying. Gram dying. Eloise dead at last. Dying pets, deer, waterfowl. Fish bending and waving their tails in death.

Dad used to say, "Don't let that scare you. It's just a reflex—nerves and muscles remembering when it was a whole fish swimming in Lake Shetek."

And when I told him why I poked the knife tip into a bullhead's air sac, he'd said, "A swift cleaning doesn't hurt them, Cal. They can't really feel pain. It just tickles a little bit."

"Are you sure?"

"Could be."

So the way it worked was this: We didn't want Dad to know he was dying. And he didn't want us to know how hard it really was. He would take it on the chin and never admit that it sure as hell didn't tickle. That was his final gift to us.

His last words to me were, "Just keep on a-goin', Cal. Keep on rowing."

I arrive in front of the apartment and slam on the brakes. Which reminds me of how Dad screeched to a halt at the entrance to the hospital in Masterton after I'd blown up my shotgun shell. And how he drove like fury the time Gram broke her hip. Anyone with me this morning would have hit the floor.

I hurry up the steps to the apartment. The door is ajar. Mom and Liz and I hug each other.

"Do you want us to go in with you?" asks Liz.

"In a minute."

I pause inside the room where Dad lay deep in his bed. Then I sit down beside him and instinctively place my hand on his forehead to feel the last of his warmth. I need to believe that his spirit is hovering, waiting for me. I whisper, "I'm here, Dad."

Mom and Liz gather round. I haven't heard them come in. My hand is still on Dad's forehead, which is now very cool. If only I could keep him warm, reverse what has just happened. But there's a knock at the door and two men come in to take Dad away.

While they wheel the covered gurney out of the apartment, down the sidewalk and into the hearse, Mom and Liz huddle together, watching from one window. I stand watch from another.

Several days after the funeral, I pull Dad's tackle box out from the back of my coat closet. The large metal box with its silver handle reminds me of a small coffin. I know by heart what is inside: sinkers and hooks, an iron scaler, Dardevles and Rapalas, gummy worms, an old petrified rubber frog, that Lazy Ike that hooked my last northern, spools of fluorescent line, a shiny fingernail clipper, a pen knife with his name—Will Lindstrom—etched into the ivory handle.

Although Dad gave his tackle box to me months ago, opening it never seemed right without him sorting through these things with me—his nicked fingers, a pipe clamped between his teeth.

The second I flip the latch and open the lid, all the old familiar smells come pouring out: rusty metal, a grimy, oil-soaked rag, oil on whetstone, flecks of Velvet tobacco. Thunder rumbles inside my head as I pick through and line everything up by size, shape, and color, the way I used to organize Grandad's empty shotgun shells when I was a kid. On the bottom tier is the old balsa lure rigged with tin fins—the one Dad placed on Uncle Ray's doorstep the day he reeled him in. After a time, I put everything back, close the lid and set the tackle box on the hearth, where I can see it.

———✦———

BECAUSE UNCLE RAY HAS BECOME QUITE DEAF, it is impossible to give him our sad news by telephone. Mom sends a letter and a package. He writes back immediately:

> *I am glad to hear about your liking Will. I miss him, also. I can visualize the place in the cemetery on the slope. You say there's a pond nearby, with some ducks and geese in season. A dandy place for a grave.*
>
> *I like those sweaters you sent and have had them on many times since you was generous to make a gift of them to me. I have the picture of Will on the counter where I can see it. That was a good trip for him to come see me. He wanted to see our house. He said several times he hoped I would get settled. And I am glad that I came to see him.*
>
> *Enclosed is a check for my brother's wreath.*

Mom reaches into her desk drawer and pulls out a folder.

"Remember this little story you wrote about Tepeeotah?"

She holds out a green-covered notebook, whose empty pages I'd filled long ago—a gift to Dad on his seventieth birthday—a memory piece about Lake Shetek and the cottage, about our family times together, hunting and fishing, playing Puccini on the upright, discovering a dead uncle's letters. It was about Dad and Mom and Liz and Gram and Grandad and Uncle Amer. And a page about Jenny. Everyone was in the story, except Uncle Ray and Aunt Eloise.

"Ray read this while he was here," says Mom. "I'd peek out from the kitchen and see him sitting on the couch, reading your piece over and over. The first few times, he didn't say anything, just put it down on the coffee table and stared out the window, looking a little sad. A while later, he picked it up again and took a long time to read. Then he said, 'Say, Emily, this is pretty good.' He even took it to his room that night. Next day, his last before returning to Sioux City, I noticed that he was reading it again. 'Say,' he said, 'we sure had a good time out there, didn't we? Callie wrote this up pretty good—that's just how it was.'"

Sitting next to my mother on the sofa, I begin to cry. Only this time without the hurt and the hopelessness. It's as if I've opened a tight fist to reveal my beautiful arrowhead whose sharp, chiseled edges no longer poke into my flesh. I have found the last piece of an exquisite and complicated puzzle, secreted away until the end.

"Ray kept reading and reading your words, Callie, until he was finally able to . . . Well, it was as if he was trying to get inside them—inside our story. In a way, he got to be with us after all."

A dandy place for a grave was what Uncle Ray had written in his letter, although he'd never seen the grave for himself.

"It meant the world to your dad when Ray came to see him. The way they were at the last gave him something to go on."

As time passes and the seasons change over Dad's grave, I think of telling my uncle about the mourning doves and yellow warblers calling out from the willow tree at the edge of the pond. I could tell him about the chorus of spring peepers and the splashdown of mallards skimming in for a rest. And about Piper barking and chasing spirits among the gravestones with a wide grin on his long snout.

I could tell him about the Norwegian god who spreads a thick, downy cover of snow. As Mom says, "We can always count on Ullr to shield Will in winter."

My uncle should know these things. Maybe he does. After all, he has made it into our story."

Thirty-Three

The Final Round ❖ February 1990

WHEN UNCLE RAY DIED, it was very cold in Iowa. If the furnace had gone out, he might have remained somewhat preserved during those weeks he lay in his bed. However, if he hadn't died during the Christmas season, he might have spoiled there a lot longer. Ben Hagen, the next-door neighbor, wondered why Ray hadn't hung his annual wreath above the front door, but assumed he'd gone away for the holidays. Long after New Year's, the locked house was still dark at night. Then, there was that strange and awful smell.

Uncle Ray was eighty-eight years old.

We'd lost touch after Dad died. Mom sent Christmas cards. I *thought* of writing to him. Had I known how alone in the world he was . . . but I never did.

Surprised that Jenny called to let her know, Mom quickly phoned Liz and me.

"She sounded tough as whang leather, the poor girl. No funeral service. Just a burial."

"I wonder if Uncle Ray has a dandy place for a grave. Remember what he wrote about Dad's?"

"How dandy could it be next to Eloise? I can just imagine her welcoming line: 'Oh, it's *you!*'"

"No, no," I counter. "It had to be, 'Oh, *shut up!*'"

"Dear me. Is that all we can remember about the woman?"

"That and her flying skillet."

"There must have been *something* good about her. We were just never privy to it."

"You know, Mom, it seems as though Uncle Ray was always leaving a place, always showing us the back of his head."

"Except the last time, when he came to see your dad. He was at ease then, in no hurry to go back to Sioux City."

I imagine what Dad would say about his brother's death: *The last of the Lindstroms. We went out in reverse of the way we came into this world—second-born, firstborn. But why the hell did he have to go like that, with no one around?* Then Dad might have repeated his story about how a mortally wounded bluebill dives deep and clamps onto a reed until he drowns. I guess Uncle Ray had found his reed.

His back was as bent as marsh grass in winter and he had to cup his hands around large, leathery ears in order to hear our words. I remember the charm and promise of his younger years, the debonair, cologne-scented affability of his middle life, and those monologues tinged with a humor I could recall from childhood—a wry lingo spoken with his trademark long, drawn-out vowels, one of the bright things left to him. He sounded like W.C. Fields, but without the artifice.

I wonder about the lost years. Time and distance were their enemies. Yet, Dad never gave up on his brother. There was the love, of course. But to let go would have been to die a little, something Dad couldn't accept until the cancer decided for him.

The last time I saw my uncle, his rank odor triggered in me an animal instinct of impending death. But I will remember the moment, because that's when the fog lifted and he and Dad could finally set anchor together.

Sometimes, I think my father got little more than a plate of crumbs for his efforts. There is, however, some nourishment in reliving old times together, filling in the missing years, erasing lines that separate the real from the imaginary. Perhaps, in Dad's mind, the long-awaited attention he got was like a feast—a platter of golden fillets.

If he had outlived his brother, he might have said, *Ray was out there in this world doing the best he could with who he was—like Grandad, Gram, Uncle Amer, Mom, Liz, you, me, Jen—like any of us . . . even Eloise.*

When I consider those words of forgiveness, I can send my uncle on his way with a wish and a blessing:

At the moment of his death, a white moon appears outside his window—a moon more intense than any he has ever seen—one that outshines the stars. Regrets and loneliness stand aside as he sinks deeper and deeper, until his spirit is transported to a northern lake in winter, where he and his brother skate down a moonbeam that shines on delicate armor.

"THOSE WERE THE DAYS," Dad had said, cradling his empty shotgun.

"Yes, sir," said Ray, "those were the days."

The blueing on the receivers and barrels of their guns had faded. Dad didn't seem to notice the crack in the stock of the Ithaca, which he used to bemoan each time he pulled the shotgun from its case. That day, their last together, the guns were flawless from years of polishing with tiny, oil-soaked remnants of cotton undershirts hooked to slender, wooden rods—into the breech, out at the muzzle.

Quirks and lead times were programmed into the brothers. They raised their guns in tandem, sighted, and drew a bead on a raven flying low above the snow-covered yard.

Click, click, snapped the pins.

The men had broken their rule—done what Dad told me never to do because it weakens the pins—they pulled the triggers without shells in the chambers.

Lowering their guns, Dad and Uncle Ray chuckled, eyes sparkling behind thick lenses. A final push on the fore-end closed the action. They polished the wood and metal one last time, and then zipped the guns into their flannel-lined cases and set them aside—one last time.

Epilogue

My Microcosm of Men ✦ February 1990

THE FAMILY LAZES NEAR THE FIREPLACE inside my cottage on Cook's Bay—Mom in her rocker, crocheting; Liz and Brian on the sofa, reading old *National Geographic* magazines from Te-peeotah; Brent and his wife, Laura, sprawled on the floor, playing with baby Willy; Josie feeding the fire with the last of our logs from Pine River.

Standing at a window overlooking the lake, I put the final notes to a piece we now call "A Song That Would Like to Make You Cry." New strings and years of practice have made Uncle Amer's violin sing. That is, *my* violin. I like to think Puccini would give us the nod. No one in my family ever applauds at the end of that song, which is how it should be.

I look down at my fingers curled around the neck of the instrument, remembering a time when Dad commented on my raspberry-red nail polish, likely worried that I might never return to the boat once I became a woman.

"Why would you want to wear that ishy stuff? How're ya gonna string worms and catch fish with that goop all over your fingers?"

Well, Dad, we caught fish for supper tonight. Josie and I snagged the most, through a hole we augured in the ice. I needn't say that aloud. It's enough to think it.

Some winter evenings, I take long walks on the bay with Piper in order to witness the spectacle of the blue hour and to sort out my thoughts. Uncle Ray's recent death has triggered memories of the four important men in my life—my microcosm of men.

Tonight, Josie wants to go along—dear Josie, who acts more like me than her mother.

I anticipate Mom's oft-repeated warning to be careful walking on the ice. Instead, she smiles and says, "Enjoy yourselves, girls. We'll be right here waiting for you."

Josie and Piper run out ahead of me. I turn for a moment to gaze at my family content by the fire. The baby toddles over and reaches out to me. I scoop him up for a big hug.

"You can go with us next winter, Willy boy, when you're a little older."

I plant a kiss on his soft cheek and lower him to the floor. Clutching his juice bottle, he jogs back to the hearth like a drunken sailor.

"C'mon, Aunt Cal," Josie calls from the last step. "Let's go!"

The crunchy hard pack along the shore thins and gives over to ice as smooth as polished granite. Here the winds have blown away the snow. Scooting over weed beds, we pause at the sight of a sunfish frozen near the surface. Josie flops down for a closer look.

"See how its scales glint in the last light, Aunt Cal?"

I glance over her shoulder as she lists the colors with a kind of reverence: "Rose and green and blue and gold."

Between swirls of snow stuck to the ice, we take short running slides out to the center of the bay—a lifeless place until April. For now, everything, except the naked trees, turns a shade of white before deepening to cobalt.

We are on time for the blue hour, that seductive transition in the cold north, when acres of shimmering snow and ice and the dimming sky come together for a brief time—a magical moment when all forms lose their color and clarity, deepen to indigo, and go down for the night.

We breathe deeply the chilled sweet air. Its frosty ozone washes through our lungs.

Along the western shore, the setting sun stabs its last fiery rays through stick trees. The opposite sky is awash in changing colors—pale blue to lavender, coral to mauve.

Alternating between the last blinding shaft of light and the calm of the eastern sky, I spin slowly from west to east and east to west, then turn my back on the last trace of sunset and look to the cool shades of evening.

With the sun gone, the temperature drops.

"Listen, Aunt Cal. Do you hear that?"

"*You* know that sound, don't you?"

"Yup. Ever since I was a little kid. Gramps taught me to listen for it."

We sprawl with stocking-capped ears tight against the surface, and absorb the reverberation of shifting ice, fissures crisscrossing the bay, a leviathan orchestra with deep, sonorous tones and sharp pings that begin at one end of the giant floe, play beneath us, and ricochet off stony masses on the opposite shore.

I roll over on the ice and look up at the darkening sky.

"Times like this I sure miss your Gramps."

"Me, too, Aunt Cal."

We sit cross-legged and talk about the usual things children learn from their parents and grandparents. And then, we detail the lessons that Dad never consciously taught us: when to cuss and talk back and when to walk away; how to listen and be soothed by the music of the wind in pines and prairie grass; applaud the free flight of a wild bird missed by shot; leave water lilies there where they grow best; know when to get off the lake and when to take it on, when to keep a fish and when to let him go. "Look to the linden tree and the stream," he said. "After all, they gave us our name." And finally, he taught us how to accept the end when there was no other way.

Josie asks about the stretches of time when she couldn't be there—about her Gramps' long, drawn-out passage—months of passage—from easy chair to walker and walker to bed. Then I tell her about the lone tree I thought would stand forever in that vast, long-ago field near Lake Shetek.

"It was a big old scrub oak and it looked kind of lonely out there. But stately, too. And then someone cut it down.

"We mourned that tree like a friend—the curves of its thick branches, the changing texture and colors of its leaves—spring, summer, fall. In winter, it seemed more alone than ever in the middle of that snow-packed field, bare-limbed, except for a few dry leaves rattling in the wind.

"A patient, old tree," says Josie, "just waiting for winter to be over."

There'll be no more stories or silly words, except the ones we've learned and those we will fashion for ourselves. And there was no fury at the dimming light. When speech failed him, he simply shrugged his shoulders, as if to say, "Doesn't hurt, Cal. It just tickles a little."

He'd pretended no pain—another white lie I was given, until he was sure I could handle the truth. And when he saw that I could, he passed into the ether.

The blue hour has nearly ended, closing down the day with a dim light that makes all things equal.

"Are you ready to go back, Aunt Cal?"

"Yes, they'll be waiting for us. See? They've turned on the porch light."

"How tiny it looks up there on the hill." Josie glances all around. "I hate to leave the lake. It's so beautiful out here."

"Don't forget, there's a blue hour in the morning, too."

"A reverse blue hour. Is it as pretty?"

"In some ways, even lovelier."

With Piper by my side, I scan the western bay and imagine Dad piloting his boat over a chop the color of gunmetal, rushing to the ends of the earth on wave after wave. Whitecaps wash over the stern and clap him on the back. Laughing, he dissolves in the rain.

I laugh, too, then raise an arm and point.

O mio babbino caro . . .

The sounds of the shifting lake deepen, as if from a great distance. With outstretched arms and an ear to the consummate music, I float above the ice in a slow dance, until the blue hour passes and the stars light my way back to shore.

Acknowledgments

Heartfelt thanks to Marly Cornell, Nancy Paddock, Faith Sullivan, and Ann Woodbeck. A special thanks to my Minneapolis and Mallard Island writing colleagues, and to family and friends, whose encouragement helped me keep my oars in the water. Finally, my homage to Scout Salvatore, a devoted sheltie who stayed by my side through eight winters at the keyboard.

About the Author

Connie Claire Szarke grew up in "The Land of 10,000 Lakes." She studied and earned degrees in French and Art at St. Cloud State University and the University of Minnesota and taught high school French for thirty years. A writer of fiction and poetry, Connie is also a lifelong classical pianist, painter, and alpine skier. She enjoys fishing from an old rowboat and kayaking with her Shetland sheepdogs near her home on a bay west of the Twin Cities.